TURN AGAIN
A NOVEL

KRIS FARMEN

Library of Congress Control Number: 2012944476

ISBN: 978-0-9850487-1-6

First Printing July, 2012

Printed in the U.S.A.

Cover design: Vered R. Mares
Editor: Stan Wise
Map created by:
Gary Greenberg, Alaska Map Co., Kenai, Alaska,
(www.akmapco.com) and used by permission.

Printed on recycled paper.

Published by:
VP&D House, Inc.
1352B W. 25th Ave.,
Anchorage, Alaska 99503
www.vpdhouse.com • www.facebook.com/vpdhouse
Phone: 907-720-7559 • email: info@vpdhouse.com

*

For the Beaudoins

and for Tim and Ruth,

with a lifetime of thanks

*

The weight of the past is heavy...
—JOHN HAINES

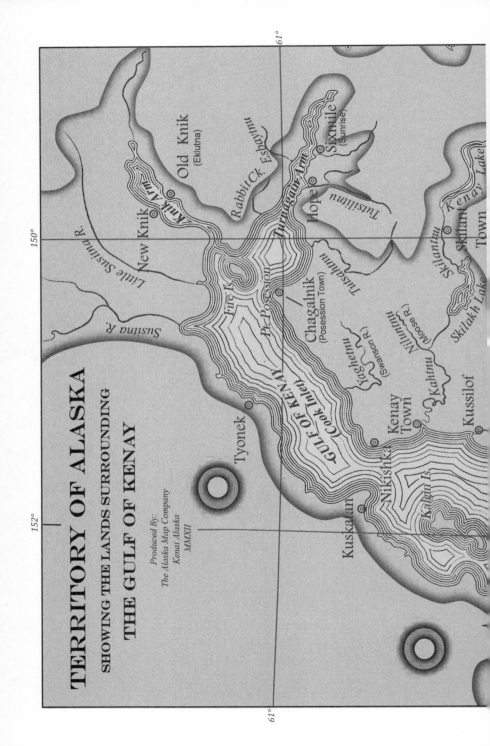

Scale of Statute Miles

0 5 10 20 30 40

Reduced from the Map Published by the U.S.G.S. 1890

Longitude West from Greenwich

Kussilof Lake

Ninilchik

Deep Ck.

Cape Starichkof

Anchor Point

Kachemak Bay

Seldovoya

Barren Ids.

Polly Ck.

60°

59°

152°

150°

*

*K*odiak town in the year of our Lord 1894. The man sits with his back against the hewn-log wall with his legs crossed before him on the floor. The spruce puncheons are dark, impregnated with grease and salt from the decades when his Russian forebears used the building as a warehouse for raw fur during an age of powdered wigs and knee breeches. There is no light save what comes from the twelve-inch unglazed window in the wall above him. Out this window is a view of the hillside and nothing more. There is a damp straw-tick mattress with a wool blanket, a bucket and an old newspaper in the far corner. Iron bars separate the man and two other empty cells from the hallway that leads to the guard office and the gateway to the world where he has lived the twenty-five years of his life.

The man has not been allowed outside in the weeks since his trial. Under normal circumstances, his skin tans in the wind and sun, but now it has faded to the ashy-gray of a mixed blood. A Creole. Or as the Americans call him, a siwash.

Beach crows caw at one another in a cottonwood tree that must be nearby, judging from the golden leaves that have blown into his cell. The prisoner doesn't move, he just listens. He is not from this island. He is from the Kenai Peninsula, two or three days sail to the north, a land his grandfather's people call Yaghanen. He knows he will never see his country again. He is to hang in one week's time for a double homicide.

His hands rest in his lap with dirt under the fingernails. He flexes them once, then lets them rest. The tips of his uncut hair fall over his face and brush at his chin.

The prisoner cannot keep accurate count of how long he sits, though it is fall, the last days of September by his reckoning. Day and night are more or less of equal length this time of year, but the grayness that passes for daylight on this isle of storm and rain offers no clues to the passing of clock hands.

His cell is the furthest from the door to the guard office. He hears the door scrape open and footsteps approach. The sound of clicking heels on the floor tells him it is a white woman. The guard Maddox appears in his blue army uniform. The woman is right behind him, smartly dressed and pretty.

"How do, Campbell," says the guard. He is fair-haired, barely old enough to shave.

"Hello, Maddox."

"This is that Russian half-breed you asked about," he says to the woman. "Aleksandr Campbell."

"Who's she?" says Campbell.

"This is Miss Ashford. She'd like a few words with you."

He tilts his head slightly. "Do I know you?"

Miss Ashford flashes him a fetching smile, all fair skin and dark eyes and chestnut hair pinned up beneath her sensible-yet-stylish hat.

"I've not had the pleasure," she says, extending her gloved hand through the bars. "I'm Rebecca Ashford from the Bureau of American Ethnology."

"The what?"

"The Bureau of American Ethnology. We're a branch of the U.S. Government that records the cultures of America's primitive peoples before they're lost."

"I see."

Several long moments of silence pass. Campbell watches her. He does not get up, and Miss Ashford withdraws her hand, an awkward gesture at best. Campbell's accent comes out as he speaks—low English words voiced with the hard, clipped sounds of Russian and the long, lisping cadence of Athabascan speech.

"You're with the Yankee government."

"I work for the federal government, yes."

The notion of an unmarried woman working a job other than laundress or salmon roe packer is beyond the scope of his experience.

"What do you want?"

"I'm travelling through the territory collecting cultural data on Eskimo and Aleut shamanic beliefs. I hoped you might be willing to let me interview you."

Campbell leans forward from the wall, his eyes fixed straight into hers. "I aint no damn Eskimo. My granddad's people are Indians."

The Eskimo and Aleut people Miss Ashford has interviewed have had nothing complimentary to say about their Athabascan Indian neighbors. Her superiors in the Bureau consider the Athabascans to have no culture worthy of scholarly study. No grass baskets, no carved masks or elaborate weaving, no stratified society. The prevailing opinion is that their aboriginal ways have been too diluted by Christian missionaries to be of scientific interest.

KRIS FARMEN

Still, despite her disappointment, she finds herself unable to look away.

"I'm sorry if I offended you," she says. "I must have been misinformed."

"It's alright. You aint the first."

"You speak very good English."

"Spasiba."

"Pazhalusta."

Campbell cocks his head, looking at her from the corners of his eyes. "You speak Russian."

"Some. I had an immigrant aupaire when I was a child."

"A pair of what?"

"An aupaire. A governess. She was from Russia."

"I see."

"I'm preparing a monograph on the spiritual beliefs of the aboriginal peoples of this part of Alaska."

"A monograph."

"It's a government report. Like a book."

"I know what it is."

Miss Ashford taps a finger against the handle of her briefcase, wondering briefly where this mixed-blood man encountered a word as obscure as monograph, and if there is enough time left in the day to locate a former shaman rumored to be living on the hill above town.

It has proven difficult to find aboriginal shamans here in Alaska willing to talk about the old ways. Their conversion to Christianity by the Russians seems to hold them back from speaking. She has been tasked with gathering such information, and it has been far more frustrating than she would have imagined. She is keenly aware of the fact that she is the only woman working in the Department of the Interior and, as such, has a lot at stake with her research.

An idea comes to her. The prevailing wisdom is that the Athabascan Indians do not merit scientific study, but there is an opportunity here, staring her in the face. She has heard a rumor about this man. Probing deeper into it could provide a needed boost to her career. At the very least it might get her an office in Washington with a window, instead of a converted basement closet.

"I was told you were a magic man, Mr. Campbell."

"Pardon?"

"They say you have the ability to change yourself into a bear."

"Who told you that?"

"I think it's best if I don't reveal my informants."

Campbell inclines his head just enough that she can see his hard eyes. He regards her for a long moment, wondering what game she is playing at.

"I'd like to ask you a few questions about your ability," she says. "And about your people's spiritual beliefs. If you'd be so generous as to share your time with me."

Campbell opens his mouth to tell her to go to hell, but thinks better of it. These are his final days on Earth, and he figures he could do worse than to spend some time in the company of a pretty white girl.

"As you like," he says.

Maddox exits the cell block and comes back a moment later with a chair. He places it so Miss Ashford can sit facing into the cell. A smirk crosses Campbell's shadow-hidden face. He can see she's well accustomed to this kind of attention, to being the prettiest girl in any room she enters, army stockade or otherwise.

"Thank you, Private Maddox," she says. Maddox looks into the cell, then back at her, trying to discover an excuse to stay. Finally he says, "I'll leave the door open, Miss. If you need anything just give a holler."

"Thank you. I will."

His bootsteps clump back down the hallway. Miss Ashford opens her briefcase and withdraws a notebook and a pencil. She flips the notebook open to a fresh page and sits with her pencil poised to write.

"Can you tell me something about where this ability comes from?" She taps her pencil against the binding of her notebook. Most aboriginals she has worked with do not respond to such direct questioning. Indeed, they seem to consider it extremely rude. But she is aware that this man is to be hanged in a few days, and there is only so much time. She repeats to herself an aphorism her mother often used: Make haste slowly.

Campbell looks at the floor.

She tries again. "Why don't you tell me something about your parents? I take it from your last name that your father was an American. Or a Scotsman."

Campbell stares into her eyes from the shadows of his unkempt hair. He begins to speak. Miss Ashford's pencil scratches as she writes.

KRIS FARMEN

CHAPTER I

*M*y dad was an American soldier. He come up to Alaska in sixty-nine with the army when they built their fort at Kenay town. I never knew him. He got my mother in a family way, then left when the bluecoats abandoned the fort the following year. I'm told that soldiers can take their wives with them when they post to a new billet, but that bluebelly colonel wouldn't let him take my mother because she was a Russian Creole and not a white lady. All my dad give me was the name Campbell. When they lit out for the States, my mother moved us into one of the abandoned cabins the soldiers had built. It was small and dark, with no glass in the window and packed dirt for the floor. There wasn't even no door, just an old piece of moosehide to keep the weather out.

My mother's father was a Kenaytze Indian from the mountains. That spring when he come downriver to sell his catch of fur and found us living in this squalor, he went to the Alaska Commercial store and paid two dollars for a glass window. He sent word up Cook Inlet, or the Gulf of Kenay as it was called then, that help was needed, and his good friend George Washington come down from Point Possession with his two nephews Petr and Yakov. The Yankees cannot pronounce our Russian names, so these two would in later years be known as Belukha Pete and Bullseye Jake.

George Washington was a *toyon*—that's what the Russians call an Indian chief—and he was a top-notch carpenter. The four of them cut logs and whipsawed them into puncheons for the floor. They built a door and trimmed the window and generally made the cabin livable. I don't recall none of this for I was barely a year old, but this was the house I lived in until I was eight. I slept in the tiny storage loft above my mother's bed. One of my earliest memories is of lying awake in the brightness of the summer nights and listening to the carpenter ants chewing their way through the walls.

My old granddad's Indian name meant something like Hawk Owl Watching, but the Yankees called him Lucky Jim. I'm told he had other names—many of the old-time Indians had several at any given time—but Lucky Jim was the only one I knew him by. He had not cut his hair for almost twenty years, since a wolverine come to him in a dream and told him he should nevermore put the shears to it. This wolverine is one of the most powerful spirits in the forest, and Lucky Jim couldn't disobey such instruction, so all those years later he wore his long hair clubbed up at the nape of his neck in a large bundle. I seen him from time to time with his hair undone when one of his wives would wash it; it trailed on the floor several feet behind him.

It was said that in his youth Lucky Jim had killed seven Esquimaux and Aleuts in combat. These people are the mortal enemies of the Kenaytze from the beginning of time. It was also whispered that he had killed three brown bears with nothing more than a spear and his axe, but Lucky Jim never once spoke of these things himself. Such boastfulness is considered unseemly among the Indians.

I did not see Lucky Jim again until the spring of my eighth year when my mother died of the consumption. She had the rattling bloody cough as far back as I can remember, but over the last year it got so bad she could barely get out of bed. Then one morning just after the start of Lent, I was up before her but decided not to wake her. She'd had so little rest. We had no samovar urn like wealthier homes, nor even an iron wood stove, so I fired

KRIS FARMEN

the brick *pitchka* furnace and boiled a kettle of water for tea. I climbed into her bed next to her to tickle her ear. This was how she woke me when I overslept, but that morning she didn't move or even twitch when I shook her shoulder. She was stiff as a board under my hand. Her soul had fled to heaven.

She didn't weigh much by then. When I managed to roll her over, her eyes was slitted open with only the whites showing. Her cheek was flattened and furrowed, stiff and froze from where her face was pressed against the spruce poles of the bed frame when she passed. Even now that memory haunts me late at night when I cannot sleep.

I was taken in by my mother's sister Klara and her husband. Aunt Klara was full blood Russian and was married to an American named Mike Morgan. Mike managed the Alaska Commercial store, or the AC as we generally called it. There is no post office on the Gulf of Kenay, so Mike let regular customers have their mail sent up care of the store, and from this he acquired the name Mailman Mike. He and my aunt lived on a little hill just north of town in a fancy two-story frame house, but sadly they had no children to fill it. Klara seemed especially pleased to have me around. It was a tough time with my mother passing on though she and Klara had not been especially close.

There was no school in Kenay town in those days, so Mailman Mike took charge of my education. I only spoke Russian, so he started teaching me American and how to read and write. I was given my assignments in the morning before he left for work, then we'd go over my work in the evening after supper. I was also required to learn three new American words each day, which he taught me to find in the dictionary. And he made a point of not letting me choose the easy words.

"Sound them out," he told me. "Sound them out bit by bit."

So that's what I done. All them words still stick with me—*pulchritude, serendipity, euphemism, monograph.* There are others, many of them. They filter into my speech at random moments. In my younger years I kept these fancy words well hid, lest my friends run me down for thinking I was better than them. That sort of attitude is common in this country, though after Polly Parker got me started reading novels, I decided I didn't give a damn about that no more.

I generally did my assignments at the kitchen table while Aunt Klara was busy cooking. I was given endless cups of tea, which she claimed was a brain stimulant.

"Chypeet," she would tell me with a tickle in my ribs and me giggling. *"Chypeet,* Aleksie." This is a Russian word that means to drink a cup of tea.

Her samovar was a beautiful appliance, the pride of her kitchen along with her big American cooking range. It had a silver stand and tap, and the urn was covered over with blue and white porcelain. She said her grandfather, who was a Cossack in the Czar's army, brought it home from Persia many years ago. We often spoke Russian when Mike was at work, and she told me stories of the Russia her parents knew, of emperors and soldiers, princes and damsels and faraway castles. Of our family history that stretched back hundreds of years to a place she called Circassia. I aint ever seen these places, mind you. I only know them from her stories.

Once when she was in a storytelling frame of mind I asked her about her and my mother's parents, where they grew up and how they come to Russian America. How it was that my mother was half Kenaytze Indian while Klara was all white.

KRIS FARMEN

She looked down at the table, and I seen her cheeks flush. "Never you mind that," she said, turning away so I wouldn't see her wiping at her eyes. "You get back to your lessons."

When the ground thawed in May we buried my mother in the Russian Orthodox cemetery. There were no priests at Kenay at that time; they had all been re-called to Russia after Seward's purchase. Sava Golinov was a Creole lay-reader and the closest thing Kenay had to a mayor, a position that in former times was called *zakazchik*. He had been standing in for church services as best he could over the years. He led the service in Russian and Slavonic wearing his best dark suit, and it was mournful indeed to see my mother's casket lowered into the earth. As always during these affairs there were the whispers among the people of how hard it was not to have a priest to help us through these times. I had never seen a priest and had only the barest notion of what one was, and this fact was a source of great distress for my aunt. As a boy I was often left thinking that the entire world the grownups had known had crumbled to pieces with the coming of the Americans.

As people started to filter away I noticed an Indian standing at the edge of the crowd. There was a six-inch shard of ivory speared through the middle lobe of his nose, though he wore a civilized cloth shirt, waistcoat and jacket. His legs was clad in caribou leather britches with the moccasins sewn onto the cuffs. These was con-sidered dowdy and old-fashioned, even in those days.

I didn't know the man, but when Klara seen me watching him she said, "Aleksandr, that's your grandfa-ther Lucky Jim."

This stranger scared me. He had been selling his furs at Knik for many years, and I had not seen him since I was a baby. It's also worth saying that this had been a difficult day for everyone, and emotions were running high. Later when Mike brought him to the house for tea I hid in the parlor while they sat at the kitchen table. Klara shoveled coals from the wood stove into the fire-pan of her fine samovar, and the water quickly boiled. She set out cookies, of which Lucky Jim partook with immense satisfaction.

He spoke no American, but he had enough Russian to get by, so Klara translated for Mike as they talked. Of course I didn't need no translation, so I heard every word twice. This stranger had come to take me upriver to live with the mountain Indians.

The grownups seen me spying on them. They all looked at me, and I ducked back into the parlor and fled. Aunt Klara found me upstairs and towed me back into the kitchen and stood me before Lucky Jim with her gentle hands upon my shoulders. I thought I might cry. I was fond of my aunt and uncle, and the thought of going away with this wildman from the mountains had me scared enough to faint.

Lucky Jim just smiled. His earlobes had holes you could see daylight through where he wore heavy earrings when he was younger and wanted to impress the girls.

He said something in the Kenaytze tongue, but I barely knew it. Mama was not fond of the Indian side of her pedigree; she was devout in the church and always told me the Indian tongue was the Devil's speech. She made me kneel down and pray for forgiveness whenever I used it. It occurred to me then that Lucky Jim had come to take me to see Old Scratch himself, and then I did start to cry, howling out loud that I didn't want to go with him.

Klara and Mike soothed me as best they could. The smile slid off Lucky Jim's face, but his eyes didn't move. There was gentleness in his look as he held out his hand to me. I kept bawling, but Klara patted my side and whispered in my ear to go to him. Lucky Jim drew me into a hug. He smelled of woodsmoke, sweat, moss and tea-bushes. I still remember the scratchy wool of his jacket lapel against my face. He patted the back of my head then drew back with a hand upon my shoulder.

"Aleksie," he said, "there are things you need to know."

———

Kahtnu is the river that flows from Skilak Lake to Cook Inlet at Kenay town. Up above Skilak Lake is the Skilantnu, which flows from Lake Kenay down to Skilak. The Yankees call the whole thing the Kenay River. It is the lifeblood of Yaghanen, the Kenay Peninsula. Lucky Jim lived at Skilant town on the upper river, and this is where we headed the next morning on the incoming tide in his birchbark canoe.

We paddled and poled up the river when we could, and when the current was too strong we had to line the canoe from the bank. It was early in May month, and the king salmon wasn't in the river yet, so we lived off dried moose meat and pilot bread. By the second bend of the river I was sullen and sulking, still scared of him and missing my aunt and uncle already. But the ducks and geese was back in the country, and Lucky Jim sang me several songs about them to the rhythm of his paddle-strokes. I kept slacking off my own paddle and resting with it across the gunwales, but when I done this the song from the stern would stop. When I finally dipped my paddle, he would start up again, and before long I decided that I wanted to keep hearing his voice so I bent to my stroke.

At our first camp, Lucky Jim lopped my hair off short with his skinning knife, saying this was how I showed I was mourning for my departed mother. Later, when we was dragging up firewood, he pointed to some square pits dug into the ground, now grown up with moss and weeds.

"Them's the old-time Indians' houses," he said. "From way back."

I looked up at him. "Before the Russians come?"

"Long time before the Russians, Grandson."

That same night he showed me how to make a fire without matches. Nothing but a piece of petrified wood from the streams near Old Knik and the spine of his knife. He struck sparks into an old tobacco tin full of rotten poplar punk that had been charred to black. It caught the spark and turned orange. Lucky Jim pulled out the glowing ember and laid it into a wad of dry grass and blew it into flame. He added shreds of birchbark, then a handful of spruce twigs, and the whole thing blazed up into a fire.

I sat watching with my eyes wide open. I'd never seen this trick done before, though of course it was commonplace not so long ago. Lucky Jim laughed and tousled my hair as he added larger sticks to the fire. He never carried matches that I seen.

On that trip he killed a little bull moose near the outlet of Skilak Lake with his Sharps rifle. I followed him on the stalk through the spruce timber, trying to move just the way he did. He was like a cat or maybe flowing water in a stream the way he used the cover and placed his moccasin feet into the moss and between the dry sticks that could have snapped and betrayed us. I was scared the whole time I would make a mistake and cost us the meat, but it was a good stalk, and his rifle cracked the silence of the woods. The moose dropped with a slug through its head.

The butchering was a lot of work with just him and me. We spent several days making the portage around the rapids above Skilak. I lost count of how many trips

KRIS FARMEN

it took. Lucky Jim packed the meat and the canoe, and I carried everything else.

But we poled into Skilant town with a boatload of fresh meat, and everyone come down to the beach to meet us. Two women, one older than the other, come trotting up to me as soon as I stepped onto the gravel. They made to sweep me up in their arms, but I dodged them, hiding behind Lucky Jim's legs. These was his wives Olga and Tasha. I'd never laid eyes on them before, nor the town we'd arrived at. Nowhere did I see an unfriendly face, but I was wary of strangers, and these Indians from upriver had a wild reputation down on the coast.

Lucky Jim put his hand at my back and gently pushed me ahead. "These are your grandmothers."

The two ladies hunkered down at eye level to me and smiled. I went to them and they drew me close and made a great fuss over me. All three of Lucky Jim's sons had died of the smallpox many years before, and my mother had been his last remaining child. For my part, it had been a long trip, and my mother's death had been a trial for such a young child, and I think I must have needed a little mothering. Looking back, my guess is that my presence helped ease the family's long-standing grief over the long-ago loss of their children.

There was maybe two hundred souls living at Skilant when I arrived there. This town is almost deserted now, not even to be found on a map. Even at that time I was told that the population was much reduced from former days when it had been one of the biggest towns on the Peninsula, owing to the bountiful salmon runs in the river and the fine weather that came from being in the mountains away from the coast.

By the time I came around, many of the town folk was living in log cabins like they had down in Kenay, though some still lived in the old style houses. These was made of pole frames with sheets of birchbark for the walls and roof, and earth and sod heaped up against them. The floors was dug two or more feet down into the ground, with several rooms branching off the main chamber where the fire pit lay. You won't be surprised to learn that Lucky Jim and my grandmothers lived in one of the old-style houses. It was dark and stuffy inside with no windows and just one little door. Our cabin in Kenay town had the glass window that let in the sunlight and made it a pleasant place to be, but them old style Indian houses was nothing of the sort. I spent all my time outdoors anyhow, as it was springtime with the sun shining.

Despite his unfortunate lack of children, Lucky Jim was a man much esteemed in the community, and I had plenty of playmates. One morning I was standing in front of Tasha's fire, poking a willow stick into the ashes while she worked nearby at scraping the moosehide we'd brought in for tanning. A thin shy-looking boy come up but stood away some distance looking at me and at her.

Tasha turned her head. "Yasha Izaakov, what are you doing here?"

The boy looked down at his dirty bare feet. He curled his toes over a stone.

"Nothing," he said.

Tasha kept her hide-scraper working. "You're supposed to be helping your mother and aunts at their fish trap."

"They said I could play."

His voice was soft and low, the voice of someone who prefers not to speak unless it's truly necessary. I could see that my grandma had her doubts about his being given leave, but she kept them to herself. She put her scraper down and come over next to me and held out a hand to Yasha.

"This is Aleksandr Campbell," she said. "From downriver at Kenay town."

"Folks there call me AC," I said.

"Aysee?" said Tasha, no doubt wondering what kind of name that was. It dawned on me that she couldn't read and wouldn't know that my initials as Aleksandr Campbell was AC. Me and my chums down in Kenay town used to pretend that I owned the Alaska Commercial store because I had the same initials, and the name sort of stuck.

"It's like the AC store in Kenay," I told them.

"Hey," said Yasha.

"Hey," I said.

"You want to see a great big pile of sheep skulls?"

I'd never seen sheep before. I knew they lived up in the mountains and the Indians there hunted them actively. I said I would very much like to see such a pile.

Tasha smiled as we took off, and Yasha led me up the river to a place where there was a deep cave, obviously man-made, dug into the side of the mountain.

"I don't see no pile of sheep skulls," I said.

Yasha grinned. "That was a fib to throw the grownups off our trail." He tilted his head toward the blackness of the hole. "We aint supposed to come here."

"What is it?" I said, peering inside. I had no notion of why someone would dig such a hole into the bowels of a mountain.

"The Russians was up here a long time ago. They come up from Kenay looking for yellow sand. They dug this big hole but they never did find what they come for."

I looked round the entrance where it was timbered up with spruce logs. The beams was rotten and beginning to sag. I kicked at a pile of dirt long since overgrown with a thatch of fireweed and grass. The new shoots of spring was pushing up through it.

There was pieces of white quartz in the dirt. I picked one up and looked at it and tossed it down into the hole. I never heard it land.

"Dare you to go in," said Yasha.

I curled my lip a little and said no.

"You scared?"

"No I aint scared."

I went down to a stand of birch trees where the bark was sloughing off like sheets of paper and stuffed my shirt full. Yasha cut a green cottonwood stick and we wrapped the bark round the stick with layers of dry moss to make a torch. We kept plenty of fuel in reserve, for birchbark burns fast. We struck a match and lit the torch and crawled into the hole. I made sure I was in the lead, for I was not going to be known as a coward. Straightaway the tunnel started to slope downward. The floor had lots of loose rock and gravel, and we had to scoot on our backsides to get down the incline.

I may have claimed I wasn't scared, but I surely was. My heart was thumping, and the sound seemed to fill the tunnel which was eternally silent but for our footfalls. Little bits of sand and gravel sifted down onto our hair and under the collars of our shirts. This was not a comforting sensation. When the opening of the tunnel slipped out of sight, Yasha stopped.

"There really aint nothing down here to see," he said.

I could hear the waver in his voice. I wrapped some more moss and bark onto the torch. "You squat to piss, then?"

That got his dander up. He pushed up next to me saying, "Well let's go then."

We scooted down further until the floor dropped off vertical. A ladder nailed together from spruce poles led down into the darkness. It was tolerably solid so we climbed down into the shaft. At the bottom of the ladder we found ourselves in a small chamber. There was tools scattered all about, we could just barely see them in the light from the torch.

I added more bark and moss. "We're getting low on fuel, partner."

"We'll have to go back soon."

We explored the chamber, looking at the tools. There was single and double jacks, hammers and picks and other things I couldn't identify. I took up a sledge-hammer with a broken handle and held it to the light. It bore Russian markings, but though I speak Russian I never learned to read it. I tossed the sledge back into the dirt.

Just then Yasha let out a yelp and I hustled over with the torch. He was froze stiff as a corpse saying, "It touched me, it touched me, it touched me!" I held the torch down to see a collapsed skeleton with its lower quarters buried in the rubble of an old cave-in. The skin was dried taught like rawhide over its limbs and face. The head still had its dark hair and beard, though the man had been bald on top. The lips had pulled away from the teeth in an eternal grimace.

One of the arms lay in a fresh posture where it must have fallen down when Yasha brushed up against it.

I recall this as a moment of raw terror. We both started screaming and flew up the old ladder like our hair was on fire. I dropped the torch but we didn't stop to grab it. We just kept heading up and up until we seen the pinprick of light at the end of the tunnel. It got bigger and bigger as we scrambled forward with rocks and dirt dropping down behind us as we bumped and banged in our panic, then we tumbled out panting and gasping into the sunshine.

Our jubilation at making it out alive was short-lived though, for both of Yasha's aunts was standing at the mine opening, waiting for us. Their arms was firmly crossed, and they wore scowls upon their faces.

"You been in that Russian pit, haven't you?" said one of them.

Yasha nodded and looked at his feet. We both knew we was in it deep.

"You know you're supposed to be helping us down at the fish trap."

Yasha kept silent.

The aunts looked over at me. "You're that boy from Kenay town."

"Yeah," I said.

"Yasha don't need you getting him into trouble."

I opened my mouth to say it wasn't my idea, but then closed it. I am many things, but a snitch is not one of them.

The aunts gave me a final look of disapproval, then hauled Yasha away. I took my time getting home, knowing what conversations was likely to take place between them and my grandmothers.

Lucky Jim was getting on in years, though he was still spry. Being in the autumn of his days he was content to leave the hunting and provendering to the younger men while he and I went travelling.

"We're going afoot," he said, pointing north. "Over the mountains to visit George Washington."

I had of course heard of this man—his name was known all around Cook Inlet—and there was the story I had heard any number of times how he and his nephews helped Lucky Jim upgrade my mother's house. But I'd not met him in person.

"Where's he live at?" I said.

Lucky Jim was wrapping up our bedding for the trip. He'd purchased quality Hudson Bay blankets from faraway Canada. Yasha's aunts had been giving me the evil eye, and I was keen to get out of town for a while.

"Up at Point Possession," he said, rolling up his own blanket and lashing it closed with leather tugs. "You met him when you was a baby, but you wouldn't remember it."

The kings was in the river by that time, so we took a sack of fresh dried fish, plus some moose meat for variety. We also took Lucky Jim's two hunting dogs. I had been given a job for this trip: Lucky Jim had traded for an old .32 caliber caplock muzzle-loader. The stock was beat up, but it had clean lines and was to me the finest gift I'd ever received. With a small horn of powder and a shot bag slung beneath my armpit it was my assigned task to kill small game for the pot, and I admit my breast swelled up at this.

Olga made me a fine cover for the rifle from the tanned hide of the moose we killed, worked over with many fringes and bangles. Tasha sewed me a pair of caribou-skin britches just like Lucky Jim's. I did not want to wear these for as I've said, such attire was considered the very mark of unfashionable, backward people. The sort of thing given to children who were too young to know the difference. But my sailcloth britches from Kenay was almost worn out, with big holes in the seat and knees. There was no store at Skilant town, so I was stuck with those home-made leather ones. This brought me grief when I seen some of the younger men who all wore store-bought britches from downriver snickering at me as Tasha checked the fit in front of the house.

She told me to ignore them, that they had no appreciation for what was good in life.

"These skin britches will keep the mosquitoes and white-socks off you," she said. "And they last longer when you're out walking through the brush. That's why

Lucky Jim wears these pants, not just because he's old fashioned."

She seen the older boys pointing at me and clucked her tongue saying, "Don't you worry about those boys. They'll be hating life when the bugs hatch."

She was right, too. The mosquitoes was awful when me and Lucky Jim set off sometime before the solstice, but they couldn't get through my skin britches. We each carried packs loaded with food and lashed to our backs by means of a broad strap across the chest. He had his axe and his Sharps rifle, and of course I carried my old caplock. The dogs carried our bedding along with the kettle and whatever odds and ends we needed. We walked up the ancient trail from Skilant town northward through the mountains along Dzadatnu Creek, where we camped the first night near a lively waterfall.

Lucky Jim's dogs was not the common malamutes one sees everywhere on the trails these days. These was Indian bear dogs. They had stout shoulders and huge jaws that could bust rocks. Lucky Jim's dogs was both bitches—he called them Camprobber and Flicker after his two favorite birds. This breed is now mostly gone, and even when I was young they had become scarce, even though they used to be common as lice. Bears was a real problem before the Indians had rifles. They would come right into town, chase the people away and eat all their fish from the drying-racks. The best weapons them old-time Indians had against such assault was dogs like Flicker and Camprobber that had no fear and could tree the bear until the men got to it with their bows and long spears. When they weren't chasing bears they had the sweetest disposition you could ask for and would push up against me and cover me with kisses. Camprobber was my favorite. She loved to chase a stick, but whether or not she would return with it was often a dubious proposition.

We was several days on that trail. I was only able to travel so fast, owing to my short legs, and would often lag behind Lucky Jim and the dogs. When we'd stop for a breather I would be tired and thinking I was done in, but Lucky Jim would just tell me to harden up and keep moving. But he did have his fun side, hardly something I expected from him.

One afternoon I was in another sullen mood, missing my mother and Aunt Klara and my grandmothers, wishing I was back in Kenay town. Lucky Jim caught my attention by asking, "What bird am I, AC?"

I looked over to see him squatting flat-footed on his haunches with his arms curled up at his sides. He watched me intently from the corners of his eyes but did not move an inch. To my mind he looked like a spruce hen that has been surprised while pecking gravel on the trail, so I told him so.

Lucky Jim laughed. "Good work, grandson. Let's say this trail is a creek. What bird am I now?"

He got down into that imaginary creek and started hopping about, flapping his wings. When he landed in a new spot he would poke his face down into the water, then flap over to the next spot. Then he lighted on a rock and made little peeping noises at me.

I clapped my hands together. "That's a dipper-bird!"

He smiled and I felt my spirits restored. "Let me do one," I said.

Lucky Jim stayed hunkered on the rock and watched me as I pointed my beak at the sky and made a long series of cawing noises.

"That sounds like the Black Bird," he said, by which he meant Raven who the old people say created the world. It is considered bad form to speak his name aloud.

"No," I said. "I'm a beach crow!"

Lucky Jim stared at me a moment, then his face split into a wide grin. He stood up and come over and clapped me on the shoulder, and I was once again happy to be with him.

———

The trail led us up the creek to a smallish lake where the timber thinned out into high alpine meadows with lovely groves of poplar and cottonwood along the way. I killed rabbits and squirrels every day with the old cap-lock, and sometimes ducks when we could find them in the lakes along the way. I allow that I was proud of my ability to stalk them down with Lucky Jim hanging behind me and shadowing my moves. Whatever game I shot was cooked by burying it in the coals of the fire, guts feathers and all. When it was done we picked off the meat and the choice bits from inside.

Nights we camped under big white spruce trees where the branches made a canopy that kept out the rain and left the ground dry beneath. The scales of the spruce cones that the squirrels pulled apart to get at the seeds made a good mattress to sleep on. Being June month the weather was fine though the mosquitoes was fierce and hungry as I've said. The dogs would curl up with us at night, but it was warm and they drew the bugs, so we pushed them away. Lucky Jim kept a smudge fire going in an old tin can which put out a thick smoke that kept the little bastards at bay. It would be an understatement to say I was impressed with his knowledge of wood-craft. There seemed to be nothing he didn't know how to do. But then the Earth and the forest was his mother and father. He'd known nothing else since the day of his birth.

We spoke only the Kenaytze tongue on our journey. In the long evenings when it didn't get dark, Lucky Jim would lean back against a tree or a log and smoke his pipe while coaching me on how to speak. He was a stickler for proper grammar and what was polite or impolite to say. Contrary to the common belief, Indians have strict rules about such things, and because of his teaching I must admit that I speak much better in the Kenaytze language than in American.

He narrated to me the old stories of the wars between the Indians and the Esquimaux and Aleuts who kept trying to push us off the Inlet. He told me all the *sukdu* stories—these are the tales of the far distant times when humans and animals could talk to one another. He told me how Raven, the Black Bird, created the world and all the animals and the rivers and mountains and trees and the bugs and the Gulf of Kenay and the Indians. I was mildly surprised at how closely some of these mirrored the Bible stories my aunt and uncle were fond of telling me.

"The *sukdu* are meant to be told only during winter," Lucky Jim cautioned me. "Usually it's bad luck to tell them this time of year. But your education has been neglected, and we have to make up for lost time."

I nodded solemnly, thinking even at that tender age that the Black Bird seemed to have created the world mainly for his own amusement, though one might well say that of God too.

We was three days going down the creek the Indians call Tutsilitnu; the Americans now call it Resurrection Creek. It runs straight north down to Turnagain Arm in a long valley with large mountains on either side. Once we got back down into the timber from the treeless heights, there was much more grass and devil's club and *puschki* weed. The grass in the meadows was taller than my head, and I have a very clear memory of standing in a patch of that grass, looking straight up at the blue sky with the stems and seed-tassels waving above me in the breeze.

It was a fine trip. We could not have asked for better weather, and we had plenty to eat all along the way. In places, the valley would straighten out and afford us a view all the way down to salt water, to the silty gray waters of Turnagain Arm. We seen the tide-bore on many occasions, a train of large waves made by the tide pushing up the shallow bottom of the Arm. Once when the east wind screamed down the Arm and we could see the whitecaps from way up in the valley, we caught sight of a waterspout out in the water that moved onto land and started stripping leaves and branches off the trees until it fizzled out. I asked Lucky Jim about that, and he told me the wind does strange things in Tutsilitnu Valley.

We camped for a few days among the cottonwoods and tall grass where the creek spills into the Arm. We was both worn down from all the walking and needed a break. The day was the hottest yet, and we stripped off our clothes and went swimming in the frigid tidal wash of the creek. The salmon felt big and slippery as they bumped against my legs and arms. There was so many of them thrashing in the stream there was almost more fish than water.

When we finished our swim I helped Lucky Jim make a fish trap from split spruce laths in the shape of a cylinder basket. We built a weir of stones and upright stakes across the creek and set the trap in the single opening we allowed. Less than an hour later we had plenty of fish. Many of them was bigger than me. Lucky Jim kept only a few kings for our cooking and to feed the dogs, and let the rest go free.

Later that afternoon I was playing among the shallows of the creek, trying to scoop up a king salmon just like a brown bear does. I splashed after one, losing my foothold and falling face-first into the creek. I opened my eyes under-water and through the icy blur I spied something yellow and shiny in the gravel. I reached out and wrapped my fingers around it and stood up to examine my find.

It was a lumpy rock, maybe the size and weight of a rifle slug. It gleamed both lustrous and beautiful, the prettiest thing I'd ever seen.

"Granddad!" I shouted, running up the bank. "Look at this!"

He set down his knife from the fish he was butchering. I handed him the yellow rock and his face turned into a scowl. He jiggled it in his palm once or twice, then turned and pitched it out into the Arm.

I cried out in protest, but he laid a hand on my shoulder. "Aleksie, that yellow rock is trouble."

"But it was so pretty!" I was upset, for I'd already come to love that rock, not knowing the pain and hardship it was to bring into my life one day.

"The Boston Men love that rock, too," said Lucky Jim. He sat down on the bank, wincing a little from the arthritis creeping into his knees. He pushed my wet hair back from my forehead. "They love it and it's all they think about. The Russians was after it as well. Thankfully they never found enough to interest them, or they would have tried to make us all slaves like they done to the Aleuts when it was sea otters they was after."

"Why do the Yankees and Russians love it so much then?" I said.

"All white men love it." Lucky Jim shook his head as his brows drew together. "Several years ago a party of Russians come up the river to Skilant town. They had been following the yellow rocks up the river from Kenay. They asked me if I'd seen any, and I said yes, I had. I took them to a bend in the river where I had found some. Them Russians cut a bunch of trees and set up all kinds of machines, digging up the river bars. The dog salmon was in the river and spawning, but the Russians didn't care. They dug up the gravel where them dogs had laid all their eggs. It's a wonder there's any left in the river."

He paused for a while, looking out at the tide flats. "I'm told you know of a big hole in the side of a mountain."

I hemmed and hawed and mumbled something non-committal.

"The Russians dug that hole in the mountain looking for more yellow rocks, but then they give up and went back down to Kenay town. They never come back, which was to our satisfaction."

He looked me in the eye. "Way up north, in the country of the Quarrelers, the Boston Men dig up whole rivers looking for those rocks. The Britishers, too. They lay waste to entire streams and kill all the fish and shoot out all the game."

"Who's the Quarrelers?" I said.

"They live on the Kwikpack River." He pointed out across the Arm where he'd thrown my pretty rock and over the distant mountains beyond.

I had heard stories of this giant river, many months travel to the north. The Yankees and the Britishers have taken to calling it the Yukon. They say it cuts across the Interior and drains into the Bering Sea.

"Esquimaux?" I said.

He shook his head. "Indians. Like us. But they speak a different language. Their rivers was all ruined. All for them yellow rocks. For something that aint got no use at all."

I toed a stick half-buried in the beach silt and said nothing.

"You listen to me, young Aleksandr," he said. "Salmon come back every year. Fur too. Moose, bears, and caribou. When you look after the country, them things will always feed you and keep you warm and supplied with ammunition and blankets. But you cannot eat them yellow rocks. You understand?"

"Yeah," I said, still thinking of my pretty pebble.

"Do you?"

"Yes."

"Them Yankees and Russians and all white men are too stupid and selfish to realize that. So I want you to promise me that you will never speak of that yellow rock to anyone. And that you will never take them from this creek to sell. Or any other stream. It will be the ruin of our country if you do."

I looked back down at the stick, at the tiny specks of glitter winking up from the silt in the afternoon sunlight.

"Promise me, Aleksandr. I want your word on it."

"Alright," I said. "I promise."

All this time Flicker and Camprobber didn't care a whit about yellow rocks. They watched the fresh fish with keen interest.

———

Two days later, me and Lucky Jim and the dogs walked down the beach around past the mouth of the Johnson River and past Burnt Island where we killed another moose. We hung most of the meat in a hemlock tree for George Washington's womenfolk to retrieve, but took with us the tenderloins and backstraps as a gift.

Chagalnik was the name of the town at Point Possession, but the Americans call it Possession town. Maybe a hundred Indians lived there. They wore store clothes and moosehide moccasins and lived in log houses like the people at Kenay.

According to custom we stopped just inside the line of the forest, and Lucky Jim fired off a round from his rifle into the air. The men of the town had seen us coming, and the shot was returned with a volley. This is an old custom going back to the Russian days—you fire off a round to announce your arrival and to demonstrate your peaceful intentions. It is considered bad manners to approach a town with a loaded weapon.

Everyone came out of their homes to greet us, with kids running around and dogs barking. Lucky Jim was greeted warmly as an old friend. Men both young and old embraced him with offers to fill his pipe, and women of all ages took him in their arms for reverent hugs.

A gray-haired man in a Stetson hat come up through the crowd with a broad smile across his face. I knew at once this had to be George Washington.

"I heard you was coming up the trail," he said.

Lucky Jim smiled and introduced me, and while this *toyon* was friendly to me, I was more than a little intimidated. He was an important and wealthy man, with influence that extended even to Iliamna Lake and the Mulchatna country beyond. His Indian name meant Spear-Breaker, which was a sideways reference to a dream his uncle had about a black bear the night before he entered the world. The Russians give him the name Georgei Wasiliev, and when the Americans arrived and saw what a powerful and respected man he was, they took to calling him George Washington. As a young man he had spent ten years in the service of the Russian America Company. He had been to the Prybilof Islands and the Yukon River and to faraway California and was considered a man of great knowledge about the world and the dealings of white men.

We was made welcome at George Washington's home, where a fire was kindled and the teakettle set to boil while the meat we'd brought was put to good use. He and Lucky Jim smoked and talked, catching up on the previous year's events and exchanging news.

After a while he looked over at me. "Your grandson is good and quiet."

Lucky Jim's eyes crinkled in a smile. "He was raised with manners."

"Will he take a smoke?"

"He might."

George Washington fished in his britches pocket and withdrew a new clay pipe. He filled the bowl from his own tobacco tin, then handed both the pipe and tin to me.

"That's your pipe and tin now," he said.

I mumbled my thanks and lit the bowl with a burning twig from the fire, feeling rather grown-up. Behind George Washington's back there came a gaggle of small children, all younger than me, sneaking up on him and trying hard not to snicker and give themselves away. I learned later that many of them were his grandchildren. He and Lucky Jim sat smoking and watching the fire as if nothing was amiss, then just as the children was about to pounce both he and Lucky Jim leapt to their feet, roaring like bears and swinging at the children with their fingers curved into claws. The children took off squealing and laughing, and Lucky Jim and George Washington sat back down with the smiles that only grandfathers must know.

————

The people of Possession Town was keen hunters of belukha whales, and while I was there I got to see the whale hunt in action. They buried drift logs upside-down in the mudflats at low tide so that the upturned root-wads spread into the air like an eagle's nest. A hunter would sit atop the roots to harpoon the white whales when they come in chasing salmon with the tide.

My uncle Belukha Pete was one of the best harpooners, which is how he acquired his American name. One morning me and the other boys of the town lined up along the shore to watch him in action. We cheered as he slung his harpoon and struck true, then leapt down into his *bidarka* nimble as a house-cat to give chase. The harpooned whale thrashed something fierce in the gray water, but Pete danced his boat round it with the utmost grace while we boys stood watching with awe and envy of the day when we would be old enough to perform such a feat.

We stayed until the red salmon showed in the Tutsahtnu River, and Lucky Jim allowed it was time to be moving on. I hated to leave my new friends, but my own feet were itching for travel. We packed our gear, and George Washington and some of the men took us in their *bidarkas* to the mouth of the Swanson River. These are saltwater boats made of skin stretched drum-tight over a wooden frame. Some have a single hatch, others have two or three to accommodate multiple paddlers. Lucky Jim and me rode in a three-seater, with George Washington at the stern as we paddled down the Inlet on the ebb tide. Camprobber and Flicker rode with me, but they didn't like being below in the dark, so they sat on my lap and poked their heads up through the hatch. I stroked their heads to keep them calm.

Just before the tide turned we pulled into shore and built a fire. We smoked our pipes and roasted fresh-caught salmon on the coals. You cannot fight that Cook Inlet tide. That's a lesson the white men learn quick, though the Indians know it from a long way back.

It took us only a day and a bit to make the Swanson mouth, but we was taking our time. The Swanson at low tide runs out into a long gutter, almost a quarter-mile from the shore. You can't walk on the mudflats on either side, for it's all slimy tidal mud, so if you get there at the wrong time you'll have to tow your boat directly up the stream-bed in water up to your thighs. Lucky Jim and George Washington knew this and timed the stages of the voyage so we would arrive with plenty of water to get us up to the beach. Also, my guess is that the men were glad to get out of town for a jaunt with the boys, and were in no hurry to get home.

Most of our friends had to head back on the next tide, but George Washington and Belukha Pete stayed behind to help us build a canoe. The three men cruised the timber with their axe-bits hooked over their shoulders, surveying the birch trees and calling out to one another when they spotted a good one. They'd get down on the ground and sight up the length of each trunk to gauge the straightness and quality of the bark. When they rejected a tree, they would pat its trunk gently and tell it what a beautiful tree it was, but it just wasn't what they needed. When they finally found good bark, they peeled it carefully with flattened sticks, talking all the while to the tree and telling it what good bark it had grown and thanking it for doing so. When the peeling was done, they blew gently on the bright green under-bark to help it scab over faster.

My job was to fetch and carry while the men peeled the bark and felled the trees and split laths, ribs and gunwales. This work took several days, and there was no time for play. All day long I was told to look here, to run and fetch something, or to come and hold something else in place. That's how I learned to build a canoe.

The morning after the canoe was finished we said our goodbyes and watched George Washington and Belukha Pete shoot their *bidarka* down the Swanson's tidal wash and out to the sea. We loaded our gear and a sack of dried fish into the canoe with the dogs and started poling up-river with me in the bow and Lucky Jim astern.

The lower Swanson's current is slow and easy to manage, though it is full of big rocks at places that require a boatman to thread a needle between them. We travelled four days up the river, then made a portage over to a series of lakes where we swapped for paddles. This was low country, lots of black spruce bog in the flats, with birch and poplar along the hills. It was Lucky Jim's favorite stretch of country. He had made this trip plenty of times and knew all the best portages and camping spots. The bugs were bad, but he said they was even worse in June month before the dragonflies hatched to eat them. We tracked several moose, but did not shoot any; it was just for the sake of my education. We caught lake trout and dollies on handlines. Lucky Jim even showed me how to make a fish snare with a loop of spruce root fixed to a canoe-pole. You spot a fish in the shallows and sneak up behind him on the bank and slip the noose over his tail and pull it tight with a sharp jerk. This is just as much fun as it sounds and is a good way to catch fish if you only need one or two and haven't the time to build a trap.

We paddled and portaged for several days through this timbered maze of sloughs, streams and lakes. The first silvers had arrived, and the fireweed was well in bloom when we cached the canoe near the foot of the mountains and made ready to walk overland to Skilant town.

On this afternoon I was chasing tiny wood frogs in the tall grass near the edge of a muskeg bog when I tripped and fell face-first into a wolf spider's nest. They are not dangerous, just big and ugly with a body the size of your thumbnail, and black and white striped legs like a witch's stockings. I rolled around in that tall grass, howling like the dickens as the spider scampered under my shirt collar. I ended up stripping off the shirt and stomping on it with both feet, screaming all the while.

I've never been overly fond of spiders, but when I'd finally smashed this one into paste I looked up to see a yearling moose calf staring at me from just a few yards away. He was barely bigger than a dog and stood watching me with big, curious eyes.

My heart slammed against my ribcage. Spiders are bad, but every child in Alaska is warned from his earliest days never to put himself in the situation where I had just found myself. I started to back away from the calf and there came a vicious snort from above me as the mother's hooves sailed past my head.

A cow-moose will only come after you if she reckons you're a threat to her calf, but the upshot is that when she does come after you, she means to kill you stone dead. I bolted, loping and screaming through the jungle of grass and teabushes. The cow-moose was right at my heels. She could sail right over the deadfalls that lurked hidden in the grass and teabushes. I jumped over one, then another, but my foot caught on a stob and I went down. I saw her brown shape above me and the shiny black of her forehooves coming straight down at my head.

I curled up to the side as her hooves slammed into the soggy moss directly behind me so close the hairs on her hocks brushed the back of my neck. Now I was directly beneath her belly with its swollen udders and teats. She reared up on her hind legs and danced back for another strike, and I scooted out fast. As I done this there came a prickly crackling sensation, like thousands of tiny bubbles popping beneath my ears where my jawbone joined the rest of my head. It got worse and worse with each heartbeat, and the heartbeats were coming fast and hard. I'd never felt anything like this before, but I didn't have no time to ponder it. The cow-moose was after me once again.

I got into some spruce timber where the going was easier, but running had suddenly got real uncomfortable. Bolts of pain shot up and down my spine and my muscles started to quiver—I thought the cow must have got me somehow and I hadn't noticed. I sank down onto all fours, certain I was done for. That same moment I was stunned to see the shaggy brown hair growing out of my arms and the dark shiny claws at the tips of what had been my hands. Not just any claws—these was bear claws.

I could scarcely believe my eyes, but the cow-moose took no notice of it. Or if she did, it only enraged her even more. By now she was on top of me once again. I can't say where the instinct came from, but I reached out and swiped at her. She was having none of that nonsense. She loosed another kick and I went sailing through the trees—hell, I wasn't any bigger than her own calf. I landed hard in a patch of cranberry bushes and there she was again, right on top of me before I could even blink, rearing up to stomp a hole in my head.

Then a Sharps rifle cracked the air and the cow-moose twisted away. Lucky Jim was shouting and the dogs was charging straight for us. He fired again, and the cow tore off through the teabushes toward her calf. But the dogs wasn't after her, they pointed straight at me. They grabbed onto me and rolled me over and over, biting and snarling, all hot breath and snapping teeth until Lucky Jim got there. He yanked Camprobber away, slinging her bodily through the air, then he cuffed Flicker so hard her head slammed into a poplar trunk.

"Aleksie!" he said. "Aleksie, are you alright?" The dogs whimpered and moaned, pacing around us.

"Granddad!" I cried, "I'm a bear!" This did not come out as words, but more of a pathetic mewling cry. I was stupefied and scared and could do nothing but sit on my haunches in the grass all confused and crying. I was, after all, just a lost cub.

Then came Lucky Jim's voice. "Look here, Aleksie."

It took me a moment but when I looked up, my granddad had changed himself into a crane. Not make-believe like before, this was the real deal. He stood there on his long slender legs, in his dun-colored feathers, looking at me with those yellow eyes set into scarlet patches. The dogs was even more befuddled at this. They danced around and sniffed at the ground. When Flicker made an advance at me, Lucky Jim flapped his wings and stabbed at her with his beak and both dogs ran off and sat down beneath some tag-alders, eyeing us both suspiciously. A crane is a big bird, mind you, taller than them dogs was, and with a beak sharp as a harpoon to boot.

He come over and stood next to me and preened my fur with his beak. "It's alright, Grandson," he said. "It won't hurt you none."

"What is this?" I cried. "What's happened to me?"

"You got the gift. I figured you wouldn't, because you're only a quarter Indian. But I'll just be damned if you don't."

He explained to me that while rare, this particular talent was known to run in his family. Some people who had it could change into birds or moose, or mink or squirrels, or whatever animal you can name.

"But can I change back?" I said. This was the overriding question in my mind at that point.

"Of course you can. I been a crane more than once."

This calmed me a little, but there was still the question of how to actually do it. Still, Lucky Jim's light-hearted manner helped me to ease up on things.

I said, "How'd you find out that you could do it, Granddad?"

"I fell in love."

"With my grandma? My Russian grandma?" I was suddenly very keen to know what he meant.

Lucky Jim winked at me. "She comes a little later in the story."

"Tell me," I said. "Tell me!"

So he told me the story of how he met my Russian grandmother.

When Lucky Jim was a young man, not much more than a boy, he fell in love with an Indian girl he met in the woods up near Old Knik. They was together all summer, busy just being young and in love, but come September month when the leaves started to turn she grew sad and wouldn't say why. When the cranes began circling overhead as they do in the falltime, she would always stop what she was doing and stare up at them.

Finally one day Lucky Jim come in from hunting and seen a crane standing by their fire pit, watching him. His heart broke right then because he knew this was his girl. When she spread her wings and took to the air pointing south, Lucky Jim sat by the riverbank and watched the water slide past, wondering how he could go on with his life not having her. Then there come a crackling sensation beneath his ears that got so unpleasant he had to lay down. He thought he was about to die, but then he woke and found that he had changed into a crane himself. He leaped up into the air, full of joy, and flew into a giant flock that was massing over Chisik Island. There, amid the thousands of other cranes, he found his true love once again.

With this happy reunion they took off together, flying south with the others. They flew and flew until Lucky Jim was sure they was going to come to the edge of the world. Then one day they was passing over some strange country full of tall trees, steep hills and clear streams when some hunters started shooting at them. Lucky Jim's girl was struck with a load of shot and fell to the ground. He cried out and dove after her, then a second shot slammed into him and he blacked out.

As luck would have it, the man who shot him was none other than George Washington who would one day be the *toyon* of Point Possession, but at this early date was just a young fellow fresh out of Alaska. He and some other indentured hunters was working at the Russian post of Fort Ross along the coast of Spanish California. And when he come trotting up to claim his kill, what should he find but Lucky Jim laying there on the ground, knocked out cold but still breathing.

"But Granddad," I said, "How did you meet my grandmother?"

Lucky Jim reached down with his sharp beak and stabbed into the cranberry bushes near my foot, catching a lady-beetle neat as you please. He tilted his head back and shook it down his gullet.

He swallowed and looked back over at me, saying, "Patience, Aleksie. Patience."

———

George Washington and the mixed gang of Esquimaux, Aleut and Indian hunters carried Lucky Jim back to the fort where he laid in a fever for several days. When he woke, he was in a bed and there was a beautiful Russian girl tending to him. Her name was Natasia, and there was a ring on her finger. She was married to a Russian naval officer and had a baby daughter—this was my Aunt Klara—but Lucky Jim was smitten and charmed her just the same. I'm told he never was one to let grief over one girl stand in the way of a gallop with the next.

Lucky Jim stayed in California, hunting with George Washington and the boys and keeping company with Natasia. Their affair was kept a close secret, for, in addition to the mortal sin of adultery, there was the unpleasant fact that he was a heathen Indian and she a Russian lady of quality. As the saying goes, she had much further to fall than did he.

Despite their precautions, it was inevitable that their secret would be found out, and when it was, the cuckold officer came tearing after Lucky Jim with his sabre. Lucky Jim got a good long run and jumped off the cliffs. Right in the middle of the air he changed into a crane once more and flew back home to the Kenay River.

Imagine Natasia's mortification when she found out her husband was transferred to the Russian post at Kenay town. By then she was heavy with child; I don't know why her old man didn't give her the boot. Perhaps he felt that true love could conquer all. In any case they sailed for the Gulf of Kenay that summer, and my mother was born on the ship within sight of the Kenay Peninsula where she would live her entire life.

———

"They say my grandmother went crazy in the winter of forty-nine," I said to Lucky Jim.

He looked sad. "The Russians made life very difficult for her after your mother was born. The next spring I come down to Kenay town to say I would take her and her girls upriver to live with me, but they wouldn't even let me see her. Her husband pointed a pistol at me and told me never to come back. They tried to catch me and put me in irons but I got away into the woods. I never went to Kenay again until the Boston Men took over."

"That why you started selling your fur catch up at Knik?"

He nodded, and I was surprised to see he was no longer a crane. He sat there in his caribou britches and waistcoat over his shirtless chest with his elbows resting upon his knees. I looked down at myself, and relief flooded through me when I seen my own fur was gone. I had arms and legs and fingers and toes once more.

I smiled, but Lucky Jim didn't. "I cautioned your mother against eating bear meat when she was carrying you, but she wouldn't listen. She never did think too much of me or my family. But you must listen to me carefully now, Aleksie. This talent will be very difficult for you to live with. Especially as you get older."

"It's scary Granddad," I said. "I don't want it."

He shook his head. "There aint nothing you can do about it. That bear lives inside your skin, just like that crane lives inside mine. But a crane is an easy fellow to get along with. That bear won't ever go easy on you, and if you change into his skin for too long you may just forget that you was ever a man. You can lose your desire to see your friends and family again, and just stay an animal for the rest of your days, wandering lost and confused in the woods with no home."

"In fact," he said quietly, "you might just become a bear that has the ability to change into a man. And that could get ugly. Real ugly."

But I had already made up my mind that I would avoid this problem by never again changing into a bear. I could only see bad things coming of it, if the experience I'd just had was any measure. The bruise spreading across my side where the cow-moose had kicked me was a good reminder of that. There was also the obvious point that I could never be friends with the bear dogs if I was a bear, the very animal they'd been bred to charge and kill.

Camprobber and Flicker had come up to us with their tails wagging. They seemed entirely unperturbed. Now that I was a boy once again, they bore me no malice. We scratched their ears and let them lick our faces. Lucky Jim smiled at this attention. He lit his pipe and put his arm around me. I felt safe and comfortable once again. Lucky Jim was all I had and I was mighty glad I had him.

✳

*M*iss Ashford returns the next morning. Campbell stands looking out the window at the storm when she arrives. He wears his black moleskin jacket over his waistcoat against the chill, and has tied a kerchief over his head to keep his hair out of his eyes.

A gale is building. He can see the wind bending the dying grass and the red-stained fireweed with the fireweed cotton drifting about in the breeze like so many loose pillow-feathers. A small fraction of the wind is deflected by the hillside and pushed into the cell through his window. He can hear the whipping branches of the cottonwood tree. He wishes he could see it, for large cottonwoods are common in his country, and he has always found their presence reassuring.

"Good morning, Mr. Campbell."

He twists around to see her. "Morning."

She sits down on her chair and studies him for a moment. "How are you this fine breezy day?"

"Well enough. Considering."

She quickly grasps his meaning. On her way here she passed the makeshift gallows now under construction.

"Marshal Tomlinson tells me you killed two men," she says.

"You get right down to business, don't you?"

"I suppose I do."

"That Sitka Marshal is a fool. I didn't kill no-one. And I god damn sure didn't kill Scotty. Hack neither."

"The jury thought so."

"Do you think I killed them?"

"I don't know. I only know what Tomlinson told me."

"You know what I just told you."

"My father is a judge," says Miss Ashford. "He taught me to make decisions based on facts. Juries do so as well."

"Maybe they do for pretty Yankee girls. But not for no Russian-speaking quadroon."

She presses her lips together.

"I'm sorry, Miss," says Campbell. "That was uncalled for."

"It's not that. I'm certainly not blind to the fact that the law is unfair to your people."

"Then how have I offended you?"

"I don't care for being called a Yankee in the tone of voice you use."

Campbell crosses the small cell to her. His moosehide moccasins whisper on the floor and his gait is the rolling bent-kneed walk of a man who has spent his life walking over muskeg and tundra.

"Don't tell me you're one of them Confederate idiots."

Miss Ashford pushes out her chin. "I am from the state of Rhode Island. But I'm an American and proud to call myself one. My father was an officer in the war and lost his left arm. Two of my uncles were killed in action at Vicksburg so we could remain one nation under God. So I will thank you to refer to me as an American and not as a Yankee."

Campbell is long since weary of hearing these Americans run their mouths about their precious war, but he keeps this to himself.

"I beg your pardon, Miss. No offense was meant. Yankees is just the name we called you folks since I was a child. George Washington and Lucky Jim always called you the Boston Men."

"We're Americans. So are you."

Campbell's face hooks into an icy smile. He folds his arms over his chest. "I am a citizen of the United States. But that's only because my dear sweet dad was an American. Most Creoles don't enjoy that privilege. And no full-blood Natives do neither."

They regard one another for a long moment until Miss Ashford realizes there is nothing to be gained from this contest, and indeed, much to be lost. She has a deadline coming up and a monograph to write.

She sighs a little and forces herself to soften. "This is silly. Shall we move on?"

"Sure. You find your Koniag shaman yet?"

"How do you know about that?"

"I hear things."

"From whom?" She is aware that a Baptist missionary has been visiting Campbell, as well as the local Orthodox parish priest. Missionaries are notorious among ethnographers for convincing indigenous people not to speak of their old ways, rendering any cultural information they might share lost and gone forever.

"A Black Bird told me," says Campbell.

"A blackbird?"

"No, a Black Bird. You'd call him a raven."

The intensity of his eyes makes her look away. She opens her briefcase. "We should pick up where we left off yesterday."

"You're writing down everything I say?"

"Yes. And actually, I was going to suggest that perhaps you'd consider writing down anything you might feel like telling me. Things you think of when I'm not here."

Campbell raises an eyebrow at her.

"You said your uncle taught you to read and write?"

"He did. I been to school and read a few books too."

"What kind of books?"

"I like Mark Twain. I read a couple of his books."

"Really?"

"Yeah. What kind of books did you think I would read?"

"I guess I don't really know. But *Roughing It* is one of my favorites."

"Mm. That is a good one. He has some sharp things to say about jury service."

"Anyway," says Miss Ashford. She pulls out a blank notebook and a pencil and passes them through the bars. Campbell flips through the empty pages as she withdraws her own work from her case.

He gestures at her notes. "Can I see your writings?"

She passes her own book through the bars. Campbell opens it and examines the pages, but he can make no sense of the markings upon it. It is a strange alphabet he has never encountered, neither Latin nor Cyrillic.

"This aint American," he says.

Miss Ashford smiles. "It's shorthand."

"Shorthand?"

"It's an alphabet that was created for people like me who write down people's words as they speak. People talk much faster than the hand can write in normal English, so each of those marks corresponds to a syllable in a word, rather than to a single letter. It lets me keep up with you as you're talking, and write your words phonetically."

"Fonetically?"

"That means that what I write down reflects how you pronounce your words. And how you phrase things."

Campbell grunts, wishing he could verify that what she is writing about him is what he has told her. He passes the notebook back to her.

"They never taught us that in school."

"It's a very specialized skill. Even students in the States don't learn it unless they go to secretarial school."

Campbell pushes his lip out slightly and nods.

"So how long did you go to school?" she asks.

Campbell laughs a little. "Until I got big enough to whup the schoolmaster."

KRIS FARMEN

CHAPTER II

I lived at Skilant town for almost five years, though I was away much of the time when me and Lucky Jim went on trips. In the summer of 1879 we paddled to the mouth of the Matanushka River and walked up to the height of land near the giant glacier that feeds the river and over the pass where we could look out over the broad Nelchina country. There we met some of Lucky Jim's distant kin, the Mednovsti Indians. These folk hailed from the Copper River and had never allowed any white men in their country, not Russians, Yankees nor Britishers. Their country appeared to my eye as an endless flat sea of black spruce and sucking bog, but the Mednovsti told stories of high mountains, glaciers, and raging rivers full of copper nuggets.

The following spring, at the end of May, we was bear hunting in the woods around Port Graham when it come to Lucky Jim's attention that we was being trailed by a party of Chugach Esquimaux. We bolted off the trail into the brush and secreted ourselves in a patch of devils club, lying still as stumps as they approached. They had rifles and was clearly hunting us. I was scared and the cold moisture seeped up from the mossy ground into my clothes. Camprobber and Flicker was next to me with their hackles up.

I almost didn't hear Lucky Jim's whisper. "If there's a fight, Aleksie, you run. I'll come find you. Don't let them get within arm's reach of you."

I glanced over at him, but his attention was fixed on our pursuers. The five Chugach filed past us on the trail we had just vacated. Lucky Jim watched them through his rifle-sights. He held three extra shells tucked into his fingers, and his axe was close at hand. I could feel my heart hammering inside my ribcage. The crackles tickled at my jawbone, but I swallowed them down.

Fortune smiled on us. They missed our sign, and we slipped away into the forest. Later, I asked Lucky Jim why they had come hunting for us. He just watched the trees and said, "I made some bad decisions when I was younger."

I pressed him for more information, but he refused to speak of it any further. I was left to figure it out on my own that those fellows were likely the sons and grandsons of men Lucky Jim had slain in combat back in the old days.

We ranged all over the Kenay Peninsula together. Them trips was the best geography lesson I could have had. I learned where to find firewood and clean water and good bark for canoes. Lucky Jim taught me which lakes was haunted and which was safe to camp on. Where the moose, rabbits, and birds like to be, and how to find a bear when you want bear meat and how to avoid him when you don't. These was the lessons I learned when I lived with the mountain Indians. Lucky Jim and my grandmothers taught me the arts of the forest and how to make a living from the country as the Kenaytze people have always done.

Lucky Jim cautioned me against speaking of my peculiar talent. He said, "You got to be careful with that big animal, Aleksie. You must never speak of something that powerful. Your mouth is too small for that."

I didn't understand at first, but then he told me the knowledge of my power was something I could and should carry with me always. In fact, during this conversation I recall him referring to it very specifically as my POWER. He said that any time a man or animal threatened me, I would know what I had inside me and what I was made of, and that knowledge would give me the means to stand up to who or whatever. There was no need to speak of it, and if I were to speak of it, then that power would vanish instantly.

"That big animal is something beautiful inside you," said Lucky Jim. "And true beauty needs no words to describe it."

This was a man who had killed three brown bears hand-to-hand and felt their dying breath upon his eyelashes. He often spoke in riddles, but I knew there was good reason to listen to what he said. Thankfully I was still young enough that he could make an impression on me. Truth be told, it seemed to me that my power was more a burden than anything, but I needed no encouragement to keep silent, as I had made up my mind never to embrace it.

———

In December of 1883 I was fourteen years old and still living at Skilant town. That month, Sava Golinov came overland on snowshoes from Kenay. The Native side of Sava's family was all Aleut from Kodiak and Kolosh Indians from over near Sitka. This caused some friction in his earlier years, which is putting it mildly, but he came from one of the oldest and most respected Creole families, whose residence on the Gulf of Kenay dated back to the days of Baranov.

Among other things, Sava had come to inform us that a school had been set up in town and that my aunt and uncle insisted I be present for the start of the term after the New Year.

We were all sitting around the fire pit in the main room of the house. Lucky Jim watched Sava as Olga served him tea in her one fancy porcelain cup and laid him out a birchbark bowl of dried fish. She poured the rest of the tea into tin spackleware cups. They was cheap things, but more durable. And it was real China tea, not bush tea.

Sava stirred sugar into his cup and sipped. "Aleksandr should learn to read and write properly," he said. "The Russians taught us to read and write and do sums when I was a lad. Didn't matter if you was Native or Creole or Russian, you had to learn."

"I know how to read," I said. "Mike taught me."

"As I recall," said Sava, "you only had a few months of lessons with him. You need more practice. And there are other things you need to know."

"Like what?"

"Mathematics," he said. "Geography. And you need to work on your American. My guess is you've hardly used it these past few years except when you've been in town."

He was right on that last point. I stared into the fire with my knees drawn up to my chest. Tasha handed me a tin cup of tea and I took it, but only to be polite. I had no desire to go to school. I was nearly a man and had acquired the reputation of being a capable hunter. I had plans to establish my own trapline and make my way in the world. Lucky Jim and I had of course stopped in to visit Klara and Mike on our travels, but Kenay town and life with what are called CIVILIZED PEOPLE had become strange to me.

Lucky Jim must have read my thoughts. "Aleksie is nearly a man grown," he said. "His home is here in the mountains. Perhaps younger children are better served by the Boston Men's school."

"Mailman Mike insists," said Sava as he peeled the leathery skin off a piece of fish and stuffed it in his mouth. "I'm just the messenger. But either way it won't do any of us much good if there is a generation of young people who don't have an education."

Lucky Jim looked across the fire at me. I stared into my cup.

Sava peeled another piece of salmon. "Son, I know you don't want to go back downriver. But the Boston Men are building their own world here, and you'll be at a real disadvantage in life if you don't know how to read or write or speak good American. I myself can only read and write in Russian, and believe me, it is becoming a real handicap not to have knowledge of American letters."

"Do I got any kind of choice?" I said.

"Well I aint going to knock you on the head and drag you back to town. But it would be a real disappointment to Klara and Mike. You're a sharp lad, and it would be a disservice to your people if you don't continue your studies."

I watched the shadows of the house and drained my lukewarm tea in a single gulp, thinking that I was tired of being torn away from my home to satisfy the desires of people older than me.

But I finally agreed to go. It was the wish of the elders, so what else could I do?

We left the next morning. The whole town come out to see me off, and it was a tearful parting. The farewells took a long time for all the people that wanted to shake my hand or give me a hug. My grandmothers Olga and Tasha was most sad to see me go. They pulled me into their arms again and again, pinching my cheeks and telling me how much they would miss me. Yasha was more than a little down at the mouth over my departure. Me and him was close as brothers by then.

Sava waited patiently, squatting on his haunches and smoking his pipe with his covered rifle stuffed barrel-down into the snow next to him.

Finally Lucky Jim come up and embraced me. "I'll see you in the spring, Aleksie."

"Promise?"

"I promise."

So I went back to Klara and Mike's fancy frame house with its two stories, wainscoted walls and big American kitchen range. The schoolhouse where I spent 1884 and 1885 was set up in a disused old cabin at the east end of town. It was a crowded house with twenty scholars aged five to fifteen crammed cheek by jowl into desks made from pearl-oil crates and spruce stumps for seats. The cabin stood so low at the eaves that the taller boys had to stoop down when they walked next to the wall. The chalk-board was nailed to the front wall, but was too wide for the space and stuck out a good six inches over one of the windows, which reduced what light there was. Each day, working on rotation, one of us boys had to stay after school to chop stove wood for heat, while one of the girls would stay and sweep the place, dust everything, and wash the windows.

Our schoolmaster was an American named Watkins. He was skinny and consumptive, with wire-rimmed spectacles perched on the tip of his nose. He would look at you over the top of those glasses the way Lucky Jim looked through the sights of his rifle. It was his habit to dress his hair each morning with an odiferous pomade. You could smell him coming around the corner.

I loathed him at first sight. On the first day of my first term I seen him dish out whippings with a green willow switch to three of my classmates for speaking Russian at recess.

"This is the United States of America, and we speak English," said Watkins to the class after the whippings was concluded. "You will not speak any of these lesser tongues while you are on school grounds."

He smacked his willow switch against his palm. "Is that clear?"

We students glanced at one another, pondering the fate that was ours to be born Russian in U.S. territory. Of course, most of my classmates had no idea what he'd said because their American was not good enough to understand his pronouncement. And none of us who did understand dared to translate. The idiocy of this situation should be obvious at face value to anyone smarter than a schoolmaster, though my American did improve with time.

———

It was early in my third term, just after Russian Christmas (which came in January that year by the old Julian calendar), when Belukha Pete drove his dogs down the Inlet from Point Possession. Klara knew we had a visitor coming because she dropped a knife on the floor while slicing the bread, this being an old superstition from back in Russia. We was just finishing our supper of moose ribs when Mailman Mike answered Pete's knock at the door. I knew something was wrong when I seen his long face through the doorway to the parlor. He doffed his parky, hat and mittens and sat at the table. He drew himself a cup of hot water from the samovar for tea while Klara fixed him a plate.

"Lucky Jim's dead," he said.

"Say what?" said Mike. Klara turned from the counter to face us. Pete looked across the table at me.

"Up on his trapline at Granite Creek," he said. "He set out one morning to check his traps and never come back. Olga and Tasha found him sitting beneath a birch tree."

"Dead?" Klara said.

"Yes."

I looked down at my plate. There was half a biscuit sitting there but my appetite had fled. I was suddenly filled with an urge to strap on my snowshoes and head upriver to ask Lucky Jim if this was true, but then there come the sinking realization that he was gone and I would never more hear his voice.

Klara set Pete's supper on the table before him, and he started into it. Grief was obvious upon his face, but he'd been three days on the trail and was famished.

"His face was all twisted up in a grimace," he said around the food.

The older Indians presumed it was sorcery, for in their understanding no death was ever from what we would call natural causes. Many years later, a visiting doctor told me that Lucky Jim most likely had a stroke that paralyzed him so all he could do was sit under that tree getting colder and colder until he froze to death.

While Pete ate, Mike poured himself a cup of coffee with a splash of vodka. He tipped the bottle toward Pete and Pete nodded and Mike poured a little into his tea. Klara dished up the dessert of bread pudding with dried cranberries. I will allow it had been a delight to rediscover such delicacies after so many years among the Indians, but it hardly helped my mood that evening.

"They're getting things together for Lucky Jim's funeral," Pete said when he finished his meal.

I looked up from my pudding where it stood untouched upon my placemat. "You mean his potlatch?"

The potlatch is the old ceremony where the Indians honor the life of the departed. His possessions are given away to friends and relations, along with other gifts accumulated by the family. I had been to a few of them when I lived upriver, but had never really considered the prospect that someday one would be held for my granddad.

Pete nodded. "Lucky Jim didn't have no sons or nephews, so George Washington has offered to step in and make the arrangements."

"Those two were always close pals," Mike said.

"They was," said Pete. He turned to me. "AC, you should come upriver for the doings."

"Yes," I said, nodding. I knew that if I went upriver I would not be coming back. But my aunt and uncle knew it, too.

"Aleksandr is a Christian," said Klara. "He does not need to be party to those ways."

She didn't say the word HEATHEN, but it was obvious that was what she meant. My aunt had been raised in a Russian household and tightly within the church. It come as no surprise to me that she would disapprove of this. Her position on such matters was that those things was fine for the Kenaytze people, but not for me.

Mike sipped at his doctored coffee. "It's the start of the new school term, Pete. And I need him to help me in the store over the summer."

This last bit of information was news to me. Resentment flared up in my breast. I had been looking forward to being in the woods all summer. I had plans to head up to Point Possession and join the belukha hunt. Now it seemed that my future was once again being mapped out for me with no consideration of what I wanted.

Pete frowned. "You could at least let him come upriver and show his face. He's got a lot of kin upriver who would like to see him."

I watched Mike and Klara. They looked at one another over the corner of the table.

"George Washington's an important man," said Pete. "It aint no small thing for him to undertake a funeral potlatch for a man who was not his relation."

Mike pressed his lips together and shook his head. "I'm sorry Pete. School is more important. AC will have to stay here."

I stared at the dark window where the glass panes reflected the lamplight and all of us sitting at the table.

As if there were a second room beyond that I might step into and live in a world where I could go upriver and be rid of my aunt and uncle and their plans for my future. This of course was the very face of ingratitude—I realize now that they loved me and were only doing what they thought best—but a young fellow on the threshold of manhood is prone to see life this way.

Klara's face grew distant as she spoke. "We shall go to church and pray for Lucky Jim's soul."

So it was that on the two days and nights of Lucky Jim's potlatch, at the very moment they lit his funeral pyre to cremate him in what was likely the last of the old-style Indian funerals, my aunt and I was kneeling in the tiny log chapel with Sava Golinov under the vaulted shingle roof topped with its onion dome and three-pronged cross. He led us in prayer, mumbling the sacred incantations in Slavonic, the high language of the church that both he and my aunt had learned as children in a world that was lost to me and all my generation.

Upriver, Lucky Jim's goods was given away to honor his life, along with piles of blankets, kettles, rifles and store clothes. My grandmothers Olga and Tasha went to live with their nieces and sisters, in keeping with a custom that dated back to a time when humans and animals could still speak to one another and rivers ran in both directions.

———

I have little to say of the summer I spent clerking for Mike in the AC store. Wage work does not suit me. I worked Monday through Saturday, ten hours a day. Mike fitted me out with a dark suit, which I had to pay for out of my pathetically small wages. He said such attire was required in the business world. Aunt Klara told me I looked handsome in it with my hair combed down and parted in the middle, but my buddies in town was of the opinion that I had no call wearing such finery while they all had to wear last year's hand-me-downs. I got in more than one fistfight over this matter.

I am not skilled with mathematics, and my ledgers was always a mess of scribbles and scratched-out computations, the fiber of the pages weakened from repeated erasings. Every single day I had to wait on friends and neighbors who came in to purchase supplies for a long trip here or there—upriver or across the Inlet or maybe up past Old Knik and the mountains beyond. They would stand at the counter in their hunting clothes while I moved about in my starched shirt and sleeve-garters collecting their purchases from the shelves. It was suggested to me more than once that I really ought to toss away my stiff collar and head out with them to wherever they were going

But I stayed. Mike kept what little money I earned. He told me I could live in his house for free when school was in session, but over the summer I was working and would have to pay for my room and board. My thinking on this matter was that the Americans might find it acceptable to charge their own kin for a bed and a meal, but such a thing was unknown among my people. To be fair, Mike was but one of a small handful of Americans living on the Peninsula. Their ways was strange and foreign to us, but he was only doing what he thought best for me in the long run. All the same, this stung me deeply.

I was released from the prison of the store at the start of the fall term only to be shut up inside Watkins' schoolhouse. This was a low point in my youth, but then Belukha Pete come to town on a supply run. He knocked on the house door and handed me two things: Lucky Jim's old Sharps rifle and a lock of his fifteen-foot hair, coiled up and sewn into a pouch made of tanned goose feet.

"You're welcome at Point Possession any time, AC," he said to me.

He spoke not a word to Klara or Mike.

———

It was the following spring that I left school. Yasha had been sent downriver just after New Year's so he could learn to read and write. A Moravian missionary had come through Skilant town and convinced his aunts that this was the right thing to do. This was a happy reunion for us, though it was destined to shatter Mike and Klara's designs for me.

Yasha didn't speak American, and he'd not had a day of schooling in his life, so Watkins seated him with the first-graders. Yasha was the same age as me, mind you. He didn't know the language, but he was no dunce, and it shamed him mightily to be seated with the little children. They stared at him as if he'd come from the moon, him being a mountain Indian and all.

Naturally, with his linguistic handicap it was impossible for him to learn anything, but Watkins wouldn't let up on him. He'd plant his palms on Yasha's desk and scream in his face, and Yasha would just sit there with his brows drawn together. He tried speaking the Kenaytze tongue to Watkins, telling him he had no idea what he was saying, and Watkins responded by ordering him up front for a whipping. Yasha learned that lesson real fast.

It was May month, maybe two weeks before school let out that we decided we'd had enough. It was just after the noon recess, and all of us kids was filing back in. I lingered at Yasha's desk in the first-grade section. We'd been talking quietly in the Kenaytze tongue about how unfair Watkins was being and about our general dislike of school. The ducks and cranes was just returned to the country, and we was itching to be out hunting.

"AC," he said, "why don't you teach me to read and cipher? I don't need to sit in this dingy old cabin to learn it."

It was a fine idea, and I told him as much. In truth, I didn't know why we hadn't thought of it sooner.

Then there came Watkins' voice from behind us. The rest of the students was in their seats and staring at us.

"Master Campbell," he said, "do you intend to join the first graders?"

"No, sir," I said. I stepped quickly over to my seat.

"Stand fast!"

He slapped his green willow switch against his palm, looking back and forth from me to Yasha. His voice was sharp as a jail warder. "You were speaking that Native language."

I didn't say nothing and neither did Yasha. Of course, Yasha couldn't understand the words, but he knew full well what was going on.

"That language is forbidden within these walls," said Watkins. "It is a dead language. Backward and savage. The English language is your future and you will learn to speak it."

He trained his eyes upon me, sighting over top of his spectacles. "Master Izaakov is new here and may not know better, but I expect more from you, Master Campbell. Now get up to the front of the room. Both of you."

Watkins ordered Yasha to stand in the corner and wait his turn while I went first. He delighted in playing this game with his victims. He never told you how many stripes you'd earned, you just had to bend over, wrap your hands round your ankles and take it lick for lick.

"You know the position," he said to me. All eyes were upon us. I stepped up to him smartly, for I am no coward, but as I bent down and assumed the position I was alarmed to feel the crackling start up again inside my jaw. Not thinking, I reached up to try and rub it away.

"Hands on your ankles!"

I done as I was told, but the crackling got worse. It spread out across the back of my head and up into my face. I most earnestly did not wish to change into a bear at that moment in time, but I had trekked to the Nelchina country and back, had shot several moose and caribou, mountain sheep and black bears. I knew the old Indian ways and the Kenaytze tongue, and I'd faced danger from the Esquimaux and built canoes and paddled to places Watkins had never even dreamed of. Had I done all of these things to be whipped like a dog before the whole class by a man I had no respect for whatsoever?

The room was silent but for the ticking of Watkins' pocket watch. I could feel all my classmates watching us, and Yasha, too. Watkins shouted at him to turn back to the corner. He drew the switch back to strike, but I wheeled round and snatched it from his hand.

He stood there blinking, a stunned expression across his face. "You give that back!" he hissed. He made a grab for it, but I quirted him hard across the face. My classmates all sucked in their breath as one. Watkins recoiled in pain as a red welt began pushing up on his cheek. Then he lunged at me, saying, "God damn you, you siwash ingrate! I'll show you how to give a whipping!"

Again I dodged his advance. The bubbles in my jaw had stopped spreading, but was growing more intense by the second. I give him another lick across the chops, then another and another until his spectacles flew from his face and he cowered down against his desk. I laid on one last strip across his backside. He let out a little whimper, and in disgust and contempt I flung the switch down at him.

Yasha watched this whole scene with open satisfaction. The movement of Watkins' timepiece was muffled by his bent posture, leaving the room quiet as the grave. He didn't look up at us.

"To hell with your Yankee school!" I shouted down at him. "I don't recall asking for your opinion on what language we choose to speak!"

The popping and crackling by now was so bad I could barely think straight. I grabbed hold of his waistcoat and made to wrench him up and really let him have it, but Yasha come in behind me and wrapped his arms around me and pulled me away.

"Let it go, AC," he said. "Leave it. You won't do no good by that."

I blinked at him for a moment, panicked to think I may have already lost control and become a bear, but looking from Yasha to Watkins on the floor, and at my fellow students staring wide-eyed at us, I seen no indication of this. I had no fur. My fingers was still fingers and not claws.

Yasha gripped my shoulder. "You alright?"

I flexed my jaw. The crackling was gone as if it had never been. "Yeah," I said.

Watkins leaned back against his desk, glaring up at us.

"We better go," said Yasha.

So we turned and walked out the door. The rest of the class followed. They was not fools. They knew there would be hell to pay once Watkins collected himself.

That was how we quit school. I'll not say with time and distance that it was the best choice I ever made, but for better or worse it is what we done. It turned into quite the scandal around town, however. The elders made no secret of their disapproval. Both Klara and Mike was fit to be tied when they found out.

"Young man, you are going to march yourself over to the schoolhouse first thing tomorrow and apologize," Mike said to me. We was sitting in the parlor, him in his favorite easy chair and Klara in her rocker. She didn't have any knitting or embroidery upon her lap like usual, which was a sure sign that this was to be a long lecture on respect for one's elders and the course of my future.

"I aint going to do that," I said.

"Don't say aint," said Klara. She was upset, and it made her Russian accent more pronounced. "You ought to know better than that after two years of school."

I might have rolled my eyes at this. Probably did, now that I think about it. "I am not going to apologize."

Mike leaned forward. "Son, you damn well better apologize."

"Or else what? I've quit that son of a bitch."

Klara flushed.

"You watch your language, Aleksandr," said Mike.

"You're the one started cussing."

"Did Yasha put you up to this stunt?"

"Nope."

"That kid is no damn good."

"Don't talk about Yasha like that."

He let out a sharp snort of a laugh and sat back in his chair and folded his hands over his stomach. "When you've apologized to Watkins, you'll go back and finish out the term. Then you'll start clerking again at the store. You'll also be helping me build an addition onto the house, which should give you no time for bad behavior."

"I aint going back to no store," I said.

"Oh no?"

"Me and Yasha are going trapping next winter. We decided we're partners in the venture. We got things to do over the summer."

The two of us had come to this decision that afternoon as we hid out in the woods. We was done with Kenay town and done with being schoolboys. We both had our own *bidarkas*, and the plan was to leave in the morning on the outgoing tide.

Mike and Klara looked at one another, and Mike propped his elbow on the arm of his chair and rested his forehead upon it.

"Well you won't be staying here then. You can just head on out that door and into the world and find out for yourself how things work."

"That's what I aim to do," I said.

I stood up and went upstairs to load my pack. I took up what was now my Sharps rifle, thinking briefly and fondly of Lucky Jim, then I went back down and out the front door. I figured I'd just sleep in the woods. Mike and I didn't shake, and Klara was sobbing into her hand as I turned my back on them and went out into what Mike called THE WORLD.

———

By the end of May month 1885, me and Yasha was living in a borrowed wall tent just north of Cape Starichkof. There's a creek that tumbles down to the sea with a real pleasant spot to camp next to a waterfall. We lived mostly off ducks and geese that we shot in the tide-slough behind the mouth of Stariski Creek.

We was not idle during this time. We was hard at work getting our grubstake together. Belukha Pete had heard of our decision to leave school, and one day he appeared at our camp and told us he could arrange for us to have a few freight dogs if we could find the means to feed them.

"Where you plan to trap?" he asked, hunkered down next to our fire in his shirtsleeves and loading his pipe. He had brought a bottle of *quass*, which is a sort of Russian wine made from fermented berries, sugar and sourdough yeast. This was shared around and before long me and Yasha was both feeling light as a feather. This was the first time I was drunk and would not be the last.

I had boiled the kettle for a *chypeet*, but we had no China tea, only bush tea. Mailman Mike called it Labrador Tea.

I added a handful of leaves to the kettle and let it steep. "We was thinking Sixmile Creek," I said, sitting back on my knees.

Sixmile is the next creek up Turnagain Arm from Tutsilitnu. Both Yasha and me had been there at various times over the years and had seen plenty of fur sign. Nobody had lived there since the old Russian days.

Pete lit his pipe and puffed out a cloud of smoke. "It's a cold spot come winter, but there's some otters and beaver there. And you got access to a lot of different country. There's marten above the canyon up near your granddad's old trapline. Plenty of rabbits around, so you might find a cat or two."

Yasha and me was pleased to have his approval.

"Takes a lot of fish to feed a dog team," Pete said. "You boys got your work cut out for you."

"The kings will be here any day now," said Yasha. "We got trap staves cut and split already."

Pete nodded. Our own pipes had gone out, and he passed us his tobacco tin, a gesture that told us we had arrived in the world of grown men. He did not mention the unhappiness we had left behind us in town.

Pete was a busy man and departed on the next tide. Said he was headed down the Inlet toward the Barren Islands to arrange a trading trip with a Koniag man he knew.

"A Koniag?" said Yasha, narrowing his eyes.

"Times are changing," said Pete. "And they aint all bad. You boys take care."

We spent the next day building the trap, and the day after that getting it set onto the beach by means of stakes driven into the sand. It was as tall as a man and nearly three *sazhens* in length, which is about three fathoms or eighteen feet. In the evenings we worked on Yasha's American.

Come the full moon when we got big tides, we left the trap and went out onto the sand-flats to dig razor clams. Just the year before, a couple big companies out of San Francisco had come up and built two new canneries along the Inlet, one at Kenay town and one at Kussilof. They paid a penny apiece for live clams. The two of us working together could dig a couple hundred on a good tide, which added up to two dollars. That was decent money for a morning's work, but we could only do it five or six times before the big tides disappeared with the half-moon. We sold our clams at the Kussilof cannery because they paid coin and folding money instead of just credit at the cannery store. Of course, we had plenty of other reasons to steer clear of Kenay. All of this is to say nothing of the fact that digging clams is a lot of fun, and they're one of my favorite things to eat.

The big tides came round again when the moon had waned down to nothing. On a lark we decided to head up to Deep Creek and see how the digging was there. The Creole town of Ninilchik was barely a mile north of Deep Creek, with better digging on its beach, but we knew folks there and figured we'd get a lecture on responsibility and the benefits of education if we showed our faces. So Deep Creek would have to do.

We jumped in our *bidarkas* that morning and paddled north with the tide. It was full when we arrived, which meant we would have to wait several hours for low tide, but it was a sunny day, and we planned to make a fire and cook some dinner. We'd been up all night cutting fish, and a snooze was also in the plan.

As we was carrying our boats up from the beach I thought I seen someone duck down into the grass. The mouth of Deep Creek is a long sand-spit grown over with ryegrass. Behind it, the stream runs parallel to the beach for several hundred yards, then bends out at the base of the bluff on the north side. Looking back, there was probably no real cause for alarm, but the youth of me and Yasha's generation had been raised with hair-raising stories of the old wars between the Esquimaux and the Indians. Every single Indian child in those days, or any Creole child with an Indian mother, was warned that if he didn't behave he would be left out in the bushes for the Esquimaux to find, cook, and eat. The old men was fond of planting the idea in our heads that with the Russians gone, the Esquimaux and Koniags might just start coming back up the Inlet looking for trouble. Of course, I was also mindful of my experience with Lucky Jim in the woods that day near Port Graham.

We both took up our weapons. I had my Sharps rifle, but Yasha had only an old British flint-lock musket. We both had our axes. We crept up into the grass, and I circled wide toward the creek while Yasha crept along the edge of the grass where the winter storms had piled mounds of kelp and drift logs.

I poked my head up over the grass to get a look around. There was a breeze to keep the bugs away, which was nice, but this made it difficult to see what might have been lurking up ahead.

I'd just ducked back down and set myself to creep forward when I heard a stick snap.

I froze, crouched down with one foot poised over the ground. There was silence and the whisper of the grass in the breeze. Then I heard Yasha's voice speaking in the Kenaytze tongue.

"It's some Yankee girl. I seen her duck down into the grass off to your right."

"She alone?"

"Can't tell."

"Miss!" I called out in American. "We won't hurt you, we're friends."

I listened for a reply but none came.

"Miss," I said, "I'm Aleksandr Campbell from down at Cape Starichkof. Over there's my partner, Yasha Izaakov. We just come here to dig clams, we won't do you no harm."

Still no reply, but I could feel her watching us. I jacked the shell from the breech of my rifle and held the weapon up so she could see the action left open. I laid it down against a drift log. From the corner of my eye I seen Yasha uncock his musket and do likewise.

We stood like that for several minutes, nobody saying nothing. Then there come a female voice:

"You aint going to shoot?"

"No," I said, "we aint going to shoot nor harm you in any way. We was just getting ready to have something to eat."

Slowly a head rose up from the grass tips, then a neck and shoulders to go with it. I walked forward real easy with my palms out. The girl looked me square in the eye, and my heart jumped up in my chest. I'd never seen such an exotic beauty. She had blue eyes and yellow hair that was full of curls. I'd seen blue eyes before—both Klara and Mike had them—but yellow hair was something entirely new to me. They say some of the Russians from the old country was yellow-headed, but they was all long gone. An urge rose within me to step up to her and touch those curls to see if they was truly real or some kind of illusion. It was only with great difficulty that I was able to push this impulse away.

"I always thought it was just a made-up story," I said, not quite aware that I was speaking out loud.

She cocked her head at me. "What was?"

I pointed over the grass. "Yellow hair."

"You mean blonde hair?"

I was suddenly aware of how stupid I sounded and could think of nothing more to say. I just stood there staring like a fool as Yasha introduced himself with his rather limited American. The girl smiled and said hello, then turned back. My face flushed hot, but then she give a little giggle. Russian girls are taught from an early age not to do this, but when this one put a hand over her smiling mouth her curls wobbled with the movement and I thought I might faint.

Yasha coughed and spat, which brought me out of my spell. I blinked a couple times, then put out my hand. "I'm Aleksandr Campbell. But folks call me AC."

"I'm Polly Parker," she said, taking my hand. "I mistook you for hostiles."

Me and Yasha looked at one another, then back at her. Her American had an odd accent I'd never heard before. She spoke in a slow drawl, stretching her words out like cold syrup. At first I thought she was a halfwit who had been abandoned by her companions on account of her mental deficiency, but further inquiry revealed that she was from Texas.

"What are you doing here?" I said.

"My papa and I come up to prospect for gold."

Despite her bizarre accent she spoke much prettier than my colonial Creole voice can render it here.

"Where's your dad at?"

"He went back up to our rental cabin in Ninilchik to fetch a couple things. He's probably waiting for the tide

KRIS FARMEN

to drop so he can walk back." She pointed up the creek to the trees on the south bank. "We're building our own place up there. Can you see it?"

I looked where she pointed and seen the fresh logs, three rounds of them, gleaming in the sunshine amid the cottonwoods.

"You're reading a book," I said.

"I am. It's called *Sense and Sensibility*." She held it up and smiled. "You made me lose my place."

"Sorry. Who wrote it?"

"Jane Austen. Men tend not to like her books so much. They're written for ladies."

"What do you learn from it?"

She laughed. "Well, not much of any practical value. I just read her books because I enjoy reading them."

"I don't think I ever seen no-one read a book for pleasure," I said. "You really like doing it?"

"I love to read. I always have. Do you read?"

"I aint ignorant," I said. "I been to school." To my surprise, I was suddenly very grateful to Mike and Klara and Sava for making me come downriver and get an education.

Yasha had by this time drifted off to examine their mining setup. He'd never seen such a contraption before. Polly followed him and showed us the big sluice-box and rocker they'd made out of whipsawn boards. Their intent was to wash fine gold from the beach sands. They had picks, shovels and pans, and there was a large pit where they'd been digging into the beach gravel. I'd seen people sluicing beach gold closer to Ninilchik. It was never much of a lucrative proposition, but the pay was consistent, which is to say it was consistently low. I said as much to Polly, but she just pushed her chin out a little and said she and her dad could do anything they set their minds to.

Yasha rolled his eyes and went off to drag up some firewood.

I thought to tell her that they could set their minds to sifting every yard of sand on Cook Inlet, but if there wasn't no gold there to begin with, they weren't going to find it. But I kept my trap shut. I had no wish to give offense to such a lovely creature as this.

"Well," I said, "if your old dad's not here, then why not sit down and have some dinner with us? We got a few hours before the tide goes down."

Polly demurred, saying something about it not being proper for her to consort with young gents like us without a chaperone. I didn't really follow that so I let it slide and said to her that she could sit here in the grass if she liked, but if she got hungry or lonesome she was welcome to come down to the fire and break bread with us. This was a bit of a fib because we hadn't no bread, just some pilot crackers, dried salmon and a couple spruce chickens Yasha had shot that morning. Still, she perked up when I mentioned food.

I picked up my rifle and walked down to the edge of the grass where we'd carried our boats. Yasha was holding a match to a pile of birchbark and kindling. He looked up as the bark caught and flared into the twigs. "She aint going to come eat?"

"No," I said. "She's shy, I guess."

"Americans."

He stacked some finger-size branches over the kindling then blew on the flame to get it roaring. Since he had the fire up, I fished our grub-sack out from the tail of his boat. I filled our tin kettle at a tiny freshwater seep that trickles down from the south bluffs and set it down atop the fire. Yasha stacked more driftwood around it. I tossed him some strips of dried salmon. He put one to his teeth and tore off the skin and ate it first, then he

KRIS FARMEN

ate the fish. I set out a box of pilot crackers with an old whiskey bottle full of seal oil. I sliced a piece of salmon and laid it on a cracker and drizzled oil over the whole thing, this being a common meal for bachelors on the trail. The water hissed against the kettle-sides.

The last of the morning clouds had burned away until there was nothing but sunshine and blue sky. The kettle came to a boil. Yasha appeared to have forgotten all about Polly, but I surely hadn't. I kept looking back, wondering if she was watching us, or more to the point, watching me. Then she was standing at the edge of the grass with her skirts blowing round her limbs and the loose strands of her yellow hair straying over her face.

"Alright," she said with a smile, "I got lonely and hungry. May I join you all?"

We nodded and she sat down on the gravel. Yasha moved the kettle off the coals and steeped it with bush tea. I handed Polly some salmon strips and the bottle of oil. She sniffed at the mouth of the bottle, and while she was polite about it, I seen her nose wrinkle up. She did like the salmon, however, and devoured it with relish.

When the tea was ready I filled my cup, then passed it to her. "I'm sorry we aint got nothing but brown sugar for it," I said. "How much you want?"

"But what will you drink from? There's only two cups."

Yasha was already sipping at his own tea and watching the purple base of Mount Redoubt on the far side of the water.

"You're company," I said. "I'll drink when you're done."

She took a sip from the cup, then swallowed and looked up. "This doesn't taste like tea."

I felt another hot flush of embarrassment at not having China tea to offer, only wild tea that any fool could pick out in the woods.

Yasha came to my rescue. "It's Alaska tea," he said. "Old time Russian delicacy."

Polly didn't see the wink he dropped at me.

"Really?" she said.

I nodded with what I hoped was a sage and expansive demeanor.

Yasha rearranged himself so he was seated comfortably with his back against a drift log. Looking at him I realized how rough the two of us looked. We'd been living in the woods more or less since we quit school, and we must have looked it. Our clothes was rank with wood smoke and fish guts. We was in our clamming trousers which was cut off at the knees to avoid the unpleasantness of wet clammy pant legs flopping around our ankles as we worked on the clam flats. We was both barefoot as well, being on the beach and all. Neither of us had a haircut in quite a while—mine was pulled back into a tail, and Yasha's blew loose under a kerchief he'd tied round his head. Quite a sight we must have been, but we hadn't really expected to encounter any damsels when we left camp. Not that we had better duds to wear anyhow.

"How long you and your dad been here?" I asked.

"Here in Alaska, you mean?"

"If you like. But I meant here where we are now." I waved the tip of my knife around us to indicate the greater Kenay and Cook Inlet area.

"We only been in Alaska since March. We come up from San Antonio. My papa had to retire from the Texas Rangers back in seventy-nine because he got shot in the knee and couldn't chase renegade Comanches no more."

I didn't know what Comanches was, but I didn't say so. She chewed on a piece of salmon and looked down at the skin in her hands. "He had a job for a while as a prison guard in California at San Quentin."

"What's that?"

"It's a big jailhouse near San Francisco. But it was just too dangerous for him with his bad knee. So we sold our house and come north to look for gold."

"What made you come to the Peninsula? There aint much gold around here."

"Papa wanted to go to the Yukon River, but it was too much of a trip for him in his state."

"That's a long way from here."

Polly drew her lips into a brief rueful smile. She looked back down at the fish skin in her hands. "So anyway, we ended up here. We'll have our cabin done by the end of the summer. And there is some gold here. We just haven't made our big strike yet."

By now Yasha was down for a nap, using his shot pouch and powder horn as a pillow. I could see his chest rising and falling in the rhythm of his breath. The tide was maybe halfway down.

I moved a little closer to her and kept feeding the fire as we visited. She told me about her departed mother and about Texas and the Mexicans, Comanches and bandits. Them last two sounded like a murderous bunch, and it made me glad we have nothing of the kind up here.

The afternoon slid by, and the tide dropped until the clam-flats started to show. I looked upriver toward Ninilchik. "How long's your father been gone?"

"Most of the morning. Sometimes he needs to rest his knee. I may just go up there and check on him."

"Come dig razor clams with us."

"Razor clams?"

"It's a lot of fun," I said, playing it sly. "We could bake some here on the beach for supper."

She seemed interested, so I shook Yasha awake, and the three of us trudged through the steep gravel of the upper beach and down onto the flats. As I've said, Yasha and me was barefoot in our clamming pants. Polly took off her own shoes and stockings and laid them in the grass. She made us turn the other way while she done this.

Yasha pointed out the first clam dimple. In a single motion he dropped to one knee and sunk his wooden clam shovel into the sand. He dug a hole in two strokes, then laid the shovel aside and thrust his hand down the hole. Five seconds later he lifted out a six-inch clam with a sucking sound. He dropped the clam into a gunnysack and slung the clinging muck off his arm.

I showed Polly how to do it again, then handed her the shovel. We stepped lightly over the sand with our eyes looking for another dimple. She tried digging the next one but made a mess of it and the clam got away. On her next try she crunched the shell to pieces which meant it was no good for the cannery because it would die before we could deliver it. By the third clam she had the digging part down, but a razor clam dives awful fast when it knows something is after it. All we seen was the clam's neck squirting at us as it slipped away into the watery sand.

But Polly was no delicate flower. "I see it, I see it!" she cried and threw herself down onto the sand, worming her hand around the hole until her arm was buried almost to the shoulder. Slowly she pulled the clam out intact and whole, and I congratulated her as she dropped it into the sack. She had wet sand down her sleeve and the front of her skirts and blouse, but she was all smiles and laughing like a loon.

Yasha was busy digging a few yards away. He'd excavated six clams by moving from one dimple to the next just a foot or so away and caving in the sand with his shovel as he went. He stuck each clam upright and neck-down in the sand so they couldn't dig a getaway, then he'd move on to the next dimple.

Me and Polly dug together for nearly an hour. Naturally I pulled up more clams than her—I had, after all, been doing this since I was a small boy. But Polly improved with each hole she dug. She had a natural touch for it though her long skirts hindered her considerably. When I suggested she might want to take off some of her petticoats or maybe even don a pair of britches, she slapped me on the arm and said, "Shame on you, AC!"

This startled me. I didn't mean nothing; it was just a logical suggestion, something any local gal would have done in a trice. But then Polly smiled at me from beneath those curls and giggled in a manner I thought rather devilish. I was, as they say, a goner.

That's when I seen two men walking across the beach toward us, each loaded down with a heavy pack.

"Someone's coming," I said.

"That's my father. I don't know the other fellow." She looked down at her filthy clothes and swore.

Down the glimmering sand-flats I seen Yasha straighten up to watch their approach. He stuck his shovel into the sand next to his clam sack and walked over to join us.

Mr. Parker walked with a somewhat wooden gait, I presume because of his bum knee. There was dark sweat stains showing around his hatband, and when he pulled it off to wipe his brow, his salt-and-pepper hair was plastered to his skull. Given Polly's concern about cavorting with young gentlemen in the absence of a chaperone, I had the impression that he might just try to tear my sweetmeats off. I kept my clam shovel handy for a swing at his knee if it came to that.

The other fellow was younger, closer to me and Polly's age but old enough to have a beard coming in. He wore expensive-looking work clothes and owned the manner of a man with money who goes around like an unshaven bumpkin to feed his image of himself as a rugged pioneer. He scarcely glanced at me and Yasha, but turned his attention straightaway to Polly. I will confess to a stab of jealousy, but this was overridden by my instant dislike of the man.

"Young lady," said Parker, "just what in the blazes are you doing?"

"We're digging clams," Polly said. She pointed at me. "This is AC, and that Indian fellow over there is Yasha."

"You're digging clams with a couple Indians?" said Parker.

"I'm a Creole," I said. "Yasha's an Indian."

His expression as he looked me up and down was not entirely unkind, but I could tell he was weighed down with worry and troubles. I would be too if I was trying to sluice beach gold for a living.

"Who's this?" Polly said, looking at the stranger.

Parker half-turned, as if he'd forgot his companion. "This is Greg Hackham. He's a mining engineer just come into the country. He's offered to look over our claims and advise us on the most advantageous way to work them."

"Most folks call me Hack," said the stranger as he offered his hand. "I specialize in beach mining."

Polly looked at her own sand-coated palm and wiped it on the back of her blouse. When she had it tolerably clean she laid it in his and shook it in a most feminine manner.

"How do," I said to this Hack fellow, offering out my own hand. It took him a second to tear himself away from Polly. He nodded at me and Yasha, and though he was cordial enough, I seen the tips of his mouth turn up as if there was something he thought funny, but chose to keep to himself. He did not take my hand.

Parker pointed down at Polly's naked ankles and bare feet. "What are you doing in such a state of undress?"

"I didn't want to get my shoes wet."

Parker started into the first line of what I took to be a harangue about feminine decency, but he remembered they had company and chose to let out a long sigh instead.

"Hell's bells," he said, "just get yourself up to the rocker."

"Boys," he said to me and Yasha. The three of them walked up toward the sluice plant.

"He's an arrogant fucker," Yasha said when they was out of earshot.

"He seemed agreeable."

"Not the old man. The other fellow."

I looked over at him. "How'd you get so good at your American? I never taught you that word."

Yasha laughed and clapped me on the shoulder. He pointed to my clam sack, which was nowhere near as full as his own. "You got clams to dig, partner. You fell way behind holding hands with that Yankee gal."

Later that afternoon when our sacks was full, we loaded up our *bidarkas* and headed north, riding the incoming tide to Kussilof. I turned to watch Polly and her dad at work. He was at the shovel and she was working the rocker. Hack walked around jotting notes in a small book. Polly looked up as we paddled past, but didn't wave. I guess she didn't want to stir her father up. The last view I had was of her turning to listen to Hack as he asked her some question. No doubt it was of a charming and debonair nature.

———

After we got back to camp from selling the clams we found a load of fish inside our trap, all of which had to be cleaned and split. It doesn't get dark that time of year, and we wanted to get it done, so we didn't get to bed until well past midnight.

It was mid-morning when I woke and went down to the creek to fill the kettle for tea. Polly had been on my mind all through the day and night, and I was plotting another clam digging mission up at Deep Creek. The moon was waxing up, and the tide wouldn't be as big, but it seemed to me that the clams there was suddenly crying out my name, begging, TAKE ME, AC! NO, TAKE ME!

Still asleep and scratching my longjohns, I shambled down to the path we'd worn into the stream bank and waded into the riffles. The roar of the waterfall filled the morning. The gravel ground up between my toes, and the icy water piled onto my ankles as I dipped the kettle. That's when I looked downstream and seen the riders. Ten men and twenty horses. All of them watching me.

The man in the lead raised his hand. "Howdy."

I straightened up and climbed out of the water and onto the bank. "Morning," I said.

"I'm Joe Cooper out of Kachemak Bay. You up at the crack of noon these days?"

This Cooper fellow was of medium build with a big moustache. The men behind him was all Americans, and a rough-looking bunch as well.

"We was up cleaning fish all night."

"What's your name?"

No local would ask such a bold question—you're meant to wait for someone to introduce themselves—but I'd learned enough about Americans over the years to know they meant no rudeness. It's just their way.

"Aleksandr Campbell," I said. "Folks call me AC."

"You an Indian?"

"I'm a Creole," I said. "My dad was a Yankee like you."

Cooper's face darkened. "Son, I'm from south Missouri. Don't you ever call me no goddamned Yankee."

"Then what should I call you?"

"We're Americans."

"Right," I said. "You care to come have a *chypeet*?"

"Have a what?"

"You want some tea."

He shook his head. "We're looking for a guide. We're headed up to look for the old Russian gold mine up near Kenay Lake. You know where it's at?"

"Yeah. I know it."

He brightened considerably. "We're packing up the Inlet beach to Turnagain Arm, then we'll head south through the mountains. If you're looking for a job, we'll set you up with a gold pan and cut you in on a share of the profits."

At first I was dubious about the prospect of abandoning the fish trap to head north on such a lark, but then things clicked inside my head. This was my ticket to Polly's heart. I could bring her back a leather sack of gold, then take her and her dad upriver to show them where they should be mining. This was a sketchy plan at best, but one is always full of optimism when young and smitten. I was too wet behind the ears to know that what Cooper offered was a sucker's deal. If a man offers to pay you in gold, you make him pay you gold in your hand, not some promise that you can dig and sluice for your own wages.

"My partner goes with me," I said. "I'll have to ask if he's game."

Cooper considered it a moment. He twisted around to look at his men, then back to me. He nodded.

"He a siwash too?" said one of the horsemen.

"He's an Indian." Considering my words with Parker and Hack on the beach at Deep Creek, there was the depressing notion that I was probably going to have this exact same conversation with every American I met for the rest of my life.

The man frowned a little, but Cooper seemed amenable.

"Bring him along," he said. "If he wants to go."

"I'll have to go rattle his cage."

"We'll wait."

I trotted up the bank to the tent and shook Yasha awake. "Partner," I said, "we got a opportunity to make some real money."

"What?" He stuck his head out of his blankets and rubbed his eyes. I seen him cock his ear and listen to the horses chuffing their hooves in the beach gravel. He stood up out of the tent and slipped into the tag-alders where he examined our new employers.

"It's a bunch of Yankees from down at Kachemak Bay," I said. "They're off to find that old Russian gold pit."

"You mean the one we crawled into when we was kids?"

"The very same."

"What are they paying?"

"A share of the gold."

He looked across the creek at the drying racks and the fish upon them. Then up at the pole cache in the trees where we'd stored the cured fish.

"We'll be short on dog feed come trapping season," he said.

"We can buy all the dog feed we want with gold."

He thought for a moment, then frowned before finally agreeing.

"So you want to go?" I said.

"Yeah. Let's do it."

So we pulled on our britches and went back down to the beach. Cooper and his men had dismounted and were milling about while the horses cropped at the grass and beach-peas. We told Cooper it was a deal.

"You speak English?" he said to Yasha.

"You bet I do," Yasha said, hooking a thumb at me. "My partner taught me."

Cooper chuckled at that. He rubbed his whiskers, looking back and forth between us. "We got two spare horses. Can either of you ride?"

Back when I was a little boy in Kenay town, Sava Golinov's half-brother Andrei had a shaggy old pony and dray he used for hauling freight up from the beach landing. Sometimes he'd let us kids ride atop the horse's back in the traces.

"Yeah," I said. "We can ride. But we'll paddle our boats up the Inlet. We can start riding when we get to Possession town."

"Possession town?"

"That's the Indian town at Point Possession," I said. "We'll leave our boats with George Washington."

"Son," he said, "you better start making sense in a hurry."

"George Washington. He's a *toyon*. An Indian chief. Me and Yasha will paddle north to Point Possession and save the wear and tear on your horses."

"Alright. Fair enough."

"Just let us pack up our camp and we'll be ready to go."

"You got a half hour."

"Don't worry," I said. "We'll be miles ahead of you by evening-time."

———

After Cooper and his men mounted their horses and got the pack string moving, me and Yasha struck our tent and piled it atop the bales of dried salmon in the tree-cache, then we threw several sheets of birchbark over it all to keep out the rain and lashed it down. We carried our *bidarkas* down to the water and loaded our travelling outfit of grub, blankets, tarps and rifles and axes. We also loaded the half-dried fish from the night before into

Yasha's boat. We hadn't the time to finish curing it, so we figured to just give it to some relatives along the way and maybe redeem ourselves a little.

We left on the next tide, paddling easy with a light breeze at our backs. Within twenty minutes we had overtaken the horsemen. They was halfway to Deep Creek, and we passed them like they was standing still.

Realizing where I was, I dug my paddle hard into the sea and pulled up aside of Yasha. "I need to make a quick stop."

"That yellow-headed gal," he said with a laugh.

"She might be lost and all alone there at the diggings. She might be in need of comfort and succor."

"Suck her? She's liable to punch you in the balls for saying that."

"Succor," I said. "It's a fancy American word that means soothing and comfort."

Yasha raised his eyebrows. "Oh, I see." He went back to his paddling, then paused to laugh once again.

"What?" I said.

"Maybe sucker's a better word."

I ignored him and worked my paddle in the gray current. Coming up on the mouth of the creek I could see Parker and Polly hard at work at their mining plant. They had quite a pile of sand, and what looked like the leftovers of a springtime flood running down where they used seawater at high tide for sluicing.

"Meet you up at Kussilof," I said over my shoulder.

Yasha nodded. "You know it."

The current had swept us up past the diggings. Polly and her dad had spotted us and stopped to watch. Me and Yasha waved, and Polly waved back. I was pleased at the enthusiasm she showed for us. I had to dig hard and lively to get up into the creek mouth, but the current evened out when I got into the tidal eddy at the base of the bluff. I beached my boat and hauled it out of the water above the tide-line, and Polly come quick-stepping down through the beach grass just as I was stretching out my back.

"AC!" she said.

"Polly Parker." There was a flutter inside me, and I felt a wide silly smile spread across my face. The sight of her was the brightest part of my day, no doubt about it.

She come up and drew me into a big hug. She was sweaty from working the rocker in the hot sun, and it made the feminine scent of her stand out all the more.

"What brings you back here?" she said.

"Me and Yasha got a job. Some fellow from down at Kachemak Bay hired us to guide him up into the mountains on a prospecting trip."

"Really?"

"It's the truth."

"That's wonderful," she said. "I'm so happy for you."

Her father come up behind her. "Mr. Campbell."

This took me a little by surprise, for it was the first time anyone had addressed me as Mister. Certainly the first time an American had done so. I wondered if maybe Polly had been talking me up.

"Mr. Parker," I said, shaking his hand. "How do?"

"Keeping busy," he said. "Lots going on."

I looked back at Polly. "I'm afraid I can't stay long. I just dropped by to see how you was getting along."

"I'm glad you stopped," she said. "I wondered if you'd ever be back."

"Well, we are neighbors. You finding any gold?"

Parker frowned a little. "Not as much as we'd hoped."

"We just haven't hit the mother lode yet," said Polly. "Right, Papa?"

He smiled down at the ground, then over at her. "That's right, hon. But it's a-coming."

"Can we take a break so I can show AC the new cabin?"

Parker looked over at the diggings, then back at us. "Oh, I suppose. But don't be too long about it."

Polly took my hand and led me up a footpath over the grassy tide-flat. Planks had been laid down over the wet spots. There was a little pang of disappointment when I glanced over my shoulder and seen Parker following at a respectable distance. Apparently, I was not meant to be alone with his daughter on this jaunt.

The trail took us up to a low hummock and into some cottonwood trees where the beach-grass ended and the forest began. Nestled into a clearing was the half-built cabin I'd spied on our first encounter with the fresh-peeled logs still shiny and bright in the sunshine. I had helped build many a cabin, and it was obvious to me that Parker was not much of a log builder. Many of the timbers was crooked, and he hadn't hewn them properly. He'd also notched the corners with crude saddle notches instead of dovetails.

Polly led me around the side and showed me where the windows had been marked out on the south and west walls. They hadn't yet installed the floor, but they had dug the hole for their cold-cellar. The yard outside was littered with sawdust, bark peelings and wood chips.

"Nice place," I said. "I like that view of the Inlet. You'll get some pretty sunsets through that west window."

She laughed. "You mean when the sun actually goes down."

"It'll be fall-time when you get them," I said. "But they're something to see. Especially when you got some clouds to pick up the colors."

"It's rather hard to get used to the sun not going down," she said.

"You think?"

She raised her eyebrows. "We hardly ever seem to sleep. I can't wait until the nights are getting dark again."

I studied her in the dappled light through the cottonwoods, not saying anything. Polly blushed and looked down at the ground.

"I guess you're used to the long daylight though," she said. "You would never have known anything different."

I tried to imagine it being dark at night in the summer, but somehow darkness and summertime just didn't fit together within the realm of my experience.

"I do alright with it," I said.

Polly stepped inside the cabin shell and took me around the packed earth inside, showing where the kitchen would go and the easy chairs and whatnot.

"We work on the cabin at low tide," she said. "Then we work at the diggings when it's high."

I noticed her hands was callused from hard labor. "That's a lot of work," I said.

"It is. I can't wait until we get it done and we have our cozy little log cabin in the woods. Then we can just focus on mining."

It come to me that by next spring a girl her age might be pretty tired of living in a cozy log cabin with her father, but I chose not to voice that opinion. I studied the hewing on the logs while nearby Parker pretended to be absorbed with reorganizing his tools. He coughed once, then again, turning his head and wiping his palm on the back of his trouser-leg.

"There aint no need to hew the logs flat all the way down," I said, pointing at their work.

Polly just looked at me.

"Just flatten down the last twelve *diuyms*."

"What's a die-yum?"

"*Diuym*," I said. I learned my carpentry from Russian teachers, and still thought in Russian measures. "That's a Russian inch."

"Is it the same as a normal inch?"

"More or less, I think. But anyway, just hew the last twelve inches of both ends, then make your notches there."

Polly looked back at the cabin, and I noticed even her father was listening, having paused from his tools. He coughed again and was seized with a brief fit that left him sucking for breath.

"You alright, Papa?" said Polly.

Parker just nodded and give a wave.

"I guess that would save a lot of time," she said, turning back to me. "You must have built a lot of cabins before, growing up here."

I smiled at her. "One or two. You finish your book?"

"Not yet, but I'm almost there." Her face brightened as she remembered something. "I got a book you might like, AC."

"To read?"

She giggled. "Of course. What else would you do with it?"

"I could use it to set a hot skillet on so it don't mark the table-top."

She frowned at me, but I seen there was a smile behind it. She stepped over to her packboard and rummaged inside it. When she come back she handed the book out at me. I took it from her and studied the title: *Treasure Island.* When I opened the front cover there was a picture of the deck of a sailing bark and this real tough-looking customer with a cutlass and wooden leg.

"I think you'll love that book," said Polly. "It's about pirates and buried treasure."

"I guess that's good, seeing as how I'm in the prospecting business."

She smiled. "I guess so."

We both studied the cabin in silence as Parker continued organizing his tools.

"So when will you be back, AC?"

"Fall. September month, most likely. Can I come calling again?"

"I'd like that," she said and drew me into another hug. I buried my nose in her golden curls and drew in her scent. It was arousing and exotic, like no other girl I'd ever encountered.

When we finally turned loose of one another, Parker was standing right next to us.

"Time to get back to work, Polly," he said.

———

Looking into shore from my vantage point on the water, I could see why Cooper and his men had chosen the beach route. It is considerably longer than going up the Kenay River, but it is the natural trail for horses or men afoot. No bogs, all easy walking, and you can wait for low tide to cross most of the streams.

Still, in the days that followed, I was glad me and Yasha had elected to take the water route. We had to camp every six hours and wait for the tide to run up the Inlet, but we was making three miles to the horses' every one. In fact, we could have made it all the way to Possession town in two long days if we'd really put our backs into it. But being young and full of beans, we turned the trip into a holiday. Sometimes the pack-string would pass us on the beach as we was taking our ease with the tide running against our destination. Then when she turned, we'd overtake the string in no time flat and have a fire made and the kettle boiling by the time the horses caught up again. Three times we seen black bears on the beach, and once a brown bear digging clams out on the flats with his claws. We made sure to pass this intelligence on to Cooper, for bears and horses make poor company.

Horses need rest and feed, so Cooper and the Yankees camped at night. When the pack train got to the big rivers like the Kussilof and the Kenay, they had to swim. Horses was a rare sight in those days, and a string such as Cooper had assembled was rarer still. The local people regarded the expedition as a great curiosity, and word spread like wildfire. This was a lucky break, as the village folk turned out with their boats and *bidarkas* to help ferry the gear across, which allowed the men to just worry about the livestock.

Me and Yasha kept going in the long summer daylight, paddling and resting in six-hour shifts with the tide. It was during these easy camps that I took to reading that *Treasure Island* book. It was painfully slow going. At first I could only get through one or two pages, but then one sunny night when I was paddling along behind Yasha, it come to me that I was eager to make camp so I could read a few more pages. Before long I was neglecting my beauty sleep to find out what happened next with Jim Hawkins and that untrustworthy scalawag Long John Silver.

We took our time as much as we could, but we had to arrive at our destination eventually. We killed a two-year-old cow moose on a small creek on the south side of the East Forelands and brought it up with us; she was scarcely more than a calf, but it was still a big load for our *bidarkas*. We rode so low in the water that there was the worry of water sloshing into the hatches, but we didn't want to show up empty-handed.

We was greeted with open arms by George Washington and his wives and everyone else at Possession town, and we ate great belly-fulls of moose meat and smoked our pipes until late in the evening when the young ladies of the town made it clear they was keenly interested in our company. It was the finest living two footloose young fellows could ask for.

Cooper and his men rode into town three days later, and everyone came out to see them. Most of the people at Point Possession had never before seen a horse, except for the older men who had worked for the Russians in California. They crowded around while Cooper and the men picketed the stock in a field of bluejoint grass. When this operation was done the Americans come up to town to meet George Washington.

The old *toyon* stood tall and formal in his frock coat as he shook Cooper's hand. "There's plenty to eat," he said. "Moose meat and lots of fish. Won't you fellows come sit down and visit."

George Washington spoke very little American, so it was my job to translate this for Cooper.

Cooper and his men made themselves comfortable in the open field above the beach that was generally used as common space for the town. The women already had fires going and meat cooking. They brought it out in short order and laid it on sheets of birchbark before the guests. Cooper took the first tray, and I seen George Washington nod with approval when Cooper chose a relatively tough cut of meat and passed the better pieces along to his men. This was something Lucky Jim and my grandmothers had always drilled into my head, a point of generosity and good form—the fellow with his hands first on the plate takes a lesser cut and gives his friends the good bits. This gave me pause to consider these Americans and their habits. They were strange and exotic to us, but I must confess some of their ways was perhaps not so different from ours.

We ate and ate that afternoon. Cooper and the boys was obviously starved for fresh meat. These was the first Americans ever to visit this part of the Peninsula, and thankfully it was good cheer all around. They was just as curious about the Indians as the Indians was of them. I was later to find out that most of the Natives down in the States was long since pacified and confined to reservations. Many of Cooper's party had never seen what they would call a WILD INDIAN, though Cooper himself seemed accustomed to dealing with them.

When we could eat no more, Cooper produced a large carrot of Virginia tobacco from inside his waistcoat and passed it to George Washington. He also handed over a bale of penny matches.

He turned to me and said, "Tell the chief to fill everyone's pipes on us, and divide it up as he likes. It's just a small gift from me to him. As thanks for his hospitality."

I said the words and George Washington nodded. He passed the tobacco and matches to Belukha Pete. Pete carved off a chunk with his knife and passed the carrot on to the next man and so on. There was still plenty left when it came back to George Washington. He filled his pipe and lit it with a match. Like many older Indians I've known, he was both fascinated by watching the match burst into flame, then reluctant to blow it out with his breath.

Cooper's men smoked their own bowls, watching the transaction. George Washington gestured with his pipe that it was fine tobacco and requested me to say as much, which I did. This pleased Cooper, and through me they exchanged a few pleasantries. There were inquiries about the trip up from Kachemak Bay and about whether or not Cooper knew George Washington's grand-niece who lived at Seldovoya.

We passed two days there at Possession town. This was the first real chance me and Yasha had to make the acquaintance of Cooper and our fellow miners. Among them was a man named Keogh. He was a few years older than me and Yasha, and while he was new to Alaska, he was no greenhorn. He had lived in Canada for many years, making his living as a trapper and lumber-jack, and had come into Alaska by way of the Yukon River.

Keogh was a jovial fellow and liked by all. Among his many talents was the ability to walk around on his hands. He could do this just as naturally as you or I might walk on our own two feet. This was a delight to the children of the village, and they fell all over themselves trying to imitate him, laughing themselves into a fit.

One evening we was sitting around a fire with this man and I asked him, "How come everyone calls you Scotty?"

Scotty Keogh looked at me very seriously and said, "Because I'm Irish." Then he laughed and passed me his bottle of home-brewed spirits, a substance he called *poteen*. It tasted like coarse vodka and might have been put to better use thinning down house-paint, but we was all too happy to grease our throats with it. I was beginning to like the feeling booze gave me.

Me and Yasha may have overstated our horsemanship abilities during the job interview at Cape Starichkof. Riding along on Andrei Golinov's dray horse as little children did not exactly qualify us as lonesome cowboys.

The sky was low and overcast when we set off from Possession town. Cooper and his men was already mounted and waiting as we sized up the task of climbing aboard our own animals. My horse was called Moonshine. He eyed the woods with a casual disinterest, chewing a mouthful of fireweed. I set my moccasin foot in the stirrup and tried to pull myself up by the saddle horn, but the whole contraption slid down cockeyed on the horse's side. When I righted the saddle Moonshine turned around and glowered at me. Again I set my foot and boosted myself up. I clawed my way onto his back but lost the reins and had to dismount to collect them. Yasha wasn't doing much better. He had managed to leap from a stump onto the back of his horse, but he ended up belly-down across the saddle and struggling to get upright.

All around us the Americans was laughing, even Cooper. George Washington and the residents of the town watched us in silence. I'd bet folding money they was wishing we would quit fooling around and represent our people a little better. What can I say? We was boatmen and dog-drivers. The only horse we knew was shanks' mare, and we knew that old nag right well.

I needed more height for standing, so I led my trusty steed over to a rock and stood upon it and finally got a-saddle. Working ever so slowly so as not to come tumbling off, Yasha righted himself and gripped his reins like he was hanging off a cliff.

Still chuckling, Cooper gigged his horse forward saying, "Let's go, boys!"

It was the start of a very long summer.

———

Though Cooper and his men was after the old Russian mine, me and Yasha was not so dumb as to think they wouldn't be interested in all gold prospects wherever they was to be located. Places, say, like Tutsilitnu where I'd found that nugget on my first trip with Lucky Jim.

To counter this we led the pack string up an old trail that runs along what is now called Big Indian Creek, a shallow stream that runs into Chickaloon Bay from the mountains to the south. There is no gold in it, which suited our purposes, but the lower reaches of the creek are full of bog and muskeg. This stretch of country is easy to get across in the winter when everything is frozen hard, but in summertime it's full of mosquitoes and a living hell for both horses and men.

Mind you, the trail was just an old footpath, not a wagon road. There was no bottom to the muck in many places, and the brush was so thick on either side of the

KRIS FARMEN

trail that the packhorses couldn't pass without snagging their panniers. Often as not we had to pilot the horses directly up the stream channel. When the water got too deep, me and Yasha was sent onto the bank with axes and saws to widen out the old trail. Once while doing this work we got charged by a sow grizzly that we disturbed at her fishing. This made for quite a dance until we could get our weapons into play.

The going got much easier once we started the climb up into the mountains. The country got more and more steep and the trail turned into easy firm footing for the horses as it wound through spruce and poplars no thicker than a man's arm. It actually became a halfway pleasant trip.

Everyone relaxed a little, and the atmosphere around the campfires was free and easy. In the long evenings after the dishes was washed and put away—this was me and Yasha's chore, by the way—the men would sit and tell stories. Many of these fellows had served in what they called the WAR OF NORTHERN AGRESSION, a title that didn't make any sense to me until the particulars was explained.

I made the mistake of asking if this was when Abraham Lincoln freed the African slaves. A general howl of disapproval went up. Several men grabbed their crutches and spat into the dirt.

"To hell with that son of a bitch Lincoln," said Cooper. There was a genuine hatred in his eyes that I'd only ever seen in the survivors of the old wars between the Indians and the Esquimaux.

A man named Mulholland leaned forward to lecture me. "That war wasn't about them damn nigras. It was about states' rights. The Confederacy seen what them god damned scalawags in the North was doing to the nation, and we didn't want no part of it. So we went and made our own country, and Lincoln wouldn't let us go."

Having grown up in a Russian-speaking world, I was and still am indifferent to the Americans' war and their stories of how tough it was for them. Folks on Cook Inlet was barely even aware of it when it was happening, and nobody could have cared less. We had plenty of our own hardships. Back when Russia was fighting the Britishers in Crimea and the supply ships stopped coming to Alaska, my people got so hard up for food they had to make soup out of their belts and boot-tops. More than one family had sons shipped out to Russia for soldiers, and most of them never came back. But the Americans don't care to hear any of that.

I looked over the top of the fire at the hard scowling faces of Cooper, Mulholland and the others. From the corner of my eye I seen Yasha moving over to Scotty's fire. I got up and joined him.

"You been listening to them secessionist fools?" said Scotty.

I sat down. "There's only so much horseshit I can swallow at one sitting."

Yasha passed around his tobacco tin. I watched Scotty tap the ashes from his pipe, then reload.

"Tell me, Scotty," I said.

He looked up and screwed the tin lid down and handed it to me.

"What side of the American war was you on?"

He lifted a flaming brand from the fire and lit his pipe. "Wasn't in it. I wasn't but two or three when it ended. But since I grew up in Boston I guess I would have fought for the North."

"How'd you wind up in Canada?" said Yasha.

"I never could handle city living. So I decided to go live in the woods. I just put my pack on my back and kept pointing north and west until I got to Slave Lake."

"Where's that?" I said.

"Straight east of here, more or less. Pretty place. Lots of fur."

"What made you leave?"

"Goddamn Britishers. Bloody Hudson Bay Company has got the fur business stitched up tight all over that country. In Canada you either sell your catch to the British or you don't sell it to no-one."

"Britishers and Irishmen don't get along?" said Yasha.

Scotty chuckled. "You might say that."

———

We moved east the next day, crossing a high pass from Big Indian Creek over to the lakes at the height of land between Tutsilitnu and Dzadatnu Creeks. Both me and Yasha was all smiles on our way down the trail toward Skilant town. It was good to see the creek me and Lucky Jim had walked up so many years ago. There was still a bit of young boy in us, and we was looking forward to riding into town with a string of horses and Yankees.

It was the following morning when Cooper announced he had decided to name the creek we was following Juneau Creek, after Joe Juneau, some prospector he knew from down around Sitka way.

"This creek already has a name," I told him. "It's called Dzadatnu."

Cooper shook his head. "We need something people can pronounce. It's called Juneau Creek now."

Yasha looked at me and shrugged. We didn't argue with him, knowing that everyone was going to keep calling it by its real name anyway.

We saddled the horses and hit the trail down through the spruce timber. It was coming on to supper-time when we splashed across the river into town. Everyone knew we was coming, there aint no secrets on the Peninsula. My guess is that George Washington sent a runner to forewarn them.

Cooper gigged his horse up to me. "So what's this place?"

"Skilant town," I said, pointing. "I grew up here."

He pursed his lips, surveying the cabins and pit-houses. The fish hanging on the drying racks and the blue smoke that hung in the air. The wood-piles and the trampled earth and the giant cottonwoods that shaded everything.

"So this Russian mine is nearby, then."

"Just upriver. Not even an hour's walk."

Both Olga and Tasha was deceased by this time, but it was a happy reunion for me and Yasha all the same. His aunts hugged him and started to fuss over him, but it quickly became obvious that he was now a man and not to be mollycoddled by the women. There was a tinge of sadness on his aunts' faces, but also a bit of pride as well. Still, they was determined to do some mothering and aimed their instincts at me, pinching my cheeks and squeezing me close in a series of big hugs that made my face go red.

Cooper and his men was made welcome, and the townfolk gawped at the horses as they was hobbled and turned out to forage. That evening after supper and a smoke, Cooper negotiated with the men of the town for access to the mine and a place to camp. It was agreed that he and his party was welcome to dig up as much gravel as they liked. Many years later, Pavil Sasha, a Creole who lived there at Skilant, told me that he knew one of the Russians who had been on the original expedition. He said this man told him there was gold in the river, but not in quantities to be commercially worthwhile. Pavil and the others figured Cooper and his boys would spend a week or two sifting and sluicing, and when the pay proved disappointing they would just head back down to Kachemak Bay.

When I asked Pavil why he didn't pass this intelligence on to us at the time, he just hooked a little grin at me and shrugged.

Pavil was half right. There was gold in the river, and it was indeed not enough to be worth the trouble. But he woefully underestimated the zeal of those Yankee prospectors. Me and Yasha worked at digging enormous holes in the riverbank while other men more experienced at mining sluiced the gravel we dug. As newcomers to the trade, me, Yasha and Scotty was the mules of the operation. We'd dug a crater near the size of Chisik Island by the time the silvers made it into the river.

We had our camp up by the old mine entrance and folks from town was regular visitors. Often they'd come in groups—the men with their pipes and the women with their needlework—and they'd lean against the cottonwood trees or squat on their flat feet with their knees around their shoulders, watching us toil away.

I will say that Cooper was no hands-off supervisor. He worked right alongside the sluice-gang, and even with us shovel-men when the need arose. He done it all without complaint, and it come to me that every time I figured these Americans for useless idiots, they would turn around and do something I admired.

At any rate, the amount of gold we cleaned up fell quite a bit shy of everyone's expectations, me and Yasha's most particularly. We'd taken to sharing a fire with Scotty Keogh, for he was good company. The other Americans often give him the cold shoulder because he was an Irishman, though white men all look alike and

I could see no physical difference between him and the others. But he was full of life and good cheer and also knew when to keep his mouth shut. I must say, he was the first American I met that I truly liked. Mailman Mike didn't count, for he was kin and I was stuck with him, like it or not.

The night we spotted the first autumn stars of August, me and Yasha got to talking, and I asked him what he thought of the placer-mining business.

"These Boston Men are fools," he said, rubbing the calluses on his hands from two months of shovel-work. "No offense, Scotty."

"None taken," said Scotty. "But you're right. This trip's been a bust. I should have gone fishing down at Kussilof when I had the chance."

"I guess we're the dumbest ones of all," I said. "We need dog feed, and all them fish go swimming past while we stand there shoveling dirt instead of putting out a trap."

"Leaves are going to turn soon," said Yasha. "We still aint got a grubstake for the winter."

He was looking at me rather pointedly as he said this, and I was keenly aware that this whole jaunt had been my bright idea. As it was, we weren't too far from where we'd planned to trap, but we still had to go back to Cape Starichkof and retrieve our stuff, then back up to Kenay town and purchase an outfit at the AC store. Then we had to get everything to Sixmile.

"We should ask around," I said. "There's probably a few folks in town that could spare us some fish. And we got all those kings we put up back at fish camp."

Scotty rose to his feet and headed for the woods to answer the call of nature. He paused after a couple steps, and we looked up at him as he turned and regarded the camp with the tents among the cottonwoods and the

KRIS FARMEN

fires spread out over the river cobbles in the grainy dusk. The shovels and picks and pans, the men stretching their cramped limbs. The hobbled horses moving through the brush just beyond sight and the loud sigh of the river as it tumbled down to the sea.

"At least fish come back every year," he said. "You always know there's going to be salmon."

We watched him for a moment, then he turned to go attend to his business.

"Hey partner," I said to Yasha in the Kenaytze tongue. "What?"

"I know a place where there's plenty of yellow pebbles. We could slip up there and gather a few and use them to buy our outfit. It's a place these Yankees don't know about."

He watched me for a moment, then reached out and placed a couple more sticks atop the fire. "Maybe it's time we took our leave."

Me and Yasha quit Joe Cooper the very next day. He was not pleased to see us go, but he knew the route back to the Inlet. Our take of the gold come to seven measly dollars for two months of backbreaking labor. I swore off prospecting at that point.

We made up our packs and shook hands with Scotty. He said he hoped to see us later in the winter. He planned to set up a trapline at Kussilof Lake, and we told him he was welcome any time at Sixmile.

"You take it easy, Scotty," I told him.

He flashed a wide grin. "I'll take it any way I can get it."

Me and Yasha shook hands with the rest of the boys, then set off downriver. At Skilant we managed to arrange for some dog feed that we could pick up later in the winter when the trails was established. The next morning Pavil Sasha ferried us across the river in his canoe and bid us good bye. We walked back up Dzadatnu Creek and over the divide to Tutsilitnu, then downriver all the way to Turnagain Arm where me and Lucky Jim had camped all those years before. It took but two days of panning to fill a baking powder can and a small leather pouch. It was money in the bank, as they say, though of course there are no banks here in Alaska. Still, there was a weight of guilt upon my soul that felt almost equal to the heft of the can full of gold.

When Yasha asked me why we had not just come to Tutsilitnu to begin with, I told him of the oath I'd swore to Lucky Jim.

He rolled a handful of nuggets in his palm. "So you've broke a promise."

"I can't see what choice we got. I think we'll be fine so long as we put this money to good use and don't make a habit of coming here for more."

Yasha grinned. "Easy money."

It did make the guilt slide away somewhat to see my partner's face turn up, but this was a moment that would haunt me in years to come. I was to learn most dearly that there aint no such thing in this world as easy money.

KRIS FARMEN

*

"*M*ay I ask you," says Miss Ashford.
"That's what you're here for."

"I was wondering what you think of us Americans."

"How do you mean?"

She pauses to think for a moment. "I mean, you said Scotty Keogh was the first American you met that you really liked. But what do you think of Americans in general?"

"As a people?"

"If you like. What's your impression of us? You seem to have some strong opinions."

Now it is Campbell's turn to think. He stares at the floorboards between his knees. Rain rattles upon the roof and wind whistles under the eaves.

Finally he looks up. "You smell funny."

"I beg your pardon?" Miss Ashford says through a lopsided smile.

"I said Americans smell funny."

Her original question is a something Miss Ashford asks of all her Native informants. A sort of control, in scientific terms. But she has never encountered this answer.

She leans forward in her chair. "How so? What do we smell like?"

He shrugs. "I don't know. You smell like Americans. It aint a bad smell, it's just different from Russians or Indians. Or Eskimos."

Campbell watches her write in her notebook. She looks up, and he notes the curiosity splashed across her face.

"Do you think Eskimos smell different from your people?"

"They stink," says Campbell.

"Actually, now that I think about it, I recall a Koniag woman telling me something similar about Indians."

"No surprises there. But that's Indian and Eskimo business. Nothing you need to worry about."

The light from the cell windows is fading with the evening. Miss Ashford looks down at her watch. Almost five o'clock. She can feel her stomach growl, and she has at least thirty pages of notes to transcribe into longhand before she goes to bed.

"It'll be suppertime soon," says Campbell.

"Yes indeed." Miss Ashford lifts her briefcase onto her lap. She slides her notes inside and notices the bound book in the main compartment. "Oh, I forgot. I brought you something."

"What's that?"

She draws the book from the case and hands it through the bars. Campbell takes it and tilts the cover to the remainders of the daylight. A smile spreads over his face.

"Roughing It," he says, "by Mark Twain."

"You mentioned it before, so I thought you might like to see it again."

He looks up, and Miss Ashford feels an unwelcome flutter of emotion inside her at the gratitude upon his face.

"Thank you, Miss. You're very kind."

"You're welcome. So I will see you tomorrow morning?"

"I'll be right here."

Campbell follows the clack of her shoe-heels upon the boards as she exits. The cellblock door pushes open, and he hears Maddox's voice speaking to her and her to him. Maddox appears a moment later with a plate of food. He carries a candle lantern against the gathering darkness. The rain on the roof swells to a roar that requires him to raise his voice to be heard.

"Howdy, Campbell."

"Evening."

Maddox slides the plate of food under the slot at the bottom of the bars, then hands Campbell a ceramic mug of tea.

"Spasiba," says Campbell as he takes the plate and begins eating. He is growing tired of the monotonous diet of beans and salt pork. He has never acquired a taste for swine flesh. He considers what he wouldn't give for a moose tenderloin or a piece of backstrap from a spring-killed black bear, or even some seal meat, though it has never been his favorite.

Maddox stands next to the bars. Usually the guard leaves the lantern, allowing him to eat, then collects the utensils later. Tonight, Maddox remains, watching him.

Campbell looks up. "Yes?"

Maddox hesitates for a moment, then speaks. "I hear you're the man who made the big gold strike up there on Turnagain Arm."

Campbell stops chewing and studies him. A laugh rises to his throat, but he pushes it down for the sake of not choking.

"You got me confused with Alex King."

KRIS FARMEN

"But they say you're the feller showed him where the gold was."

Campbell shakes his head and looks down at his plate. He takes another bite of food. Silence. Maddox sits down in the chair Miss Ashford has just vacated. It is still warm from her residence. Finally, he says, "You know where there might be any more gold? Gold them boys up there aint found yet?"

"Where you from, kid?"

"Scranton, Pennsylvania."

"Scranton, Pennsylvania." Campbell doubts the word Pennsylvania has rolled off his lips since the days of Watkins' geography lessons. He is fairly sure that Pennsylvania is somewhere in the faraway land the Americans call Back East. There are so many states down in America, and he marvels that anyone could keep them all straight.

Maddox leans forward in the candlelight so that his face is pressed in between the bars. He casts a glance around to see if anyone is listening, but the room is just as empty as it was a moment ago.

"My enlistment's up in the spring," he says. "I aim to go prospecting up in the Yukon country. Strike it rich, you know?"

Campbell polishes his plate with his cornbread and slides the plate over the puncheon floor. It clinks against the bars. The sound barely registers in Maddox's eyes. He blinks a little, then leans back and reaches down for the empty plate and brings it up, slapping it absently against his knee.

Campbell's tea has cooled. He takes a sip and begins loading his pipe.

"Gold," he says.

"That's what I'm talking about."

"Tell me something. You ever seen a golden-haired girl?"

The change of subject takes Maddox aback. His brow furrows as he perches on the edge of the chair.

"Why, yes," he says. "There's plenty of girls back home with blonde hair. Both of my sisters have it. It's fairly common."

Campbell leans his head back against the log wall and tries to imagine a land where there are blonde-headed ladies standing at every tree and creek-mouth. He rolls his head over toward Maddox.

"Do me a favor?"

"What?"

"Leave the lantern. I'd like to read a little."

CHAPTER III

*W*ith our grubstake set, we packed further up the Arm to Sixmile Creek, then turned upriver to have a good look at the trapping prospects. Belukha Pete was right, there was good fur sign everywhere we looked, both above and below the canyon. We spent several days cutting beetlekill spruce logs for a cabin and dragging them up to a building site on a long bench above the creek with a south exposure and several giant old cottonwoods.

We stacked the logs so they wouldn't pick up moisture from the ground, then we walked back down to Possession town and spent a couple nights with George Washington and his family. Yasha in particular caught the eye of a girl named Fedosya, and I didn't see much of him until it was time to leave. My thoughts was fixed on Polly Parker as we greased our *bidarkas* and paddled around the point on the ebb tide.

Fedosya stood on the beach for a long time watching us go. When we was out of earshot, Yasha told me he hoped for a good trapping season so he could present himself to her family as a potential groom.

We pushed hard and made Kenay town on three tides, stopping only to kill a mess of geese on the grass-flats near the mouth of the Swanson with my old caplock .32. We was walking like kings as we lifted our *bidarkas* onto the beach landing at Kenay, loaded with fresh fowl and gold. Folks crowded around us, shaking hands and clapping us on the back. Nobody had any news of Cooper's expedition since we passed through in the spring. At first all this attention threw me off my guard, for quitting school had made me and Yasha *persona non grata*, which Scotty Keogh told me means unwelcome.

Evidently, while our actions was by no means forgotten, the worst of the scandal seemed to have blown over. I figured the people of Kenay had found newer fodder for gossip, which was confirmed when I seen a fresh coat of paint on the chapel.

"New paint," I said to Sava, pointing at the church. It looked more active and spruced up than I had seen it in years. The blue of the onion dome gleamed in the sunlight.

He smiled broadly. "They finally sent us another priest."

"Really?" I was unsure what to make of this. "You mean from America?"

"From Russia. Just like the old days."

I couldn't recall ever seeing Sava so pleased with life. Because there was no priest at Kenay during my childhood, I hadn't been baptized into the church. Klara and my mother raised me to be devout all the same, but it never really took.

We divvied up the fowl among our kin and friends, and Yasha went off with some relations. For my part, I swung a brace of geese onto my shoulder and carried them up the hill to Mike and Klara's house. I had amends to make.

The door stood open for the late summer breeze, and I could hear pots and pans rattling in the kitchen. "Hello the house!" I called inside.

Klara appeared in the kitchen doorway wiping her hands on her apron. Her face lit up when she seen me, which was a relief.

"AC," she said, pulling me into a hug.

"How's my favorite auntie?" I said in Russian.

"Wonderful now that you're here." She stood back, taking me in. You've gotten taller."

"Could be. I brought you some birds."

"That's lovely. We're just finishing dinner, but I can fix you a sandwich."

"Mike's here, then?"

She nodded. "It's Saturday."

Mike had Saturday afternoons off work, and of course, the store was closed on Sunday. I had completely lost track of the days of the week, and it took a moment for this information to soak into my head.

Inside the kitchen, Mike sat picking his teeth with his chair pushed back from the table.

"Look who I found," said Klara.

"AC," said Mike. "How are you?" His disapproval filled the kitchen.

Klara fired the samovar, then went to the counter and began slicing leftover roast and bread for my dinner.

"Hello, Mike."

"So where'd you blow in from?"

I got a cup from the drain-board and filled it with hot water and tea. "Sixmile. Up on Turnagain Arm."

"I know where it is."

Several seconds ticked past. Mike made no motion to say anything more, so I told him of me and Yasha's plan to build a cabin and trap over the winter. I thought he would be pleased at the initiative and pluck we'd shown, but he just kept picking his teeth and wouldn't meet my eyes.

Klara ladled pea soup from a pot atop the range into a bowl. She set it before me with the sandwich on a plate to the side and a glass of water. I sipped at my tea.

"There's oatmeal cookies if you'd like when you're done," she said. These was an American favorite she had learned to bake for Mike.

"Thank you."

Still standing, she leaned into me and give me another squeeze. Mike still hardly looked at me, and I could feel Klara trying to bridge the gap between us.

I took a bite of the sandwich and chewed and swallowed. "How's business at the store?"

"Plenty of work." He looked directly at me. "I sure could use another clerk."

I held his eyes for a moment, then dipped my sandwich into my soup. I was inclined to say he should go tell it to someone who gave a damn, but there was also a sting of guilt. My uncle worked hard and could probably use a couple days off here and there. Still, I had no intention of ever clerking again.

"I imagine so," I said to my plate.

After dinner we hung the geese in the ice-house to season, then I went out back to give Mike a hand with the wood-chopping. They had a good six cords stacked up, which was enough to see them through the winter, but Mike liked to keep ahead on his wood budget. He had a pile of spruce rounds almost as tall as the shed, so we set to work. Mike would wrestle a round onto the block, and I'd whack into it with the splitting maul. Then he set the halves on the block, and I split them down to quarters, and so on. When we'd done several rounds we picked up the split stacks and piled them in the wood-shed.

Mike hardly spoke except one or two words here and there, just what little communication was needed for the job at hand. Finally his silent treatment was too much to bear, so I leaned the maul against the block and asked him what the hell was eating him.

He carried a round over to the block in a giant bear hug and set it down, tipping away the maul handle as he done this so that it fell into the dirt.

"I think you know," he said, straightening up.

I looked down at the fallen maul, then back at him. "I aint a mind reader. Why don't you enlighten me?"

"You watch your tone, son."

I said nothing. I just watched him.

"You should have stayed in school."

"It wasn't for me, Mike. Besides, I can read and write and do sums. There wasn't no reason for me to stay."

"AC, having an education is your ticket to a better life."

"You mean clerking in a store? I didn't want to come downriver to go to your damn school anyway. That was your big idea. I got my own plans in life, and now I aim to go make them happen."

"How? By living in some one-room shack in the woods with a bunch of mangy Indians?"

I took a step toward him. "Don't you ever speak of my kin that way."

Mike rolled his eyes to the sky. "Hell's bells, AC. I never should have let you go upriver with Lucky Jim in the first place. I'm your kin, too, and I'm trying to help you."

"Help me do what?"

"To see the benefits of American civilization! Jesus Christ, if we'd left this country to the Russians you'd all be a bunch of pig-ignorant savages."

"You run that sentiment past Klara?"

"She knows it as well as I do. You ask her sometime what life was like here back in the old Russian days. I mean what it was really like. Now that there's an economy you have the opportunity to wear a clean suit and work in an office and go home to a nice house. Instead of living in some hovel in the woods trying to scrape by from year to year."

"I like the way I live, Mike. All things considered, you've been very kind to me over the years. And because of that I'll forget what you just said about my grandparents and their people."

I turned to walk away and leave Mike to his chopping, but he laid a hand on my shoulder.

"Wait," he said.

"What now?"

Mike let out a long sigh. "Look, AC. You're a man now, so you can paddle your own canoe. Let's not let this turn into something we wind up hating each other over."

I watched his face for a moment, then I put out my hand, and we shook on it.

———

We tarried in Kenay for only a day. The season was advancing and we had things to do. At the AC store we bought traps, grub, tobacco, matches, ammunition and quality winter clothes as well as other odds and ends as we saw fit. Mike totted up our bill on a pad of paper. We paid eleven dollars of folding money from our spring clam-diggings and filled out the balance of the two hundred and eighty-seven dollars with gold from our baking powder can. This excited no small amount of interest on Mike's part. His eyes lit up when he seen the nuggets we tipped onto the troy scales.

"Where'd you find all this?" he said, working the weights. "Upriver?"

"In a creek," I said.

"Cooper and his boys must be doing well then."

"Could be."

On top of our bill Yasha paid twenty-one dollars of his share of the cleanup for a Winchester Model 76 repeater and six boxes of forty shells each. I had to make the purchase for him as the Americans have a law against selling repeating rifles to the Natives. This law is widely ignored, however. Yasha was standing right at the counter as I handed his money to Mike, and he passed me the rifle over the counter, which I in turn handed to Yasha.

"Maybe you'd be good enough to carry this rifle outside," I said to him with a wink.

Yasha took the weapon and winked back at me. This was a proud moment for him. His family had always been too poor to afford such gadgetry.

We left town the next morning bound for our fish camp at Cape Starichkof. I departed with a kiss from Klara and a handshake from Mike. He still wasn't exactly pleased with me, but at least we were no longer at war, which made me feel good about the world once again. That and the fact that I was headed in Polly's direction.

We wanted to make it down to fish camp on one tide, but we hit a strong headwind down near Kalifornski town which slowed us considerably. The turning tide caught us just south of Kussilof so we beached and made camp. When we had everything set up, Yasha fired off his old musket one last time over the Inlet and threw it down into the grass. Then he picked up his new repeater and caressed it like he would a woman. He loaded up the magazine with the full fifteen rounds and we took turns shooting at a tin can. The can jerked and danced on the gravel as he blasted it again and again. There was quite a cloud of smoke when he finished and worked the lever action to eject the final spent shell.

He was grinning from ear to ear as he handed me the rifle. "Give that a try, partner."

He trotted down the beach to position the can while I recharged the magazine. When he returned I took aim and went for a repeat performance. I missed four times— the speed of shots at my command was so amazing I kept forgetting to aim. Still I made the can dance aplenty, and I admit I was a little jealous of his new weapon. Yasha took a few more target shots at a drift stump in the grass, but we didn't do no more can shooting. At thirty cents for a box of shells it was easy to see it could become an expensive hobby.

The next day we shot straight past Ninilchik and Deep Creek on the tide. Polly and her father was working the diggings, and it looked like they'd dug out half the sand on the beach. I waved as we sped past and Polly waved back, but we was a long way offshore and I wasn't sure she could recognize me. We made it to fish camp on the same tide and collected our outfit that we'd cached back in June month. Yasha spied a moose track up in the woods above camp, a young bull by the shape of it. We trailed him a half-mile south along the bluff edge and caught up to him in a little draw full of willows. Yasha of course wanted to put his new rifle to use but the bull knew something was up, and I had the best shot so I took it. We flayed the hide and cut him up and packed him down the gully to the beach with the eagles wheeling in the sky above the kill-site. We cruised northward that same evening on the tide carrying a moosehide and more meat for our families, less a hindquarter which I had marked for a special purpose.

I peeled off from Yasha at the mouth of Deep Creek while he continued up the Inlet toward Kenay town where he would meet me the following day. The Parkers had left the diggings for the evening, and I could smell coal smoke coming downriver on the breeze. I stopped under the bluff for a quick and very chilly bath, after which I put on the brand new duds I'd purchased at the AC store: a white shirt with a collar stud, dark sailcloth britches, black waistcoat and jacket. I tied a new kerchief smartly round my neck and topped myself off with a silver-belly Stetson hat like George Washington wore.

A magpie flew down from the bluff and lighted on a cottonwood branch above me. I studied my reflection in a pool of the creek by the fading light, wishing I'd thought to buy a looking-glass. I could see the magpie watching over my shoulder in the surface reflection. Bent over at the waist, I turned my head this way and that to study the combing of my hair. I can be something of a peacock when I buy new clothes, but I was going court-ing, and any young fellow wants to look smart for such an occasion.

"How do I look, Uncle?" I said to the magpie.

He told me I looked good, then let out a couple squawks and took off, flying his bobbing and dipping path through the sky with his long tailfeathers stretched out behind. I got back into my *bidarka* and paddled up the tide-flooded stream to the Parkers' landing. As I came round a bend in the estuary I seen their new cabin was finished with a roof of cut-up pearl oil cans. The light of an oil lamp glowed in the squares of their west window next to the door.

I dragged my boat up into the grass and withdrew my heavy pack from inside. I lashed the moose ham onto it, then stood the whole works on the cutbank, hunkered down and shrugged into the straps. Near the Parkers' tied-up skiff I found a trail through the grass and fol-lowed it up to the cabin. I stopped halfway to pull a comb from my jacket pocket and give my hair a final slicking with a little seal oil, after which I carefully re-set my Stetson hat. I had no boots, only moccasins that wrapped round my calves, but I'd pulled my trouser-cuffs down over them to look as dapper as I could. I wished I had some flowers to bring her, but they were out of season. And anyway I had the heavy leather sack of gold for her, bumping against my belly in my waistcoat pocket.

I took a deep breath and called out to the house.

The door opened a moment later, and the shape of Mr. Parker stepped out. "Who's there?"

"It's AC. Aleksandr Campbell."

"Why AC! How you doing?"

I come up and stepped onto the porch-boards. "Doing good. I brought you some meat."

Parker was seized by a fit of coughing and had to lean against the doorway for a moment to recover himself.

"'Scuse me," he said. "I've been a bit under the weather."

"Nothing serious, I hope."

"Nah," he said wiping his hand on his britches. We shook and I unlashed the ham and hung it from the heel tendon on a nail against the wall. He ushered me inside.

The furnishings of their house was rough and the walls were lined with canned goods, tools, and other paraphernalia. I seen a guitar standing in a corner. Small and rough as it was, the place had a woman's touch, and the lamplight cast a soft glow over the whitewashed log walls. It was evident that as a housekeeper Polly knew how to do a lot with very little.

The coal stove was going, and it was plenty warm inside. Polly was at the kitchen table winnowing cranberries from the leaves and stems that had accompanied them into the berry bucket. She looked up from her work and smiled when she seen me, and I got that fluttery feeling inside me once again, as if nothing else in the world mattered so long as she kept looking at me like that.

She got up and come over to give me a hug. She felt so nice pressed up against me that I thought I might swoon.

"How are you, AC?"

"Fit as a fiddle and right as rain."

"He brought us some moose meat," said Parker.

Polly's face split into a smile. "That's so kind of you. We haven't had any fresh meat for a while now."

"It's my pleasure," I said, smiling back at her and feeling like I was floating in the air with my feet six inches above the floor.

"Will you take some coffee?"

Russians drink tea, and I've never been partial to coffee, but I accepted all the same. I would have accepted a mouthful of burning coals from the stove if she'd offered them.

Polly filled the coffeepot with water and set it atop the stove. Then she opened the firebox and scooped a shovelful of fresh beach coal into it. Looking around, it struck me as odd that they didn't have a samovar for hot water, but this was an American household. This notion made Polly seem all the more exotic and alluring.

Mr. Parker settled into his easy chair made of bent willow wands and returned to his magazine. The date on the cover was ten months old, which is fairly recent for this country.

"How'd your digging go this summer?" I said to Polly.

"Not as well as we'd hoped. We got pay in almost every cleanup, but no big strike. But I guess there's still another month left in the season."

"Beach mining is like that."

The days are starting to get short though," she said. "There's so much to do before winter, and it gets nearly impossible to get anything done when it gets dark so early."

"I seem to recall you not liking the long days,"

She rolled her eyes to the ceiling and smiled. "I know, right? Can't nothing ever satisfy this girl."

We had a chuckle over that as the coffeepot began to hiss.

"Hack was a big help to us," she said. "He really showed us how to make the most of our claim."

The mention of this popinjay stuck at me like a rose-hip thorn in the thigh of my trousers. "He got a mine he's working around here?"

"He owns a series of beach claims down near Anchor Point with a sluice plant like ours." Her face glowed with admiration as she said this. "Some up at Ninilchik, too. He's a professional miner with a college degree in geology. He says there's plenty of gold in these beaches, but it takes a large-scale operation to make it pay."

I frowned. "What do the folks down at Layda town think of his operation?"

"What's Layda?"

"That's the Indian town at Anchor Point."

"Gosh," said Polly, "I don't really know. He says he offered jobs to a few of them, but they don't seem interested in working."

"Maybe they just don't care to work for him," I said. Straightaway I wished I could stuff those words back into my mouth.

She looked askance at me. The coffee water boiled and she got up to add the grounds, then sat down again.

"I was hoping you'd come back so we could dig clams again," she said. "That was much more fun as far as digging up the whole beach goes."

"I wish I could have."

"How'd you do up in the mountains?"

"About the same as you folks, I guess. There's a whole bunch of fresh-scrubbed gravel up there at Skilant town. I think we cleared seven dollars between me and Yasha for the season. For two months of hard labor."

Polly's blue eyes danced in the lamplight. "At least there's someone who did worse than we did."

"Well, I do what I can to make your life more pleasant." I laid my hand on hers and she giggled, but Mr. Parker cleared his throat rather conspicuously. I withdrew my hand.

When the coffee was ready she poured it into cups and set the pot back on the stove. From under a dishtowel made from a flour sack she produced half a blueberry pie and cut off three slices. She set one before me and carried another with a cup of coffee to her father, then she sat down with one for herself.

"Did you finish *Treasure Island*?" she said.

"I did. Just the other day, in fact. I got it out in my pack for you."

She forked some pie up to her mouth. "Did you like it?"

"I did. That Long John Silver and his boys was a pretty rough bunch. I kept staying up late to keep on reading. Seemed like a sure thing Jim Hawkins was going to get his throat cut."

Polly smiled as she chewed and swallowed. "I love it when a book is like that. When it grabs you and you can't put it down. That's why I read."

The pie was quite good and I ate two mouthfuls, one after the other.

"You got another book you aint reading at the moment?"

"To borrow?"

"Surely."

She waggled her fork between her thumb and forefinger, then got up and reached to a shelf over the west window where a couple dozen books were stood with their spines facing out.

"Try this one," she said, pulling out a volume and handing it to me.

I tilted the cover toward the lamplight so I could see. It said *Typee* by Herman Melville. I was so eager for another story that I opened it and started into the first page, completely forgetting my manners.

Polly sat at the table again, crossing her arms on the checkered oilcloth and leaning over toward me so that her bosom rested upon them. "You can take it with you, AC. You don't have to sit and read it right here."

I looked up and felt my cheeks flush. The view before me had a distracting effect and when I managed to find my voice it come out in Russian.

"*Iswinie.*"

"Pardon?"

I flushed again and managed to find my American. "That's Russian for sorry."

We sat there quietly as I sipped at my coffee. Polly cleared away the dishes and asked me about my plans for the winter.

"Trapping," I said. "Me and Yasha got logs cut for a cabin at Sixmile."

"Where's that?"

"North of here. Up on Turnagain Arm. Plenty of fur."

About then Mr. Parker closed his magazine and began making ready for bed. I took this to mean it was time for me to skedaddle. I stepped outside and dug *Treasure Island* out of my pack. Polly came out after me with a candle. She paused for a moment to study the moose ham hanging on the wall.

"Thank you so much for the meat, AC."

"My pleasure."

"Where are you sleeping tonight?"

"I'll just camp down by the creek if that's alright with you folks."

"You don't have nowhere else to stay? Papa would probably let you bed down on the floor inside."

"I'll be fine," I said, tilting my face up to the moon and stars. "It's a fair night and a northwest breeze. That means clear and cold with no rain."

She looked at me with concern for my welfare, and I must admit I swelled up a little at that.

"Don't worry," I said. "There's plenty of moon for light."

Through the window I seen Parker's shadow moving in the amber lamplight as he crawled into his bed on the main floor. Through the walls I heard another coughing fit, and Polly's eyes flicked toward the glass. There was a loft above the kitchen which I took to be her bedchamber. I dearly wished for an opportunity to spend the night up there, with her father somewhere far away.

"I brought you something else, Polly."

"What?"

"Open your hand."

She done so and I cupped it in mine. I withdrew the leather sack of gold from my waistcoat and laid it in her palm. She almost dropped it, it was so heavy.

"Oh my stars, AC," she said. "Is this—"

"Take a look."

She dribbled a little wax onto the windowsill and pressed the candle down into it, then she opened the drawstring and tipped a few pea-sized nuggets into her palm. She stared at them a moment as if not knowing what to believe, then she looked up at me.

"Alex."

"Take it," I said, smiling at her. "Flowers are out of season, but that stuff's awful pretty. I hope it will do."

"But where did you find this? You said you only cleared seven dollars working for Cooper."

"That's the truth. But this gold come from someplace where Cooper and his boys wasn't looking."

"Where?"

"I can't say. I promised someone I'd never tell."

She looked at me, then down at the gold in her hand. There was probably three hundred dollars in that poke. It was more money than she and her father would have made in five years of beach mining.

Finally she pressed her lips together and pushed the gold back at me. "AC, I can't take this. It's too much."

I took her hand in both of mine and wrapped her fingers closed around the sack. "I want you to have it, Polly. That's what I brought it for."

She opened her mouth to speak, but didn't. Instead, she pressed up against me. I bent down to fill the space and gave her a kiss. She returned in kind, and I almost fell off the earth.

That night I lay on my side in my blankets where I had bedded down in the beach-grass by the creek. I couldn't sleep so I watched the half-moon, trying to find Polly's face upon it. The Big Dipper hung in the northern sky, and the wind was still, save for an occasional puff out of the northwest as I had forecast. The tide was out, and the rustling of the creek next to me was mixed with the pulse of a light surf breaking across the sand-flats.

I wanted Polly very badly, more than anything I had ever desired, and I was trying to talk myself into staying nearby for the winter so I could be close to her. But the trapping grounds was all staked out and claimed on that part of the Peninsula, which meant there was no opportunity for me there. There was no wage work of any kind over the winter unless I wanted to surrender myself to Mailman Mike and go back to clerking. Hindsight has shown me that perhaps I was being young and hard-headed about things, but in the Russian and Indian world I was raised in, hunting and trapping was the measure of a competent man. The thought of being shut up inside all day, having to do sums and once more live my life on a schedule dictated by another man's whim made me feel like the ground might just open up and swallow me whole. Clerking at the AC store might keep me close to Polly, but how was I to win her heart and hand if I could not even stand to look at myself in the mirror?

I sighed and rolled onto my stomach. The wind rustled the grass, and I thought I heard a whisper. I raised my head from my rolled-up jacket and cocked my ear.

A foot crunched in the gravel nearby. There came the whisper again.

"AC?"

I got up on my knees, feeling all fluttery. I scanned the tops of the grass, and there was Polly in her night-dress with her father's oversized coat and her golden curls let down in the silver air.

"Polly," I said.

She turned, and we stood there watching each other in the moonlight. Then she walked up to me. We lay down, and I wrapped the blankets and tarp around us. My hands found the hem of her gown. She lifted her arms over her head then wrapped them around me as I lay it aside.

Later, when we lay with our faces turned to the stars with her snuggled up against me, she asked me to tell her about Sixmile.

"It's a pretty spot," I said. "Lots of hemlock trees down near the beach. Cottonwoods as you get upstream. There's spruce and birch further up the valley above the canyon. We got a nice spot on a bench about a mile up from the mouth where our cabin is going to stand."

"It sounds lovely," she whispered into the night.

I looked down at her and seen she was looking across my chest and through the stems of the grass next to me.

"What's on your mind?" I said.

"Nothing."

"Nothing? Not a single solitary thing?"

She curled her fingers against me, then relaxed them. "I was just wishing we didn't live so far away from one another."

"Come with me," I said. I was not sure how we'd get there—both Yasha and me had only single-hatch *bidarkas*. But there had to be some way to make it work.

Polly was silent for several moments. "I can't."

"Why not? Because your dad will get mad?"

"He would be mad. But that's not it."

"What then?"

Polly took a long breath, then let it out. "He's got the consumption."

Now it was my turn to be silent. I rolled over on my side to face her. I wanted to tell her that my own mother had died of consumption, but death seemed the wrong word for the moment.

"You're certain?" I said, but even as I spoke I thought of Parker's coughing fit when I first come onto the porch. And when he climbed into bed.

"He had it before we come to Alaska," Polly said. "But he just started coughing up blood a few weeks ago."

"They got hospitals down in the States for consumption. He could go there."

"We've got no money to pay for it," said Polly. "He sunk everything he had into our mine here. I think he was trying to make me a grubstake for when he's—"

Her voice dipped away as she finished the thought, as if she spoke as much to herself and to the night as to me.

"—For when he's gone."

I gently pushed her hair back from her forehead. "Don't worry about that. I got you taken care of. You won't never go hungry or cold with me. You have my word on it."

There was a little sting in the back of my mind as I said that. It was hard not to think of Tutsilitnu and Lucky Jim and the notion that my word probably wasn't much good.

Polly said nothing. She just curled her fingers against me once more, then kissed me.

"I have to go," she said. "Before he misses me."

"I'll be back for you in the spring, Polly. I'll have a good stake for us then. We'll find a way to make it all fit together."

"In the spring then," she said in a voice that was not much louder than the whispering of the grass stems in the breeze. "I'll wait for you."

She kissed me once more. Then she got up and slipped back into her night-clothes and was gone. I lay there for a long time looking at the stars and the bluffs. I finally caught a few hours sleep just before the dawn.

———

At Kenay everyone gathered on the beach landing to farewell me and Yasha. Mike couldn't be there; he was waiting on Hackham and some other mining customers up at the store. Such is the life of a store-keeper. Klara sent me off with several pairs of new moccasins plus some new moosehide mittens and a heavy wool cap she'd knit for me. I wouldn't need these things for a couple months yet, but it was nice to know I was loved.

"Tell Mike I said good-bye," I said to her in Russian.

She planted a kiss on my cheek. "I will. You be careful."

"You know I will."

There was still a few late-run silvers in the rivers when we made it to Point Possession. George Washington invited us to stay at his house, but Yasha was off straight-away looking for Fedosya. The nights was getting dark and cool, but people still gathered round their fires as much as possible. They knew there would be plenty of indoor time over the coming winter, and there was the rare delight of being able to sit outside and watch the stars without freezing. This of course can only be done in the autumn when the sky gets dark but the temperature has not yet dropped for the winter.

Those dark evenings were pretty, but they filled me halfway with melancholy. Fall brings golden leaves, no bugs, and good hunting, but you always know that several months of winter are on the way when you see those first stars overhead. The days get short, and all of a sudden there is plenty of time to sit around brooding on all the things you have done wrong in your life. Even young people are not immune to this change of season.

George Washington had his grandchildren around the fire that night. I sat across from him, smoking and listening as he told the *sukdu* tales, and they sat watching him with wide eyes and gaping mouths, just as I no doubt had when Lucky Jim first told them to me. Later, when the children was bustled off to bed, George Washington's three wives come and sat with us and Belukha Pete. Pete had my old favorite dog Camprobber with him. He had been looking after her since Lucky Jim's funeral. Sadly, Flicker had been killed a couple years earlier in a fight with three freight dogs. She had fought bears all her life and didn't know what fear was, but she also had no appreciation for the cunning teamwork of malamutes when off their tethers.

Camprobber came up to me and lay down with her head on my thigh. She looked up at me with her big wet eyes and let out a long sigh. I was the only one she would ever do this to. Indians don't waste a lot of affection on their dogs, but she knew I was a soft touch. She was getting on in years and was still fit, but the hairs around her muzzle was going gray. I scratched her ears as I listened to Pete and George Washington talk of hunting and trapping.

George Washington's youngest wife was called Yelena; she was only ten years older than me. She sat next to me on the other side from Camprobber and tapped my free leg, saying, "Fedosya and Yasha make a handsome couple."

"I suppose," I said.

"It's your turn next," she said, drawing on her pipe. "You need to find a nice girl to look after you."

"I've got one."

"Why isn't she here with you?" said Maria. This was George Washington's eldest wife. Her hair was gray, but you could tell she had been a great beauty in her youth.

"She's living with her dad down at Deep Creek," I said.

"Who is she?" Both Maria and Yelena studied me with a very coy look, along with Gavrila, the second wife.

"She's not Creole," I said. "Nor Kenaytze."

By now Pete and George Washington was listening in. It made me uncomfortable to be the center of attention like this.

"She's Ulchena then?" said Pete. *Ulchena* is a common Indian slang word for Esquimaux and Aleuts, and I could feel everyone's curiosity growing more and more keen with each heartbeat.

"She's a Yankee," I said.

There was naught but silence and staring eyes.

"An American?" said George Washington.

"Yes. I aint asked her the question, though. When Yasha and me get back from trapping in the spring, that's when I aim to do it."

Gavrila smiled. "I suppose that explains those fancy new store clothes you been wearing."

I blushed, then smiled in spite of myself. This lightened the mood a tad, but there were looks exchanged across the fire that I could not ignore.

"Do you mean that girl with the ugly yellow hair?" said Yelena.

Gavrila's eyes lit up in recognition. "That girl?" She made a face at Yelena. "Isn't that hair hideous? All wrinkly the way it is?"

"And those blue eyes!" said Yelena. "AC, I don't know how you can stand to be around those eyes. It's like she's blind or something."

I looked down at Camprobber. She blinked her own dark eyes at me and I stroked her ears.

Maria shifted her position so she was facing me more directly. "Don't let them bother you, AC. You know I came here from the Mulchatna country, right?"

I was aware of that fact and I told her so.

"Georgei here," she said meaning George Washington, "come over to our country from the Gulf of Kenay when I was a little girl. He was a young sprout himself, just a boy playing with his bow and arrow. We were chums when we was growing up, and when we got older the elders told me that I should find a nice boy from the lake country. They said my mother and father and my aunts would never allow me to marry some skinny smart-mouthed kid from the salt water."

I looked over at George Washington. He shrugged. "I was known to be free with my opinions when I was younger."

"So what happened?" I said.

He smiled. "She couldn't resist my charms."

Maria arched an eyebrow at him, then turned back to me. "My point is that you shouldn't ever let no-one tell you that you cannot be with a girl just because you're different than her. Love is love, and we cannot deny it when it visits us."

I nodded at this and asked George Washington how he came to grow up over on the Mulchatna.

"There was smallpox here on the Gulf when I was a boy," he said. It spread upriver from Kenay town so my folks took me and my sisters across the water. We stayed at Kuskatan for a while. Then we walked over the mountains to Kijik town, then over to the Mulchatna River. My mother had kin there."

He put his arm around Maria and favored her with a large smile. "Maria was one of the three best things to happen to me."

All three wives rolled their eyes at that, and I decided then and there that I only needed one wife.

Later that night when the women had gone to bed, still discussing George Washington's various shortcomings and Polly's supposed lack of pulchritude, he sat down next to me and Camprobber and filled my pipe. He lit his own with a brand from the fire, and I watched the light pulse upon his face as he drew it into the bowl again and again.

"AC," he said, tossing the flame back into the fire, "regardless of what the women say, there is something I must tell you and I suspect your ears will not want to hear it."

"Tell me what?"

He exhaled a cloud of smoke from deep in his lungs, holding his palm before his face for a moment to catch the aroma.

"If you want this girl," he said, "then you're going to have to be prepared for the anger it will cause among the Boston Men."

I was not such a fool as to think a girl as fetching as Polly was not the object of desire among all the American fellows from Knik Landing to Kodiak town, and I said as much to George Washington.

"I think this was meant to be," I said. "I can't help it if other men are chasing her. I'm headed up to go trapping so her dad will know I can take care of her."

He watched me for a moment in the firelight. "You're a Creole, AC."

"I am. What of it?"

"The Boston Men are sensitive about the mixing of races. I seen it happen when I was in California. I watched a Spaniard get hanged by the Americans because he chased after an American woman. I haven't met this girl's father, but I doubt he would consent to such a marriage. She herself may not even be willing."

"I know she's willing," I said. "She said she'd wait for me to come down in the spring."

"Women are known to change their minds."

"Yankees marry Native women all the time," I said. "So did the Russians for that matter. There aint no shortage of Creoles running about."

"That's different," said George Washington.

"You're thinking of my grandmother and Lucky Jim? My Russian grandmother, I mean."

He stared into the fire.

"What?" I said.

"That was an ugly time for everyone involved."

"But she was white and Lucky Jim was an Indian. The sun didn't fall out of the sky because they got together. Hell, for that matter, I'm three-quarters white myself."

"It's just different," said George Washington. "The Boston Men make the rules and their women follow. That's their way."

He put a hand on my shoulder. "I've not said this to give offense, mind you, AC. I just want you to have a good long think about what you're getting yourself into."

I thought of the devilish look in Polly's eyes as she leaned over the table telling me I could take *Typee* with me, that I didn't have to sit and read it at her table. Of her breath against my neck under the half-moon. There was love there. Of this I was certain.

We smoked one more pipe, talking about Iliamna Lake, which he told me was all fresh-water, yet nearly as wide as a sea. He told me old stories of hunts and wars and other doings long ago. When at last he retired for the evening, he said, "Take heart, AC. The world is full of pretty Creole and Indian girls who can warm your bed better than some funny-looking American."

He left me sitting alone under the stars by the fire. The flames died down, but I made no move to add more wood. I had an urge to jump in my *bidarka* and paddle back down the Inlet to ask Polly if what George Washington had told me was true. Perhaps I should have done just that, considering what was to come. But I stayed by the fire. It was fall, and there was a lot of work to do before freeze-up.

———

Me and Yasha headed up Turnagain Arm the next day. It was just the two of us though he told me he had tried mightily to get Fedosya to come along. He'd even approached her aunts and her parents, but got only a firm "No" for his trouble.

Her father told Yasha, "You call yourself a trapper, and you got American money and fine store clothes and a repeating rifle, but I aint seen you bring a single pelt out of the woods. And until I do, my daughter aint going nowhere with you."

It's true that Indians don't put a lot of effort into marriage ceremonies the way Russians or Americans do, but this does not mean a father takes lightly the betrothal of his daughter. Her aunts, who actually had more say in the matter than he did, was of the same mind.

So it was just the two of us with the team of four dogs that Belukha Pete had gathered for us. They wasn't exactly thoroughbreds, but they was adequate for our purposes. We cut cards to see who would walk them up the Arm and who would paddle with our supplies. Yasha turned a jack and me a six, so I leashed the dogs and slung my Sharps rifle over my packboard and started walking to the mouth of Sixmile Creek. Yasha paddled his *bidarka*, towing mine behind by a line. This was no mean feat of boatmanship, especially in the treacherous currents of Turnagain Arm, but he had the easy end of the deal—he made it to camp in a couple hours while I spent two days hoofing it with four badly-behaved malamutes.

When I arrived at Sixmile he had a comfortable camp set up and had shot some ducks and geese and caught and dried several dozen silvers as extra insurance on our dog-feed pile. We lined our boats upstream to our cabin-site under the cottonwoods where we found our stack of house-logs just as we'd left them. A squirrel had been using them as a dining room, and there was mounds of spruce scales everywhere. We built a fish trap for the late silvers, then slabbed and notched the logs with dovetails. To fortify ourselves when the nights got cold, we put up a batch of *quass* made from several gallons of crowberries and blueberries mashed up with sugar and yeast.

We had the walls up by the time the leaves started to drop. The scent of cranberries hung heavy in the air. The puschki weed was dead and brown like cane by the time we had the sod roof in place and the sheet-iron wood stove set up. This was real deluxe living for us. Prior to our cleanup at Tutsilitnu we had been planning to build an old fashioned pit-house with a Russian *pitchka* furnace. Our plank door had rawhide straps for hinges, but we had brought up a real glass window, and let me tell you, that made all the difference. Yasha and me was agreed that those old pit houses was not a healthy place to dwell if you had any choice in the matter. As it was, it had been a real trick getting up there with the stove and the window. Yasha had the pane lashed to the deck abaft of his boat-hatch while I paddled with the stove thrust down before me, my feet pushed into the firebox through the open door. This was every bit as awkward and un-comfortable as it sounds.

We killed a moose for meat, then a black bear that come to investigate our comings and goings. We made daily patrols through the woods, scouting the best trapline routes and cutting trails as we went. Stove wood was sawn and split. Traps was boiled and dyed, snow-shoes made, and also a good trail sled out of split spruce. The ponds was froze hard by the time we was ready to go, and we watched the sky every day for snow.

Much of this work would have been considerably easier if we'd had women along, but we knew we had to bach it for at least that first winter, so we didn't complain. In the evenings I got into Melville's book *Typee*, which is a story of an American sailor jumping ship in the South Seas and being held captive by the Natives there until he could escape. Melville spared no expense of words to describe this island tribe and their habitations, and of course the free behavior of their women was of no small interest. There was also a recurring daydream of having Polly with me, alone, on just such an island.

We started dipping into the *quass* as soon as it was ready. This beverage is not as potent as vodka or even Scotty Keogh's *poteen*, but it does get the job done eventually. I was coming to love the buzzy sensation that it brought me, though waking up the next morning could be something of a trial. That first batch went fast, so we picked a couple more buckets of late-season cranberries and set them to ferment.

I could see that Yasha missed Fedosya already, but I told him to be glad she was only a short trip away where he could see her whenever the urge took him. My girl was all the way down at Deep Creek, so far away she may as well have been in Frisco. I often wondered how she and her dad were getting along. His illness was no doubt becoming a real hardship, and it pained me that I could not be there to help her.

The *quass* loosened our tongues on these matters. "You really think Polly would marry a Creole like me?" I asked Yasha one night. It was dark, the candles blown out for the night. We was abed in our bunks with a skin full of home-brew and I was holding on tight to the wall.

"If she loves you she will." He had the top bunk; he'd offered to take it since he got the easy ride up the Arm. There was a little patch of moonlight that spilled onto

KRIS FARMEN

the floor through our glass window. The dogs was quiet outside for once, and there was no noise but the whispering of the fire in the stove flue.

I heard the springy spruce poles squeak under his blankets as he rolled over and hung his face over the edge.

"The room spinning?" he said.

"Yeah."

Yasha listened to the stove for a moment. He hadn't drunk as much as I had, and I was suddenly envious of that.

"You really think she'd want to come live up here?" he said. "A Yankee girl like her?"

The room slowed itself down somewhat, so I loosened my grip on the logs. "I hope so. She's got pluck."

In the dimness I seen Yasha cross his arms and rest his chin on them. He looked out the window at the moonlight on the brown fall-time grass.

"We could build another cabin come spring," he said. "Me and Fedosya could take this one and you two could have the other. Nice and close so the girls can keep company. We could just fish and hunt and trap. Live good and easy up here, you know?"

"There's those yellow rocks to be had if fur comes up short," I said.

Yasha's voice was muffled by his mouth pressing against his arms. "I say we forget about that. You promised Lucky Jim. I've heard George Washington say more than once that the Yankees will wreck this country if they think there's gold to be found here. And if we start paying our bills in gold every year, folks will start to talk."

"I don't want to be no prospector," I said. "Only a fool would shovel sand all day when he could be out hunting and trapping."

Yasha laughed. "Tell that to a prospector. Belukha Pete told me they call us cat stranglers."

"You and me?"

"I mean trappers. The miners call us that."

I watched the moonlight on the floor. The room had finally settled down to sleep.

"I reckon you might be on to something, Yasha. Not the prospectors, but all of us living up here. You, me, Fedosya and Polly. It would be like having our own little town up here, but with just the people you want to have around."

"That would be nice."

I rolled onto my stomach and closed my eyes with this pleasant thought in my head. It was a night for dreaming.

KRIS FARMEN

*

*T*he storm continues into the next day. Campbell has been talking for much of the morning, with Miss Ashford writing in her notebook. After a while he falls silent.

"Cat got your tongue?" she says.

"What?"

"It's a figure of speech. You've never heard it?"

"Not that I can recall."

Miss Ashford looks over her notes. She is rather pleased with his descriptions of the village at Point Possession and of George Washington's wives, though she is not fond of the concept of polygamy. On a personal level, she is glad it is being eliminated by the efforts of local missionaries, even if their efforts do make her job harder. Human society at large has a way to go before she will be truly happy with it, even if she has been trained to look at these things with professional objectivity.

As a scholar, however, she is keenly interested in the presence or absence of romantic love among primitive tribesmen. She opens her mouth, intending to ask Campbell more about George Washington and Lucky Jim's multiple wives and the nature of the relationships between them, but he beats her to the punch.

"Can I ask you something, Miss?"

"Certainly."

"I been wondering how it is that a woman is allowed to work for the federal government. Especially to be talking to a condemned man in a jail cell. That aint the way things generally work among you Americans."

"Well," she says, "I guess you're right about that."

"So why aint you in the States looking for a husband?"

Her eyes narrow down to slits.

"Easy," says Campbell. "I didn't mean nothing by it. It's just been my experience that most young ladies are more concerned with love and children. Hearth and home and all that."

Miss Ashford says nothing for a moment. She waggles her pencil between her thumb and forefinger, a gesture that reminds Campbell of Polly Parker and her fork.

"I never said I wasn't concerned with love," she says, looking down at her notepad.

"Scholarly investigations don't count. Not when you haven't been in love."

Miss Ashford's head snaps back up. "Just how do you know these things about me, Mr. Campbell?"

He shrugs. "A jaybird mentioned something about it."

"A jaybird."

"Yeah. Dark blue and black, half again the size of a camprobber." He voices the Kenaytze name for the bird, unaware that Miss Ashford would know it as a Steller's jay.

"You seem to spend an awful lot of time conversing with birds, Mister Campbell."

"They're more interesting than people most of the time. Besides, any fool could figure it out from the questions you been asking me. Lucky Jim and George Washington's wives and all that. And me and Polly, and Yasha and Fedosya. We're always the most keenly interested in what we don't have."

Miss Ashford smiles and looks at the ceiling. "Am I that obvious?"

Campbell laughs, meeting her eyes.

"So how did you come to this line of work, Miss?"

"I found a college that would accept women and studied my little heart out. I was fortunate to find a mentor in the field of anthropology."

"Who was that?"

"Professor Franz Boas."

"That aint no American name."

"He's from Germany, originally. He's done a lot of work among the Canadian Eskimos.

Campbell crosses his arms over his chest, thinking.

"I imagine you've had a pretty tough road getting to where you are now," he says.

"You could say that. Many men are intimidated by the idea of a woman asking these kinds of questions."

"To hell with them," says Campbell. "I like a woman who's got brains to go along with her looks."

She is unsure how to take this comment. A warm blush creeps up beneath the collar of her blouse.

Bootsteps come through the open cellblock door. The second guard, Heinz, enters with a plate of beans, two flour biscuits, and a cup of coffee. He is older than Maddox, thirtyish, spade-bearded and heavy of frame.

"Dinnertime, siwash," he says, placing the plate on the floor and sliding it through the slot. He passes the cup to Campbell through the bars.

Miss Ashford sits with her notebook on her lap, watching them, glad she has her professional demeanor to hide behind. Heinz favors her with a greasy smile as he turns to leave.

"You require anything, Miss?"

"No, thank you. I brought my lunch with me."

"We got coffee if you like."

"I'm fine."

She can see Campbell standing back from the bars, out of arm's reach. He has pulled his food inside but left it on the floor as he watches. His face betrays no emotion, but she can plainly tell he does not think much of this man Heinz.

Heinz turns and leaves with a final hostile look over his shoulder at Campbell. He enters the office and leaves the cellblock door open as usual, but they can hear the front door open and shut. Probably Heinz going to the necessary house.

Campbell mutters something after him in what she takes to be the Kenaytze language.

"Pardon?" she says.

"That Heinz is an asshole. Pardon my French."

"He does have a certain manner about him."

Campbell seats himself once again at the sidewall of his cell and begins shoveling beans into his mouth. Around the food he says, "I only got my dinner on a plate because you're here. Usually he just pitches it through the bars at me."

"How do you mean?"

"I mean when he's on duty I usually end up licking my grub off the floor like a dog."

Her eyes travel to filthy, grease-sodden floor with lingering salt crystals in the cracks. "You mean he literally throws it at you?"

There is the scrape of his fork against the tin plate and the hammering of the rain against the roof.

"Yep. But it aint all bad. I got flour biscuits today instead of cornbread. Must be a ship from the States come in."

Miss Ashford reaches into her briefcase and produces a sandwich wrapped in wax paper. "Would you like half of this?"

"What is it?"

"Egg salad."

Campbell frowns a little, but extends his hand. She passes him one of the halves, and he brings it to his nose and sniffs it.

She smiles. "You're not a devotee of egg salad?"

"It's alright. My aunt used to make it every now and again." He takes a bite, then another. "Where'd you get this? I didn't know there was an eating house here in Kodiak town."

"There isn't. My landlady, Mrs. Rudikov, made it for me."

"Rudikov, you say?"

"Yes. She rents rooms in her house. I've been staying there since I arrived."

"I know her family," says Campbell. "Or her husband's family anyway. They live up near Seldovoya. What's this lady's Christian name?"

"Anna."

He nods. "Semyonov was her maiden name. She married Konstantin Rudikov, but I don't think I've met her in particular."

"That's right," says Miss Ashford. "Her husband's name was Konstantin. I recall her saying as much."

"Was?"

"She's a widow. But it's funny that you know her family."

Campbell shrugs. "Alaska's a small place."

Heinz comes back into the office as they're eating. Not long after, they hear the front door open again and a second pair of shoes on the floor. Heinz's muffled voice speaks, but they cannot make out what he is saying, only that he sounds exasperated.

"Who's that?" says Campbell. "Can you see?"

Miss Ashford shakes her head. "I don't know."

A moment later, Heinz enters with a smallish gray-haired Creole man behind him. He waves a hand at Campbell saying, "There he is." Then he turns and walks back into the office with no explanation of the man's business.

The newcomer wears a dark suit and black woolen clerk's cap. Old-fashioned muttonchop whiskers gone gray, dripping from the storm-lashed rain. There is a very plain-looking watch chain across the front of his waistcoat. And while Miss Ashford does not spot it, Campbell sees at a glance that the Native part of the man's lineage is all Aleut.

The elder Creole doffs his cap and favors Miss Ashford with a rather courtly bow. He says something to her in Russian, but his accent is so thick she can't make out his words. She realizes that he

KRIS FARMEN

speaks no English. He returns his cap to his balding head then turns to Campbell and addresses him.

Miss Ashford watches from her chair as the two Creoles speak. She is distressed and more than a little annoyed that she cannot keep up with their bizarre-sounding Russian. The dialect she has encountered here in Alaska bears only a passing resemblance to the language her governess spoke to her when she was a little girl in her parents' house in Rhode Island. One word, however, catches her ear: Grob. *Coffin. The gray-haired Creole is the undertaker.*

A stricken look crosses Campbell's face but is gone just as quickly. The undertaker reaches into his jacket pocket and withdraws a rolled-up cloth measuring tape. With an extended index finger he indicates for Campbell to turn around and press his back to the iron bars. Campbell complies. The undertaker stands on the metal tip of the tape with the toe of his shoe and stretches it upward to measure the height, then makes a series of lateral measurements of the feet, hips, back and shoulders, all the while giving direction to his customer in Russian.

He jots figures on a pad of paper with notes in Cyrillic. Campbell turns his head and asks a question. The undertaker's response brings a frown to his face. He asks another question, to which he gets only a shrug and a short, apologetic answer. Campbell turns his face to the undertaker and speaks sharply to him, but the undertaker only presses his lips together and shakes his head. He puts away the tools of his trade and turns to Miss Ashford and lifts his cap again, bidding her a wordless good-day. Then he is gone.

"What did he say to you?" Miss Ashford asks.

Campbell's voice is surprisingly passive considering his ire just a moment before. "He was measuring me for my coffin. I told him I wanted to be cremated in the old Indian way."

"Like Lucky Jim."

"Yes."

"You don't want a Christian burial?"

"Not really. The Russian fathers won't like that. But I guess I think of it as a way to stay close to Lucky Jim and all the things he taught me."

"I see. But what did he say to you?"

"He said he could arrange it, but I'd have to pay for the fuel and for his helpers to tend the fire and dispose of my—"

His voice cuts off sharp, and he looks Miss Ashford straight in the eyes. "My ashes."

"And you don't have the funds."

"Not a lousy red cent."

Miss Ashford looks down at the half-eaten sandwich still in her hand, her appetite suddenly gone. Quietly, she wraps it back up in the wax paper and returns it to her briefcase.

Campbell sits down in what has become his customary position when talking with her, his back against the side wall of his cell, in front of her chair, so he can admire the tiny bit of ankle that shows below the hem of her skirts and imagine the shape and softness of the leg connected to her. So close he could reach through the bars and touch her.

They sit like that for several minutes as the rain continues to beat against the roof. A trickle rolls down through the window and drips onto the floor. Miss Ashford takes a drink of water and arranges her notebook once more.

"So I'm curious to know what happened with you and Polly," she says.

KRIS FARMEN

CHAPTER IV

I never did get a chance to return Polly's copy of *Typee*
that winter. We were too busy with the fur harvest.
There was beaver dams all through the lower valley and
down the Inlet at Tutsilitnu as well. Early in the season
we took turns shooting them with my old .32. When the
ice got thick enough we plugged their escape chutes and
chopped into their lodges and lifted them out one by one.
We ran a string of traps for river otters and mink, too. As
predicted by Belukha Pete we seen good lynx sign, and
we made sets for them with a duck wing hanging on a
string to catch their attention. Curiosity killed the cat,
as they say. We caught five big toms that winter and several females to make a baker's dozen, and there was still
plenty of sign about. There was no marten in the lower
valley, but they was thick above the canyon, so we cut a
trail and ran a line of twelve pole sets. Every couple days
we'd drive the dogs up there and camp, then check the
traps the next day. We'd sleep out one more night, then
go back home on the third day.

Trapping is hard work, but we often ran the lines together. It was a pleasure to be working in the woods, just
us two young bucks with the dogs and the mountains
standing high above us.

We finished up at the end of March month by heading inland to go ratting. Muskrats was our last chance
to make cash money for the season, but they was not in
abundance along Turnagain Arm. So we drove our dogs
down around Point Possession and across Big Indian
Creek and out onto the flats along the Swanson River,
breaking trail as we went. The rivers and lakes was still

froze over, but the days were long and warm. We ran alongside the sled in our shirtsleeves, and there was more than one day when it got so warm we travelled bare-chested, with four feet of snow all around us.

We stopped at Skilant town, but didn't stay long. They had the whooping cough there, and neither of us wanted it for ourselves. I was dismayed to find that Lucky Jim's old house had collapsed into itself from neglect. The fish runs had diminished considerably on account of the cannery traps across the mouth of the Kenay, and more and more people was moving downriver. Those that stayed were mostly living in log cabins; nobody wanted to live in the old-style houses anymore. I stood in front of my grandparents' hearth for some time, feeling disconnected from the world, as if I might go tumbling into the sky without the tether of their old home, dark and dank though it was.

"I need a drink," I muttered to the ruins.

Yasha was in a foul mood when we pulled out. He hardly spoke except for whatever words was needed on the trail. I figured it might have been the news of so many sick people or maybe a disagreement with his aunts that I had not been party to, but I kept my own council and figured he'd either get past it or bring it to light in good time.

I, for my part, was eager to get back down to Deep Creek to see Polly. I'd had no word from her, and I am not nor have I ever been much inclined to letter-writing. Not that there was any postal service to deliver it anyway. We had made a very respectable catch, and I was looking forward to town and to feeling her in my arms once again. I had high hopes that I would never again need to be gone so long from her, or so far away.

The sunshine felt good on our skin as we made camp at Broken Dog Lake and set about scouting for pushups where the rats do their feeding. We also kept an eye out for any spring beaver we might chance across. Over the coming days we shot several dozen rats and chopped into three beaver lodges. Spring was around the corner, and the days was full of warmth and light. The ice made for easy travel, but there wasn't much to eat, so our desire for beavers and rats was just as much about food as it was fur.

Our original plan was to head straight back north to spend breakup at Sixmile, but come early April, after several weeks of beaver and rat meat, we hankered for some variety in our diet. We decided to detour over to the hills above Skilak Lake to try and find some caribou.

It took us several days of beating out a trail on snowshoes to get across the Swanson flats, but when we hit the upper Kenay River we found the snow packed down like a highway all the way to the lake. It was starting to get slushy during the day, and we knew we would have to make it a quick trip.

We set up a camp at the southeast side of the lake where the foothills began. Behind us were the high mountains with their glaciers and snowfields. To the south was the broad table-land between Skilak and Kussilof Lakes.

We left on foot the next morning long before sunup when the snow was still frozen and easy to travel upon. We walked up onto the table-lands, cutting for sign all the way and pushing for high ground where we could gain a good prospect of the country below and any game that might be seen.

On a high knoll on the side of a mountain we found a good view to the south and west. The sun had not yet cleared the mountains, and we sat on our snowshoes in cold blue shadow though the country below was bathed in warm light. We watched for movement, munching on left over roast muskrat.

"I think I'm going to have Mike order me a pair of field glasses," I said. "It would make spotting a lot easier."

Yasha just give a little grunt and pulled off another string of meat and pushed it into his mouth. We was so hard up we hadn't any seal oil to dress it, nor even any pilot bread.

I watched him as he chewed. It had been several weeks of his sullen attitude, and I was growing weary of it. I was even starting to worry that he was mad over something I had done although I could think of no slight I might have given.

"Yasha," I said, "what the hell's eating you? You aint said more than a dozen words since we left Skilant."

He kept chewing the stringy rat meat until he could swallow. For a moment I thought he wasn't going to say anything.

"My aunts told me that Fedosya's family has arranged a marriage for her."

This was a common practice, though by our time it had begun to die out. Then again Lucky Jim was hardly the only one who kept some of the old ways.

"And I take it the groom aint you," I said.

"Nope."

"Who then?"

"Ilarion Lebedev. From over at Kuskatan."

I moved my gaze down-country below the patch-work of creeks, woods and ponds with the river cutting through it all. It was a fine morning, and you could see all the way across the Peninsula and the Inlet to Mount Redoubt.

"That's a hard piece of luck," I said. "But maybe you could head up there after breakup when we sell our catch and deliver her aunts a boatload of cloth and beads. Maybe change their minds."

"We aint made that good of a catch."

"There's always Tutsilitnu."

"We aint doing that no more, AC."

I considered our alternatives. "You want to go down to Kenay town and get loaded?"

"Maybe," he said. He nodded his head toward a distant pond. "I see gray hairs."

I looked where he indicated. There was maybe fifty caribou milling over a broad flat, digging for lichen where the wind off the mountains had blown the snow thin.

We moved fast, staying in the shadow of the mountain where it was cold and we could go at a dogtrot on our snowshoes, barely sinking into the snow. Even so, it took us a solid hour to get into position. I let Yasha do all the shooting. He dropped three animals, a cow and two small bulls with three shots, one two three, slick as you please. He was all smiles at this, and it was good to see his mouth turn up once more. I had to admit the value of his repeater—he could have kept on killing caribou all day if he'd a mind to.

While we was butchering the first kill we spotted two sleds and four men moving toward us from the south. We straightened up to watch them with our sleeves rolled up and the bright blood running off our forearms.

"Any idea who that is?" I said.

Yasha shook his head and kept watching, then I seen him draw up sharp.

"What?" I said.

"Shit. It's Big Nick."

Nicolai Andreivich stood six foot six in his stocking feet, something quite unusual for a Creole. His mother, who was half Kenaytze and half Aleut, had left Alaska with his Russian father when he returned to St. Petersburg in the aftermath of Seward's purchase. Nick was sixteen years old at the time.

His father had told him that a junior commission in the Imperial Navy had been arranged. Big Nick had never been to Russia; he was colony-born and had no desire to move to this faraway city his parents said was his home. And he certainly had no desire to serve in the Czar's navy. He took off for the woods in the middle of the night and made his way to Kussilof Lake where he had good friends among the Tustumena Indians. He married a Kenaytze girl from the lake and lived the kind of life the Russian colonials had always known, despite the coming of the Americans. He was a man much admired for his hunting and trapping abilities, but he had the reputation of a quick temper.

Big Nick's appearance that day drew such a response from Yasha because we was at the edge of the Tustumena people's territory, and they was known to be jealous of their hunting grounds.

We worked fast, but they approached even faster. We was just cutting off the last fore-quarter from the third carcass when Big Nick called out to us in the Indian tongue.

I sliced through the final bit of muscle that held the shoulder and Yasha stood it on the rib-cage. Big Nick and his companions was on snowshoes, maybe a long stone's throw away. We watched as they pulled their rifles from the scabbards and fired a volley into the air, as custom dictated. But times had changed, and I noticed they was all shooting repeaters.

"*Kak sebya chustwesh?*" I called out. This is Russian for How do.

"Doing just fine," said Nick. "Is that Yasha Izaakov and Aleksandr Campbell?"

"It is. How you been, Nick?"

"We're wore out. We been trailing some caribou."

I looked over at Yasha and him at me. This had the potential to go badly, but we'd been caught red-handed and there wasn't much we could do about it.

KRIS FARMEN

"Come up for a *chypeet*," I said. I wondered how much, if any, of the kill we would be permitted to keep. Most likely Nick and the Tustumena Indians would help themselves to the hides and the lion's share of the meat and leave us a single front shoulder. If we were lucky.

Then there come an American voice: "AC and Yasha! Good to see you boys!"

Nick and the Tustumena Indians turned toward the American to whom the voice belonged. The sun had found us, and I had to squint over the brightness of the snow-glare.

"Scotty Keogh?"

"That's my name. How goes the battle?"

"Well I'll just be damned," I said. It was a great relief to see a friendly face.

We found some dead timber and got a fire going. With the tea made, Nick produced a bottle of his home-brewed vodka and poured a dose into each man's cup. We charged our pipes and sat on our snowshoes smoking and chatting. Scotty made a sort of bridge between us, for Nick and the Tustumena boys seemed quite fond of him, and he was obviously a good pal of ours. He always was a gregarious rascal. He could charm the bark right off a tree.

Even more surprising, Scotty had learned enough of the Kenaytze tongue to communicate, even if his grammar left something to be desired. He told us that he'd established a trapline along Kussilof Lake, and Big Nick and his relations had been kind enough to invite him along on their caribou hunt.

This caused me and Yasha to share another uncomfortable glance. There was still the worry of what they were going to do with us.

Finally Nick fixed a hard eye on me. "You're that kid who beat the hell out of the schoolmaster up on Kenay town. Klara Morgan's nephew."

"I am."

A grin spread across Nick's face. "I never liked that son of a bitch."

He poured us another round of tea and vodka while Yasha and me cut up the tenderloins and tongues from all three kills and skewered them over the fire on green willow sticks. When done, these morsels was cut up and passed around to a general murmur of agreement.

Scotty chewed and swallowed his last mouthful then said, "Wasn't you taken up with that pretty little blonde gal down at Deep Creek? What's her name."

"Polly Parker," I said. "I'll be down to see her as soon as the ice goes out."

Big Nick looked at me sideways as if he hadn't yet made up his mind. In fact his two companions, plus Scotty, all looked like the cat that swallowed the canary.

"You might want to head straight down to town," Nick said. "She's getting hitched in a couple weeks."

"What now?" I figured I must have heard him wrong.

"She's getting married. To that Yankee beach miner. The one who thinks he knows everything."

"You aint too good with names, are you Nick?" said one of his Tustumena friends.

Nick chuckled and refilled our cups with good cheer; though, to be honest, the cheer was rapidly draining out of my day.

"Greg Hackham," said Scotty. "You know him, AC?"

"Yeah," I said. "I know him. But that can't be true. I told her I was coming back for her. She said she'd be ready for me in the spring."

"Women are known to change their minds," said Scotty.

"So they tell me."

He shrugged. "Happens to the best of us. Hack's a big wheel, and he's got a lot of Back East money behind him. He's been scouting out gold prospects for the big mining syndicates."

"That supposed to make me feel better?"

"Nope. But I figured you should at least know what you're up against."

Big Nick slapped the ashes from his pipe. "I thought you would already have heard about it."

I just stared at my feet. Later I would find out that Belukha Pete had in fact drove his dogs up to Sixmile to inform me of this development, but we had already left for rat camp.

"We been on the trail a while," said Yasha.

Nick nodded and stood up. The others followed suit. Scotty laid a hand on my shoulder. "It happens, bud. That's all I can tell you."

"You going to tell me she ditched me because I aint white?"

"I don't think she's that kind of gal. A lot of them are, no question about it. But not her."

A grunt was all I could manage.

Nick turned to me as Scotty knocked his snowshoes together to clear them of loose snow. "The wedding's on the twenty-ninth of April," he said. "So you boys better make tracks. The snow's already melting in the low country and you got a long way to go."

"You going?" I said.

"I am. Everyone's invited. I been told these American weddings are something to see."

"What about the hides and meat? You all need grub?"

"We'll take a couple quarters off your hands. But you go ahead and keep most of it. You boys did all the hard work."

"The hides?" said Yasha.

Big Nick looked real sly at him. "Fedosya's going to be down for the wedding with her folks. I reckon she could use them. Maybe her mother and her aunts too. Might even soften up her old dad some."

"No secrets around here," Yasha muttered.

"You're always going to be the last to hear, living way the hell out in a place like Sixmile."

I looked west down the slope of the land toward the river. There was still snow, but it looked warm and slushy on the flats.

"What about you, Scotty?" I said. "You going?"

"Wouldn't miss it for the world."

He moved away to strap on his snowshoes. Nick leaned in, and after a quick glance around he spoke to me quietly in Russian.

"AC, you make damn sure you don't tell that Hackham clown about the gold at Tutsilitnu. You hear?"

"Yeah," I said. "I hear."

———

It was a rough trip down to Kenay town. We was almost two weeks on the trail and just as Big Nick said, the spring that year was a warm one. The trail across the flats to town was in awful shape, with bare ground showing in the south-facing stretches and all the creeks filled with overflow. We almost didn't make it across the Niluntnu River. The ice was busted and jumbled up at its mouth where it dumps into the Kenay with big open leads. The ice on the Kenay River was even worse. We had to detour almost a full day up the Niluntnu to find ice that looked solid enough for us to cross. I fretted every step of the way that we might have been trapped and might have to stay there until we could build a canoe or even a log raft, and I didn't have that kind of time.

We made it across eventually, though we busted through the ice halfway over and had to splash and wade and lift each of the dogs and the sled on to the shelf ice on the far side. Then we lost several more hours building a fire and drying out. Thank God it wasn't January with a cold wind blowing. After we got everything dry it took us yet another day to get back down to the main trail again.

We took to running at night when it was cooler and the trail was still froze, but the weather quickly warmed to the point where even that didn't help. We spent an ungodly amount of time shouldering our heavy sled across bare mud and muck with our winter moccasins squishing in the melt-water and the dogs all panting and surly.

The snow finally give out just three miles from town. We sat on the bare brown grass of the riverbank, cussing the spring and the snow and everything around us. The wood frogs was already singing in the forest. Our load of caribou meat was about to spoil even though we had it wrapped in a tarp with several chunks of river ice. Out on the river, the ice was busted up and grinding against itself, but there was still too much of it for navigation. Not that we had a boat anyway.

We'd been sitting there on the riverbank next to the last of the disappearing snow for most of the morning when Yasha cocked his ear and said, "What's that?"

"Nothing," I said, not even bothering to listen. The dogs behind us lay on the ground in their harness with their ears pricked, but I took no notice of them. I was fuming because, among other things, we had no way of knowing what day it was. We hoped we had at least two or three days before the big event. Nobody at Skilant had any idea what the calendar date was when we passed through. Indians are generally not bothered by such notions. The upshot was that we had no way to mark off the days as they passed. We was dead reckoning through time. By and by it dawned on me that maybe we'd miscalculated and was actually overdue by a couple days, that the moment of truth had already come and gone.

This started me to cussing all over again, but Yasha told me to shut up.

"I hear a woman's voice," he said.

I swallowed my bile and put a hand behind my ear. "Kenaytze or Russian?"

"Can't tell."

I listened. Fortunately it was a calm day with no wind. I heard the ice grinding in the river. I heard a dollop of wet snow plop onto the ground from an overhanging bank. An early robin sang from a nearby tree.

Then it hit my ear—a voice, only it belonged to a man, and he was speaking American.

"It's Yankees," I said.

Yasha nodded with his eyes fixed on the ground as he always did when he was listening intently to something. By now he had both his hands cupped around his earlobes.

"There's a Yankee woman too," he said. "How many Yankee women you know here on the Peninsula?"

"Polly!" I said.

I moved my hands to my mouth and let out a sharp high-pitched cry. It cut through the springtime air and was followed by several seconds of silence. Then there come a deeper cry, the HAWLOO favored by American woodsmen.

We tied off the dogs and pushed through the brush. The call seemed to have come from along the river, so that's where we looked. Yasha let loose with another whoop, and it was followed by another hawloo. We was bashing through a thicket of doghair black spruce when I spotted a man's coat-sleeve. I called out and he stopped short. It was none other than Greg Hackham.

"Hello there," he said.

"How do," said Yasha.

I didn't answer. I just watched him, trying to hold down the ire that had been building inside me over the last several days.

"You two look familiar," said Hackham. "Did we meet down at Seldovoya?"

"The beach at Deep Creek last summer," said Yasha. "We was getting clams, and you was helping old man Parker with his beach diggings."

"Yes, that's right." Hack's demeanor was that of a man talking to small children, though he wasn't that much older than us. He spoke as if he owned the entire forest. You will notice that once again he did not offer his hand to either of us.

"We should find some decent color there if we really work at it," he said.

"We?"

"My company purchased the Parker claim not long before he passed."

"Passed?" said Yasha. "You mean Parker's dead?"

"He is. The consumption took him back in February."

This of course come as a shock to both of us. For all my anger, my heart went out to Polly, for I know firsthand what it is to lose a loved one to this dread disease.

Hack shifted his weight a little. "I guess you've come down for our wedding."

"You could say that," said Yasha.

"What were your names again?"

"I'm Yasha Izaakov."

"And who's your sidekick here with the long grim face?"

"That's my partner, AC."

"So we haven't missed it," I said.

"No. In fact, you're a couple days early."

Yasha pointed back to the river. "We got a load of meat that's going to spoil if we don't get it into a cold-house soon."

"That shouldn't be any trouble. My fiancée and I rode out here for a picnic. We can give you a hand."

Yasha turned to me and said in the Kenaytze tongue, "What's a *feeyahnsy*?"

I gritted my teeth against the crackling in my jaw. It was there, but it was manageable, and I pushed it away.

"It means the gal he's getting hitched to," I said in American.

"That would be Polly Parker," said Hackham.

———

Polly was sitting on a cottonwood log at their picnic site when the three of us joined her. She had a fire going and watched as we approached, having heard us in the thick brush.

"AC," she said when she seen me. "And Yasha! Where did you two come from?"

She stood up to greet us, and I noticed right away that her belly was large with child. She was quite spry, though, considering her state. She rushed up to us and give us each a hug, first Yasha, then me. I held on to her a moment longer than was proper, and she put her hand against me to push me away.

"What are you doing with this joker?" I said hooking a thumb over my shoulder at Hack.

There was perhaps three-quarters of a second where her eyes held mine, then she looked away. "Greg is my fiancé. We got engaged back in February."

She made a point of not looking at me, though I was looking at her most directly. Behind me I heard Hack take a step forward, but I knew Yasha had an eye on him. He stepped in and blocked Hack's play, so I paid it no mind.

Mind you, it was not as if I had given Polly that sack of gold in the fall to purchase her affections. It was a token of my feelings. Now, looking at the swelling beneath her dress it dawned on me what must have happened—Hack must have come along right after our night together on the beach. Hell, maybe he was there before me. I was not the first man whose touch Polly had known, that much she could not keep hidden from me.

The smoke from the fire smelled sour, which suited my mood. I grabbed Polly by the arm. "What the hell is this? I come back for you just like I said I would. You said you'd wait for me and that you'd come away with me to Sixmile."

"AC," she said. That and nothing more. Her eyes looked into me, and it was like a knife sliding between my ribs. Hack watched us keenly, not liking it one bit.

"I asked you a question, Polly." She tried to twist away, and I clamped my hand down harder on her arm.

"Stop it AC. You're hurting me."

Hack finally shouldered his way past Yasha and grabbed onto the lapel of my waistcoat.

We didn't even bother to draw a scratch-line in the dirt—he raised his dukes and I done the same. He was older than me, but I was taller by a couple inches, and I was fit and hard from a winter of snowshoeing and running dogs. The crackling and popping roared back to life in my jaw, worse than it had ever been. It felt like hot sparks fizzing and shooting into the back of my neck and under my ears, and there was the thought of two boar grizzlies I had once seen battling over a sow.

It was all I could do to control this sensation. I blinked once, then again, which Hack took as an opportunity to puff himself up, but Polly seen her opening and pushed herself in between us before a single punch could be thrown.

"Greg," she said. "Give us a minute. Please?"

She had a hand against each of us while we both pressed at one another. The crackling was about to get the best of me, so I pulled away. To this day it still irks me that Hack thought he won because he was the better man, when the truth of the matter was that I just barely managed to keep a pissing match from turning into a bloody confrontation that would likely have ended with his guts dangling from the spruce limbs above.

"Greg," said Polly, still looking at him.

His eyes flicked down to meet hers.

"Give us a minute."

He backed off, gloating at me all the while. Then he turned and walked toward the river. Polly pushed me back into the woods in the opposite direction. As we left I seen Yasha hold up his axe and incline his head toward Hack, but I shook my head no. We didn't need that kind of trouble.

Polly drew me into a stand of big cottonwoods, and we sat beneath them in the paper-dry leaves.

"AC," she started, but I cut in.

"You said you'd wait for me, Polly."

She looked down at her belly, then back up at me. It was all she needed to say.

"Were you carrying on with him before I come around last fall?"

"That's not really your business."

"It damn well is my business."

All the same, her response told me what I wanted to know. She would have denied it flat-out if it weren't true.

"Hack decided to do the right thing," she said.

"You saying I wouldn't have?"

She waved a hand in the air. "I'm not saying that at all."

"So just what the hell are you saying then?"

"God dammit, AC! Just what is it you want me to tell you?"

"I want you to tell me why I aint good enough for you. And why you got to go running off with that knuckle-head! Because he's got money and a college degree? That why you bedded down with him after I left? So you could keep your options open?"

This cut her to the quick. But seeing it didn't make me feel any better. In fact, it made me feel even worse.

"AC, I meant to tell you. I wanted to. But you were gone."

"I was gone trapping so I could show your father that I could provide for you. I went to Sixmile to make a start for us."

She blinked and a tear dropped from her eyelashes. Another followed, and she put a hand over her face while the other rested upon her belly. To his credit, Big Nick had not mentioned her being with child, but there was no doubt in my mind that Polly Parker was the talk of all the towns up and down the Inlet.

"I heard about your dad," I said. "I was very sorry to hear of his passing."

Polly said nothing. She just sat there letting the tears spill out from under her hand. I reached for her, but she threw my arm aside and wouldn't let me touch her.

"Polly, my mother died the same way. I know what it's like, believe me."

I reached for her again, but she stood up and stepped away. I rose to my feet after her, and we stood there apart for several moments until she got herself under control. I wanted to pull her into my arms and wipe her tears away but it was evident that she had no desire of my comfort.

She took a long breath. "Alex, I didn't have anyone left to take care of me. My dad sold our beach claim and cabin for money to go to a sanitarium, but then he died, and I was all alone and knocked up, and I didn't have anywhere to go. Then Greg comes along and sees my state and proposes to me. What was I supposed to do?"

I took a step toward her. This time she held her ground, looking up at me. "Polly Parker, you don't need him. I've come to take care of you. That sack of gold was a token of my love for you. It shined bright even in the darkness in your front yard, but it pales compared to the light of my love."

This speech seems a bit silly and youthful to me now, but at the time it was the best American words I could muster. For the record, it would have sounded a lot better in Kenaytze.

I pointed north toward Sixmile. "Me and Yasha got a good cabin set up for us. He's going to marry a girl from Possession town named Fedosya. We can all go up there and live together. It'll be like our own little town. There's plenty of fur, and I can make us a good living. I'll love you and your child. And I'll give you more children and plenty of money to spend on all of us."

She stared at me as new tears slid down her cheeks. "AC, how was I to know? I didn't have any word from you."

"You could ditch him. You aint spoken the oath yet."

Polly looked out at the forest. "I gave him my word."

"Your word."

"He asked me to be his bride and I said yes."

I wanted her to look at me, but she wouldn't do it.

"There's gold at Sixmile, Polly." My pulse pounded in my ears as I said those words. This is what the Americans call going for broke.

"I don't give a fig for gold. That was my father's obsession. And Hack's."

I could think of nothing more to say. I now had the burden of knowing I had not fulfilled a promise, both to Lucky Jim and Big Nick. We stood there listening to the breeze in the bare cottonwood branches, and I started thinking that maybe I should have been less worried about a good fur catch and allowed myself the luxury of a trip or two to see Polly over the winter. Or perhaps swallowed my pride and asked Mailman Mike for a job at the AC store. Ever have I been the type to fixate on a goal and then blind myself to everything else in life.

"So did that night on the beach last fall mean anything to you?" I said. There was more bitterness in my voice than I meant for there to be.

"It was wonderful, AC. But what is done is done."

Again we was left in silence with nothing more to say on the matter.

"We'll give you a hand hauling your meat into town," Polly said.

More than once I'd heard talk of heartache in poems and songs, but I never understood what it was until that moment when I had to stand there and watch Polly walk away from me. Even then I suspected there was something she was not telling me.

Back at the fire, Hackham and me eyed one another as he and Polly shared their picnic lunch with us. Fair's fair, and I must admit that was rather gracious of them considering the circumstances. Still, it was hardly what you would call an enjoyable meal. I ended up with an egg salad sandwich, which to this day has left a bad taste in my mouth.

They had come on this excursion with Hack walking and Polly riding his saddle horse. Even with child Polly didn't weigh very much, so we tied several of the hind and fore-quarters over the saddle. There was a brief tiff between the betrothed when Polly suggested they each load their own packboards with meat. Hack dismissed the idea on account of her state, but this was a thin excuse. He could have easily taken a load on his own back, it would have done him no harm. I recall thinking that such a disagreement on virtually the eve of their wedding did not bode well for their future together, but I kept this to myself. All the same, we was grateful to have the help of the horse, though the fact that Hack could afford to keep such a rare and expensive animal made me dislike him all the more.

They left with the barest of good-byes, thanking us for the meat we gifted them for their wedding supper. They said they would spread the word in Kenay that we was in distress and in need of, shall we say, succor.

After they departed, me and Yasha cut some spruce poles and knocked together a platform cache for our outfit. We made heavy packs of the rest of the meat and the hides, and led the dogs by lines tied to their harnesses. We would have had them carry part of the load, but we had no dog-packs for them. They seemed satisfied with that arrangement.

Our plan was to deliver the meat and hides, then walk back up and retrieve our gear. But on the way to town we heard voices among the trees and suddenly found ourselves surrounded by a gaggle of Creole and Native women, all aunts, cousins, or family friends, come to fetch us and our baggage. There was a festive spirit in town on account of the wedding, and this attitude prevailed as they took the heavy loads from our backs and left us with just the dogs. We described where we'd left our things, and some of the younger women continued upriver to collect them.

The word festive would not precisely describe my own sentiments at the time. I was in a dark mood when we finally stumbled into town that evening. Even the fine spring weather and the sight of the ice pans flowing out from the river mouth could not lift my spirits. Kenay town had swelled to perhaps five times its normal size. A wedding, be it Russian or American, means a party, and folks had come from all around.

Word had spread about our arrival from upriver, and we was greeted by a jovial crowd. I found my aunt Klara in the second place I looked, that being her sewing room upstairs in the house. Little did I know when I padded up the stairs that my day was about to go from bad to worse.

"AC!" she said when I tapped on the door and stuck my head inside.

I smiled in spite of myself, but the corners of my mouth turned back down when I seen the swollen figure of Polly Parker standing in the light near the window. She was in her white dress holding up her hair as Klara stood behind her, pinning up some pleats or darts or some such.

Klara crossed the floor and took me into a hug, being careful not to stick me with any of the pins. It had been a long time since I'd seen her so happy. Weddings always bring smiles to the faces of the women-folk.

"Isn't she beautiful?" she said.

I mumbled an answer and Klara glanced over to see Polly staring down at the floorboards. She quickly put two and two together. For my part, I'd had no inkling that my aunt was acting as Polly's seamstress. Neither Polly nor Hack had mentioned it, but then we'd all had other things on our minds.

"I tell you what, my dear," Klara said to Polly, "I've got all the measures I need, so why don't you get changed and I'll finish this tonight."

She got no argument from Polly, who stepped behind the modesty screen of painted birchbark panels. Klara steered me out into the hallway, closing the door behind her and switching to Russian.

"Thank you for the meat," she said. "Polly and Hack brought it around to keep it in my cold-house."

"Klara, what's she doing here?"

"I offered to make her wedding dress. Mike and I took her in when her father passed away so she could have someplace to stay until the wedding."

"You mean here in the house?" The thought was almost more than I could bear to contemplate.

"We gave her your old room. I hope that's alright. The poor thing hasn't a soul left in the world except for Hack."

"Right," I said. "Her state must be the talk of the town."

"Never you mind that. She's hardly the first young lady to find herself in such a fix."

By this I knew she was referring to my own departed mother. My cheeks flushed with shame that I had even brought it up.

"At least Hack did right by her," Klara said. "That's what matters."

I nodded, looking out the glass window at the end of the paneled hallway. The pale light of the sunset filled the air around us and the glare hid the faces of the icon paintings that lined the walls. The hard floorboards were strange under my moccasin feet, and I felt out of place in my trail clothes, lacking of soap and water. I could hear the floorboards creak as Polly stepped out from behind the screen, and the knowledge that she had been undressed on the other side of the wall made my pulse race and my blood boil all at the same time.

"So it's alright if she stays in your room?"

I nodded. "I'll camp down by the beach."

"You don't have to do that. I can make you up a bed in the parlor."

"Yes I do," I said. It was only the appropriate thing, as well as a move to preserve what remained of my sanity.

Klara's eyes flicked to the door, then back to me. "I have to take some berries over to Iriana Golinov. Would you like to walk with me?"

It had been a long day, but I said I would. We went down to the kitchen, and Klara sent me into the cellar with a birchbark basket. Iriana's special recipe for blueberry glaze had been requested for the wedding cake by the bride herself. Iriana was out of berries, so Klara had volunteered the last of her preserves from the previous summer. I filled the basket with the last five lonely Ball jars, then we went out the door and along the trail to town, down the little gully then up the other side onto the bluff. The entire population of sled dogs put up a chorus of howling at our approach.

"I know you were sweet on her, AC," Klara said when we was out of earshot of the house.

"I wanted her to be my wife. I was making a start for us." As I spoke these words I realized for the first time just how hollow Polly had left me feeling. My life suddenly seemed to have no direction at all.

Klara reached up and pushed a lock of my hair back from my face. "I'm so sorry, honey. This must be very difficult for you."

I shook my head. "Don't worry over it."

"Would this be a bad time to tell you there are other fish in the sea?"

"Yes."

She pinched my cheek, which took me by surprise and made us both laugh.

"I know you don't think much of Hack," she said.

"I'll behave myself. I aint going to ruin her big day just because it's not me she's marrying."

We walked past the Russian chapel and down Front Street along the bluff. None of the side streets had names in those days, they was just dirt tracks running back from the bluff and grown up with grass and fireweed along the edges. There was two new buildings going up. One was a two-story log house behind the AC store and the other a frame place with a false front at the south end of Front Street where it turned into a foot-trail that wound down the bluff to the river. When I asked Klara about them she said the log place was a new Creole family just arrived from Sitka, and the false front was to be Greg Hackham's new office. Apparently his business had grown to where it needed a fancy headquarters. We stopped to have a better look at these new constructions.

"Aunt Klara," I said, "do you think things was better before the Americans come?"

She turned to me, squinting against the evening sun that shone straight into her face. "What makes you ask that?"

"Just wondering. I mean, I was born after Seward's Purchase. I speak Russian, but I don't have any memory of the old Russian days."

She held a hand up over her face to shield her eyes from the glare. "Well, it was very different back then. The Russian America Company owned everything, even the houses we lived in. They was the only game in town, and you couldn't do anything without their say-so."

I chewed on this for a moment, studying the new log house with the spruce peelings lying all about and the gin-pole planted in the yard for hoisting the logs. It was built Russian-style, with dovetail corners.

"We did get an education though," Klara said. "Children learned to read and write and speak proper Russian. They were catechized by the priests. The boys were taught trades and some of them even went to St. Petersburg for college. We all got a smallpox inoculation. And the company made laws so that hunters couldn't just keep killing fur animals on whim so they could re-populate themselves."

"You mean the animals," I said. "Not the hunters."

She laughed. "Yes. The hunters didn't need any help repopulating themselves."

"I used to lay awake at night terrified of the Americans. You know, all those stories we used to hear of drunkenness and gunplay and the wicked behavior over in Sitka.

I recall being scared to death of every American other than Mike."

"You used to run and hide," she said. "But you came around eventually."

The new priest came strolling past in his dark cassock and collar with his hands clasped behind him. Klara turned to greet him.

"Good evening, Father Ludinov."

He smiled and responded in very fancy-sounding Russian. "Madame Morgan, good evening."

"This is my nephew Aleksandr."

I greeted the priest as my aunt had, though never having seen one before I was unsure of how to act. He was cordial, but he was on his way to the chapel and stopped only long enough to pass the time of day.

"It's so lovely to have a priest in town once more," Klara said when he had continued on his way. "It's been far too long."

"He called you Madame," I said. The usual form of address for a married Russian woman is *gospozha*.

"The nobility from the old country do that," said Klara. "It's considered more high class to use the French." A wistful smile crossed her face. "I've never actually had anyone call me Madame before. All the people from Russia went home before I married Mike."

I watched after him as he walked with the hem of his cassock swishing around his legs. "Would you go back to the old Russian days, Klara? If it was available to you?"

"There are days when I think I would. But there's plenty of good things the Americans brought to us and lots of things I certainly don't miss about the old empire. I do know you wouldn't have been allowed to live the life you're living now up at Sixmile. You would have had to serve the company for ten years to repay the debt for your education, and you would have no say in where they sent you."

"So you're glad the Americans bought our country," I said.

"What I think," she replied, "is that the Americans are here now, and we don't get much choice in the matter. We've got to make the best life here that we can. I'm glad Mike came to Alaska. He's the love of my life, and we would never have met if Seward's Purchase hadn't happened."

I was about to ask her what she didn't miss about the Russian administration when another figure came strolling down the street.

"Scotty Keogh!" I said.

"AC!" he said with a wave. He was carrying his fiddle in a case and shifted it to his left hand so he could shake with his right. He touched his hat brim at my aunt.

"I see you and Yasha made it to town alright," he said.

"Barely. The season caught up with us, and we run out of snow. We had to pack everything in on our backs."

Scotty blew some air out between his lips. "Nick was worried about that. The ice was out of the Kussilof River early this year, so we come down by boat."

"Lucky you."

He laughed and held up his fiddle case. "I got to run. My presence is required down on the beach. Come on down and have a smoke with the boys."

"The wedding's not till tomorrow," I said.

"This is band practice."

I knew Scotty probably had a supply of quality vodka or his homemade *poteen* on hand, but he wished to spare me any lecturing on the topic of Demon Rum.

I looked down at the basket of preserves, thinking that Klara was probably smart enough to know what his invitation was all about.

She watched me with a smile. "Go ahead, AC."

When I handed over the basket she snuck her hand out and pinched my cheek again.

"For luck," she said.

———

We took a few nips from Scotty's flask as we made our way down to the beach landing where the revelry was concentrated. This American wedding was quite the affair—Ephim Lebedev and all his people from Tyonek was there, and George Washington with everyone from Point Possession, too. There was some Skilant folks, but the sickness over the winter had left many of them in no shape to travel. Several Creoles and transplanted Aleuts had come up from Ninilchik, along with more Creoles and Indians from Anchor Point. And of course there was Big Nick and the Tustumena Indians. The canneries hadn't yet opened for the season, so the China gangs was not yet arrived. It was all locals, which was good, for them fellows who come up to work the slime-line are wont to cause trouble at a party.

Some of the Americans from Kachemak Bay turned up as well. There was a new family with a homestead down there, a Mr. and Mrs. William Davis and their three daughters: Candace, Martha, and Urilla. The oldest was seventeen and the youngest thirteen, and they was the cause of great interest among the single men. It will come as no surprise that these girls did not want for company.

I took a couple more pulls from Scotty's flask and wandered around in something of a daze. This was more people than I had seen in several months, and it had me almost wishing there was a hole I could bolt into. I was thinking of going to set up my camp when I was surprised by a familiar American voice.

"Alex Campbell."

I turned around and was startled to see Joe Cooper standing at the beer keg, drawing himself a libation. He waved me over and grabbed a fresh tin cup from a pile inside a pearl-oil box. He handed me the beer he'd just drawn and started pouring himself another. We clinked our cups and drank, and I asked Joe what he was up to and how he'd done up north after we departed.

"Lousy," he said shaking his head. "Hardly a speck of color after you left."

"I guess that's why the Russians didn't stay there."

"Well, there's going to be a big strike on the Peninsula soon, you mark my words." He was a good three sheets to the wind and hanging on his own words.

"You think?" I said.

"Oh hell yes. And I tell you what," he said leaning closer. "When the strike gets made it's going to be Greg Hackham that makes it."

He gestured with his cup to Hack's half-built office on the bluff above us. That Hack is a real wildcat. Prospecting's just a job to me, but he's going to open this country up. He's been looking in every single stream up and down the Inlet.

This was not joyous news to me. "That's an awful lot of country for one man to cover, Joe."

"He aint just one man, AC. He's grubstaking prospectors left and right. He knows there's gold out there. He can smell it. It's only a matter of time."

Just then Scotty come up next to us. He had his arm around a girl I knew slightly from Nikishka named Suzanne McCoy. She was an American Creole like me and widely regarded as one of the prettiest girls on the Peninsula. They each had a cup of beer, and Scotty was rapidly catching up to Joe. I myself was starting to feel fine and happy all over.

"Jesus Joe," said Scotty. "You're not off on that HE CAN SMELL GOLD thing again are you?"

He shifted his cup and threw his free arm around me. "Aleksandr Campbell, how are you, me lad?" His Irish accent, normally dormant, was much more out front when he was in his cups.

I caught a whiff of his odor mixed with the much more pleasant one of Suzanne. "Doing good, Scotty. Looks like you're flying pretty high yourself."

"I'm fit as a fiddle and right as rain." He clinked his cup with Suzanne, then with me and Joe, and raised it to his lips. "I'm just taking a little break from the Devil's Box."

"Your fiddle?" I said.

"Yes indeed. There's naught but sin that follows wherever I take it."

Suzanne laughed at that and I seen her looking at me.

Scotty remembered something and fished in his jacket pocket, producing a second pint flask of dark brown glass which he pressed at me. "That's some of Big Nick's finest. A present from him and me."

"How do you and Nick make this stuff?" I said.

"Easy. You make a batch of *quass*, then distill it."

"Distill it?"

"You boil off the water and the slurry. The alcohol condenses inside a coil of copper tubing. Come find me later, and I'll take you up to the store and get you lined out."

This seemed to me like a capital idea. It's illegal to buy and sell booze in Alaska, and why should I wait for the random bottle to come my way when I could make all I wanted from the bounty of the forest?

"Shit boys," said Scotty, "I'm dry. Let us onto the beer tap, Joe."

Joe laid a hand on the bung. "Allow me the pleasure, my good man."

Scotty held his cup under the tap as Joe poured. When it was full we all clinked cups again and took a drink. Suzanne come up behind Scotty and clapped her hands over his eyes.

"Who's there?" said Scotty, feeling the empty air around him like he'd been struck blind. Suzanne grinned at me over his shoulder.

"It's President Arthur, aint it? God damn, I've writ you letter after letter about how you've run this whole country into the ground. I knew you'd finally come face me man to man."

I believe Chester Arthur had already left office and been replaced by Cleveland at this point in time, but news from the States only comes north in a slow trickle. All the same, Scotty's comment produced a general round of laughter, and when Suzanne joined in I seen her looking once again at me. It made me wonder if perhaps my fly was undone.

I drew myself another beer and took my leave, walking down to the water. A band had been formed for the evening, consisting of whichever musicians had come up to the party and brought their instruments. They hammered their way through a fast jumpy version of "Sleepy-Eyed John," minus Scotty who was busy recovering his good form. Couples consisting of various combinations of Americans, Russians, Indians and Aleuts swung each other round and round on the beach gravel while everyone else hooted and hollered, clapping their hands and singing along. All races was having a grand time, and it must be said of the Americans that they certainly know how to throw a party.

I said hello to Swedish Mike, Russian Mike, and Mike the Finn. They was all middle-aged immigrant bachelors, shaky in their American and lacking in dancing ability. They eyed the girls like they was gold bullion, something beyond their mortal reach. I stood with them for a few minutes, but they didn't have much to say, and I got tired of watching them suck the beer suds from their droopy moustaches, so I moved on. It filled me with melancholy to think that I might just be looking at my future written across their dour faces.

I confess I was halfway looking for Polly. I wanted to see her, but also dreaded the prospect. She was nowhere to be found, and the thought of her sleeping in my old bedroom made me want to collapse into myself. Then again, I was new at love.

Out beyond the edge of the goings-on I found a drift log to lean against and sat myself down in last summer's dead grass. I filled my pipe, then lit it and sat there smoking and nursing my cup of beer with my eyes drifting back and forth between the bonfire and the sunset over the mountains on the west shore. The sight of the revelry and all those couples enjoying themselves cast a shadow on my soul that the colors in the sky could not chase away. I kept coming around to the question of whether Polly had been with Hack before she was with me or if he'd come along right after I left. Or if she'd taken up with him because he was white and I wasn't. Not that it really mattered. It was all just the same mosquito bite to pick at.

These of course was the most selfish of thoughts. I think it may have been the Devil himself I heard whispering into my ear: *That's right, AC. That's why she didn't want to take that sack of gold back in September. She didn't want to be beholden to no brown-skinned siwash like you.*

I slugged back the rest of my beer, then went to work on the flask of Big Nick's vodka. Before long there was the feeling I loved of being able to just float away from my troubles, and I was grateful to the world for providing me with such medicine. When the pint was nearly done

I laid down in the grass and gravel, looking straight up at the sky. The last stars of spring was coming out. Soon we wouldn't see them again for three months.

It goes without saying that I was pretty well-marinated at this point. The Dipper started to spin, and the stars got all streaky from their revolutions as the ground turned beneath me. I was more accustomed to this sensation by now and felt like an old hand at drinking as I reached out and planted a palm on the log behind me. I was feeling all alone in the world, but the booze had me convinced that everything was going to be alright.

Yasha's voice: "AC?"

"Yasha," I said. "And Fedosya. Partner, you found yourself a real keeper, you know that?"

Fedosya raised an eyebrow at me, then looked over at Yasha. They come closer, looking down at me. I was still working to keep the world from spinning too fast, and I could hear myself slurring my words.

"You're loaded," said Fedosya.

I held up my thumb and forefinger, a pinch apart. I started laughing, but I felt just as much like crying. It can be hard to tell these feelings apart sometimes.

Yasha bent down and grabbed me by the armpits and propped me against the log. My arms flopped around like a rag doll, but I managed to stay upright. The two of them sat down next to me, one on each side.

"How's things with you two?" I said.

Fedosya coughed a little and looked again at Yasha.

"AC," he said in the Kenaytze tongue, "we got something we need to tell you."

I think I must have slapped him on the thigh. I was feeling rather convivial. "Shoot, partner!" I said in American.

"We're getting out of here. Me and Fedosya."

"What?"

"We're leaving. Tonight."

"Where you going to?"

"Seldovoya," said Fedosya. "There's a preacher at the Methodist mission there. We're going to have him marry us."

"Well damnation," I said. "Everyone's getting hitched."

They was quiet as I fumbled around trying to load my pipe. Finally Yasha reached over and done it for me. My mind turned in slow circles.

"But Yasha, you aint Methodists. You're Orthodox. That parson in Seldovoya town won't marry you if you aint of his church."

"We are now," he said. "We both took the Methodist sacraments from that travelling preacher who's going to marry Polly and Hack."

"So what's a Methodist?" I said.

Yasha shrugged. "I aint really certain. But one's the same as another, I guess."

"They got that new priest here," I said. "Why can't he marry you?"

"He's away at Nuchek," said Yasha. This is a Chugach town over in Prince William's Sound.

"And besides," said Fedosya, "if we do it here there's too much chance for my aunts to get in the way."

"So you're going to Seldovoya."

"That's it," said Yasha.

"Folks won't like it that you changed churches just to get married against your family's wishes."

"To hell with them," he said.

"You want me to come along and stand up for you?"

"I don't think you're fit to stand up anywhere," Fedosya said with a smile.

"You're probably right about that."

"If anyone asks about us," said Yasha, "tell them we went up the Susitna River."

"You got it. Susitna River. When you leaving?"

Yasha sat up from the log and pushed himself around on one knee so he was facing me. "Right now. We'll meet you back up at Point Possession in a couple weeks."

Looking down, I spied a couple fingers of hooch left in the flask. I held it out to him. "Have a drink, pard. We'll toast your new life together."

He shook his head. "I aint drinking no more."

"What now?"

"I quit drinking."

I would find out later that Fedosya had told him she wouldn't marry him if he drank.

"That's a shame," I said.

He reached out and took Fedosya's hand. "I got something better than booze."

"Oh. Right."

We shook hands and Fedosya give me a hug. "I'm real sorry about Polly ditching you."

I squeezed her a little harder, then let her go. They headed down the beach with a final wave, and I was left alone once more by my drift log with my two fingers of booze and my unsmoked pipe. The crunch of their feet in the gravel faded into the night.

"Lucky bastard," I said to the sky. Then I laughed, cackling at the stars and the moon for no reason. Lucky bastard indeed.

I must have passed out then, because when I woke it was full dark and very chilly. I lay with my jacket pulled tight around me and listened to the waves lapping at the sand-flats. I felt less drunk, but my head had started to hurt and my tongue seemed to fill my mouth. It was maybe three in the morning, judging from the position of the Dipper, and the town was silent, even the dogs at their tethers.

I found my flask where it had dropped from my hand and drained the last of the vodka. It eased my head some-what. I got up and stumbled back to the beer keg. I rocked it to see if there was any beer left, then I filled my tin cup and drank a long draught. I let out a long belch that was swallowed by the breeze, thinking of Polly sleeping in my old room and wondering what position she lay in beneath the quilts. Face up, most likely, or on her side, given her condition. Then I thought of Greg Hackham, the son of a bitch who had stole her from me.

I shambled up the hill to the wall tent where Hack was staying while his office was under construction.

"Hackham!" I called. My voice sounded huge in the night. There was only the stars and the wind and the trace of light spread over the mountains to the east where the sun was slowly peeking up behind them.

"Hackham!" I was still flying high and slurred his name a little.

There come a stirring inside the tent.

"I'm calling you out, Hack!" I said. "Get your ass out here if you think you're man enough!"

Hack struck a match, held it a second, then let it go out. I heard the sounds of clothes being pulled on and composed myself even as I heard two voices murmur-ing. Polly was in there with him. She must have snuck out from Mike and Klara's house seeking his arms. In my addled state I felt a flare of anger at her for behaving so dishonorably toward my kin who had taken her in. I later realized that was a pretty stupid way to look at things. The dishonor had already been done; why shouldn't she share a tent with him?

The tent flap moved and Hackham ducked out in his moleskin britches and union suit, barefoot with his braces hanging down. There was a pistol stuffed under his waistband.

He stepped up to me, so close I could smell her scent upon him. "Go home, Campbell. You've had enough for one night."

I pointed at the tent. "Polly's in there, aint she?"

"That's not your affair."

"The hell it aint."

"She don't want to see you."

"She can tell me herself if she don't want to see me, damn you."

"I'm telling you. Now get the hell out of here."

"Polly!" I called over his shoulder. "Polly, I love you!"

Hackham took a step back and pulled his revolver. He pointed it straight at my breast and thumbed back the hammer in one slick motion.

"Not another fucking word, Campbell. Or by god I'll shoot you dead."

I stared at the tent where my gold-headed gal lay, then looked back at Hack. He meant business. Even drunk I could see that.

I turned and lurched back down the road to the beach. I passed out in the grass, next to the creek below Mike and Klara's place.

Not the proudest moment of my life, I'd warrant.

———

Mailman Mike, being one of the leading citizens of the town, had lent his and Klara's ice cream churn to the wedding enterprise, along with several gallons of fresh cream that come up on a refrigerated cargo ship from San Francisco.

Klara drafted me into service on the morning of the wedding to crank the churn. She said she needed a strapping lad like me. The machine sat down inside a big wooden piggin, and she packed the space between the chamber and the wood staves with chipped ice and rock salt. I cranked that contraption for almost an hour in the

KRIS FARMEN

kitchen, with her continuously re-packing the salt and ice. She said this lowered the temperature the cream froze at. I was hung over and feeling none too jolly, and the effort demanded of my arms seemed an extravagant outlay of capital for a rather dubious reward. But when she handed me the first spoonful of the finished batch, I knew straightaway what all that cranking was for.

"That's good," I said licking the spoon, my throbbing head momentarily forgotten.

Klara laughed and carried the dasher out the back door of the kitchen where a gaggle of children waited eagerly. Evidently, word had got out that there was ice cream being made. She handed them the dasher in a big copper pot and they dove into it like a gang of beach crows, scooping up the scraps of frozen cream with their fingers like it was manna from heaven while I leaned in the doorway nursing a lukewarm cup of tea.

We made three more giant batches, during which Klara recited some of the old Russian fairy tales she used to tell me when I was a boy. On the final batch, there was the story of the fool who sold his ox to a birch tree, and when the tree wouldn't pay up, he chopped it down and found a cache of gold coins hid inside the hollow trunk by some robber. This was always one of my favorites, maybe because birch trees are such a familiar sight to me.

As I cranked, I told Klara about how when I was very little I used to go around peering into woodpecker holes in the sides of the ancient dying birches, trying to see if the hollow space inside held any gold coin. This made her laugh, and she reminded me that when I was very young, maybe five or six, I was always bringing her clumps of rotten wood and telling her I'd found a paying tree.

"If only it was that easy," I said, switching hands upon the crank.

"You had quite the imagination when you were young, AC."

Klara moved off and scooped some coals from of the kitchen range into the samovar. Then she came back and pried open the churn lid.

"I think this is done," she said.

She got no argument from me. We carried the churn out to the cold-house, which was filled with blocks of river ice packed in sawdust and would keep everything froze.

"I hear Yasha's gone missing," she said as she scooped the ice cream from the churn into the heavy five-gallon crock that held the other batches. I held the churn for her easy access with the bottom resting upon my knee and my foot propped up on a block of ice.

"He mentioned something about going up the Susitna River," I said.

Klara fixed me with a look that told me she knew something was up, but she said nothing more on the subject.

———

Greg Hackham and Polly Parker was joined in matrimony that day at two in the afternoon. The crowd watched in silence as the Methodist parson said his ceremonial words. He married them outdoors because he couldn't very well do it inside the Russian chapel and because it was almost May and the weather was warm and sunny, with no bugs, and nobody wanted to be cooped up indoors on such a fine day.

This was a great curiosity, being the first American nuptials anyone had ever been invited to, and everyone remarked on what a fine ceremony it was. Many of the ladies in the audience wept as they often do at a wedding. Then there come a great whoop and holler when Hack kissed Polly to seal the deal. I turned away and looked into the forest, for I did not care to witness it.

A series of tables and benches had been laid out in the grass above the beach for the wedding supper. The women of the town had been busy preparing food since the previous day. Most of the caribou meat me and Yasha brought down was slow roasted in large underground pits filled with hot stones. There was also half a cow moose brought in by a Tustumena Indian named Fedor Fedorov and several dozen ptarmigan from Big Nick, as well as large slabs of broiled halibut caught in the Inlet the previous evening.

There was wheat bread and fry bread. Bean salad and also roasted turnips and parsnips kept in people's cellars over the winter. The last of the previous season's potatoes had been cut up and fried in bear fat in every Dutch oven available in town. Some of the families from Ninilchik kept a few shaggy Siberian cows for milk, and they brought up some cheese which was a rare treat. I can only recall having eaten cheese four or five times in my life, including that day. Scotty and several of the men had got up early and boated down toward Clam Gulch to dig the season's first razor clams while I was churning ice cream. Scotty dipped them in a mix of egg and canned milk, then rolled them in meal and fried a stack two feet tall. This appetizer went like hotcakes.

Food and libation flowed like water, and a lovely atmosphere spread through the crowd. Kids of every race ran about yelling and laughing together, and the dogs charged back and forth, barking and sniffing as everyone sat at the long tables to eat, drink, and laugh. It was as fine a feast as I've ever been party to, even if I spent much of the time sulking at the edge of things.

The wedding cake was baked special by Mrs. Davis in Mrs. Golinov's *pitchka* furnace. It had three tiers, the top one the exact size of Mrs. Davis' Dutch oven and the lower two each bigger again. The whole thing was slathered with creamy white frost, then drizzled with the aforementioned blueberry glaze. Following the Yankee custom, we all watched in silent anticipation as Hack and Polly cut into the cake, each with a hand around the knife. It was the selfsame knife that had been used earlier to bone out the halibut, but nobody cared. They each took a piece of cake in their hands and fed it to the other, and Joe Cooper let out a sharp, shrill cry he called the Rebel Yell. In an instant everybody was once again whooping and hollering and clapping. Many of the men fired their rifles into the air in jubilation, and the traditional cry of *gorko!* rang out from the Russians over and over to encourage the newlyweds to share another kiss.

The ladies served out the cake with ice cream for all. The ice cream was quite popular, and Klara made a point of telling everyone that I did all the hard work. A general applause went up, dedicated to me and the ice cream, and I cannot say it was entirely unpleasant.

My memory of that day gets a little hazy by the early evening. I was under the influence of a full belly and large amounts of beer. At some point the tables was carried away, and the makeshift band began tuning up. There was three guitars, a banjo, two *balalaikas*, a washtub bass and of course Scotty's fiddle. Polly and Hack shared the first dance, then everyone got into the act, and the gravel was trampled into pavement by at least fifty pairs of brogues, caulk boots, moccasins, hip boots and fashionable ladies' pumps ordered from the catalogs special for this event. Both Big Nick and Russian Mike got well-lubricated and started doing Cossack squat-kicks with their arms crossed over their chests until they fell over, which brought plenty of cheers and laughter. The Davis girls was allowed no rest during all this; they was flung around the dance floor until they was in a lather.

A bonfire was lit, and at one point I found myself standing next to Scotty as he took a beer break. I had asked him about his boat that he was building, and he explained the finer points of the boatwright's craft—along with some random points on the distilling of vodka from *quass*—shouting into my ear over the music and gesturing wildly with both his cup and his free hand. That's when I noticed Suzanne McCoy standing nearby. The band was on a fast number, and she clapped her hands, bobbing to the rhythm and watching the dancing couples. She seemed to be pointedly not looking at me.

Scotty favored me with a catty look. "You better quit ogling her and go ask for a dance."

I looked at Suzanne again. I almost thought I caught her watching me from the far corner of her eye.

"I figured she was with you, Scotty."

"Nah," he said. "Nothing between us. She's just a pal."

"Whatever you say."

"Bud, she's been giving you the hairy eyeball all afternoon."

"She don't want to dance with me," I said. I had plenty of beers in me and was chewing snoose mixed with gudge ashes. This is an old Indian vice—you mix the ashes with your chaw, and it makes the world around you turn different colors.

"Oh trust me, AC. She wants to dance with you."

"What if I don't want to?"

Scotty shrugged. "Suit yourself. But standing around moping aint going to make Polly any less married to Hack. You got to get back up on that horse and ride."

"Right."

"Hey, up here you don't lose your woman, you lose your turn. So when a turn comes up with someone new, you'd best take advantage."

That got my dander up, for it was all the American fellows coming into the country that was making single girls harder to find. I pulled out my chaw and drained the last of my beer and pushed the cup into Scotty's hand.

"Hold that," I said.

He grinned as I sidled up to Suzanne.

"You want to dance?" I said in Russian.

She shook her head and my heart sank, but then she said, "I don't speak Russian."

This made me feel dumb, and I almost left it at that, but I seen Scotty standing where she couldn't see him and gesticulating most pointedly for me to get her out on the floor. The expression on his face as he silently shouted the words ASK HER! ASK HER! made me bust out into a grin. Suzanne frowned, and when she turned to look behind her Scotty snapped himself into a posture to suggest innocent contemplation of the beauty of the mountains. He turned and waved at us.

I repeated the question to Suzanne in American.

She laughed. "I'd love to, AC."

I aint the best dancer, though I like to think I can hold my own when the occasion demands. The band went into a waltz, so that's what we danced. Suzanne smelled lovely and feminine, not foreign like American girls. She smelled like home, and that was arousing in an entirely new way. She smiled and rested her left hand delicately upon my shoulder, with her right hand holding mine as we glided along. I was heartsick and blue and didn't know what to say to her. It took a lot of effort to keep my eyes from sliding over to stare at Polly and Hack. The two of them was spinning round and round, and despite her swollen belly she was quite light on her feet. Hack leaned into her and put his lips to her ear and whispered something that made her throw back her head and laugh.

The smoke from the bonfire drifted over us as we danced two more numbers. When everyone stopped to applaud, Suzanne laid a hand to her chest.

"I need some air," she said. She had a genuine Chinese fan that she was working to try and keep the smoke away.

"Let's take a walk down to the water," I said.

She hooked her arm into my elbow. "It would be nice to get away from all this commotion."

We went down onto the beach in plain sight where there was no need of chaperones, then slipped into the woods. I think you can guess the rest.

———

Later, as we lay together under a spruce tree, Suzanne asked me if it was true that my dad had run off before I was born.

"Well," I said, "he didn't exactly run off. He was in the army, and he got shipped out somewhere."

"But he never come back?"

I stroked her dark hair. It was hard not to dwell on the texture of Polly's curls, but thinking of Scotty's advice I pushed that sentiment away.

"No," I said. "He never did."

Suzanne slid her arm over my chest. "My dad was a Yankee market hunter. He run off when my mother died."

"He just up and abandoned you?"

"He did."

"How old were you?"

"Nine."

Naturally my heart went out to her. We was both orphans left adrift on the shores of the Gulf of Kenay.

"At least you knew him," I said.

*

*O*utside, the storm has broken and sunlight streams through the tiny windows in the makeshift cellblock. In the cell closest to the office door lies a drunken Revenue Service sailor who overstayed his shore leave, got drunk, and threatened a local fisherman and his wife with an axe. He waits for the shore police to pick him up and take him back to the cutter, snoring loudly.

"So it doesn't sound like you change into a bear very often," says Miss Ashford. She watches him, thinking of a Haida shaman she interviewed back in the spring who was said to have the ability to breathe underwater and walk across the bottom of the ocean from island to island. When she asked him to perform this feat, he said he could not do it at that time of year, due to a certain species of shark that was particularly fond of human flesh after the snows melted.

"I think I already told you that I decided not to do it no more. That time back when I was a kid."

"You seem to be ashamed of this ability of yours."

"It's been a burden and a curse all my life."

"How do you do it? Do you just think about it?"

Campbell shakes his head. "It happens when I stop thinking about it."

Miss Ashford taps the eraser of her pencil against the notebook binding. "Could you change into a bear for me?"

"You mean right now?"

She nods.

Campbell frowns and stares across the room, a gesture she has seen before. It means he does not care to discuss what she has asked about. The Haida magic man wouldn't meet her eyes either, which left her with the distinct impression that he was making up excuses. Briefly, she wonders if the new science of psychoanalysis might yield some insight into this phenomenon. She jots a note to this effect in the side-margin of her notes.

"So, there's an obvious question that I have to ask you," she says.

"What's that?"

"If you can change into a bear, then why haven't you done so and escaped from jail?"

"It doesn't work like that."

Miss Ashford watches him.

"It's pretty tough to make yourself stop thinking about something. If I order you to stop thinking about bears, then bears are suddenly going to be the only thing you can think about."

"I see your point." *She writes as she listens.* "But you said Lucky Jim changed himself into a crane."

"He must have had more control over it than I do. Like he told me, a crane is a much easier fellow to get along with when he lives inside you. A big animal just does whatever he will. He don't give a damn about what you want."

Miss Ashford lowers her pencil again to the page.

"That time at Skilant, when Sava came up to fetch me."

"When you were still living with Lucky Jim."

"Yes. Late that night when everyone was asleep I went outside and tried to change into a bear. Tried to make myself do it. But I couldn't make it happen. I just ended up staring at the Dipper."

"Why did you want to change? You said you decided never to do it again."

"I was confused. I didn't want to go downriver."

Miss Ashford crosses her arms and leans back in her chair. "This crackling sensation you describe."

"Yes."

"It always precedes the change?"

"It does."

"Does this change happen during the full moon?"

Campbell frowns at her, annoyed. "It aint lycanthropy."

Miss Ashford laughs a little. "Where did you encounter a word like that?" *Instantly she wishes she hadn't said it. The condescension, accidental though it is, hangs in the space between them.*

Campbell seems untroubled. "I read it in a book about werewolves."

"Really? Which book?"

"The Book of Were-Wolves," *he says.* "I think the author's name was Gould."

She looks up at the ceiling. "I have to say, Mr. Campbell, you never cease to amaze me."

"Well, I am pretty amazing."

She cocks her head at him, wondering how serious he's being. His face splits into a wide grin.

"Right," *she says as a smile spreads across her own face. She closes her eyes and laughs, and there is a fluttering inside her. A hot flush over her chest and under her collar that she wrestles down to the ground.*

She clears her throat. "So where on earth did you find a copy of Professor Gould's book? It's a rather obscure title."

"Scotty give it to me."

"I didn't realize he was so widely read."

"Scotty? You kidding me? He wasn't no keen reader."

"Could he read?"

"He knew his letters," says Campbell. "He just didn't like doing it. He was using that werewolf book to prop up a broken table leg when I found it."

"And he gave it to you?"

"Yeah. I was out of reading material at the time, so I fixed his table, and he let me have the book."

"What did you think of it?"

Campbell shrugs. "A bit dry. Like I said, I didn't have nothing else to read. You read it?"

"No, I'm afraid not. But I've heard of Gould's work."

They both fall silent. Campbell fingers the edge of the pages of Miss Ashford's copy of Roughing It. *In the far cell, the sailor snorts, moans, then starts snoring once again. Miss Ashford riffles through her notebook. Campbell loads his pipe and for the umpteenth time admires the turn of her ankle and lower calf. He wonders if she is showing it off on purpose to get him to talk, but then he decides he doesn't really care.*

"You don't got a match, do you?" he asks.

"I might. Don't they allow you to have matches for your pipe?"

"They're afraid I might try to set the jailhouse on fire."

Miss Ashford pauses from digging through her purse. Her eyes travel up to the ceiling and around the room.

"You'd burn yourself alive. If you could even find any kindling."

"That's what I keep telling them. When you're not here I have to call the guard in to light my pipe for me."

She rummages again then withdraws a penny box of matches. She hands them to Campbell.

"Good job," he says.

Miss Ashford smiles. "A lady never knows what she might need."

A distant look washes over Campbell's face.

"Have you written anything in the notebook I gave you?" she says.

KRIS FARMEN

He shakes his head. "Aint thought of anything to say. My hand's not so good anyway. I had good penmanship when I was clerking for Mike, but it's gone downhill lately."

"Why?"

"Things."

Campbell lights his pipe and passes the matches back, watching the blue smoke curl in the shaft of sunlight from his window. He is quiet for a long time.

"Penny for your thoughts," Miss Ashford says.

Several heartbeats go by before Campbell answers. "I dislike this island intensely."

"Whatever for? I think Kodiak is quite lovely. It reminds me of our summer home on the coast of Maine."

"There's a miasma of sadness that hangs over this rock," he says. "All them bad things the old-time Russians did to the Koniags when they first got here."

"I've read Bancroft's history of Alaska," says Miss Ashford. "It does sound like a truly awful time. I read about one Russian officer who lined up several Aleut men front to back and fired into them point blank to see how many a musket ball would go through."

"Yeah, I heard that story many times. Us Indians never got on well with the Aleuts. Koniags neither. But that don't make those doings any less awful. And it surely don't make us any better."

Miss Ashford watches him.

"When I was a boy, Belukha Pete told me about one time when George Washington and Lucky Jim led a war party down to Naknek Lake. This was before George Washington become a Christian, back when they was both just young bucks. It had come to Lucky Jim's attention that an Ulchena sorcerer had worked some black magic against one of his favorite aunts, so he figured to go get even."

"Where is Naknek Lake?" says Miss Ashford. "I've heard of it, but I can't picture where it is."

Campbell holds up his right hand with the thumb and index finger pointing down to the floor and the remaining digits curled into his palm. He points at the thumb. "This is the Alexander Islands, where Sitka is. My pointer finger here is the Alaska Peninsula and the Aleutian Islands. Naknek Lake is south of Iliamna Lake, right here at the knuckle."

"Got it. So what happened?"

"Long story short, they killed sixteen men and their dogs. Stove in their houses and burnt everything they owned. All the pretty Ulchena girls decided to follow them back north."

"That seems rather odd," says Miss Ashford. "I mean, considering what had just happened to them."

Campbell's mouth hooks into a half-smile that is less than pleasant. "That's a polite way of saying they dragged those poor girls up to Iliamna Lake with moosehide leashes around their necks."

"Oh." Miss Ashford waggles her pencil between her fingers. "This sounds like it might have been one of those bad things Lucky Jim said he did when he was younger."

"That's my guess," says Campbell. "But they didn't kill all the Ulchena men. Two Indians got killed in this fight, so they saved the fellows who did the killing and give them some special treatment. They took them down into a big muskeg flat where the bugs was so thick they nearly blocked out the sun. Not just mosquitoes, but whitesocks and horseflies, too. They stripped these fellows naked and staked them out to die."

"Did they die?"

"As far as I know. Apparently Lucky Jim and the brothers of one of the dead Indians stuck around to listen to their suffering. Pete told me that after a while the two brothers took to peeling their skin off in strips, but I don't know if that's true or not."

Miss Ashford props her chin upon the folded over fingers of her left hand. Something about his story strikes her as fishy. "I would bet," she says, "that any Native, be he Ulchena or Indian, would be well-inured against mosquito bites."

Campbell looks hard at her. "We'd like to believe that, too, wouldn't we? But we're as human as you are. I've seen dogs that was bit to death by mosquitoes. Seen it with my own two eyes. Even if those fellows didn't get sucked dry by the bugs it would hardly have been pleasant to starve to death staked out on the ground. But my point here is that whatever else they may have been, those two Ulchena was also every bit as human as us Indians. Or the Russians, or you Americans. An evil deed is an evil deed, no matter who it's done to."

"Do you think what your grandfather did was evil?" In the back of her mind is the notion that this man has been convicted of a double homicide.

"I'm sure he had his reasons," says Campbell. "I know he was eaten up with regret toward the end of his life. The world he was born into was a very different place from the one he died in. George Washington told me he found forgiveness from the Lord when he became a Christian, but Lucky Jim always stayed with the old ways."

"What happened to those girls?" says Miss Ashford. She can't help but put herself in their shoes, and shudders to think of what an awful time they must have had.

"Sold off for wives and slaves most likely," says Campbell. "The Kolosh was always in the market for slaves in those days."

"You mean the Tlingit?"

He shrugs. "Don't know that name. Kolosh is the only word I know for them. They live in the Alexander Islands."

Miss Ashford scribbles in her notebook for several minutes. The revenue sailor stirs again, but does not wake.

She looks up. "What are you thinking now?"

Campbell reloads his pipe. "Actually, I was thinking of how much you remind me of Suzanne. Physically, that is. Behavior-wise you aint nothing like her. Could I get another stick of that timber?"

She hands him the box. "Keep them. But if you decide to burn down the jailhouse then you didn't get them from me."

Campbell stares at her a moment with his pipe poised before his lips. He looks up at the ceiling and chuckles. "I'll remember that, Miss."

"So would you tell me what happened after the wedding? It sounds like you found love again."

He snorts out a sharp laugh. "You mean Suzanne?"

CHAPTER V

"*A* lady never knows what she might need." These was the words Suzanne said to me as I stared at her enormous pile of belongings on the beach at Nikishka. We had decided to shack up together at Sixmile, and I had borrowed a double-hatch *bidarka* to come down and fetch her.

She had all manner of wares—her kitchen kit of dishes, pots, pans and the like filled three pearl-oil crates alone. Then there was her bedding and her clothes. Good Lord, her clothes. And the box of rocks and seashells she insisted she just couldn't live without. She'd grown up poor as church-mice, and you wouldn't think a girl so poor could acquire so much stuff. About three quarters of my own belongings could be lashed to my packboard, and the remaining quarter consisted of my *bidarka*, which was presently stowed on the beach at Possession town. Anything else I needed I made on the spot from what the woods provided.

Suzanne's outfit amounted to nearly three times the cargo space available in the borrowed *bidarka*. The bugs had hatched early that year and there was not even a breath of wind. They clouded around us so thick it seemed they might actually pick us up and carry us away.

"So what now?" I said, looking at the pile and waving at the mosquitoes that crawled in my hair and whined at my ears.

Suzanne was cross for some reason I couldn't divine. She let out a loud sigh and pressed a hand to her forehead. "You'll have to make several trips, AC."

"Me?"

She looked at me as if I were some dim-witted school-boy. "I'll be busy setting up house at Sixmile."

"You aint got any kin that could help us out?"

"Not really, no. My aunts won't talk to me no more since they found out I'm moving in with a man I aint married to." She gestured at the *bidarka*. "You can make a few trips. You'll be able to haul more if I aint in the boat with you."

Paddling a double-hatch *bidarka* on your own with a heavy load inside is a real chore, but that wasn't the point. I had things to do back home. The roof on our new cabin was not yet finished, and I was still living in a wall tent, taking my meals with the newly-wed Fedosya and Yasha. Then there was the coming belukha hunt and summer fishing, both of which required extensive preparations. I had planned to be away only a day or so to retrieve Suzanne, and now it was looking like I would lose almost a week to this enterprise.

I studied the glassy water. I had been warned that women could be like this, but it was hard not to think that Polly would have been much easier to deal with. She would at least have helped me carry her things down to the beach. But it was May month, sunny and bright, and we was on the way to set up our own household together, so I let it go. I knew I had to, for Polly was lost to me, and it was time to move on, to get back on that horse and ride, as Scotty would have it.

———

The two subjects on everyone's lips at Point Possession was Yasha and Fedosya's elopement and the crash of the fur market. We had grown accustomed to high fur prices since the Purchase when there was several American traders around the Inlet clamoring for our custom. Times had been good—everyone had warm blankets, stylish clothes, and plenty of ammunition. Now the corporate offices of the Alaska Commercial Co. had bought out all the competition and substantially lowered the prices they paid for fur. Many trappers had for the first time in memory failed to make enough money to see their families through the coming year. The talk among the residents of Possession town was almost exclusively of what they could do to make ends meet. Many of the young men had decided to leave for the canneries at Kenay town and Kussilof to seek wage jobs on the China gang. For several years now the canneries had sent a boat around to the towns every spring looking for men who wanted work. They never got many takers, for we had a good living from the land, and who wanted to leave home to work like a slave on the slime-line when you could be hunting belukha whales and catching your own fish for dog feed?

Now many people had no choice. Folks was down at the mouth over this, for how were families to get by over the summer without their menfolk? Many of the older men of George Washington's age had been indentured by the Russian company to hunt fur and work as laborers at their far-flung posts, from the Prybilof Islands to faraway California. Many of them was gone for years at a time with no contact with their families. One of the great benefits of having the Americans in our country was that men could make a living at home, but now it was whispered that the Americans was conspiring to enslave the Natives by paying a pittance for furs and only allowing us to work at the canneries on shifts of seventy hours per week.

Part of the reason cannery work was so onerous to the people was the fact that canneries only paid Natives half the wages earned by American and Chinese laborers. When asked about this, the cannery managers said it was the only way they could keep Natives on the job for the whole season. If an Indian knows he needs to make a

KRIS FARMEN

hundred dollars to purchase his outfit for the year, he'll work until the day he makes one hundred dollars, then quit and go home. This usually happens toward the end of July or early August when it's time to head up into the mountains to go sheep hunting. Your average Indian is a busy man with places to go and things to do, and once his money is made, working for more money falls pretty low on the priority list.

The Americans tend to shake their heads and roll their eyes at this. The cannery foremen act as if they are great benefactors, saying we should be grateful for the opportunity to hitch our wagons to the star of mercantile capitalism and help them destroy the fishery that has sustained us for so many generations. The upshot of all this is that when you're only paid twenty dollars a month, you have to stay until the end of September when the canneries close down to make the cash you need. Not surprisingly, the Indians don't think too highly of this system. But the options seemed to be getting pretty limited.

As for Yasha and Fedosya, opinions was divided like rabbit paths through the willow-brush. Many people condemned them for going against the wishes of their elders. They said that what they'd done would never have been permitted in the old days, that they would both have likely been killed by Fedosya's family. Furthermore, the Orthodox church is a long-standing institution among the people of Cook Inlet, and their leaving it was widely regarded as an unpardonable sin. During all this hulla-baloo, nobody bothered to mention that Yasha had given up drink. It's worth saying here that many of his worst critics were individuals who themselves had an intimate relationship with the bottle.

Others, many of them of the younger generation, thought it romantic and inspiring that two young lovers would do something so bold. Fedosya's parents, oddly enough, was on this side of things. Her mother and father seemed genuinely impressed by the lengths Yasha went to in order to prove his devotion to her, though her father did disapprove of her leaving the church. In the end, however, his daughter's happiness won out, and he give them his blessing, though her aunts always regarded Yasha as something of a pariah for defying them.

The cannery boat come around at the end of May month and left with probably two thirds of the men in town. Me and Yasha was not among them. We elected to try our luck at trapping once again. We had dogs to feed, and that meant fishing. The lesson we learned shoveling gravel for Joe Cooper while thousands of salmon swam freely past was still with us. Besides, Sixmile was our home, and we quite naturally wanted to be there with our ladies.

The spring belukha hunt went on as usual when the whales followed the kings into the upper Inlet. Belukha Pete done me and Yasha the honor of asking us to partner up with him for the hunt. We took turns with him atop his spearing tree while the third man waited below in Pete's three-hatch *bidarka*. When a whale was harpooned, we jumped into the boat to give chase. Some of the younger men had taken to finishing off the whales with a rifle, but Pete disapproved of this. He made me and Yasha learn to kill them the old-fashioned way. I must allow here that Yasha possessed much greater skill with a harpoon than I ever have. Before long he acquired quite a reputation for the accuracy of his strikes, but in keeping with good form he never spoke of it.

While at Point Possession, me and Suzanne lived with Yasha and Fedosya in a tent camp at the edge of town. It was a fine place, and there was always friends and relations over at our fire. It felt good to have our own

KRIS FARMEN

household. We men would come in from the whale hunt and sit and smoke our pipes while the women got supper going. The gals would chatter away as we spun the tale of each day's hunt. Oftentimes there would be a dozen of us there. Everyone was poor on account of the low fur market, but we had tobacco and plenty to eat.

I had a supply of booze that spring, thanks to the distilling kit Scotty had helped me piece together out of what was available at the store. This of course was entirely my operation, not Yasha and Fedosya's. I made my first batch of vodka from a half-tank of *quass* that Belukha Pete had given me. I set up out in the woods where I could be alone with my thoughts. I had a big copper pot with a lid, then a vapor coil of copper tubing. The booze dripped down from the coil into some old catsup bottles I'd scavenged. I was somewhat disappointed with how little alcohol I got out of five gallons of *quass*, but I figured I had to start somewhere. There was a certain satisfaction in swallowing the first mouthful of my own product. It was pretty rough and raw, but I convinced myself it was smooth as bourbon, and I sat there drinking most of the first bottle and listening to the wind in the trees.

During this period I learned to not just pour the stuff into me until I was stumbling drunk. This was in no small measure out of respect for Fedosya and Yasha. One time I showed up for supper loaded to the gills, and Fedosya chased me away, whacking at my backside with a stick of firewood and telling me in no uncertain terms not to come to her fireside when I was drunk. This got me seeing red, and I grabbed the stick and went to wrest it from her grip, but Yasha stepped in and pushed me back.

"Go sober up," he said, and I felt the sting of shame rising all through me. Even in the state I was in I could see this was no way to treat my partner's wife, who was also my good friend. So I learned to just get myself to the point where I felt all happy and buzzed, then drink at a pace that maintained that feeling. This had two distinct benefits: the hangovers weren't as bad, and it also gave me some distance between myself and Polly. It helped me to see the whole thing in a philosophical frame of mind. It bothered me a little that Yasha didn't see the virtue in this accomplishment, but I kept that to myself.

"You'd be better off quitting," he told me more than once. He wasn't preaching, mind you, just stating what he saw as a simple fact.

I always dismissed this notion with a wave of my hand. It still troubles me that I acted that way, but as I think I've already said, stubbornness has always been one of my faults. Americans often express this by the phrase STUBBORN AS A MULE, but I aint never seen a mule except for a picture in a book once. I tend to think of it as STUBBORN AS A BEAR, for obvious reasons. Lucky Jim said it would be hard for me to live with that big animal inside my skin, and he was right.

Suzanne, by the way, loved a drink and would at times go at it even harder than I did. Among other things it increased her appetite for my affections to a fever pitch, which I did not really mind. All the same, though, I think it was a relief when we ran out of vodka and decided to head up the Arm to Sixmile so I could finish our new house.

We borrowed Belukha Pete's two-hatch *bidarka* once again and freighted her stuff up to the river landing. When this was accomplished I left Suzanne and returned the boat, then scooted back up the Arm with my own craft on the next tide. I took Camprobber along for companionship, as our freight team provided none worth speaking of. Being malamutes they was dumb as dirt and owned the personality of tree stumps.

I let the dog ride in my lap as I paddled. She whined and licked my face with pleasure. Unlike the common freight dogs of today who dislike the water, the only thing them old bear dogs loved more than a fracas with the man in the fur overcoat was a boat ride.

The tide carried us all the way to Sixmile in just over an hour. Suzanne was catching a snooze on the beach when we arrived, and it irked me some to see that my old lady was such an idler. But it was a beautiful bluebird day with the sun lighting up the white snow on the mountains slopes above, so I decided not to taint it by getting into an argument.

She yawned and stretched her arms when I sat down next to her. "So when can I see my new house?"

"Tomorrow," I said.

"Why not today?"

"It's getting late, and we got a ton of gear to carry. Best to camp here for the night and enjoy the evening. We can get a fresh start on it in the morning."

"You didn't bring no booze with you?"

"We're all out. I'll make some more once we get things squared away."

"Zachar Ivanovich was making *quass*," she said. "You could have got some from him."

"He didn't offer it."

She frowned a little. "I'd rather go up and see my new house tonight. We got lots of daylight."

"It's late," I said standing up. "I'll make a fish snare."

I could feel her frown against the back of my head, but I paid it no mind. I was thirsty for a drink of vodka, but of course I didn't have none, so there was no help for it. I cut a stout birch pole then dug up a supple spruce root and fashioned it into a snare on the end of the pole just as Lucky Jim had taught me to do. It didn't take very long to catch a good twenty-pound king. The fish fought so hard I feared it would break the snare but I managed to wrestle it up onto the beach and club it across the head with a stick.

Suzanne cut up the fish and buried it under the moss in a shady stand of hemlocks to keep cool, then we took Camprobber for a ramble up the creek. We didn't go far, maybe a quarter-mile, just long enough to make the dog forget about the fresh fish. Despite our earlier disagreement she was in a good mood, all coy and flirty, and I enjoyed walking behind her and studying her fine figure. I threw Camprobber's stick, and she chased after it and brought it back no matter where it landed. Each time her tail wagged for another throw. I have never met a dog with as wonderful a disposition as that one, but the problem with bear dogs was that when they didn't have a bear to chase they got into mischief.

We was walking along the southern side of the creek where snow still clung in the shady northern slopes when we come upon a large patch of deep soft snow that hung out over the water on a shelf of rotten ice. There was no way around it, we had to wade. We took off our moccasins and stockings, and I pulled off my britches and pushed my longjohns up to my thighs. Suzanne rucked up her skirts and stepped in after me. Camprobber bounded through the snow until she was buried almost to her shoulder hump, then she favored me with an exasperated look and charged for the water. The ice shelf broke under her weight and she vaulted into the stream, pointed at me. She bowled right into me as the ice shelf splashed down into the water. The creek was not deep there, but the ice made a wave that when combined with forty pounds of dog slamming into me knocked me right off my pins. I managed to keep my rifle and cartridge bag above the water, but in doing so I dropped my moccasins and rolled-up britches and had to splash downstream after them. Suzanne, of course, managed to stay mostly dry.

Camprobber swam downstream and climbed out on a sandbar on the sunny north bank and give herself a mighty shake. I caught myself against a knob of bedrock that poked up from the stream and snatched up a handful of gravel to throw at her, but she scampered into the brush before I could let loose.

I cussed and called her every kind of filthy name there is in both Russian and American. I was wet all through, only my right shoulder and my hair stayed dry. The water was very cold, only a couple degrees from being ice itself. Suzanne thought the whole scene was pretty funny. She laughed with her hands over her mouth, and this didn't help my humor none. I cocked my hand back to throw the gravel anyway but the weight of it stopped me. When I opened my hand there was sand and peagravel and three rocks. One of them gleamed yellow. It was a nugget of gold nigh the size of a tablespoon.

"Hell's bells," I said to the current. I dropped the rest of the gravel and hefted the nugget in my hand. It was lumpy and pitted, and the pits was packed full of grit from its time in the creek-bed.

Suzanne found Camprobber waiting behind a drift log. The dog give itself another shake, sending out a spray of water, then she come up and licked at Suzanne's hand. Suzanne cooed at her and scratched her ears while I sloshed my way to the bank where they stood. My feet was numb as ice blocks from the cold water.

"What's that?" said Suzanne, looking down at my hand.

I opened my palm for her to see. She sucked in her breath.

"Is that what I think it is?"

I nodded.

"Can I see it?"

I handed it over and her hand sank down from the weight of it. "It's so heavy," she said.

"It is."

I watched as she turned it over and over in her hand, admiring its lustrous surface. When I held out my hand for it she didn't want to give it back.

"Is there more?" she asked.

"Probably. But you can't tell people about it."

"Why not?"

"Because if the Yankees find out there's gold here they'll come and wreck this whole valley."

Her eyes travelled back to the stream. It wasn't hard to divine the nature of her thoughts. Down below us, Camprobber's eyes were wet and expectant with her tongue hanging out.

"Dog," I said, "I don't suppose this gold nugget can buy me some dry clothes?"

She just jumped around in a circle and give a little yip saying, Let's go find us a bear to chew on, AC!

We got onto the main trail down the creek where I walked barefoot and barelegged all the way back to camp, with my toes slipping and sliding in the cold mud, moss and runoff. I tucked the nugget into my cartridge bag that hung by a strap under my right arm. It added considerably to its weight, and I kept reaching in to fondle its smooth stream-worn surface.

Back at camp, Suzanne built a fire and hung my clothes and moccasins up to dry. I retrieved the salmon we'd cached and fed part of it to Camprobber who gulped it down. Suzanne set the rest of it in the coals atop a flat slab of slate, along with the backbone meat. I lay back against a drift log and juggled the nugget from one hand to the other as the fish sizzled and baked.

My thoughts was jumbled up like broken river ice. After I'd bought our outfit for the summer—new clothes, ammunition, grub, tobacco, mosquito nets, and materials to finish the new cabin—I wound up with two dollars and sixty cents in my pocket. That meant two-sixty to purchase our winter outfit unless I could come up with some more cash. The summer was set aside for catching fish to feed the dog team. Yasha had told me he had about five bucks to his name.

This did not leave us in much of a position for the winter. Truth be told, I had started to regret not going on the cannery boat down to Kussilof. Now here was this lump of money in my hand. Gold sells for twenty-six dollars and change per ounce, and that nugget had to weigh at least a pound. That meant more than four hundred dollars, a sum that fairly made my head spin.

Yet I had made a promise to Lucky Jim.

I closed my eyes and asked him to tell me what to do, but there was no response. Only the heat of the fire against my knees and the evening breeze in the hemlocks.

"Supper's ready," said Suzanne. She pulled the rock slab out of the coals with a heavy rag, then sliced off portions with her butcher knife and slid them onto two sheets of birchbark. I slipped the nugget back into my cartridge bag and turned my attention to eating. Out of sight, out of mind.

When we'd finished, Suzanne put a kettle of water on the fire for tea, then snuggled up next to me. I lit my pipe with Camprobber curled up on my other side. It was a pleasant evening, with orange sunlight splashed across the peaks on the north side of the Arm.

The water had just boiled when the dog jumped up and started growling with her hackles raised.

Suzanne sat up. "What's going on?"

I grabbed my rifle and axe. "Likely the man in the fur overcoat. Go find somewhere to hide."

She moved away from the smell of our supper and got into the woods above the beach-line. I jacked open the breech of my rifle and slid a shell into the chamber and tucked extra rounds between the fingers of my left hand as I slipped through the moss and trees, up behind a tall wedge of slate that jutted out into the sand.

I watched Camprobber as she stood looking eastward up the Arm. My pulse whooshed in my ears. I expected her to charge at any moment.

Suzanne crept up beside me. "You see that big animal anywhere?"

I shook my head. It was an annoyance that she had not stayed put like I told her.

The minutes drew out as we watched the beach and the forest. Then there come the sound of footsteps crunching in the gravel.

"Look," she said, pointing. Two figures walked toward us, picking their way through the drift logs and skirting the sticky mud at the water's edge.

"Who is it?" she whispered.

I shrugged, squinting through the branches and boughs. By and by I seen it was a young girl leading a man by his hand. Then I seen their sealskin boots.

"Ulchena," I said.

We held our perch and I kept my rifle sights on them. They looked harmless enough, but I was wary. I scanned the distant shore behind them for hidden riflemen.

The man and the girl stopped short when Camprobber started barking and snarling at them. The girl reached out and tried to calm her, but the bitch snapped those killer jaws at her hand and the girl backed away. The man said something to her. She shook her head.

I called out to them in Russian, "What do you want?"

The girl started in fright at the sound of my voice. Camprobber kept barking, and I shouted for her to shut up.

"Who are you?" the girl called back in American. Camprobber continued to growl at her.

"I asked you first, girl. This is Indian country. What are you doing over here?"

"We're just passing through." I could tell from the way she looked around that she hadn't spied us, but the man listened closely to me like he knew exactly where I was.

I shimmied down behind the rock wedge and come up behind its mossy toe with my weapon up and cocked. I eased around behind Camprobber and pressed myself belly-first into the crumbling slate for what little cover it would give. I peered over my rifle sights to get a better look at them, and I seen right off what the deal was. The old man was blind and the girl was leading him. He leaned on a stout stick and carried a large pack. She carried a lighter one. They looked wore-out, ill-used, and hungry.

"We're looking for somewhere to camp," said the girl. Her American was quite good.

"You alone?"

She nodded. "Aint but the two of us."

My heart went out to these two wretches. Their clothes was ripped and threadbare, and they looked about as ragged as any two folks could be. They must have come a fair piece, for the closest Ulchena settlement was over the Kenay Mountains on Prince William's Sound. The portage through those mountains is a tough journey, even for fit young men. Lots of snow, and brushy as all hell, with nothing to eat along the way. For a small girl to lead a blind man over those mountains was nothing to sneer at.

We stood there for several heartbeats watching each other, and the blind man listening. Suzanne came up next to me. I glanced at her, then back at our visitors. I tipped my head toward our fire and the girl led the man forward. Camprobber barked once more, but I clouted her across the chops and she kept quiet. I watched the dog to see what she would do, if she sensed any skulkers in the woods, but she just turned and followed our guests to the fire.

They dumped their packs, and the man sat down heavily with his back against a boulder. The girl sat in the sand next to him. Suzanne fed more sticks into the fire and got the kettle going. She served up the remainders of our evening meal for them which they devoured quickly, starting with the head.

I have known some Creoles of Chugach and Esquimaux extraction, Sava among them, but I'd never seen no full-bloods up close before. The man was gray-headed and wore a bushy moustache. There was ivory plugs set into holes in his cheeks. I had been told of this practice by Indians who'd had dealings with these folk. The girl was no more than seven or eight years old. She was skinny as a stick, with long hair in a plait behind her. Their faces was much rounder and more flat up front than those of an Indian, their eyes narrower and shaped like those of a Celestial. The blind man's eyes was heavy-lidded, and I could see his milky irises in a crossed posture behind them.

When the water was up, Suzanne put in the tea and set the kettle away from the fire to steep. We filled their cups, then our own. Suzanne passed around a can of sugar with a spoon, then sat down next to me where she had been before their arrival. Camprobber curled up across the fire, but she never took her eyes off the strangers.

"I'm Opal," said the girl when they'd finished their meal. "This is Muscle Sam."

"I'm Aleksandr Campbell, but folks call me AC. This here is Suzanne McCoy."

They nodded, saying nothing.

I took a sip of tea. "This is a long way out of Chugach country for you to be wandering around."

"We're on a pilgrimage," said Opal.

"A pilgrimage."

Muscle Sam said something in the Ulchena language, and Opal responded in kind. Suzanne looked at me and I at her—neither of us could make heads or tails of it. There didn't seem to be no words, just clicks and gargling noises.

"My uncle says he had a dream that he would find a birch tree growing out of a glacier on the south end of the Peninsula. A halibut told him this."

Suzanne looked unconvinced. She had been taught nothing of the old ways, though of course their beliefs was as foreign to me as they was to her.

I could see Sam listening to us. "What will you do when you find this birch tree?" I asked him.

Opal translated, and he give his reply, which she then translated for us. "He aint sure. Halibut told him he'd go up into the sky. Sam reckons he's going to see if the white men's god really lives in the clouds as they say."

This was an interesting notion, but I reckoned I was happy here with my own feet on the ground. I pulled out my tobacco tin and rapped it with my knuckles to loosen the contents. Muscle Sam knew that sound. He drew an old calabash pipe from his jacket pocket. I filled it for him and passed him a handful of matches. He nodded at me and said something which I could only assume was his thanks.

I filled Opal's pipe as well, then lit my own bowl. A robin called in the forest behind us, and we all cocked our ears to listen.

Muscle Sam said something.

"He says it's good to hear the songbirds again after a long winter," said Opal.

"Aint that the truth," said Suzanne. "How long have you two been walking?"

Opal counted on her fingers. "Two weeks."

"And you walked all this way? From Prince William's Sound?"

She nodded.

"You got a long and dangerous journey ahead of you," I said. "This is Indian land."

Opal watched me over the fire.

"Things aint like they used to be in the old days, but there's still more than a few Indians would just as soon cut you up and feed you to their dogs."

Opal translated my words to Sam, then listened to his response.

"Sam says that halibut told him the trip wouldn't be easy."

"You didn't bring much of an outfit with you," Suzanne said. "You don't even got a rifle."

"That halibut told him to go unarmed," said Opal. She tapped the ashes of her pipe into her palm and turned them onto the sand next to her, a rather delicate gesture. "But we also had to git in a hurry."

"Why's that?"

"Missionaries. They got everyone else in our town to leave the Russian church and go Catholic. The head preacher said the Orthodox faith was the tool of the Devil. They run Sam out of town because he wouldn't go Catholic."

I was unsure what to make of this, but I knew Suzanne's dad was a Catholic, so I kept my mouth shut. I refilled Opal and Sam's pipes.

"Did you convert as well?" Suzanne asked.

Opal nodded.

"So how come you're helping one of the infidels?" I said, nodding at Muscle Sam.

"He's my uncle. My folks died of diphtheria. He's all I got left."

I pulled on my pipe and mulled that over, thinking what a shame it was that the doings of missionaries should have forced this poor girl into such a desperate course of action.

The fire crackled and flared as some pitch caught flame. Opal spoke of her own accord, sounding ten or fifteen years older than her age.

"The Yankee storekeeper at the cannery in our town, he's Catholic, too. That missionary preacher come to him one day and said he'd throw him out of the church and damn his soul to eternal fire if he sold any more goods to Sam. He said the only way Sam could buy supplies at the cannery store was if he went Catholic like the rest of us."

All I could do at this was shake my head. When the Russian fathers first come to Alaska, they put a stop to the bad things the fur hunters was doing to the Natives. They helped us, so we took the Orthodox faith as our own. It mystified me that American missionaries reckoned they could save souls by treachery.

"I'm betting that has something to do with your halibut visiting Sam here," said Suzanne. There was a tint of sarcasm in her voice that I didn't care for. I glared at her, wishing she would keep her mouth shut. As I've said, she knew nothing of the old ways, and it irked me that she would inquire so freely and with such impertinence about these things when she knew nothing of the potential consequences.

Suzanne just kept her eyes on Opal, going merrily along with her joke.

Opal nodded. "Sam's a seer. He can tell the future."

"Really now."

I looked across the fire at Muscle Sam. He nodded sightlessly at me, which was more than a little unsettling.

"Can you see our future?"

"Cool it, Suze," I said.

"I want to know, AC. If this fellow has such a power then let him show it off."

I lowered my voice and spoke in Kenaytze. "You're being rude."

Suzanne ignored me and fixed her eyes once again on Opal. "Ask him."

Opal hesitated, then translated the question while watching me with a mixture of wariness and reproach.

Muscle Sam drained the last of his tea. I expected him to utter some sort of incantation or go into a trance like I once seen a magic man do at Skilant town. Instead he groped around the fire until he found the kettle where it was set back from the flames to stay warm. He found the bail and lifted it toward his cup. We watched as he handily poured himself a fresh cup.

He pointed his sightless eyes at me and spoke. I could feel Suzanne watching him. My own pulse was racing, for this was somehow more frightening than the thought of ambush from the woods.

"He says he can see what lies ahead for this place," said Opal.

This wasn't really what had been asked, but Suzanne told him to go on. I was now dreadfully curious myself and didn't stop her.

The blind man spoke at length in their garbled lingo.

"Sam says there will be Yankees here," said Opal. "Real soon."

"There's already Americans here," said Suzanne. "Down at Kenay town and Kussilof. Kachemak Bay, too."

Opal shook her head. "No, Sam means here on this creek. He says they will be like the stars. Like the sparks that fly up into the air when you throw a log onto a spruce fire."

It was late and the stars above had disappeared for the summer, but the mouth of Sixmile Creek faces north and it was just dark enough for the firelight to glint upon the girl's eyes. She looked not so much like a slip of a girl, but like some being come to Earth from a world unknown to us. I caught myself staring and feeling like I was about to go tumbling into her, but then I blinked and shuddered and caught myself. When I glanced down I seen that Suzanne was in the same trance. I nudged her out of it and she shook her head, blinking.

Opal went on as if nothing had happened, speaking directly to Suzanne. "My uncle says that your old man here has something in his pocket that them Yankees want badly. He says the streams will be turned inside out and that your desire of material goods will be the end of you. Of all of us. Because of this, your man will become a bear in a prison with no walls."

This took me aback, for I never spoke to anyone about the affliction passed on to me by Lucky Jim. Suzanne never knew of it, and I certainly hadn't mentioned it to our visitors. I looked into the fire and took hold of Suzanne's hand while working hard to keep my other hand from slipping into my cartridge bag. Camprobber watched me from her bed on the sand with her head upon her forelegs. It was hard not to think of the time she and Flicker had attacked me back on the Swanson Flats. When I was a bear.

Perhaps I should have dropped the nugget back into the stream. I could feel Sam's sightless gaze upon me along with the dog's. What else did he know? And what did Camprobber know? It was more than unsettling—this time around it was downright unpleasant.

"What else?" Suzanne said softly, as if not sure she really wanted to know. All jest was vanished from her voice.

Opal shook her head. "That's all he's got to say."

——

Neither me or Suzanne felt much like chatting after such a prophesy, so we made up our blankets and turned in. Suzanne kept Camprobber next to her, and we three huddled together. I didn't get much sleep. I heard Muscle Sam snoring peacefully. I could only presume he enjoyed the sleep of the just. Suzanne tossed and turned, but eventually her breath settled into the rhythm of sleep.

Sometime in the wee hours of the morning, having slept not a wink, I decided to get up and catch a few fish so Opal and Sam could have some grub for their trip. I went down to the beach where my fish snare was propped against a rock and fiddled with the snare loop. When I had it set the way I wanted I looked up and there was Opal, standing next to me without a stitch of clothes on. There was nothing untoward in this, mind you, she was just running around in her birthday suit as young kids will do when they play on the beach. There was just enough grainy light for me to see her, and I kept my eyes averted out of concern for her modesty.

"Maybe you better put some clothes on," I said. "If you're going to help me fish."

She swiveled her head around at me, then looked back at the Arm, studying it like she was party to some secret it bore that I could never know.

She stepped into the icy gray water, wading out to her ankles, then her knees, then her waist. I started to get worried, for those mudflats along Turnagain Arm are treacherous and full of quicksands if you don't know where it's safe to wade and where it aint.

"Opal," I said, "you ought to come back in. Those mudbanks will grab you."

She half-turned, watching me over her shoulder, and that's when I seen that her back was white. Not white like a white man, I mean white like a bed-sheet. This white color ended in a sharp line that travelled down her shoulders, her sides, and down each arm and up and down each finger. Just like a halibut. I cocked my head at her, not knowing what to make of this deformity and puzzled that I'd not noticed it before. She shuffled her feet, turning around to face me. Then as I watched she splashed backwards into the Arm. She swam a backstroke for a few yards, then slipped under the water and was gone.

I jerked awake in my blankets at the call of a thrush. The bright swell of the dawn was showing over the mountains to the north. Suzanne and Camprobber both snored next to me. I sat up, looking at my moccasin prints in the sand. I rose and walked over to the water's edge, but I could see no trace of Opal's small feet. I listened to the morning sounds. The creek tumbling, the mosquitoes all around, the thrush still singing his mournful song that seemed to come from every corner of the forest all at once.

When I looked back at our camp, Opal and Muscle Sam were both gone. His tracks was the only ones to be seen; he'd packed up and left some hours before. I followed them up into an alder hell, but they disappeared. I never did find no trace of Opal.

Suzanne was awake when I returned. She was in a fever over what had happened to our guests.

"You didn't find them?" she said.

"No."

I hunkered down by the fire. She made no move to build it up for my comfort, so I laid several sticks on it myself.

She hugged herself against the morning chill. "How hard can it be to track a small girl and a blind man?"

I shrugged. "It aint always laid out for you like a book."

"Well, what if they find the gold there in the creek?"

I still had the image of Opal diving backward into the water. Suzanne's mundane question annoyed me.

"What if they do?"

"They might tell others about it. That Muscle Sam fellow said the miners are going to run all over this country."

The flames licked up into the fresh fuel. "Suze, I doubt they'll even stop to look for it. Placer gold aint the sort of thing you just stumble across. You got to be really looking for it. There any tea?"

She ignored my request. Tending the fire and getting the morning tea is women's business, and I was rapidly growing annoyed at having to perform this task. Any woman other than Suzanne would have been mortally ashamed to have her man getting his own tea at her fireside. But as usual, Suzanne had other things on her mind.

"Don't tell me you can't stumble across it," she said. "You done just that yesterday. What if they find our gold?"

"So now it's our gold, is it?"

She looked away.

"Don't you go messing with things you don't understand," I said.

I made my own tea that morning while Suzanne sat in bed. But I was still thinking of my dream, and of Opal's white back, the line that separated the white from the other half.

It took us six trips to backpack our outfit up to the cabins. The plan was for us to stay in the first cabin while I completed the roof on the new one. Yasha wanted to finish the belukha hunt at Point Possession, so he and Fedosya would be along in a couple weeks.

We arrived to find the door busted open and most of me and Yasha's things scattered all about the front yard. A black bear had broke in sometime recently and torn the place to hell. The glass window and the wood stove was thankfully intact, but just about everything else was smashed to pieces. It could have been worse, though. Our tree cache was unmolested.

Camprobber knew straightaway what had happened. She sniffed at everything, whining and growling with her tail wagging and her hackles straight up. I had to put a lead on her and drag her with us back down the trail so we could finish packing our gear, but the next day we set off in search of the bear while Suzanne went about straightening things up. The tracks showed it to be a smallish boar. It had spent three or four days at the cabin, then moved on. Camprobber's nose led us upstream following his scent. The second run of kings was in the creek so I kept a weather eye on the banks as we proceeded, lest we stumble across our visitor at his fishing.

The bear had wandered through the open meadows and cottonwood stands toward the canyon, munching on the new blades of green grass that poked up through the dead thatch of last year's growth. I found a bed up in the hillside hemlocks where he'd spent a night. Then Camprobber led us down toward the creek again. I had a light travelling pack, just a blanket, a small kettle with some tea, and a little dried fish. That night it turned cold and rainy, so I used a trick Lucky Jim taught me: I built a tiny fire inside a hat-sized hole scooped into the dirt at the base of a cottonwood tree. I covered the coals with cottonwood bark and loose dirt, then poked a couple air-holes. I spent the night sleeping with my back against the tree and my calves on either side of the fire-pit with my blanket wrapped around me to catch the heat.

We was up and moving early, pushing upstream on the scent trail. We found the bear about midday. He was ambling along the stream, perhaps pondering the meaning of his life. Even though we was well hid, he caught our wind and wheeled and bolted for the hills. I told Camprobber to get after him and she needed no encouragement. I ran after her, listening all the while for the particular bark that would tell me she had him treed.

It took only a few minutes. When I heard the call I wanted, I slowed up and crept through the woods with my rifle at the ready. I came into a stand of big cottonwoods with devils club beneath, watching sharp. Camprobber danced round the base of one of the trees, snapping and snarling at the bear perched high in the limbs. I took a rest against another tree and fired. He crashed to the ground but jumped up ready for a fight. He charged straight for me but Camprobber jumped onto his back and clamped her rock-breaker jaws onto his throat.

I snapped off a second shot as the bear roared and batted at Camprobber. This was a ticklish proposition because of course I didn't want to shoot my dog. The bullet punched into the upper part of the bear's back as he was twisted away trying to sling Camprobber off him. I jacked out the spent shell and thumbed home a fresh load as he turned back to me and charged again, dog and all. I loosed the third shot into his head and he fell dead.

Camprobber was slow to turn loose. She kept her jaws clamped shut, twisting and worrying the dead bear's throat. Her face and neck was covered in bright red blood and she was growling for all she was worth. I had to calm her down so she could get her jaws loose and I could pull her away. I expected her to start panting and wagging her tail as usual when we killed a bear, but instead she limped a few steps and slumped to the ground. I knelt down to examine her and sucked in my breath when I seen the ragged bullet wound.

It must have been the second shot, when the bear spun around and slung her with him as he went. That Sharps was a .44-65, that's a caliber that will damn near shoot through a brick wall. The slug must have gone straight through the bear and into the dog. It had entered just above her shoulder and plowed straight down into her guts. Gently, I felt around and discovered the slug pressing against the inside of her skin down at the back of her hams.

I swore in American. Then I switched to the Kenaytze tongue and spoke to her in soothing tones. She whined piteously, and I don't mind saying that I had tears pooling in my eyes. She was not only my favorite dog of all time, but also one of my last tangible links to Lucky Jim.

Beneath my hand I felt her flesh tighten in a spasm. She went into a fit of coughing, hacking up great mouthfuls of blood. She looked at me and wagged her tail one last time. Then the light fell out of her eyes and she was dead.

A good dog does not deserve such a death, especially when there are so many men who have it coming.

I laid Camprobber to rest under those same cottonwoods where she died. Then I packed the bear meat and hide back to the cabin. I took the time to flesh and salt down the hide, for it was worth at least five dollars. The older Indians disapprove of selling bearskins to the fur buyers; they say such hides are sacred and full of power. But I was quickly learning that sacredness and power don't buy flour, tea, and ammunition.

We got the original cabin fixed up, then I went to work building the gables on our new house. Suzanne worked the fish-trap, catching and splitting kings by the hundred as I laid a ridgepole and purlins, then peckerpoles and tar-paper with sod over the top of it all. Yasha and me had whipsawed a pile of floor-boards prior to the belukha hunt. I laid them out and spiked them down, then I installed the stove and the smokestack. Suzanne was delighted when I told her it was time to move in.

"I love it!" she said, planting a kiss on me.

It was a good-sized cabin—twelve feet by sixteen, with a big glass window in the south wall. I had learned a lot from building the first cabin, and it showed in this new one. I followed her inside, smiling at her happiness. She went immediately to the kitchen counter.

I pointed to the east wall. "I spaced the spikes on the wall there so that we can cut out and install another window to get some morning sun. Maybe after trapping season when we got more cash. And I still need to knock together a table and some chairs."

Suzanne rocked up and down on the balls of her feet, clapping her hands together. "It's wonderful, AC. We'll need oil lamps and a table-cloth. And I've always wanted real china dishes." She pointed at the back wall. "I think we could have a nice hutch for the kitchenware right over there."

This desirous nature of hers made me uncomfortable. "We don't really have the funds for that right now. But we got some pearl-oil crates. I can make shelves and cupboards out of them. Candles will have to do for light."

Suzanne seemed not to hear me. She just slipped her arms around me and gave me another kiss. God help me, I thought everything was going to be alright. I really did. The cabin's walls was still bright, and the inside smelled of fresh-cut spruce. Those are always the best days in a cabin. It's all downhill from there as the age and acrimony builds up on the walls.

———

Yasha and Fedosya arrived just a couple days after we'd moved into our new home. He shook his head when I told him about the bear busting in, but we'd cleaned the place up good as new, and I'd done some more carpentry to make our bachelor shack into a proper home for his bride.

This was the first time Fedosya had laid eyes on her new digs. She was every bit as delighted as Suzanne to have a real kitchen to cook in and not have to stoop and bend over an open fire all day long. She and Suzanne chatted away like two chickadees in a tree as she took Fedosya to show off our new house.

Right away Yasha noticed Camprobber's absence. The tale was still a little too fresh and raw inside my head, and it was hard to get through it. There was only silence at the table when I was done.

Yasha pulled at his lower lip the way he always did when thinking deeply. "I guess rifles and bear dogs aren't such a good combination," he said. "Shooting your dog by mistake wasn't such a concern back when the old-time Indians was still using spears. Now that we got rifles there aint really much need for those dogs."

"Lucky Jim was always old-fashioned," I said. "I don't know anybody who still keeps bear dogs."

"I guess his times are long gone," said Yasha. "Camprobber's too."

And with that we closed the subject.

"*ell me more about your people's beliefs regarding bears*," says Miss Ashford.

"*I can't.*"

"*Why not?*"

"*Bear hunting is men's business. We don't discuss it with women.*"

Miss Ashford presses her lips together, and her eyes narrow. Campbell recognizes the expression.

"*No offense meant.*" he says.

"*I understand, of course. If it's taboo, then it's taboo.*"

"*But you still don't like it that I won't talk to you about it because you're a woman.*"

"*The oppression of women is hardly limited to civilized nations.*"

Campbell opens his mouth to speak, but there are footsteps in the hallway. Several men enter. Leaning his head into the bars he sees Maddox and Heinz's commanding officer, Lieutenant Henderson. With him are Maddox and two men in Revenue Service uniforms. They take long notice of Miss Ashford, then stop in front of the cell containing the offending seaman, who is now awake and moaning over his aching head.

"*Here he is,*" says Henderson.

"*On your feet, Phipps,*" says one of the shore police. The other seems to be having difficulty keeping his eyes off Miss Ashford.

Phipps moans again. Campbell cannot see him through the timber walls, but he can hear him slowly drag himself upright as Private Maddox works the keys to open the door. The shore police grab Phipps by the arms and drag him out into the hallway. His bleary eyes land on Miss Ashford.

"*Hey,*" he says, "*she's a peach.*"

"*Eyes front!*" says one of the shoreys.

Phipps tries to straighten up and summon a fetching smile for the lady, but instead his eyes go wide and he bends over and vomits violently on the floor. The two shoreys let him crash face-first into the rank puddle where he continues to retch and heave. Finally, they pull him upright and frog-march him outside. Maddox glances at

Campbell and Miss Ashford, then turns to follow the Revenue men. He returns a moment later with a bucket and mop.

Lieutenant Henderson steps up to Miss Ashford and touches the brim of his hat. "My apologies for that, Miss."

She smiles up at him. "It's quite alright."

"This really isn't an appropriate place for a lady."

"I'll be alright. I've seen a few inappropriate things in my line of work."

"What do you call it? Enthopology?"

"Anthropology. Ethnology, to be more specific. Mr. Campbell has been kind enough to allow me to interview him about his people's culture."

Henderson looks down at Campbell, then back at Miss Ashford. "Be careful with this man. He's a violent criminal. He murdered one of the territory's leading industrialists."

It occurs to Campbell that every one of the American officials he's encountered seem greatly concerned with the demise of Greg Hackham, yet none seem to care a whit about his close friend, the Irishman Scotty Keogh. "He's been quite docile, I assure you," says Miss Ashford. "Very cooperative."

Henderson glances again at the condemned man.

"How do, Lieutenant," says Campbell. "You know I aint supposed to be held in no Army jail."

Henderson rolls his eyes to the ceiling. "Not this again."

"Your American congress made the Organic Act back in eighty-four. It says I'm supposed to be held in a civilian jail."

Henderson crosses his arms. "And I've told you any number of times that there is no such facility here in Kodiak or this side of the capital that is appropriate for a violent offender such as yourself."

"My dad was American. I'm a U.S. citizen and I got rights."

"Yes, and you're going to hang in four days, so I suggest you not trouble yourself with it."

Campbell throws up his middle finger.

Henderson flushes. "There is a lady present here, Campbell! At least try to have a little decency in your final days."

"She's seen a few inappropriate things in her line of work."

The lieutenant turns back to Miss Ashford. "Once again, I apologize. You can't expect much from these Russian siwashes."

Miss Ashford raises an eyebrow.

"Right then," he says. He turns to leave, but turns back again. "I almost forgot. My fellow officers have asked me to inquire if we might have the pleasure of your company for supper tonight."

"That would be lovely. What time?"

"Six o'clock sharp. Private Maddox can escort you to the officers' mess."

"Thank you, Lieutenant. That's very kind of you."

Henderson nods, then exits the cellblock.

"Can I ask you about books?" says Campbell.

"That's a change of subject."

"It is."

"What's on your mind?"

"I been wondering what books you've read."

As a general rule Miss Ashford dreads these kinds of questions.

"Cat got your tongue?" says Campbell.

She laughs. "No, it's just that I'm not very good at being put on the spot like this."

"Give me a title. You obviously done some reading in your time."

"I've read Typee," *she says. "I read it when I was fourteen, in fact. It's the book that made me want to study indigenous cultures."*

"That's a pretty racy book for a young lady of quality."

Miss Ashford smiles up at the ceiling, a frequent gesture that Campbell finds beguiling. "Especially since it was the original uncensored edition. I snuck it from my uncle's bookcase when we were over for Christmas supper. It was quite the scandal in our house when my governess found it in my room."

"You got in trouble for it?"

"You bet I did. But the worst was that my mother tore into my uncle for having such a licentious volume in his house. She blamed him for me getting my hands on it. Thankfully I'd already finished it."

"The good old fam-damn-ilee," says Campbell, laughing.

"Yes indeed."

Their eyes meet through the bars. Miss Ashford looks away.

KRIS FARMEN

CHAPTER VI

*W*e managed to scrape by that year. The summer of 1886 saw a good fish run, and it was a humpy year to boot, which was a considerable help in the dog feed department. We even had a surplus of fish and were able to sell some for cash. This worked well, for with the men of Possession town gone to the canneries there was a shortage of labor in the town. This in turn meant the workload was doubled on the women and old men. But Indians look after one another, and everyone made sure that everyone else had enough fish and a share of what supplies there was, so me and Yasha was able to go down to the AC store in Kenay and buy a halfway decent winter outfit. The heavy gold nugget stayed hidden inside my cartridge bag.

Not long after they arrived at Sixmile, Fedosya discovered that she was expecting, which was cause for jubilation. Yasha, naturally, was all smiles. It was getting difficult to move our outfit with *bidarkas*, what with all of Suzanne's worldly goods plus a baby on the way. Come August month we felled some beetle-kill spruce and whipsawed them into lumber to build a sailing dory. Back in the Russian days people used to ship large freight using an open boat called a *bidarra*. This craft had a wooden frame covered over with walrus hide that was obtained in trade with the Esquimaux of the Behring Sea. They were commonly rigged with a sail, oars, and a tiller. You still see them on the Inlet sometimes, but walrus hide has been hard to get since the Russians left, so they've been mostly replaced by the American-style wooden dories. Walrus hide may be scarce, but there's no shortage of wood for planking.

When it was finished, our new dory could carry twenty times as much gear as a single-hatch *bidarka*, plus a cut-up moose for good measure. We could sail it or row it, depending on weather conditions. We still used the *bidarkas* for catching belukha whales and for quick runs along Turnagain Arm, but the new dory quickly became the workhorse of our tiny fleet.

For her maiden voyage we took the girls and a camping outfit across the Arm to Kiskabetnu Creek where we spent a fortnight hunting sheep on the rocky slopes above tidewater. Both Fedosya and Suzanne was partial to sheep meat, and it's a particular favorite of mine as well. It was a fine holiday with our wall tents set up in a stand of spruce and poplar above the cataract where the creek tumbles down into the Arm. We hunted early in the mornings and late in the evenings, and to fill the midday hours I brought several bottles of my latest batch of vodka, made from mashed up raisins, blueberries, and dried apples. Fedosya had made it clear that she and Yasha did not care to have us getting tight around camp, so me and Suzanne did our drinking by ourselves in the woods. I have to say I was a better drunk than she was. She never did learn the trick of nursing a good buzz; she just guzzled away until she was sloppy drunk. Fortunately it didn't take much to get her to this point, and I could generally get her sobered up enough to function when it was time to take her back to camp so I could go out on the evening hunt.

As I've said, booze always filled her with a ravenous appetite for my affections. She would get a couple slugs in her, and then she would be tugging at my waistcoat buttons, giving me that coy little look. This was not unpleasant given my own appetites, but there was also the fact that my heartbreak over Polly, which still troubled me on a daily basis, faded into the background when I had a few drinks in my head and Suzanne's lovely curves pressed up against me.

This tactic for preserving my sanity worked well enough so long as I didn't have any contact with Polly, a point that was driven home near the end of our sheep hunting holiday. We spied another dory coming up the Arm on the tide one morning. We was curious as to who it was, so we put out after it.

It turned out to be Scotty Keogh's boat, with Greg and Polly Hackham as passengers. It was her golden hair I spotted first. The sight of her put a stone in my stomach. Yasha was at the oars, and we caught up with them at Esbaytnu River which is the first big stream east from Kiskabetnu on the north side of the Arm. They was just starting to set up camp when we rowed into the river mouth and beached next to them.

"Scotty!" I said. "Aint you just the bad penny."

"Always," he replied as we shook hands all around.

"What you doing up here?" Yasha said.

"We come to look for some sheep. Hack hired me as a camp hand."

Hack himself seemed somewhat less than overjoyed to see me, though he was cordial enough. Polly was newly slimmed down and holding a live bundle in her arms. She smiled at everyone except me.

"Hello, AC," she said with her eyes somewhere else.

"How do, Polly." I wished mightily for a drink.

"Who's this?" said Fedosya.

Polly smiled and tipped the bundle down so we could see. "This is Maxim. We call him Max for short."

The girls cooed at the baby and Polly beamed. Yasha stepped up for a closer look and slipped his arm around his bride. Young Max had dark hair and eyes, and his hair had already started to form into curls. There could be no doubt where those come from. He looked familiar to me in a way I couldn't place, but then all newborn babies look more or less alike.

"So why'd you come all the way up here?" I asked. "You can hunt sheep with Big Nick down at Kussilof Lake."

"Prospecting," said Hack in a flat, disinterested voice. "I'm on the lookout for a big strike up here, so it seemed like a good time to have a look around."

"I thought you had men out doing that for you."

"Well, I do like to get onto the creeks myself from time to time." He looked down at the child. "We've been itching to get out of town for a while, so we decided to make an outing of it."

"I see." From the corner of my eye I seen Yasha glance across the Arm toward Tutsilitnu.

"So I keep hearing rumors that you got a secret gold mine up here, Campbell."

I could feel Suzanne pull her attention from the baby and fix it on me, but I paid her no mind. "You shouldn't put no stock in rumors, Hack. There aint no gold around here that I know of."

"Well, they tell me you paid for your outfit last fall in gold, so I'm betting you got something up your sleeve."

He was smiling as he said this, but I seen his true nature behind it. Right then I decided that if Polly was the kind of woman who was enchanted by such a selfish and conniving creature as this, then she was welcome to him.

Hack crossed his arms and looked down his nose at me. "You do know you're supposed to tell other miners when you make a gold strike, don't you? That's the way it works in this country."

"I never been informed of any such notion," I said. I was sorely tempted to inform Hack that I would tell him how things worked in my country, not the other way round, but the ladies was happy and chatting over the new baby, and eager for a visit, so I held my tongue.

"Well you been informed now," said Hack.

I restrained myself from cold-cocking him right there. I'd had a lovely two weeks of hunting and had no desire to mar it with a fistfight. The girls returned to making a fuss over young Maxim, and Scotty had moved off to work on the tents. Hack took a step toward me and Yasha, speaking quietly so the ladies would not hear. "I aim to find your gold stream, Campbell. And I will, sooner or later. You can bank on it."

He favored us with an unfriendly smile, then went to help Scotty with the tents. Me and Yasha looked at one another. Each of us knew this was not good news, and I was suddenly thinking again of Muscle Sam and Opal the halibut-girl. To my knowledge, there is no gold at Esbaytnu, but the idea that Hack was even sniffing around Turnagain Arm did not sit easy. But we decided to keep our mouths shut and not make any waves.

We'd brought a seasoned sheep ham from our camp. When the tents was set up, Fedosya and Suzanne peeled the meat off the bone in a single sheaf and set it to roast over the coals. Polly had not spoken to me again since our arrival, but I still had her copy of *Typee*. Unfortunately, it was back at Sixmile. This was a little embarrassing, but it seemed that I should at least mention it. Hack was down by the creek scrutinizing the gravel, so I took a seat next to her and offered my apology for being so slow to return her book.

Polly seemed surprised, as if she had expected me to mention something else. "That's quite alright," she said. "There's no hurry to get it back."

"Well, I'm done with it. And I shouldn't be such a laggard with someone else's property."

"It's just a book. I'm not worried about it. Whenever you're in town next."

She shifted young Maxim on her lap. The lad still watched me like he knew me.

"What have you been reading these days?" I said.

She blew a little air out between her lips. "Not much time for reading these days, what with little britches here. But I finally managed to finish Mark Twain's new one, *Adventures of Huckleberry Finn.*"

"What's that about?"

"It's about a boy and a Negro man that float down the Mississippi River on a raft and the adventures they get into. Actually, I think you'd really like it. It made me think of you when I was reading it."

"Really?"

I must have spoken too quick, for Polly looked away. We listened to the meat sizzle over the coals. "I've got it right here if you'd like to borrow it."

"Sure thing."

She reached into her baby-bag and withdrew the volume, handing it to me. I started to thank her, but just then Fedosya and Suzanne come up bearing sheets of birchbark and green willow wands.

"What's all this?" Polly said with a smile.

Fedosya held up a coil of spruce roots saying, "We can show you how to make a baby-carrier so you can keep him on your back."

Suzanne fixed me with a sharp look. "So you don't have to leave him sitting on the ground where he can get into mischief." It was Polly she spoke to but it was plain the words was meant for me. Of course, she knew me and Polly's history, as did everyone else on the Inlet with ears.

Polly was delighted with the prospect and paid close attention as the girls showed her what to do. The manufacture of baby-tack is women's business, and I quickly lost interest. Hack had moved up the creek with his gold-pan, out of sight around the next bend. Yasha had taken to the woods on the pretense of looking for a spruce chicken, but my guess was he was shadowing Hack to see what he got up to.

Scotty come up as I was bent over my pack, putting away my newly borrowed book. "They tell me you're the next big thing in bootleg liquor," he said.

"Where'd you hear that?"

"A robin flew up and told me."

I laughed. "I've heard that one before. I got a little bit left if you want a taste."

Scotty rocked back on his heels and hooked his thumbs into his waistcoat pockets. "Don't mind if I do."

I pulled the last catsup bottle from my pack. It had maybe three fingers left in the bottom. I pulled the stopper and handed it to Scotty. He toasted me with the lip, then took a drink. I was keen to hear his opinion of my product, but his eyes bugged out and he started coughing and sucking wind.

"Jesus Christ," he gasped. "AC, I love you like a brother, but that's some pretty raw stuff."

"Really?" I said. "I thought it was pretty good. I've had your hooch, remember."

By now the girls was looking over at us, so I took the bottle from Scotty and led him down to the sand at the edge of the creek.

Scotty drank a couple handfuls of water, then rubbed his mouth with the back of his hand. "Don't tell me you actually been drinking that stuff."

By now I was more than a little crestfallen. I shrugged and took a drink from the bottle. Scotty shook his head. He held his hand out for the bottle, and I passed it over. He held it up to the light.

"You're on the right track," he said, "but you need to filter your hooch to pull out the toxins. You can lose your eyesight from drinking this raw booze."

"You're boshing me."

"I've seen it happen."

"So how do I filter it?"

"You run it through a bucket full of charcoal," he said, shaping the bucket with his hands in the air as he spoke. "Save the cold ashes and embers from a big campfire, or scoop them out from under your still. You want to break it up into clumps the size of your thumbnail, then put it in the bucket and wash it with water to get out all the ash and dirt. Then let it dry."

He went on to explain the process of rigging a funnel to catch the filtered booze and channel it into a tank, drawing diagrams with a stick in the sand. We had moved on to the finer points of setting up the condensing coil when a commotion over by the girls caught our attention. Hack had returned and was arguing with Polly in front of everyone, waving his hands and pointing at Maxim. Scotty and I trotted over to see what the fuss was about. As we done this Yasha came out of the woods, and I knew he had indeed been watching Hack.

As we got closer we could hear what they were saying. Hack was not impressed with the Native-made baby carrier. He had a hold on Polly's arm and was shaking her, shouting, "I will not have my wife packing my son around like some damned squaw with a papoose!"

The word *papoose* was new to me, but the meaning was clear enough, and of course we all knew the word *squaw*. Fedosya and Suzanne was insulted by this and quite rightly so. Polly herself flushed with embarrassment, and even Scotty seemed to think it was a bit much.

"Greg," said Polly, "I think maybe you're overreacting."

"You mouthy bitch!" Hack said, then he reached out and smacked Polly hard across the face. It caused her to stumble, and she would have fallen with the baby if Fedosya and Suzanne hadn't caught her. Hack stepped in for another go at her, but me and Scotty grabbed him and pushed him away.

"Whoah!" I shouted at him. "Aint no call for that!"

Hack moved to throw Scotty off and lay into me, but Scotty held him tight. "Easy now, Hack," he said. "They was just being friendly."

Yasha examined Polly's face. It was already starting to puff up. She walked off crying with the baby. Fedosya and Suzanne followed.

"I think you owe someone an apology," said Yasha in a very cool, level voice.

Hack made a lewd suggestion about what Yasha could do if he meant to interfere between a man and wife.

Once again I was tempted to give Hack a thrashing. It was only my feelings for Polly that stayed my hand.

"Steady, Yasha," Scotty said.

"We should go, partner," I said, pushing my palm out onto Yasha's chest.

"It's alright," he said, though his voice made it clear it was anything but alright. "I reckon we'll just go and leave this son of a bitch for whoever wants to deal with him. Scotty, you're welcome at our place any time, but if I see Hack set foot on the south side of the Arm he won't like it none."

"That's pretty bold talk," said Hack stepping forward.

"I wasn't talking to you, son," Yasha snapped even though Hack was a almost ten years his senior.

Polly wouldn't look at me as we loaded into our boat and shoved off, pulling the oars downstream on the slack tide.

———

The incident at Esbaytnu was a down note to start our winter on, and things sort of went further downhill from there. Suzanne couldn't read, and she greatly resented the time I spent with my nose buried in *Adventures of*

Huckleberry Finn by candlelight after supper or on days when it was snowing too heavily to go out. Of course it didn't help none that it was Polly that lent me the book. Suzanne took to interrupting my study from across the table as she sewed, always breaking right in at an exciting part in the story to needle me with some trifling matter. It was pretty obvious she was doing this by design.

By February month we was fighting almost every day. She was, among other things, not satisfied with the material status of our lives together, which is to say she was displeased that she was not able to have her china dishes and a hutch to keep them in. I pointed out that there was no space in the cabin for such an extravagant piece of furniture, and in any case there was far better things to spend twenty bucks on than fancy supper-ware. She couldn't seem to get it through her head that our breakfast wouldn't taste any better eaten off Wedgwood than it did off our blue tin spackleware.

Finally Suzanne had enough of this line of argument. "Well maybe if you would get off your lazy ass in the summer and go get a job at the cannery, then you could make the money to buy us some nice things!"

It was early evening when this happened. I was just back from a three-day trip up above the canyon to check the marten line. I was exhausted and in no mood to have my old lady call me a loafer.

The warmth of the cabin had me drowsy after so many days in the cold. I rubbed my eyes with my thumb and forefinger. "Christ almighty, Suze, why you always got to be such a goddamn materialist?"

"I beg your pardon?"

"How come you're always bitching about all the things you aint got? All you ever seem to think about is your precious damn money and what it can buy you, just like some Yankee. Why can't you just be good with what you have?"

That made her nostrils flare. She leaned over the table. "I'm proud to be an American, AC. All you ever seem to think about is ways to tell people that you're not one. You keep saying Russians this, and Indians that. But I got news for you. You're about as Russian as a pig in a poke!"

"Woman, don't you even presume to tell me what I am or what I aint."

Suzanne didn't seem to hear this, she just waved a hand out toward the creek. "And as for money, you've got a whole stream full of gold right there, and you won't lift a finger to dig none of it up."

"How many times do I got to tell you? I made a promise to my grandfather."

"Don't you give me that! Everyone knows you and Yasha paid for your outfit with gold back in eighty-five. You already broke your promise, so you might as well partake of the rest of that gold because you can't unbreak it now!"

The cabin had suddenly become a very small place with her glaring at me. I stood up.

"Just where are you going?"

"Out. I got a batch to check on."

I pulled on my sweater and my waistcoat over top of it and stepped into the snowy dark. Sometime earlier George Washington had counseled me that a woman always has to have the last word in an argument, so you're better off just letting her have it. With three wives, he surely knew that tune.

The freight dogs started yowling and yapping as I walked past the dogyard, headed up the small footpath that led to my still. It had snowed while I was gone, and my moccasins made no noise as I shuffled through three inches of powder. I'd set a batch of booze to filter through charcoal before I left, just as Scotty described it to me. This was the second batch I'd done that way, and it improved the flavor considerably. It was a bit shocking to realize just how awful the unfiltered stuff I'd been drinking really was. Scotty's charcoal filtering made my finished product smooth as silk on the tongue, and I had it in mind to maybe take him a couple special bottles later in the winter.

The night was cloudy, but with the white snow all around there was enough light to make out the dark shapes of the still and the filter beneath the pole roof I'd built to shelter them. I nudged the bucket below the filter to see that it was full, which it was, then I fished a bottle from my pile under the snow, brushed it off, and dippered it full. I stuffed it under my armpit for a moment to warm it, for drinking ice-cold booze is a bad idea. It will freeze your innards and kill you.

Suzanne was right, though I could scarcely bring myself to admit it. About not being Russian, that is. Like I said to my aunt on the way to Iriana Golinov's place, I was raised in a Russian world, but I was born after they'd already left. And I wasn't exactly an Indian neither. I was only a quadroon with a dangerous affliction that I could tell no one about, lest they laugh in my face. My dad was American, and I knew several Americans who I greatly admired, but try as I might, I could not find a way to think of myself as one. I had seen no more of America than I had of Russia.

And yet, while I spoke three languages, I used American at least half the time. Maybe more. All the books I read was in American, for it was the only language I could read. And I almost always cussed in American. I was about seventeen at this time—Creole people tend to start young—and in my short span of years I had seen the

American language go from being rarely heard to what is called a *lingua franca* among the people of Alaska.

Knowing that you're the one who is wrong has a particular sting that is hard to ignore. Still, it mystified me why Suzanne was so stubborn in her love of a place she had never seen and likely never would. She had known her American father for a little while before he took off, and they must have had happy times together at some point. Perhaps that had something to do with it.

I took a drink and swallowed the smooth fire. Off through the snow-laden trees I could see the yellow square of light that was Yasha and Fedosya's glass window. They was inside with their baby due before long, basking in the warmth and anticipation of their new family. The warmth, light and love in that window was all the gold I ever wanted or needed, but that just wasn't ever going to be enough for Suzanne. For once, the booze couldn't chase away my thoughts of Polly, which was unsettling in and of itself. I wished things could have been different for us.

But as for me, if I wasn't Russian and I wasn't an Indian, and I wasn't precisely an American, then what was I?

I took another drink. The forest offered up no answers, but at least I was starting to feel warm, if not happy.

———

That was a bad argument, but we got past it with the help of a bottle or two. Then later that month, we was fighting again over the gold in the creek and I asked Suzanne why she couldn't be more like Polly. That proved to be a big mistake. Suzanne rolled over in bed and wouldn't let me touch her no more. The next day she started packing her things. I tried to get her to stay, but it was no use. She said she was done with me. I loaded up the sled and hitched the dogs and took her to Point Possession where she stayed until spring when she moved back into her old cabin at Nikishka.

My thoughts on this trip out and back was a mixture of gloom and lightheartedness: Gloom heading out with Suzanne, then light-hearted on the way back.

So I was back to being a bachelor, but it wasn't all bad. I suddenly had all the uninterrupted reading time I desired. That April I got caught in a late snowstorm up on Granite Creek and had to tear out half the pages of *Adventures of Huckleberry Finn* to get a fire going. Thankfully I had just finished the story, but I had to send a note down to Kenay town with one of Belukha Pete's cousins requesting that Mailman Mike order a replacement copy. In any case, the mood at Sixmile lightened considerably with Suzanne's departure, and I gradually came to realize that Yasha and Fedosya had been as tired of her as I was.

Still, I must confess that I did miss her at times. We shared our lives together for the better part of a year, and that is no small thing. By Fedosya's invitation, I started taking my meals with her and Yasha. It was a delight when their son Semyon was born, and I was honored to be named the child's godfather. Yasha and Fedosya had become my family, and now we had a new member.

———

For all his tough talk, Hack steered clear of Sixmile. The next time I seen Polly was on the porch of the AC store in town that May. Yasha and Fedosya had taken baby Semyon in the dory to visit relations in Tyonek, so I paddled my old *bidarka* down to Kenay to start getting our summer outfit together.

The AC Company had finally sent Mike an assistant, a young clerk from Portland named Hewitt. He was alone at the counter when I entered. He informed me that Mike had taken the day off. He found Polly's replacement copy of *Huckleberry Finn* beneath the counter and handed it over, marking up the cost to my account. I turned to go

KRIS FARMEN

find Polly, but she saved me the trouble. She was just coming in the door with young Max slung on her hip as I was headed out. I had to backpedal so I didn't crash into her.

"Polly!"

She smiled, and despite my most noble intentions my heart jumped up in my throat when I seen her golden curls and blue eyes. There was a dark bruise along her eye, but she allowed me no time to inquire.

"AC, how are you?" She gave me a one-armed hug, then looked down at young Max. "Can you say hello to Mr. Campbell?"

Max was now over a year old. He babbled a little, then managed to say the word.

"How do, son," I said in return. "He's talking already?"

Polly was obviously proud of this. "Yes. He's been saying words here and there for almost a month now."

"Smart lad."

"And handsome, too, don't you think?"

"I brought your books back," I said, handing her the padded shipping envelope with the brand-new book inside.

"What's this?"

"I had to rip up that Mark Twain book you loaned me to get a fire going."

"Rip it up?"

"Got caught in a snowstorm with no birchbark. So I tore a bunch of pages out for firestarter. It was either that or freeze to death."

I had already torn open the envelope to inspect the contents. Polly stuffed the hem of the envelope under the arm that held Max, then reached inside and drew out the shiny new volume.

"I made sure they got you the deluxe edition though," I said. "It's got pictures and everything."

"That's very nice of you, AC. I guess the old pages made a good fire since you're still here with us."

"Believe me, I was real happy to have a book with me just then."

We'd moved out to the porch for the sunlight and fresh air, but we was not alone. Swedish Mike, Russian Mike, and Mike the Finn was sitting on upturned buckets around a wooden cable spool playing dominoes. Young Max started fussing, and I heard the old bachelors' tiles stop clacking, which told me they was watching us. From the corner of my eye I seen Mike the Finn looking back and forth from me to Max. Swedish Mike whispered something at him, and there was the faintest of smirks.

"Let's take a walk," I said. "It's crowded here, and I got your Melville book in my boat down at the beach."

She kept a proper distance from me as we ambled onto Front Street and turned for the road that led down the bluff to the beach. The cottonwoods had shed their sticky spring buds, and they stuck to the soles of her shoes and my moccasins, so that we had to stop frequently to scrape them off.

"I'm sorry about last fall," she said. "I've been wanting to apologize ever since."

I looked again at the faded bruise beneath her eye. "You mean Esbaytnu?"

She nodded. It took her a moment to find the words she was searching for. "It was a bad scene."

"How long you been putting up with that kind of thing?" I said.

"He calmed down later."

"That aint what I asked you, Polly."

She didn't respond, and we walked along not saying anything until the beach trail leveled out into the grass.

"Did you hear Yasha and Fedosya have a new son?" I said.

"I did. They named him Simon, right?"

"Semyon. That's Russian for Simon."

"That's wonderful," she said. "I'm so happy for them."

"We aint seen Hack up on Turnagain Arm again," I said. "I take it he's still looking for his big strike."

"He's been building up the sluice plant at Anchor Point. His idea is to use the beach gold to finance prospecting and investing in stream placers further up the Inlet."

"That's some big plans," I said stepping over a drift log.

Polly shifted Max around to her other hip, which meant she had to talk at me over the top of his head. "It's nice now that he's working more in the office and less on the end of a shovel."

Not for the first time that day I noticed her skirts, blouse and jacket was of expensive fabric and fashionable cut. Hack's new ventures was evidently bringing in some good coin. Still, she was the same old Polly.

She started to giggle when she seen me watching her. "What?"I grinned. "I'm just wondering what book you might recommend for me next."

"You can find books on your own," she said, laughing. "I'm going to start charging a ten-cent recommendation fee pretty soon."

Across the river-mouth the cannery was gearing up for the season. There was boats tied up at the wharf, and I could just barely make out the forms of men moving to and fro, looking like ants in the distance. The smell of coal smoke from the boilers drifted on the breeze. Out in the water, work gangs were building two new fish-traps, giant platforms set upon pilings driven into the sand, with twenty-fathom nets strung out along them. We walked through the last of the grass to the edge of the beach where my *bidarka* rested.

"I hear you and Suzanne split up," Polly said.

"We did."

I sensed she was curious to know more, but I really didn't care to discuss it. She stooped to pick up a piece of blue glass. The sharp edges was ground away from its time rolling in the sand and gravel, so she give it to Max. He promptly put it in his mouth and started sucking on it.

"I hear she's taken up with Scotty Keogh," she said as she pulled the glass from his lips.

"That's news to me. She living down at Kussilof Lake then?"

"I don't think she's there with him now. But I got a hunch there might be wedding bells in the future."

I had my doubts about this. Along with being a good trapper, fisherman and fiddle player, Scotty was known for cutting a swath through the single girls of the Peninsula. I once asked him if he ever thought of getting married, and he said to me, "AC, why would I make one girl miserable when I can make them all happy?"

"That don't really sound like Scotty," I said.

"People change. Besides, Suzanne is expecting."

That caught my attention.

"How far along is she?" I said as I mentally counted back the months since we'd last been together.

"Only a month or so. She just found out."

This of course was a relief. I hadn't even seen her since early March month when I drove her to Point Possession.

I ran my arm up into the tail of my *bidarka* and withdrew the seal-gut bag where I kept my important treasures. Polly set Max down in the gravel and readjusted her Stetson hat on her head as I withdrew her copy of *Typee* and handed it to her.

"Is Hack down at Anchor Point now?" I said.

She shook her head. "He's gone down to Kodiak. He had to see the customs director about some mining claims."

"The customs director? Mining claims aint really his department."

"There's no other federal official this side of Sitka."

"I reckon we're pretty low on the governor's list out here," I said. "But I figured you two would have moved down to Frisco or someplace by now."

She watched Max grabbing handfuls of gravel and throwing them at his feet. "We don't really want to move Outside. Alaska's full of opportunity for young people, and there's such a positive spirit here. Greg and I aim to stay and help make something of this country."

"It already is something. It was something when you got here."

"I mean a place with good jobs where people can raise families. Greg and I are Alaskans now. This is our home."

"Alaskans?" I said, trying not to laugh as I stuffed the seal-gut bag back into its hiding place. "What pray tell is an Alaskan?"

"You're one. You're as Alaskan as anyone I know."

"I aint no such thing. You Americans can call yourselves whatever you like."

Polly studied me rather queerly, holding the two books before her. This was still the girl I'd met on the beach, but her world was now one of marriage and motherhood, of white picket fences and fancy American frame houses. It suddenly seemed rather silly that I had ever thought she might come with me up to Sixmile to live in a one-room cabin. And here was me, a bachelor trapper living alone in the woods because he hadn't been able to keep his own woman satisfied. That was probably all I would ever amount to.

"What is it, AC?"

"Did Hack put that bruise on your face?"

She turned from me and crossed her arms before her, looking down at Max again.

"Did he? I seen what he done to you there at Esbaytnu."

"That's not your concern," she said quietly.

"Yeah, I guess it aint," I said looking straight into her. She wouldn't meet my eyes.

Down the Inlet the white cone of Mount Redoubt stood stark against the sky. The new moon had brought a big tide, and the sand-flats was exposed a long way out.

"Good clam digging these next few days," I said.

"We've gone out clamming when Greg's around for a good tide. He grew up near Cape Cod, and he loves his clams."

"Any luck?"

Polly shrugged. "A little. Not as much as we'd like."

"How about you and me head down to Clam Gulch?"

"You mean now?"

"Of course. There'll be another good tide tomorrow."

"Alex."

"Why not?"

"You know why not."

"I aint scared of Hack," I said. And I wasn't. It was one thing for him to pull a pistol on me when I was stumbling drunk, but I was big for my age and pretty certain I could lick him in a fair fight.

Polly took a step away from me then turned and scooped up Max. "It was nice visiting with you," she said. She turned away, leaving me there on the beach wondering among other things if I would ever get another book from her again. Then there was that bruise. I had been hoping that the incident at Esbaytnu would prove to be a one-time thing, but that did not seem to be the case. I pottered around my *bidarka*, checking the seams and the joints in the frame for wear and tear. The more I thought about the bruise, the more worked up I got. At base was the simple fact that she was my friend, and it was hard to stand by and watch her get hurt like that.

Eventually I headed up to Mike and Klara's house. It was good to see the old place again. They'd had it repainted sometime recently. It was now a pale green-blue color with blue trim.

Mike answered the door in his shirtsleeves, looking like he had just finished a nap. "AC!" he said shaking my hand. "I figured you'd turn up sooner or later."

"I'm just here for a couple of days. Alright if I bunk here?"

"Sure thing." He stretched and smiled. I was relieved to see no ill will upon his face. Perhaps he had finally accepted the fact that I was not bound to be a store clerk. Or maybe he was just pleased to finally have some help at the store.

He stood aside from the door. "Come in son, come in."

I done so and dumped my things next to the sofa. "So how are you, Mike?"

"I'm good. Nice to have a day off for myself every now and again. I was just fixing to head down to the river for some fishing."

"I hear the first kings are in," I said. "Careful you don't snag one of them fish traps."

I doffed my hat and jacket and hung them on the rack by the door. I could tell summer was on the way because Klara had the top of the disused parlor wood stove piled with dishes of fragrant herbs. The room was awash in the pleasant light of May, and Mike had his fishing tackle spread out over the coffee table. He appeared to have been tying flies when the urge for a nap overtook him.

"Is Klara around?" I said.

Mike clamped a hook in his fly-vise. "She's upstairs sewing. Go on up."

The door to Klara's sewing room stood ajar, so I crept up and silently poked my head inside. She sat in her rocking chair bent over some embroidery and didn't notice me. I tapped on the door, saying in Russian, "Hello Auntie."

She looked up from her embroidery hoop and smiled when she seen me. She set her work aside and come over to give me a big hug.

"I was hoping we might have a chat," I said when she was done fussing over me.

"Of course. What about?"

"Polly Hackham."

Emotion passed across Klara's face like the shadow of a cloud on a sunlit beach. "I see," she said. She went over to a spare chair and lifted several bolts of fabric that was piled there and set them on the table.

"Please sit," she said, extending a hand. I thanked her and took my ease as she returned to her rocking chair. She folded her hands over her lap, waiting.

"Hack's been whaling on Polly," I said.

Klara nodded. "I know."

Silence occupied the room like an extra person. I considered what I wanted to say. "How do you know?"

"A magpie flew up and told me."

"Did this magpie tell you how long it's been going on?"

"For quite a while."

"She's got to quit him."

Klara studied me for a long moment. "AC, I'm going to tell you something, and I don't want you to take it the wrong way."

"I'll keep an open mind."

She formed her fingers into a steeple below her chin. "This isn't really your business."

"Beg your pardon?"

"What goes on between a man and his wife isn't any of your affair."

It seemed to me that I was hearing that sentiment an awful lot these days. "It damn well is my affair," I said. "She's my friend."

"And she's Greg's wife."

"Oh come on. You must have seen the bruises on her face. Hell's bells, he smacked her right in front of me and Yasha up on Turnagain Arm last fall."

Klara give a slow nod, then listened as I told her the story.

"Aleksandr," she said, "you mustn't think that Polly's situation doesn't make me feel awful."

"Then we should do something about it. She can sue for divorce on grounds of abuse."

Klara did not move her hands, nor did her gaze waver from mine. "It's not that simple."

"Well it aint exactly complicated neither. He's a louse, and she needs to shake loose of him."

"AC, the reason it's not simple is because Polly loves him."

"How can she love a man who smacks her around like that?"

She lifted her eyebrows and gave a little shrug. "Love is complicated. Sometimes you can love someone but not like them very much."

That made no sense to me, and I said as much.

"Have you ever been in love?" said Klara.

I shuffled my feet on the floorboards. "Of course. With Suzanne."

"You never loved her. You and I both know it was a relief when she left you."

I felt my stomach churn a little at that. I had, in fact, never spoken of Suzanne with my aunt. I looked down at the floor. "There is Polly."

"Polly doesn't count."

"Why not? I loved her. Hell, I still do."

"That's just it. You love her, but the two of you are not in love together. So you don't truly know what love is."

It seemed to me that she was talking in circles. "So Polly stays with Hack and takes his beatings because she loves him? Jesus Christ, Suzanne pissed me off plenty of times, but I never once laid a hand on her in anger."

My blasphemy drew a pained look from Klara. I had slipped into American for the sake of the cussing, but she kept on in Russian. "Well, you could say that, but again it's much more complicated. A woman needs to feel needed."

"Do you think Hack loves Polly?"

"I don't know. Maybe. Probably. Some people are mixed up in their feelings."

I was more confused now than when I arrived. "I just can't understand why she'd stay with a louse who treats her like that. Or why he's so awful to her. If Polly was mine I'd treat her like a queen."

Klara smiled at me. "Aleksandr, I've no doubt that whatever girl you find to marry, you will treat her well. But in this world women often have to make very difficult choices that men simply do not understand."

"You mean she doesn't want to leave his fine house and wind up working on the cannery line."

"That might be part of her thinking. But she also has her son to consider. The boy would stay with Greg if they divorced."

We fell silent for a while. I listened to the clock downstairs chime four-thirty. I had just started thinking I might go find Mike and see if he wanted some company for his fishing when Klara spoke again.

"How is it you're still hung up on Polly Hackham?"

"I'm not hung up on her. I love her."

"I don't think it's healthy for you to be in love with another man's wife."

"Love is complicated," I said.

She eyed me with a rather motherly look. "So it is. Are you staying here tonight?"

"If it's alright. The next night, too, probably. Yasha and Fedosya have the dory."

"Of course it's alright. I'll go make up your bed. Will you be here for supper?"

"I hadn't really thought that far ahead."

"I'm making battered halibut," she said. This was among my favorite things to eat, and she knew it. Still, I hemmed and hawed.

She looked at me from the corner of her eye. "There might be some French fried potatoes, too. And lemon cake for dessert."

That sealed the deal. That lady always did know the way to my heart.

————

The years 1887 and 1888 was good to us there at Sixmile, even with low fur prices. George Washington died in his sleep late in the summer of eighty-seven, which was a low point, but his funeral potlatch the following spring was one of the biggest ever held. Everything from cooking pots to guns was given away—Belukha Pete must have spent almost a thousand dollars on goods, which is to say nothing of the contributions of other relatives. Every single person who attended, including myself, Yasha, Fedosya, and Semyon, came away with a new suit of clothes. Fedosya was pleased to receive a pile of new housewares. I was given a new twenty-gauge fowling piece, which was a welcome addition to my outfit, along with new blankets and an axe.

The pattern of our lives became a pleasant round of fishing and belukha hunting in the summer, sheep hunting in the fall, then trapping and moose hunting in the winter, with ratting and bear hunting in the spring. I had no great difficulty finding girls to keep me company from time to time, but I kept away from the idea of marriage. I had settled into bachelorhood. I spent much of my spare time reading books I ordered from the AC store. I was particularly fond of Washington Irving's stories such as "The Legend of Sleepy Hollow" and "Rip Van Winkle." It was during this time that I first read *Roughing It* and also *1001 Arabian Nights, Don Quixote,* (which I confess I thought was about a fellow named Donald Quick-sote, until Mailman Mike set me straight) and a number of others. I tried reading Fenimore Cooper's *Leatherstocking Tales,* but found them dull beyond measure. I never in my life met an Indian who acted like the hapless rubes in those stories.

During this time I also refined my distilling to the point where I could honestly say my favorite booze was the stuff I made at home. This should not be taken as boasting; I only bring it up to say that I got reasonably good at it. Connoisseurs that they were, Scotty and Big Nick started asking whenever they saw me if I had any of my product to pass around, which I took as a high compliment. In all truth, I probably could have made pretty good money selling the stuff, but the Indian side of my upbringing has always inclined me toward sharing the good things in life with my friends. In any case, I would have been my own best customer. Bachelor solitude was tolerable only with a free supply of alcohol to keep me filled up with that feather-light feeling. I always ran my traps and hunted actively. I kept my bills paid, and I made a point of never being drunk around Yasha and his family. But in the evenings when I was alone in my cabin with my books, I was finding the more I drank, the more I needed to drink to keep the buzz going. And when I was out on the trapline, or in a tent camp somewhere, the desire for a drink filled my thoughts more and more.

Booze also made it much easier to push away the crackling in my jaw when it come around, which in turn made it so that I didn't have to dwell on my affliction. I can see now what an unhealthy habit my drinking had become, but I was blind to it then. As Scotty would say, I just kept pouring more whiskey in the jar-oh.

Suzanne McCoy delivered a baby girl in February of 1888. Scotty was not around. I only heard this through the moccasin telegraph, and did not lay eyes on Suzanne or her child during these years.

That same spring, not long after George Washington's funeral, me and my family sailed for Polly Creek on the west side of the Inlet for a clam-digging holiday. It was the first big tides of the year, and we all needed some fun after the long winter.

But the wind died halfway across, leaving us becalmed on the southbound tide just north of Kalgin Island. We had only an hour left before the tide turned north, so me and Yasha took turns rowing for the island. I was on the oars pulling us round the north point when Fedosya, who was in the bow with Semyon, pointed to shore, saying, "Look!"

Yasha stood up, and I rested my oars, twisting around with a knee on the seat. As we drifted, the gravel spit peeled away to reveal a fleet of maybe a hundred *bidarkas* and dories, all beached to wait out the tide. There was a multitude of driftwood fires up and down the strand. The people huddled around them looked forlorn and miserable.

"Who are they?" said Fedosya. Little Semyon was fussy in the cold wind and she was bouncing him on her knee, trying to keep him quiet.

Yasha shook his head. "Don't know. Can't tell from this far out."

The tide was rapidly pushing us southward past the encampment. "Hey, Yasha," I said, "you want to put in here, or keep going until we hit the Barren Islands?"

"Hell with it," said Yasha, "let's go in and see who they are."

I bent to the oars again, and we made our landing with help from the strangers. They turned out to be most of the population of Layda town at Anchor Point. Their *toyon* was a Creole named Silas Petrovich. We knew him only by his reputation, but it turned out that he knew both Big Nick and Scotty Keogh quite well.

He invited us up for a *chypeet*, and when we inquired about what such a multitude was doing on the island he informed us that the residents of Layda been evicted from their homes by none other than Greg Hackham. Apparently their town was perched right atop a patch of beach sand that he coveted for his sluice-plant. He already had a giant fish-trap across the river to catch salmon to feed his work gang and had leveled most of the trees both for building timber and boiler fuel to power the steam machinery he used to dig up the sand and dump it into the rockers. Given all this, the Layda people had come to the conclusion that their best option was to cut their losses and move someplace new. Except for a few holdouts, they had left *en masse* two days prior.

"Where you all bound for?" I asked.

Petrovich pointed to the northeast. "I got kin among the Mednovsti. Over on the Copper River. We'll go see if we can start over again up there."

"That's a long trip," said Yasha.

Petrovich just stared at his fire.

The inmates of this encampment looked even more dejected up close. They sat hunched against the world, staring into their own fires and paying us little mind. Everywhere I heard the rattling cough of consumption, and I seen more than one face with measle spots. Nowhere did I see a smile, hardly surprising given their circumstances.

They departed on the flood tide while we stayed behind to wait for the next ebb. Me and Yasha helped them launch, and as the fleet paddled off bound for Old Knik he turned to me and said, "You see them measle spots?"

I nodded. "You think they'll make the Copper River?"

He shrugged, not wanting to commit to an answer. Behind us, Fedosya sat on our grub box with Semyon on her lap, watching the boats pull away into the distance.

———

We spent two days digging clams at Polly Creek. Fedosya baked them in the coals, and we ate them dipped in seal oil until we was sick of them. Then we dug several crates full of live ones and crossed the Inlet to Kussilof where we sold them to the cannery for nine dollars and twelve cents.

Scotty was there, getting his boat ready for fishing season. He had scraped and caulked the hull, and was busy laying on a new coat of paint. He paused to give Semyon a stick of peppermint candy, which made the lad happy as the proverbial clam. The four of us had a visit, during which I noticed Scotty kept avoiding my eyes. After we'd caught up, Yasha and Fedosya and Semyon drifted off to chat with other friends while I stayed behind to help Scotty.

"I hear you may be getting hitched," I said.

This, of course, was old news. Scotty dipped his brush and kept painting. "So you heard about me and Suzanne then."

"A chickadee flew up and told me."

"Those birds never know when to keep their mouth shut," he said. He stood his paintbrush inside the can and set the can on the gravel. He leaned against the unpainted portion of the hull and folded his arms over his chest.

"We split up," he said after a while.

"She's delivered the baby," I said. "It's a girl."

"I heard."

I dug my toe into the gravel. "You ought to be thinking about marriage."

Scotty flashed me a rueful grin. "I aint going to marry that cooze."

I was happy to be shed of Suzanne, don't get me wrong. But this was a personal matter to me. You'll recall that my own sweet American dad went off and left me, his bastard son to grow up without him. Still, Scotty was a good friend, and it did pain me to see him in such a fix.

"Why not?" I said.

"You got a lot to learn about women, AC."

Good friend or no, I did not care to be talked down to in such a manner. "I shacked up with that gal for almost a year. So tell me if you will what exactly it is that I got to learn about women."

"She done it to trap me, brother. She was on the make for a husband, and she decided I fit the bill."

"That aint your child's fault, Scotty."

"That's true. But I aint going to share no roof with that bitch. Hell, you know what she's like. Maybe you should take her back if you're so damn worried about it."

"Don't you try to shift this off onto me," I said. "You're the one stuck your dick in her after she left me. It's your kid and your responsibility."

Scotty's eyes hardened. "My my, aint you just the crusader for morals and virtue."

"It aint about no morals and virtue. Suzanne's a pill, I grant you that. But she don't deserve to be left with your bastard child because you're too goddamn selfish to do the right thing."

Scotty launched himself from the boat and clocked me hard across the chin. I was startled enough at this that he managed to get in close and land two fast punches to my gut and one across my chops. I slipped a punch to my nose, then palmed the side of his head, catching him off balance. I slammed a hard right into his kidney and drove my knee up into him. He went down, but grabbed my ankle and pulled me right off my feet. I crashed onto the gravel, trying to scramble back up, but he leapt onto me swinging hard. I grabbed his fist in my palm. He pushed down, glaring into my eyes and me glaring right back.

Several of the nearby fishermen had seen us by then. They came running and grabbed Scotty and pulled him off me. He struggled against them as I stood up and wiped the blood from my mouth, but I could see it in his eyes that he didn't have it in him to really hurt me.

We kept staring at one another. Then I straightened my waistcoat and walked off with Scotty's apology hanging in the air behind me as I worked my jaw to and fro.

———

It was the usual summer routine that year for us as we repaired our fish trap and started hauling in salmon. Fedosya's sister Agrafina came up to help her with the cutting, drying, and smoking. She brought her two sons Demid and Ephim with her. They was both Semyon's age, and the three of them ran around like a pack of feral dogs. Aggie and Fedosya was always close, and they chatted all through their work as womenfolk are wont to do.

Word had long since gone around about me and Suzanne splitting the sheets, and of her bearing Scotty's daughter. Naturally, this was fodder for the gossip mill, people on the Inlet lacking for entertainment and all. During her stay at Sixmile, Aggie and Fedosya called it to my attention that Suzanne wanted me back, but I was not especially interested in returning to where I'd already been.

Still, Fedosya kept bringing it up and hinting that I ought to stop in to Nikishka and look in on her. So come the fall supply run in September, I towed my *bidarka* behind the dory as we rowed south. When we passed Nikishka I pulled my boat up abeam of the dory and climbed in and paddled to shore where I called upon Suzanne's ramshackle cabin. I won't claim this was the right move, but I had been several months without a woman's affection, and I am, after all, only human.

The child was in her arms as she opened the door on its leather hinges. She watched me a moment, then smiled.

"Hello AC."

"How do, Suze."

"This is Lindsay," she said bouncing the baby up and down.

"Hello baby Lindsay," I said. The child stared at me with wide, dark eyes.

Suzanne stepped aside and invited me in. She put the baby down to sleep and made me some coffee, this being a taste she had acquired from her American father. She fed the wood stove and set a Dutch oven of leftover *parok* atop it to heat.

It didn't take us long to fall into each other. We had to do it quietly so as not to wake the child. Afterward, Suzanne propped her chin in her palm and contemplated me. "So you still wish I was like that other girl?"

By this of course she meant Polly.

"I'm past her," I said.

And God knows I thought I really was, and it felt lovely to have a woman snuggled up close to me with the scent of her filling my mind. I rolled my head over to watch Lindsay sleeping by the stove in her crib fashioned from a pearl-oil crate. The stove was a rickety old thing made from an oil drum. It was full of holes, and the light that escaped through them cast flickering shafts across her sleeping form and the walls and the water bucket on the kitchen counter.

"Her husband's been sniffing around here looking for gold," said Suzanne.

"You mean Hack?"

"Yeah. We told him we don't want him doing no mining here."

"What'd he say to that?"

"Nothing to mention. He and his two workmen just packed up and left."

"Nothing good happens where that man sets foot," I said, thinking of the people of Layda town.

She rolled over with a sigh and pressed her soft backside against me. She was soon breathing long and slow, and I knew she was asleep. I listened to her breath and the whispering of the stove. I thought of Hack and of fatherhood and Suzanne and the fact that baby Lindsay had come barely eleven months after we was last together.

Poor little thing, I thought, for I knew what it was to be in that child's shoes. Yet when I closed my eyes all I could see was Polly smiling on the beach that day when we first met. It took me by surprise, and a wave of the old loneliness broke over me.

All those hard choices women have to make. Lindsay and me was much the same. We was both bastards in an old land with a new name. I felt awful for the child, but I knew it was not me who was going to take the place of her father. It was pretty obvious that was what Suzanne was angling for.

So I made my own difficult choice and left the next morning. Suzanne was down at the beach with me as I loaded my travelling things into my *bidarka*. She'd left Lindsay with her sister-in-law for the morning.

"When are you coming back?" she asked, running her hands up and down the lapels of my jacket. She smiled up at me and straightened my collar.

The tide had turned, and I was ready to shove off for Kenay town. There was a stiff breeze out of the north, so I had my Stetson hat stowed in the hull and a kerchief tied round my head. She kept brushing my hair back from my face.

I coughed once. "I aint coming back."

The sultry smile vanished from her face. "What do you mean?"

"I mean we aint right for each other. We never were. I love you, Suze, but I don't love you enough to be your husband."

I expected a more dramatic reaction. Instead, she just took a step back and said, "You'll be back."

She spoke with genuine certainty. I didn't understand it at the time. I just shrugged and got into my *bidarka* and paddled off with the tide.

Any of you young gents who read this, take heed. If you split up with your old lady and then sometime down the road she suddenly wants to climb you like a randy sow, don't go there. Don't ride that horse, because nothing good will come of it.

I was about to learn this lesson for myself.

❋

*C*ampbell lies on his back upon his mattress, reading Mark Twain's description of the Hawaiian countryside when footsteps approach his cell. He closes the book and slides it beneath the blanket and looks up, expecting to see Rebecca Ashford. Instead there is a tall American in a dark suit. He carries a battered copy of the King James Bible against his chest.

"Not you again."

"How are you, Mr. Campbell?"

"Tired of being in jail. What about you?"

The visitor is the Reverend Robinson, the local Baptist missionary. He holds up a steaming ceramic mug. "Would you like some coffee?"

Campbell grunts, then sits up and rubs his face. He rises, steps over to the bucket and pisses. When he is finished he crosses the cell and takes the mug, then he returns to the mattress, sitting beneath the light from the window as he sips at the coffee.

"What is it you want, Parson? I told you I was raised in the Orthodox Church."

Robinson dislikes being called Parson. He gestures at the chair Miss Ashford normally occupies. "May I sit down?"

"What is it you Boston Men say? It's a free country?"

Robinson sits and hooks one leg over the other. "I dined with Miss Ashford and the officers last night. I wanted to speak to you about some things she said you told her."

"Like what?"

"Mainly your notion that you can change yourself into a bear. And that your grandfather could turn into a crane."

Earlier in his life, Campbell might have flushed with embarrassment at being outed. But with his execution just a few short days away, he finds he does not really care anymore.

"What of it?" he says.

Robinson's mouth turns up into a knowing smile. "You can't actually expect us to believe that."

"Why not?"

He coughs a little, as if waiting for Campbell to pick up on something glaringly obvious. He cocks his head. "You have to admit, it is a pretty childish notion."

"You shouldn't speak so freely of things you can't understand."

Robinson lifts his Bible. "I was wondering if I might read some passages to you."

Campbell takes another sip of coffee. "Don't think I don't know that you Yankee missionaries have a quota of converts that you're required to make when you get sent up here. So you can get a transfer back down to the States."

"That's just a silly rumor."

"Has it ever occurred to you that I might be perfectly happy in the Orthodox Church? Or do you even give a shit?"

"I recall you telling me you were never actually baptized into the church. My primary concern here is that you will not be admitted to heaven because of that. Committing your life to God in any church is better than living in darkness."

He rotates his foot on the end of his leg. "And in any case, we feel the Orthodox Church has been much too permissive with respect to the Native people's old heathen ways."

"We?"

"My superiors and I. And the churchgoers of Illinois who sponsor my mission. It's obvious that you people have been allowed to continue with your devil-worship, and this state of affairs has gone on long enough."

"We was doing just fine before you showed up."

Robinson places a hand upon the cover of his bible. "This book holds the true word of God and his only son Jesus Christ. Your soul cannot be saved if you do not take these words to heart. You have the opportunity right now, this very morning, to be born again unto Christ."

Campbell drains the last of his coffee, wishing idly that he could get some tea. "And all this time I thought God spoke Russian. Or Slavonic, to be more precise."

"God speaks every man's language."

"Now you're talking like a priest."

There is Heinz's voice from the office, too muffled to make out. Footsteps on the floorboards and a swishing of skirts. Campbell half expects it to be the local Russian parish priest in his cassock, but it is his interviewer.

KRIS FARMEN

The Reverend stands up. "Miss Ashford, good day to you."

She looks from Robinson to Campbell then back again. "What's going on here?"

"I'm doing my best to make sure Mr. Campbell is admitted to paradise."

"I told you last night I prefer you not speak to him until I'm through, Reverend."

"I do have a job to do."

"As do I. When you missionaries get hold of these tribesmen they start refusing to speak of their traditional beliefs. I have not yet finished interviewing this man."

"This man is to be executed on Friday. I think his immortal soul is slightly more important than your—"

He waves a hand in the air, searching for the right word.

"—Than your folklore studies."

Miss Ashford's face sharpens. She steps toward him. "Now you listen here. I am an employee of the United States government, and you are interfering with my work."

Campbell watches as the Reverend cuts her off, stabbing a finger into her face. "No, you listen here, young lady. I am a man of God, and I am charged with the responsibility of delivering the souls of these savages to heaven. You are interfering with my work. And I will not be ordered about by some misguided young hussy who should be busy finding a husband!"

Robinson's eyes go wide, then clamp shut as Campbell's hands yank him back against the iron bars. Before the Reverend can react, the prisoner has a forearm wrapped around his neck, both cutting his air and squeezing his temple against the unforgiving metal. He claps his other hand over the Reverend's mouth so he cannot cry out.

Campbell hisses something in Russian into his ear, then switches to English. "You don't speak to her like that, Parson. Got it?"

Miss Ashford stands with a gloved hand over her own mouth. Robinson's arms flail about as he grunts and gasps.

Campbell tightens his grip but keeps his tone level, barely audible. "I said do you got that."

Robinson manages the barest of nods. Campbell gives him an extra squeeze for good measure, then drops him. The Reverend wheezes for breath as Campbell picks up his Bible and hands it to him.

Miss Ashford watches as Robinson straightens himself, then leaves the cellblock with what little dignity he can muster. She turns to Campbell. "You just assaulted a man of the cloth!"

Campbell leans his forehead against the bars, working his jaw up and down and from side to side, as if it has come unhinged and he is trying to pop it back into place.

"To hell with that fucking clown," he moans.

His eyes are clamped shut, his face a mask of agony and concentration. Miss Ashford studies him as he kneads the flesh below his ears. She recognizes these symptoms from the things he has told her. One of Campbell's hands grips the bars to keep himself from falling to all fours. Her heart begins to pound, and her empirical defenses wobble. Her lips part as she realizes what is about to happen right in front of her.

Campbell straightens up. He flexes his jaw one last time, then hooks his thumbs into his waistcoat pockets. "How was your supper with the officers?"

Miss Ashford blinks, pulling her scientific training back around herself like a cloak, or perhaps as she might have drawn the bedcovers up over her head when she was little and scared of monsters in the night. Still, her heart pounds inside her chest as she sits in the chair.

"I'm sorry, what?"

"Your supper with the officers," says Campbell. "How'd it go?"

She draws a long breath. "Very nice. Though I'm afraid none of them have anything very complimentary to say about you." She blinks again as her pulse settles and her composure returns.

"No surprises there. I bet they couldn't tell you enough about me."

She flashes an impish smile. "It's a natural enough subject for conversation, given my work with you."

She stands her briefcase on her lap, both hands primly holding the top handles. Campbell can tell she's trying to form her next question carefully.

"What is it?" he says.

"One of the officers named McNaughton mentioned the fisticuffs between you and Scotty Keogh. He said it demonstrated that you were a violent man."

Campbell purses his lips, then folds his arms over his chest. "Americans get in fistfights all the time and it don't mean anything. I don't reckon I'm any more violent than the next man."

She adjusts her fingers on the leather briefcase grips. "Yes, well, Lieutenant Henderson told me about another fight you had. With Greg Hackham."

Campbell looks stricken. "Yes," he says in a downcast voice, "they love to talk about that one."

"They said you almost beat him to death."

"That was a long time ago. I forgave and forgot and made my peace with it. And with him."

Miss Ashford is less than convinced. She watches Campbell, wondering in all frankness how much peace he made with Hackham before killing him.

"You don't really think I'd harm you, do you, Miss?"

"I don't know. Given what I just saw happen."

"Well, I wish you'd stay. I enjoy visiting with you."

"Really? I was under the impression you were just tolerating me."

Campbell lifts a little grin. "I do wish we'd met somewhere else other than this jailhouse."

"Tell me about the fight," she says. "And I've been wondering."

"Wondering what?"

"Did you change into a bear at all as a grown man?"

CHAPTER VII

It was late in October when fresh word reached me about Suzanne. Yasha was off somewhere trailing a moose, and I was busy cutting cordwood for the coming winter.

Sometime around mid-morning Fedosya come out to find me with fry-bread and a pail of tea and Semyon tumbling along behind her. He was just starting to get his legs under him but still had trouble negotiating the slash and stobs that littered the woodyard. The days was drawing short, and there was a lot to do, so I kept working the bucksaw and cutting rounds as they came. It was a warm cloudy morning, and I was looking forward to taking a breather before the rain started to fall.

When they arrived I laid the saw on a stump and sat down on the ground to load my pipe. I poked at Semyon's ribs to make him laugh and squeal as Fedosya set out the tea and poured me a cup. I dug a thumb into the sugar-dusted fry-bread, and Semyon busied himself with blowing the cottony fireweed-down into the wind where it drifted across the yard. This made me wonder idly if Polly's son Maxim had discovered this delight.

Fedosya drew herself a cup of tea then arranged her skirts and sat on a nearby hemlock stump. She had something big to say, I could see it written across her face. Finally at my urging she come out with it.

"Suzanne's with child again," she said.

My guts give a little twist. "Oh?"

"She says it's yours."

It took some time for this to sink in, but before long it became clear to me what had happened. Scotty had run off and left her with their daughter, so Suzanne set a snare for me.

I said as much to Fedosya. She drummed her fingers on the side of her cup and watched Semyon for a moment.

"She may very well have," she said. "Stranger things have happened. But now it's all about the child."

"So this is fatherhood," I said.

Fedosya smiled at me, and I could see she was putting the best face on it that she knew how. I looked down at the fry-bread in my hand. My appetite had vanished.

"I thought I'd gotten shed of her," I said.

"I know you'll do what's right, AC. But you're not alone in this. You're family to us. Me and Yasha will find a way to help you make it work. "

"No man is an island," I said, thinking of my beloved bachelor life whose days was now numbered.

She cocked her head at me.

"It's from a book."

"Ah," she said. She couldn't read, so the reference was lost on her. I didn't bother to tell her I'd never read John Donne's work, but knew the line only as a random quote.

"Suzanne might have to come live up here," I said. "Lindsay, too."

"I know. But search your heart, AC. Semyon would have some playmates. That's a good thing. And you'll be doubly blessed with a son and a daughter."

"Yeah," I said. "Sort of."

Looking back over the years I suppose this was one of those difficult choices that Klara spoke of. But at the same time I couldn't see why it should be me who was left to pay Scotty's bill. Then again, I could hardly refuse my own child in the same manner that my own father done to me.

We sat there on our stumps for some while, not talking, just watching young innocent Semyon as he ran about with no inkling of what was happening. He had only the world in front of his eyes to be concerned with. At last Fedosya stood to go and drew me into a hug. She called Semyon to her and they walked back to the cabin.

There was so many thoughts crowding my head at once, it was hard to get a handle on any one of them. I had no intention of moving to Nikishka. Sixmile was my home. But the other side of that coin was that Suzanne was never happy there when we was together, and I knew that her presence at Sixmile was likely to make everyone miserable. It would be hard on me, but it seemed like an awful lot to ask of Yasha and Fedosya. Little Semyon, too.

Now it seemed that life was suddenly moving much too fast around me. I buried my axe in a stump and walked down the path to my cabin. I had just put up a fresh batch of vodka and had a good dozen bottles packed inside a box beneath the table, waiting to be drunk.

I picked up the bottle I was currently working on and studied its contents in the light from the window. I pulled the cork and poured a cup and sat down at the table. I looked around the cabin that I'd built for me and Suzanne, the house that had become my solitary domain. The thought of her being here again pressed upon me like steel and made the cabin seem like a prison. There was the thought of Muscle Sam's prophesy that I would wind up in a prison with no walls. My cabin of course, had four solid walls and a good roof, but I decided he was probably speaking in higher terms.

I studied the stack of books and my reading lamp next to it and lifted the cup to my lips. It tasted good. The only good thing in my life, it seemed.

Yasha returned two days later with a boatload of moose meat. We went to work again in the woodyard, and when I explained the situation he just shrugged and said, "You wear the pants. Tell her this is your home, and she and the children can come stay here with you. Nikishka's a shithole, and there's no doubt the children will have a better life with us."

I went to bed that night expecting to feel good, or at least less bad about my situation. Still, I lay awake in my bed thinking of how unlovely me and Suzanne's last months together had been in that selfsame house. It was not a pleasant night, but little did I know at that very moment a boat was putting into Nikishka that would change all our lives forever.

————

Two nights later, after a big snowfall, all of us sat round the table in Yasha and Fedosya's house talking over what needed to happen for the future. It was agreed all around that Suzanne should come back to Sixmile where we would all try to make the best of her presence among us once again.

"I think I should go down to Nikishka to help her with the baby," said Fedosya.

"You'd do that?" I said.

"She had it rough when she was carrying Lindsay, and I think she could really use an extra pair of hands. And while I'm there I can maybe work on her and soften her up to the idea of coming back."

"Would you take Semyon or leave him here?" said Yasha as he held his son on his knee. The lad was too small to know what was being discussed; he just grabbed Yasha's tea-spoon in his fist and waved it around like a magic wand. The thought of life with Suzanne was a burden, but the sight of my godson there at the table suddenly made me eager to see my own child and hold him on my knee at the table with my family. Quite unexpectedly, I looked forward to taking him to Point Possession where Belukha Pete could tell him the old *sukdu* stories, and to Mike and Klara's house where Klara could fuss over him like she once done to me. It brought a smile to my face, the thought of the light I would see in their eyes when they held their grand-nephew for the first time.

"He should be with me," said Fedosya. "If I leave him with you two, the only words he'll know when I get back will be filthy ones."

Yasha and I grinned at one another over the table. Three babies in Suzanne's tiny shack at Nikishka seemed like a real handful, but if Fedosya was game, then so was I.

"You should come down after trapping season," she said to me. "But before the ice goes out. That's when she'll be due. When the baby is strong enough to travel we can all come back here together in the dory."

"So it's agreed?" I said.

"Agreed," said Yasha.

Fedosya smiled and tickled Semyon's chin. "Agreed," she said.

———

We sent word down the Inlet to Suzanne, and a couple weeks later when the trail was in decent shape Yasha took Fedosya and Semyon down to Possession town in their freight sled. From there, Belukha Pete give them a ride to Nikishka. By then we'd acquired two teams of dogs, so while they was gone I started dragging in more firewood and breaking out the trapline trails with my team. When Yasha got back we boiled our traps and started laying out our lines.

The snow come down heavy in November that year. By December month we had nearly three foot on the ground. It was tough going on snowshoes—we had to break trail almost every single day. First we'd go out to make the trail, then we'd come back to pack it down, and then we'd turn around and go back a third time, bringing the dogs and sled behind us. This meant that we walked three miles to the dogs' every one.

The fur catch wasn't so good that year, but we had a pleasant time all the same. It was a return to our first days there at Sixmile without Fedosya to worry over us. We was baching again, smoking and using foul language at our pleasure. We had no news of Fedosya, Semyon and Suzanne, though this was not unusual. Neither of the girls could write, and Sixmile was a long way from the rest of the Peninsula's goings-on.

It was a late December evening just before Russian Christmas (as I recall, it came a week after American Christmas that year, right before the New Year) when we heard our dogs set up a howl, which told us someone was coming on the trail. We was just home from running the lines, and the last light was leaking out of the day. We'd brought in a cat and two mink, and I had set them by the stove to thaw while Yasha filled a lamp and got it lit. He stepped over to the window and peered out while I fed the stove, then we went outside to see who our visitor might be.

There come a call to our ears over the frozen stillness: "Hello the house!"

"Scotty Keogh!" said Yasha.

"What's he doing way up here this time of year?" I said.

Yasha shrugged.

There was a clear sky that evening with a full moon. The stars were just beginning to poke out for the night as Scotty and his dog team materialized from the gathering shadows. He set his snow hook and waved a greeting. His handshake was a tad wooden with me. We had not laid eyes on each other since the row at Kussilof.

"It's late for travelling, Scotty," Yasha said. "You have trouble on the trail?"

He'd been jogging behind his sled, and there was heavy frost collected on his otter fur hat and around the collar of the Yukon-style buckskin jacket that stopped at his waist. He brushed it away with his mitts and shook his head. "No, but I'm afraid I got some bad news. They got the whooping cough down at Nikishka."

"Whooping cough?" I said.

Scotty's face was grave. "They reckon it come in with a boatload of Hack's prospectors that showed up back in October."

"Fedosya and Semyon are down there," said Yasha.

Scotty opened his mouth to speak, then he looked at the snow. We watched as he pressed his lips together and looked back up. "Yasha, I hate to have to tell you this. They both got it. And they're not doing well."

"No," said Yasha.

"Father Ludinov told me, bud. His word's good as gold." Scotty shook off one of his mitts and went to lay a comforting hand on Yasha's shoulder. Yasha stepped away.

"It can't be," he said.

"I'm sorry."

Anyone who knows anything in this country knows that full-blood Natives are always the first to fall prey to sickness. It is as if the ground falls right out from under them. And for a Native, getting sick generally means a one-way ticket to the graveyard. I knew, as did Scotty, that it was entirely possible they were already dead, for it's a three-day dogsled run from Nikishka to Sixmile, and that's if you're really making tracks.

All the ill will between me and the Irishman was forgot in that moment, for both our hearts was broke for my partner. His domestic happiness was about to be torn asunder.

A light breeze blew through the treetops. Across the still silence there come the boom of the ice buckling and cracking from the tide out in the Arm. Scotty blew on his cold fingers. I could see he had more to say.

"What is it, Scotty?"

He stuffed his hands back into his mitts. "Suzanne is dead. The child inside her, too."

"My God," I said. It was all the words I could find.

"It's real bad," said Scotty. "It's already took most of the young kids. Plenty of strong healthy men and women, too. Ludinov put the whole town under quarantine."

I was getting cold, so I suggested we all go inside. Scotty give me no argument there, but Yasha didn't move. He just stared into the bleak evening forest.

"Come inside, Yasha," I said. When I laid a friendly hand between his shoulder blades his flesh was tight from the cold, and he was shivering.

He turned to face me. His eyes was numb. "Have we all got to get sick and die, AC? Is that how it is now?"

"I don't know. I really don't."

"I swear," he said. "I wonder if there will even be any more Indians left in another ten years."

I didn't know how to respond to that, so I just told him to come inside and get warm. He turned, and I followed him into the cabin where Scotty stood in the doorway, watching us from the rectangle of amber lamp-light.

———

It was the draught of icy air from the open door that told me Yasha was up and moving around. We was all bunking together in my cabin, with me and Scotty sleeping off a healthy round of booze on the floor by the wood stove. It was the wee hours of the morning. Moonlight streamed through the window. I opened my eyes in time to see Yasha close the door behind him. At first I figured he was just gone to answer the call of nature, but as the minutes dragged on and the dogs started yowling outside it dawned on me that something else was afoot.

I got up and stepped into my britches and slid on my moccasins. I pulled my sweater over my head. My head hurt, but I was well-seasoned to living with a hangover. When I stepped outside I seen Yasha's sled and his dogs harnessed up and waiting on the tug-line. My own dogs and Scotty's was jumping up and down on their chains and circling around their houses, wanting to go.

Yasha had a big tarp laid open in the basket of his sled and was loading gear into it. I reached the sled just in time to see him come up with a gunnysack full of dried fish.

"Where you off to?" I said.

"Where do you think?" He didn't look at me, but shouldered his way past, intent on his packing.

"Yasha, you can't go to Nikishka. It's under quarantine."

"I don't give a god damn about no quarantine," he said. "I got to see them."

"You know what's going to happen if you go there."

Yasha didn't respond. He tied up the mouth of his dog-feed sack with a length of copper wire and stuffed it down into a space between his sleeping robes and grub-box. He folded the tarp down and started lashing it in place with a moosehide line.

"Look at me, partner," I said.

He knotted the rope, then stopped and met my eyes.

"You go there, and you're liable to get sick, too. You know as well as I do that full-bloods always get sick first."

"You aint going to stop me, AC."

"Alright," I said, "then what if Fedosya and Semyon get better, but you get sick and die? You will have widowed your wife and orphaned your son because you wouldn't listen to reason."

"Fuck you," he said. He pushed past me and made for the steering board to pull the snow hook and tell the dogs to hike, but I launched myself at him and threw him to the ground.

"Yasha, you can't go there!" I was trying to push him down into the snow and hold him, but he slipped free and come up swinging at my nose. I ducked the punch but he caught me with another to the gut, and I fell assward into the snow.

He looked down at me. "Easy for you to tell me not to go there when it aint your woman and child!"

I picked myself up. A load of snow had found its way under the collar of my sweater and I shivered as it melted against my skin. Yasha was a hard puncher. I felt queasy and couldn't quite stand up straight.

"Don't you give me that shit!" I shouted. "I've already lost my old lady, and my child! You heard Scotty, they're both dead!"

"Suzanne wasn't your old lady, she was the mother of your bastard kid. You and I both know the thought of it aint ever been nothing but a burden to you!"

That made me see red. I lunged at him, and this time I belted him hard across the face. He went down and I sat a-straddle his chest to pin his arms to the ground, but he slipped an arm out from under me and squirmed away.

The crackling burst into my jaws as I grabbed the back of his parky and pulled him back down, but my wits had fled, and I could not be bothered with pushing it away. Yasha twisted around and drove his elbow into my face, then pushed himself on top of me. The crackling sparks grew harder and hotter until they was gushing out from my ears, down my neck and into my head. Yasha drew his fist back to deck me, but he stopped short. His eyes got wide as dinner-plates and his mouth dropped open. I seen my chance and smashed him across the chin, but I was horrified to see that it was not a fist I swung but a huge shaggy paw with long dark claws streaked with ivory.

Yasha ducked away and rolled off me, backing up across the hardpack. He almost stumbled over the sled, but righted himself as I roared with anger and frustration and crawled to a snowbank and buried my head to try to cool the sparking in my jaw. Our dogs and Scotty's team was all going berserk, barking and snapping and lunging at their tethers.

I willed myself back into human form. Behind me I heard Yasha screaming at his dogs to hike and lashing them with his whip. When I finally could look up all I seen was his backside disappearing down the trail in the moonlight.

The cabin door was flung open, and Scotty come running out bare-chested and barefoot in the snow. I looked down at my hand. Once again it was just skin and nails, no hair or claws to be seen. I rolled over onto my back and let my head drop against the hardpack as I stared up at the Big Dipper.

"AC, what the hell is going on?"

I tried to respond but had a hard time recovering my voice. I was scared that all I might find was a growl.

"AC?"

"Yasha's gone," I whispered.

"Gone?"

"To Nikishka."

Scotty cussed in American, and when he run out of vocabulary he switched to Irish and cussed some more. His dogs was still howling and barking, filling the night with their frustration.

"We got to go catch him," he said.

"Yeah."

He peered down at me, and for an instant I was seized with panic, thinking I might still be a bear after all. But when I examined myself once again there was only the form of a man with his clothes wet from melting snow.

— 264 —   KRIS FARMEN

Scotty hunkered down next to me. "You alright there?"

I nodded. Scotty stood up again and put out his hand. I gripped it and he pulled me to my feet, saying, "Let's get moving."

———

We took Scotty's dogs and sled. Yasha had a good two hour lead by the time we was loaded up and on the trail. The midday sunlight was painting the high slopes across the Arm when we came around the toe of the mountains at Tutsahtnu and found where his track split off from the trail to Possession town. He'd taken the little-used route from Chickaloon Bay up the river and overland to Nikishka via the headwaters of the Swanson. It was the route Scotty had used coming to our place, and the broken trail and Yasha's faster dogs gave him the advantage. We was still well behind him when we spotted weather moving in from the southwest. By noon it was snowing so thick we could barely see the trail. A couple hours later, as the gray evening grew dim, we had slowed to a crawl from new snow filling up Yasha's track. To make it worse, the wind came down from the mountains and blew the snow all around us into a white-out.

Scotty went ahead trying to feel out the trail with his snowshoes while I jogged behind the wheel dogs with my hand on the gee-pole to keep the sled upright and moving.

Scotty stopped and twisted around, looking back at me. I called the dogs to a stop.

"We're going to have to hole up," he shouted over the weather. "We can't keep going in this shit."

"We'll never catch him if we stop!" I called back.

"AC, I can't see the fucking trail to break it out!" The fringes on his jacket was standing straight out in the wind, and he had his dark goggles on against the blowing snow. I had snow piled up on the shoulders of my sailcloth parky, and both of us had our fur hats lashed down by the chin-ties.

"Fuck!" I screamed at the wind. "Son of a bitch!"

Scotty tramped his way back to the stern of the sled. "Look, Yasha won't be able to move in this shit neither. We'll wait for it to blow over, and then we'll get moving again."

"He won't stop," I said. "You know he won't. He'll just keep moving until he gets to Nikishka. Or until he freezes to death on the trail, whichever comes first."

"Well we aint going to help things none by getting ourselves froze to death! Come on, AC. Use your head."

"Fuck!" I said again, but I knew Scotty was right.

We was out in a wide-open flat with nary a tree in sight, so we tied the sled off to the biggest willow-bush we could find and left the dogs in harness. We tossed them each a dried salmon, which they gulped down before turning themselves around and bedding down with their shaggy tails over their noses. Using our snowshoes we shoveled up a mound of snow as tall as a man, then hollowed out the inside and spread a tarp with our sleeping robes over it. We had no fire save the stub of a candle. That plus our body heat kept the small space tolerably warm. Inside there was no trace of the wind that howled outside. It was quiet as a womb.

When we was settled in I blew out the candle, but neither of us could sleep. Scotty tossed and turned within his robes and eventually stayed still, but I could hear from his breath that he was still awake.

"Scotty," I said.

A heartbeat of silence. "Yes?"

"What was you doing up at Nikishka? I mean, this time of year?"

More silence. I had begun to think he wasn't going to respond, but then he said, "I come up to see Suzanne."

Now it was my turn to be silent.

"AC?"

"What business did you have with her?" I said.

"I reckon you know."

"I reckon I don't."

"I went to do the right thing. But I found her dead and Lindsay in the care of the neighbors."

We stared at the ceiling for a while. Then Scotty said, "Look, when they turn him away because of the quarantine he'll probably just come on back."

"Maybe," I said.

"You don't believe it."

"He knows how to sneak around. If he wants to see his woman and child, then he will."

We said nothing more that night.

That storm kept us pinned down for most of two days, which believe me is a long time for two men to spend together in such a tiny space. When we finally got moving again there was two foot of new snow over the trail, which made it hard going. It took us two more days to travel a distance that should have taken a half-day. Then we run out of dog feed—we had not foreseen that we would be on the road so long and had packed for speed above all else. By this point it was rapidly becoming obvious that we was not going to catch up to Yasha.

We cursed all of God's creation as we turned the team around and started back. We hardly spoke during the time it took us to return to Sixmile. Frankly, I expected to never see Yasha again, and I spent the days and nights trying to prepare my mind for the news that he had died of the whooping cough. This was just as difficult as it sounds.

Back at Sixmile my tethered dogs had not eaten in several days. They was curled up on the hardpack and barely stirred when we drove in. I fed them up, letting them recover strength while I stayed more or less drunk for a couple days. Scotty took his leave, and I went back to the trapline, but I was so encumbered with melancholy that it frequently took me three days to run a one-day line. More than once I found myself standing along the trail and staring at the snow upon the spruce boughs with no recollection of stopping or of how long I had been there. When I made camp I would linger over my fire, lost in my thoughts, drinking cup after cup of tea. I took to bringing a bottle with me to the woods, something I had always made a rule of not doing. At first I put just a splash into my tea, but only during the evenings. Then I started doctoring my tea at midday, and whenever I stopped to boil a quick kettle along the trail.

By the start of Lent, every single cup of tea I drank was spiked. More often than not, I was drinking equal parts booze and tea. This of course made me clumsy on the trail, but I had ceased to care about such things. The woods had become empty to me, and the birds refused to speak. The light feeling the booze give me was the only thing that made my days bearable. More than once, when I was way out in the bush with no one to hear me, I contemplated putting my Sharps rifle under my chin and pulling the trigger. Just to relieve myself of the pain and sorrow. No more worrying about my affliction and whether or not that was what had caused Yasha to abandon me.

Truth be known, I did put the muzzle under my chin once. It was a dark moonless night with the rare sight of the aurora overhead. The ring of steel was icy against my skin, and I sat for a while with my thumb on the trigger guard, looking down at the battered stock and the firelight that glinted on the barrel. I have no idea how long I sat like that. In the end, I think the only thing that kept me from going through with it was the thoughts and memories of Lucky Jim that was connected with that gun. He had bought it on the sly from an illegal Yankee trader on Prince William's Sound, paying a stack of marten skins as tall as the muzzle. The selfsame muzzle that rested under my chin.

Also, there was the notion that if I offed myself I would never get to have another drink. You may take that as a mark of just how low I had sunk.

So I didn't do it.

Hardest to bear was that because of the quarantine I had no way to know what had become of my family. No news was coming in or going out. Anyone who has been through such a trial will know about this firsthand. Then finally word come over the trails that Fedosya and Semyon had both succumbed to the whooping cough. This piled grief upon grief. All my dreams of a son of my own, and my godson Semyon, and me and Yasha teaching them how to hunt and trap and build boats was gone, swept away like a leaf upon the current of a stream, and I was left to carry on all alone.

Of Yasha I had no word until the spring, just after Russian Easter when Belukha Pete come out to Sixmile for a couple days.

"Yasha's gone," he said as we sat at my table. His hair was gray at the temples, and the lines in his face had deepened.

"Gone?" I thought he meant that Yasha, too, had died of the whoop, but this turned out not to be the case.

"He went down to the coal station at Kachemak Bay," said Pete. "There was a whale-ship that had called in there."

"What do you mean?"

"He signed on."

"You mean he's gone to sea?"

Pete nodded. "They was bound for the Beaufort whale-grounds."

I did not know what to make of this, other than it calling to mind Melville's *Moby-Dick*, a book I had tossed into the kindling bin because it kept putting me to sleep. My partner was not dead, but he was gone nonetheless, and the last words I had said to him was spoken in anger.

"Did he get sick?" I asked.

Pete wasn't sure. He'd heard a couple different stories, none of which agreed with one another.

For three nights after he left I had the same dream: Yasha was drowning in the Inlet, and I come floating up to him on a pan of river ice. Seeing him in distress, I crawled to the edge of the ice and yelled out for him to grab my hand. In every single dreaming, Yasha looked up at me and said, "Let me go, AC. Since you only care about yourself. Go get drunk."

Those words exactly. Then a salmon shark come up and dragged him under, and when I looked down the ice pan was no longer ice but a giant halibut with eyes that I recognized straightaway.

"Opal!" I would say. Her two eyes would roll around to look into me. Then she would dive down with me holding onto her gill-plate. She took me to the bottom of the sea where I could only lie flat on the gravel and kelp, not knowing what was to become of me. It was cold down there. Very cold.

But I always woke up sweating.

———

Normally spring is the sunshine season, but the spring of 1889 came wet and rainy. The weather did not help my mood none as I pulled into Kenay town, alone in what was now my dory. It was a lonely voyage without my family. It was too quiet in the beach camps along the way without Fedosya bustling about and Semyon making noise and playing games while me and Yasha smoked by the fire, keeping him entertained so his mother could fix supper.

Now it was just me, and the loneliness was a test that I was gradually failing. Often I wouldn't even bother to cook a meal—I just went hungry because the sight of a cheery campfire made me think of all the happiness I had lost. I drank my supper. Sometimes I took a little dried meat. I slept very little.

On the way I called in at Nikishka to pay my respects to the graves of Fedosya, Semyon and Suzanne. They was not the only fresh graves in the cemetery. Father Ludinov was still there; he had not been back to Kenay town since the sickness started. He told me they'd had three funerals every Friday since the ground had thawed enough to permit the digging of graves. Orthodox funeral rites are extensive, and he told me three burials per week was all he could handle without breaking his sanity.

He had on a passive face as he told me this, but I could see it had been a very difficult winter for him. I've never been as devout as my mother or Klara would have liked, or Father Ludinov for that matter, but my heart went out to the man. The previous fall there had been fifty-seven souls living at Nikishka. That spring there was only twenty-nine left above ground. Half the town was gone. Only three children under the age of ten had survived the sickness.

Father Ludinov had the look of a man who has not smiled in a very long time, but then I saw very few smiles in Nikishka that spring.

Fedosya and Semyon was buried next to each other in the tiny graveyard out back of the chapel-house. It drizzled rain as I stood at their graves for most of the afternoon, studying the three-pronged crosses that marked their final resting place. I tried to work up the fortitude to gather materials to build them a grave-house, this being the custom among the Kenaytze people, but fortitude was in short supply. Of course they had been Methodists, but I was told Fedosya had re-taken the Orthodox sacraments just before she died and had Semyon do the same.

After a while I went and found Suzanne's plot in a small clearing at the edge of town where a handful of Lutherans and people of other denominations was buried. Her wooden head-board was rounded at the top and bright with fresh white paint. I felt numb all over. Though she'd been carrying our child I could not help but feel that I'd dodged a bullet, and I hated myself for that. I know that when I die I will have to stand before God and explain that to Him, and I do not relish the prospect.

I heard someone coming behind me and turned to see Scotty walking up the trail. He looked wet and miserable, like he'd been out in the rain as long as I had. A half-drained bottle of whisky hung in his hand.

"Hello, Scotty," I said.

"Howdy, AC."

He shifted the bottle and put out his hand. "No hard feelings?"

"About Kussilof?"

"Yeah."

I couldn't find my voice, so I just nodded. I gripped his hand and we shook. "No hard feelings."

"Want a drink?"

"Shit, why not."

Drinking in a graveyard might just be bad form at its very worst, but me and Scotty was both past caring about such things. He handed me the bottle, and I took out the cork and lifted it to my lips. The warmth of the liquor spread down through me. It was top-dollar stuff. I took a second pull and handed the bottle back to him.

Scotty stared down at Suzanne's wooden headboard.
It read:

Suzanne Belle McCoy
AND CHILD
B. 1870
D. 1889
BELOVED MEMORY

"Who put it up?" I said.

"I did."

Scotty made the sign of the cross over his chest, and I wondered if being Catholic was what had drawn them together. This, however, was not my business, so I didn't ask.

"I heard she was talking about moving back to Sixmile," Scotty said.

"She was expecting our child."

Scotty shook his head. "Poor gal."

"You wasn't much of a help to her, Scotty."

For a moment I thought he might get mad, but then I seen he was as somber as me.

"I know," he said. "But that don't mean I didn't love her."

I looked over at him and him at me.

"I did love her you know, AC. I know it now more than ever." His voice hitched a little as he said this.

We took another drink and watched Suzanne's headboard. The rain drummed on our hat-brims. God help me, I started thinking that I was once again free to dream of Polly.

"So you heard about Yasha," Scotty said.

"Yeah."

"I seen him at Kussilof when he passed through on his way to Kachemak Bay."

"He have anything to say?"

"I asked him where you was. He said you didn't care enough to come see Suzanne's—"

Scotty's voice cut off. He couldn't bring himself to say the word GRAVE.

"We tried to stop him," I said.

Scotty lifted the bottle again to his mouth. "I know it, bud. It's God's own grace he didn't get sick."

"He didn't?"

He passed me the bottle. "He was healthy as a horse when I seen him. But he was drunk off his ass. First time I'd seen him that way since him and Fedosya got hitched.

"He was drinking?"

Scotty nodded. "He said he was going to see if he could fall off the edge of the world and join Fedosya and Semyon. Said he was going to find a place where God couldn't find him."

I didn't know what to say to that, so I just took a drink.

"He also said something odd about you."

"Oh?"

"He said you turned yourself into a bear. Some kind of hocus pocus magic. That last night when you two were punching it up."

My pulse pounded inside my ears. "He was loaded. He must have just been talking crazy."

Scotty tipped the bottle to his lips, keeping his eyes on me. "Must have been."

The whiskey sloshed inside the bottle as he handed it back to me. "He sounded like a completely different person, not the Yasha I knew."

I took a drink and wiped my mouth on my jacket sleeve. "Loss changes you, I guess. Drink, too."

"It does."

"Don't spread that around about him," I said.

"What?"

"That he was drunk and talking crazy. Folks don't need to know that."

"I wasn't the only person in the room, AC."

I looked over at him.

"Don't worry. Hell, it wasn't like anyone believed him." Scotty shuffled his feet upon the previous summer's dead grass. We listened to the rain for a while.

"So I come to take Lindsay to the new Catholic mission school in Sitka," he said.

"She's your daughter then?"

"Yeah, she's my daughter. Lindsay Elizabeth Keogh."

"That's good of you, Scotty."

"Fatherhood," he said.

"I was almost there."

He looked over at me, and I passed him the bottle.

———

Scotty and baby Lindsay sailed for Kodiak town in his dory the next day. They were bound on a steamship across the Gulf of Alaska to the capital where he had a job lined up guiding wealthy sport hunters from the States. Europe too, he told me. He said he was leaving Kussilof Lake and Cook Inlet so his daughter could have a proper education in a school with painted walls, not just a few years in the dingy Kenay school.

I pushed him off from the beach with the morning tide. He stood at the tiller with Lindsay in his arms and waved back at me. Then he lifted his daughter's tiny hand and gently waved it in the air. I could see him smiling over the distance as I raised my own hand in farewell. There was a pang of jealousy knowing that, unlike me, Scotty had not lost all. He still had something to live for.

I was in low spirits when I made it to Kenay town. Scotty had informed me that the fur market was down again that year, owing to what he called a FINANCIAL PANIC in the States. I asked him what that was, and while he seemed to understand the concept he was hard-pressed to put it into words. He said when he'd started downriver from Kussilof Lake he reckoned he'd taken about five hundred dollars in fur. But when he got to Kenay, Mailman Mike could only offer him one-fifty.

"Don't make no plans for a pleasure cruise to the capitals of Europe," Scotty told me.

Mike was behind the counter when I hauled in my catch and laid it across the fur counter. He smiled and raised a hand, but he was busy helping another customer, some white-haired American gent I'd not seen before. He appeared to be going over a long list of supplies with Mike. I wandered around to the gun rack and examined the Winchester repeaters. There was a card tacked to the rack that labeled the new Model 1886 in .45-70 government caliber. I had it in mind to retire Lucky Jim's old Sharps rifle, not the least because the sight of it reminded me too much of that awful night by the campfire when I'd almost made my very last shot.

I drifted over to the optics case and studied the binoculars. There was a pair I'd had my eye on for several years; they was made in Switzerland and cost twenty dollars. You will recall I had coveted this item since that day above Skilak Lake when me and Yasha run into Big Nick and Scotty and the boys, but I never had been able to afford them. I had high hopes that this year would be different.

The white-haired man finished his accounting and shook hands with Mike. He nodded at me as he exited, and Mike come over to the fur counter. I had ten red fox and three silver, twenty-seven marten, fifty beavers, two wolves and eighty-seven rats. I'd got no cats that year; they had declined in number since the rabbit population crashed back in eighty-seven. I also had four black bear hides and one grizzly bear to sell.

Me and Mike visited as he sorted through the pile, grading each pelt in turn. He said fur prices was the lowest he'd ever seen. I leaned over the counter and pulled a fresh tin of Prince Albert from the shelves, making sure Mike seen it so he could tally it with my bill.

"Who's that white-haired fellow?" I said while charging my pipe. When I was a boy there was so few Americans on Cook Inlet that I knew them all on a first name basis. Now it seemed there was more and more of them coming into the country every year.

"His name's Alex King," said Mike as he shook out a marten pelt to grade it. "He's a prospector who just got a grubstake from Hack."

I struck a stick of timber and lit my pipe. "Another one?"

"You hear that Hack's planning to set up a new placer operation at Nikishka?"

I recalled Suzanne saying something about it, and I said as much.

"Should be work available there for any man that wants it," said Mike.

"I reckon I can do better than working for that Hack."

"You might want to wait and hear your total before you make that call."

"How do you mean?"

"Hold on," said Mike. He licked the tip of his pencil and totted the sums on a tablet. I watched as he made his final total and checked his math. He looked up at me with an apologetic frown.

"What's my tally?" I said.

"Ninety-seven dollars."

"Ninety-seven dollars? Mike, you got to be kidding me."

He shook his head. "Ninety-seven bucks. Sorry AC. Like I told you, it's a lousy fur market this year. I know you're reliable, so I'll extend you credit if you need it."

I had no desire to be in debt to the AC Company, particularly when the man in charge was my kin. Red ink has been the ruin of many a trapper. Still, what other option did I have? I'd come down from Sixmile with my heart set on a repeating rifle and a pair of binoculars, but now it looked like I'd be lucky to get a fresh pair of longjohns out of the deal.

"Let me think about it," I said.

"You staying at the house?"

"Figured I would. I'll go haul up my gear and say hello to Klara. Then I'll let you know about credit."

"If you won't work for Hack, the canneries are hiring men for the China gang. You might go talk to them."

"We'll see," I said.

Out the door and on the porch I seen Russian Mike, Swedish Mike, and Mike the Finn had begun the summer's game of dominoes. I looked across the river mouth toward the cannery but decided to leave that conversation for later. I turned along Front Street which was now being called Mission Street, then walked down to the beach and watched the women working at their fish racks. Iriana Golinov had a moosehide stretched up on a framework of poles for tanning, and was scraping it with her niece and daughter. Kids ran about, chasing each other with fireweed whips until their mothers and aunts yelled them back into line and put them to work.

The news that Hack was planning to set up shop at Nikishka weighed heavy on my mind. I kept picturing Suzanne that last night we was together in her cabin when she told me he'd been sniffing around.

I cupped the weight of my cartridge bag where it hung at my right side. It was still much heavier than it needed to be after all these years—I'd not once removed the gold nugget I found that day with Suzanne at Sixmile. Watching the children, I came to a decision.

The nugget made a dull thump when I laid it on Mike's counter. Both his and Hewitt's eyes lit up like a sunrise.

"Holy cow," Hewitt said, crossing the empty store for a better look.

Mike picked up the nugget and hefted it. "Jesus, AC. Where do you keep finding this stuff?"

"Secret Indian place."

"I recall you said the same thing back in eighty-five."

"I might have."

Mike stepped over to the troy scales and laid it in the tray. It dropped and he added ballast to the opposite side. I turned my back as he weighed me up. This is only the polite thing to do. I had no cause to accuse my uncle of sticky fingers.

"Well," said Mike, "that nugget weighs in at thirty-two ounces and nine grains."

"What's that in dollars?"

"Just a minute." His pencil scratched as he scribbled on his tablet. I tried to ignore the unpleasant feeling of a thorn in the side of my soul. I was breaking my oath to Lucky Jim for a second time, but then what else had I to lose? Maybe it was time to return to the placer-mining trade.

Mike cleared his throat. "You got six hundred eighty-one dollars and forty-five cents."

"That's more like it," I said.

In truth, it was a fantastic sum. I handed over my list of supplies. Then I went and examined my brand new binoculars and repeating Winchester.

———

I made it home to Sixmile by the third week of May month. The early kings was just coming into the creek, but I didn't stay long. The whole place was suddenly too quiet for me to handle. I stood in the doorway with my morning tea and vodka, staring at Yasha and Fedosya's empty house. I'd left my dogs at Possession town in the care of some friends, and the valley seemed strange without the noise they made. The birds was returned, and the air was filled with song, but I could find no joy in it. I suddenly wished for nothing so much as to be away from that place. The sunshine on the rocky poplar slopes of the far side of the Arm beckoned me.

I loaded up the dory that same day and rowed for Kiskabetnu Creek where I made camp in the usual spot next to the cataract. The sound of the rushing water was good for me. It seemed to block out all the ill thoughts that plagued my soul.

The day after my arrival I climbed up the rocky crags above my camp and studied the hillside through my new glasses, looking for a sheep. I found a band of rams down near tidewater, cropping fresh spring grass. I studied them and the country between us with a smile of satisfaction—the glasses made all the difference in planning a stalk. I slipped through the cottonwoods and poplars, then crawled across an ancient landslide piled with boulders as big as a cabin until I was within fifty yards of them. I took aim and fired, dropping one ram as he stood looking in my direction, then the second as he bolted for the ridge beyond.

The weather was fine, and I took a couple days to dry and smoke the meat. All the while I dined on the choice cuts until I was fit to burst. I had ordered several books from the AC store, and during this time I had my nose buried in Mark Twain's *Adventures of Tom Sawyer*, whom I was pleased to recognize from the last chapters of *Huckleberry Finn*. I had not done much reading in the previous months, and it made me feel somewhat normal again to be carried away by a book. When the meat was cured I built a platform up in some spruce trees and cached it in a canvas sack.

Somewhere during these days it occurred to me that I had not thought of the weight in my heart for a couple of hours. Then a few days later, I realized that I had gone a whole day without dwelling on it. I was learning how to smile once again, but my mind was still fragile and it was a slow process.

I stayed at Kiskabetnu for several more days, climbing high on the slopes and dozing in the sunshine. When I wasn't napping I glassed the country looking for a spring bear. I was ignoring my fishing, and the belukha hunt, but a man does need a holiday every once and again, and I do believe I had it coming. I'd brought no booze with me on this trip. It was the longest I could remember going without a drink in many a year. Being sober for more than a week give me some perspective on what I had been doing with my life. I was pleasantly surprised at how nice it was to wake up in the morning without a hangover, and there was the thought that maybe the light and loose sensation I got from drinking might not be worth that burden alone. From time to time I pondered the possibility of leaving Sixmile and maybe building a cabin somewhere there on the north side of Turnagain Arm. Or maybe moving down to Kussilof Lake near Big Nick, though I knew that was likely to kick my drinking habit back into full-swing.

Then one afternoon as I was just waking up from a nap and thinking of starting down the mountain to my camp, I spied a row-boat coming around the point, headed up the Arm. There was stiff east wind coming down from the portage, and the sunlight glinted off the whitecaps. The boat was bucking the weather, and though it had the tide behind it, the incoming current made the water quite rough.

That east wind is notorious on Turnagain Arm. It blows hard enough to peel the scalp from your skull. The poplars and scrubby trees on the exposed hillside was bent over nearly double from its force, and it pasted the shirt to my skin as I climbed to a better lookout. I trained my glasses on the boat, but I was too far away to see much detail. I could make out that it was one man with a pile of gear. He looked like an American, but I couldn't be sure at such a distance. Whoever he was, he knew how to handle a boat. He rowed standing up, with short strokes, bending his knees for power on the oars.

A seasoned boatman he may have been, but he didn't know Turnagain Arm. It is by far the most treacherous stretch of water in Alaska. As I watched, he come hard aground on a mud bank. I was sure he was a goner, for that mud is slippery as fish guts and sticks to a boat bottom like shit to a blanket. The man climbed over the side to try and shove himself free but quickly figured out this was not a smart move—he almost lost his boots in the muck jumping back in. Waves was breaking hard over the gunwales, splashing all over him. I feared I was going to have to try and row out to him and lend a hand, but before long the tide rose enough to unstick him, and he continued eastward into the wind.

I watched him with great interest as he put into the mouth of Tutsilitnu Creek. I lowered my glasses and rubbed the stubble on my jaw, cogitating for several minutes amid the rattle of the poplar leaves. I had no idea who this was, but down in the pit of my gut was an unpleasant feeling that I could not escape. Muscle Sam's prophesy from all those years ago, something I thought I had managed to outrun, flashed once more across my mind. I had forgot the most important part of what he said: the Boston Men would come and turn the streams of my country inside out.

The man in the boat turned out to be none other than Alex King, the codger from the AC store. I rowed across just before high tide and landed next to his boat. Up the beach and through the grass he had set up a wall tent in the cottonwoods, right next to the selfsame fire ring where me and Lucky Jim had camped more than ten years before when I found the yellow pebble. Most of his stuff was still packed away.

I called out in American, but no-one answered so I walked up the creek. I spied him just as the forest changed to birch and spruce. He was bent over a gold pan in a riffle of the stream in a pair of rubber hip boots. I called out again, and his head come up sharp. I seen his eyes as he recognized me.

He splashed to the shore, and I put out my hand. "You're Alex King."

"I am," he said. "And you'd be Alex Campbell, Mike Morgan's nephew."

"Folks call me AC," I said. "I live up on the Sixmile."

King must have been about fifty. His movements were those of an old man with aches and pains. His watery blue eyes followed my every move. I asked him his business even though it was obvious enough. I wanted to hear how he reacted.

"Prospecting," he said. "I hear you delivered a big thirty ounce nugget to Mike."

"Who told you that?"

"Greg Hackham."

"You shouldn't believe everything you hear. There aint no gold in this creek."

"He said you'd be cagey about it," said King. "He told me you and your partner threatened him."

"That a fact?" My holiday mood was rapidly fading.

"He said you told him not to show his face on this side of Turnagain Arm."

You will recall it was Yasha who said that, not me, but it made little difference standing there next to the creek.

"That was a long time ago," I said. "But my guess is that Hack sent you because he aint got the balls to come up here himself."

King leveled his eyes at me. "You can think of it whatever you like, young feller. He staked me and said that if I followed you I was likely to find some color."

My blood was coming up. Of course I knew there was color to be found in Tutsilitnu Creek, and once King found it that would be all she wrote.

"Prospectors aint welcome here," I said. There was the crackling in my jaw, and I knew it would be harder to control with no booze in me.

He snorted and looked at me like I was some foolish boy. "You don't own this creek, son. This is my placer claim under the mining laws of the United States. So you just keep your halfbreed ass off it, you hear?"

I took a step toward him. "This is my country, not yours. I come to this creek when I was eight year old, and I'll come and go as it suits me. You don't like that, I got a hundred people down at Point Possession who'll back me up."

"You mind your manners now, Campbell," said King. "And you tell them Nates down there at Possession to do the same. I get any guff from you, I might just have to send word down to Hack and have him bring up a load of special blankets for your people. As a token of his good will."

"What the hell are you talking about?"

He favored me with a greasy smile. "You don't think that whooping cough last winter in Nikishka was an accident, do you? Them ice niggers thought they'd keep Hack out of their creeks, so he had them blankets shipped in special from St. Michael where they had the whoop back in eighty-six."

This brought me up short, and King chuckled most heartily. The crackling and sparking in my jaw was nearly as distressing as his speech. We was both unarmed, and for a moment I seriously considered getting my rifle and bushwhacking him right there. It wouldn't have taken much to make sure his carcass was never found. But murder is not in me, and I managed to keep my wits collected. It was clear to me that I had to go to the source of this poison spring, to kill the snake by cutting off its head.

King watched me as I backed into the woods. I took a well-concealed route through the trees back to the landing but as I passed his empty camp I spied something inside the open flap of his wall tent. A bottle of scotch whisky, standing atop his grub chest next to a tin cup. Two fingers' worth had been drunk. Evidently he had toasted his success at not drowning in the Arm.

I looked around, then snatched up the bottle as payment for what was about to happen to my home. It turned out to be not much of a trade, but the sparks beneath my ears faded away by the second swallow.

———

I was back on the water with the ebb tide, bound for Kenay town and Greg Hackham's office. It was a fast trip down Turnagain Arm with both the tide and the wind behind me, though I had to stay lively on the tiller to keep from being pushed aground. Down below Point Possession the east wind from the Arm disappeared, and I picked up a good north breeze that filled my sail overnight all the way down to Kenay.

I recall that it was a Tuesday morning when I fetched up at the beach landing. Folks was surprised to see me back in town. They paused at their fish-cutting to ask me what had happened, but I walked right past them, straight up toward town and Hack's office. I could see the roof-line behind the edge of the bluff. The empty bottle lay on its side in the bow where I'd pitched it.

The fine weather was still with us, and Hack's secretary—a man named Chalmers—had the door and windows open. I strode in over the jamb and planted my palms on his desk.

"Where's Hack at?" I said.

Chalmers tilted his head back and sighted down his nose at me. "What do you want?"

"That don't concern you. Where the hell is he?"

"He's out."

I glanced over at Hack's inner office where his door stood open. He was indeed not in.

"Out where?"

"That doesn't concern you, Campbell."

"Oh," I said reaching for his collar, "aint you just the clever one."

He pushed his chair back so that my hands just missed him. He stood up sharp and pointed at the door. "I suggest you leave immediately."

Footsteps crunched on the gravel outside. I looked out through the door and there was Hack, coming up the street. He wore an expensive suit of English tailoring and carried a bundle of rolled-up schematics under one arm. He stopped in his tracks when I come out and stood on the porch-boards.

"Hackham!" I said.

"Alex Campbell," he replied in a voice that dripped with false cheer. "What can I do for you?"

"You got a placer miner working up at Tutsilitnu."

His brows drew together. "Where now?"

"Resurrection Creek, god damn you!" I shouted. "Whatever the hell you Boston Men are calling it now. Next door to Sixmile."

"Oh, you mean Alex King. What of it?"

"He tells me you sent hospital blankets from St. Michael to Nikishka to give them all the whooping cough. Because they wouldn't let you onto their creeks."

Hack hooked a little smile at me, but he owned the demeanor of a serpent. "Oh that," he said. "Come to think of it, I did get those blankets from St. Michael."

I stabbed a finger at his face. "My family died there at Nikishka! Close to thirty people died because of what you done!"

He shrugged as if this was some trifling objection. "They were standing in the way of progress, Campbell. The gold is out there to be found, and I'm here to find it. These resources were put here to be used."

My heated words had not gone unnoticed. A crowd of passers-by had started to gather around us, Americans, Creoles and Indians, all hovering in a loose ring.

I got into his face. "Damn you Hack, you son of a bitch. You stole Polly from me all them years back, and now you murdered my family. By God, you set up shop on Turnagain Arm, and I'll make you pay dearly for it!"

He smirked at me. "Is that what this is all about? Polly? Jesus Christ, Campbell. Why do you always have to be such a fucking child?"

I took one step back and traced a line in the dirt with the toe of my moccasin. I cocked my fists for action. "You just step across that line if you care to find out what kind of child I am."

He studied me for a moment, then he moved past me onto the porch. The crowd moved to make way for him. I thought maybe he wasn't man enough for a fight, which pissed me off even more—I was going to have satisfaction, one way or another. But instead he stood his drawings carefully up against the window trim. He turned to face me and peeled off his jacket, then took off his hat and laid them both over the small bench out front where he liked to take his coffee in the mornings. He removed his tie and loosened his collar, then pulled his cuff-links and slipped them into his jacket pocket.

He turned up his sleeves as he come back to the scratch-line. He raised his fists with the broad-legged stance of a prize-fighter.

"You fucking pansy," I said, "you squat to piss." Then Hack crossed the line, swinging a hook at my jaw. I found out later that he had been the vice-president of the Columbia University Pugilistics Society, which is a fancy name for a boxing club. He was game, I'll give him that, and he knew how to fight. But he wasn't up to the job. He shuffled papers at a desk all day, and I worked in the woods.

I wasn't quite fast enough to get out of the way, and his hook clipped my jaw. He come in close and landed a hard right to my stomach which almost took the wind out of me. I pushed him back, slapping aside another punch as I slammed a fist into the tender spot above his gut. I bashed two hooks into his jaw, and I heard a crack on the second blow. He screamed, but I paid it no mind. I caught him with an uppercut that smashed his broken jaw back together, and then I jammed him hard in the gut.

The crowd was screaming and shouting by now, with the Americans yelling at Hack to shake it off and kick my ass. He staggered back with one hand holding his jaw, and the other held out at me to stop. I give him no quarter. I laid two more punches into his kidneys. Then I clocked him hard across the face, and he hit the dirt.

Booze might make it easier to push away the sparking in my jaw when it comes, but it doesn't by any means give me total mastery over it. I should have let things go then and there, but the bear inside my skin was roaring. I could actually hear him in my head, though this may have been the crowd. A spark shot out from beneath my left ear like a bullet, then another from the right. In the space of a second it had become an explosion. I clamped my teeth down against it as I got down on top of Hack. He struggled, trying to get out from under me, but I got a knee down over one of his arms and then the other. I grabbed a handful of his hair with my left hand and started bashing his face with my right, blow after blow after blow. I broke his nose, and then I smashed it to bits. Then I went to work on his pretty mouth. At first he tried to scramble away, but he got weaker and weaker with each hit.

I am not proud of this, mind you.

By now the crowd was silent and looking anxiously at one another. Sava Golinov and Russian Mike pushed their way through the mob and tried to pull me off. I fought them away, screaming at the top of my lungs, cursing first in Russian then in American, saying, "GOD DAMN YOU HACKHAM! GOD DAMN YOU, YOU FUCKING MURDERER!" Spit flew from my mouth, I was in such a rage. More men piled onto me, dragging me away. I flailed at them like a cornered animal as the crackling and sparking started to take over, shooting all through me. I only stopped struggling from the need to get control over myself. After the incident at Sixmile I had enough sense to know that no good would come of me changing into a bear on the streets of Kenay town.

I heard a woman cry out. It was Polly, screaming, "Oh my Lord! Greg!"

She sprinted up, holding her skirts. Then she was down on her knees before him, caressing him and holding him close with her golden curls spilling all around his bloody and broken face. It was more than I could stand to see. Men was running to and fro. Kids was suddenly crying. There was my aunt Klara staring at me with a hand clapped over her mouth in horror at what I'd done. Sava was yelling something at me, pointing at Hack and Polly, but the crackling sparking popping in my head had got so bad, and I was fighting so hard to stamp it down that I could not hear what he said.

I turned away and stumbled toward the bluff trail, cradling my right hand against me. A roaring pain had begun to build in it so bad that my stomach turned, and I thought I might faint. I heard Polly running up behind me, and I turned to see her just as she smashed against me and shoved me so hard I almost lost my feet.

She flailed her fists at me, screaming, "Fuck you AC! God damn you to hell!"

I'd never seen her like that. I tried to look at her, but I couldn't. Swedish Mike and Mailman Mike ran up and pulled her away, but not before she'd landed a hard stinging slap across my chops. Wailing and crying, she fell into a heap next to Hack.

Sava knelt down and examined him. His face was pulped, and there was the chilling thought that I might actually have beaten him to death. It was plain that people in the crowd had this same thought. They whispered to one another in hushed tones as Sava held his ear above what was left of Hack's nose and mouth. Several agonizing seconds ticked by as he waited, and I could feel disgust building among the onlookers who only moments before had been cheering us on.

Sava looked up. "He's breathing!"

Hack let out a moan and inched one of his legs to the side.

"Don't try to move," Sava said.

Several of the men rolled Hack gingerly onto a tarp and carried him into Sava's house. I stood alone, watching them. I seen young Max staring at me, but there was no malice in his gaze. He seemed merely puzzled as to why this had happened. I tried to smile at him, but it felt wrong. Then Polly come back to collect him, and when she seen me she spat at me. She swept her son up into her arms and hustled back up the street toward Sava's.

I staggered down the beach and plunged my aching hand into the Inlet. I sank to my knees in the lapping waves, breathing long and slow. Then I lowered my head into the water to hide my grief and shame as the sparks finally, thankfully, faded from my body.

*

*C*ampbell slowly reloads his pipe as Miss Ashford watches with a hand over her mouth in shock.

"Was he alright?" she says through her fingers.

"Eventually. His jaw was a bit crooked after that. And his nose was pretty well flattened out. But he lived."

"Why in heaven's name would you do such a thing?"

He tamps the fresh tobacco down with his index finger then digs the box of matches from his waistcoat pocket. Lucky Jim's words from so long ago fill his mind, the warning that his life was bound to be difficult because of the bear that lives inside his skin.

Methodically, with the ritual of habit, he strikes the match and raises it to the bowl, puffing the stem so that the flame is pulled down in rhythmic pulses as the smoke rises around him.

"Mr. Campbell?"

"I don't know why," he says. This is a lie, and he knows it.

"You don't know," says Miss Ashford.

"That's what I said."

"But he sent those infected blankets to Nikishka."

"He did."

Campbell smokes in silence, staring out the tiny window at the flaming crimson of the dying fireweed. Miss Ashford watches him for a few moments, thinking about how his grandfather told him never to speak of the bear. How the source of whatever power he had in life would disappear if he did so. It dawns upon her that it must be one of the greater burdens upon his soul that he has never been very good at living up to his grandfather's advice.

"What is it your grandfather said to you?" she asks.

It takes Campbell a moment to respond. "When?"

"What he said to you when you first changed into a bear."

"True beauty needs no words to describe it."

"Yes."

"You're beautiful," says Campbell.

Miss Ashford feels herself flush, unable to stop it this time. She studies her shoes. Her ship back to the States is scheduled to sail on Friday, the same day as Campbell's execution. She lifts her

KRIS FARMEN

briefcase onto her lap and digs through it, looking for her pencil sharpener even though her pencil does not really need sharpening.

"He killed my family," says Campbell.

She looks up. "Pardon?"

"Greg Hackham killed thirty people in cold blood. Almost half the folks at Nikishka. And for what? So he could make money. My family died so he could turn a profit, and it's me that sits here waiting for the gallows."

The breeze outside has blown bits of fireweed fluff into the room once again. His right hand reaches out and snatches a clump from the air. Gently, he rubs it between his fingers to feel the downy softness.

"You have every right to feel the way you do," *Miss Ashford says.*

"Truth be told," *says Campbell,* "I've regretted that fight all these years. Every single time I think about it."

"It had nothing to do with Mrs. Hackham?"

He looks up, his brow creased. "Polly? No, not at all."

"But she was the source of the bad blood between you and Hackham."

"Don't talk at me like you're his lawyer. That fight was about Hack murdering my family. And about what Lucky Jim made me promise all those years ago when I found that little nugget at Tutsilitnu. And the fact that I wasn't man enough to live up to my oath, but took the easy way out."

He looks down at the fluff between his fingers. Miss Ashford swallows hard, fighting the urge to cry. It would, after all, be unprofessional. She sets her briefcase on the floor and re-crosses her legs with a long, deep sigh. She suddenly remembers a conversation in the officers' mess last night, something she meant to mention to Campbell.

"Captain Rubin said last night that he didn't think you committed the murder."

Campbell seems not to have heard her.

"Mr. Campbell?"

"Would you call me AC?"

"If you like. AC."

"And may I call you Rebecca?"

She smiles. "Actually, I prefer Becky."

"Becky," *says Campbell.* "Like Tom Sawyer's sweetheart."

She smiles again. "So did you hear what I said? About Captain Rubin?"

"You said he doesn't think I killed Scotty and Hack."

Becky nods. "He said as much at the table, but the other officers shouted him down. They said you were a violent savage. That's when Lieutenant Henderson told me of your row with Mr. Hackham."

Campbell studies his pipe. "Well, like I said. That was a long time ago."

"How long?"

"Five years."

"Five years? Where were you in the meantime?"

"I took off. Spent some time on Kalgin Island."

Becky Ashford's interest is piqued. "Really? What were you doing there for five years?"

He watches her for several heartbeats, studying the color of her irises. Becky feels her lips part ever so slightly. Just as she is about to look away, he speaks.

"I was a bear."

CHAPTER VIII

*W*hen I finally got hold of myself I went up to Mike and Klara's house. Nobody was home. I got a dish towel from the cabinet where Klara kept her kitchen linens and went out to the ice-house. I chipped a pile of ice into the towel and wrapped my hand, then I went back into the kitchen and fired the samovar for tea. The pain was so great I thought I might have broken the bones inside my hand, but after several minutes in the ice wrap I found that I could move my fingers just a little. Still, the digits looked like sausages, and I couldn't close my fist. The pain sobered me up considerably.

The water in the samovar was just boiling when the door opened and Mike came in. He entered the kitchen and sat at the table, not saying anything.

"Where's Klara?" I said.

He doffed his hat and laid it on the table before him. He rubbed his eyes. "She's helping see to Hack."

"You want some tea?"

"Sure."

I filled Klara's small kettle from the samovar, then lowered the tea-ball into it. I leaned against the countertop as the tea steeped, trying to ignore the pain in my hand.

"How is he?" I said.

"He'll live."

"Good."

"That was quite a beating you give him."

"I guess."

Mike drew his pipe and tobacco tin from his jacket pocket. He unscrewed the lid and loaded the bowl.

"They're going to take him down to Kodiak town on the next tide. He needs a doctor."

I said nothing. For a brief moment I considered telling Mike about my affliction, but in the end I just looked away. There was no way I could phrase it that wouldn't sound like an excuse. A pathetically fanciful one at that. Even so, I couldn't help but wonder if Yasha's drunken account of our fight at Sixmile had made it to Mike's ears. I doubted he would believe it if it had. He was not the type to put any stock in such things. I wished Lucky Jim was still with me so I could speak of my troubles to someone who understood.

"There's some men in town talking about rounding you up and taking you with them," he said.

Desolation flooded my soul as I poured the tea into cups. "What for? My hand hurts, but it aint broken."

"They aint taking you to the doctor. They aim to turn you over to the federal marshal. If they don't lynch you first."

"Aint no marshal in Kodiak town," I said. "He's way over in Sitka."

"True," said Mike. "But he comes through Kodiak every year about this time on his patrol. If nothing else, they'll hand you over to the customs commissioner. Or the Revenue Service. Hell, they even asked me to keep you locked up."

"Are you going to lock me up?"

"I told them you was my nephew and I would have no part of it." He eyed my battered hand. "But there's plenty of men willing to testify that you assaulted Hack. Bad as you done him, you could get sent up for attempted murder."

"To hell with them. It was a fair fight."

"A fair fight's one thing. But people reckon you went a bit overboard."

I stirred sugar into both mugs, then retrieved Mike's stash of vodka from the back of Klara's spice chest. I poured a healthy dram into each cup. Mike watched me as I done this.

"How much you been drinking these days?" he said.

"Some."

I set his cup on the table and sat down across from him with my own. He raised his weary eyebrows in thanks and took a sip. I done likewise. It tasted like poison on my tongue, but I loved it all the same.

I swallowed. "What do you think, Mike?"

He set his cup back on the table and rotated it on its base. "I think you might better skedaddle, AC. Get gone while the getting is good. And I don't mean up to Sixmile. It won't take them long to find you there."

"I might go over the mountains to the Iliamna country. Maybe look up George Washington's relations there."

"I'd prefer not to know where you go," said Mike.

A cold weight settled over me. "You mean really gone, don't you, Mike?"

"Yeah," he said. "And I think it's best if you don't come back."

———

I laid low the rest of the day and left that night after the town had gone to bed. I didn't say goodbye to Mike and Klara, but I did sneak his bottle of vodka with me. I felt guilty about it, but told myself that I needed it far more than he did.

I sailed for Kalgin Island on the outgoing tide. Then I let the incoming tide push me back up the west side of the island in the grainy light of the dawn. I anchored my dory in a small cove behind a gravel point and flopped down onto the sand above the tide-line. I took a long drink, then stared straight up at the sky.

The morning was overcast and looking like rain though none had yet fallen and the sand was dry. I watched the gulls and listened to their mournful cries as they flew overhead and walked to and fro upon the beach. I would never see Sixmile again, most likely. I had not even stopped there for a change of clothes on my way to Kenay to confront Hack. Now I was bound to live the life of a homeless renegade. My repeating rifle and expensive field glasses offered no comfort in this.

I took a second drink and thought of me and Yasha's empty cabins and all of my possessions still piled and stacked within those four walls. Who might go to live there one day, I wondered, and what would they think of what they found? What would they have heard of me, the man who called that valley home since he was fifteen? That I was a bachelor trapper and a drunk who had once had friends and kin, but then nearly beat a man to death and ran off to parts unknown?

These thoughts plunged me into a terrible melancholy worse than any I had ever known. I wished so much for Yasha to come walking out of the bushes and say something cheerful, but this of course did not happen. I knew where I was upon the earth, but I was lost all the same. Maybe I could start over again on Iliamna Lake, make my life anew. But this thought just made me weary, and there was the memory of how cold the muzzle of the old Sharps rifle had felt under my chin. I looked down to my boat, where my new repeater lay. If only I could muster the energy to get there.

I took another drink. I had half a bottle to get through first.

It caught me unawares when the crackling started once again beneath my ears, but this time I was mentally too weak to stop it. The drink hadn't dulled it like normal, but perhaps the bear had just been kept too long

KRIS FARMEN

inside his cage. I no longer had any reason to resist. He was part and parcel of my nature and always had been, so I gave myself over to him as the sparks spread through me, laying there in the sand with the sea-birds wheeling high above and my hands pressed over my eyes until I noticed the morning had become uncomfortably warm.

I sat up to shed my jacket but stopped when I seen the brown fur that covered me.

So this is how it will be now, I thought. Then I stood up on my hind feet and roared at the sky and at God and all his saints in heaven, not knowing or caring what else to do.

I stayed near the boat for several days eating grass and new poplar leaves. I barely even noticed when a big storm blew up with a huge tidal surge that drug the anchor and carried away the dory and my whole outfit, never to be recovered. I wandered up the beach and found some harbor seals hauled up for pupping season. I pounced on one and bit him on the neck, slinging him to and fro until his spine snapped. I ate on him for a good while, not minding in the least when the carcass started to smell.

One evening, a raven came and landed nearby.

"You gonna eat that?" he said.

I was rolling on my back on the beach cobbles to scratch an itch. I turned my head and saw him—upside down from my point of view—perched on a nearby drift stump, cocking his shiny head this way and that.

"This place must be like a prison for you," he said.

"What?"

"You know. Like a prison with no walls."

I sprang to my feet, and he shot into the air with a loud *Ggwaakk!* The air whistled under his wings as he flew off. But he was right. The last conscious human thought I recall having was of Muscle Sam and the fact that an island is as good as a prison. I was marooned there all alone, for there are no bears on Kalgin Island. Not until I got there. I guess it was as good a penance as any.

––––––

The years I was alone on Kalgin Island are difficult to reckon in human words. When you have changed into a bear, or any other animal for that matter, time moves differently. There is no past, no future. Your life is about what is there in front of you at that moment, be it food to eat, a river to cross, or the November snowflakes sifting down through the trees to light on the tips of your fur coat.

I fattened myself over the summer on seals, salmon, and berries. Come falltime when the creeks was full of ice I dug me a hole in a cut-bank deep in the woods on the south lobe of the island. I filled it with dead grass and fireweed down for a mattress, then I crawled in and went to sleep until spring.

A bear spends his whole winter lost in dreams. Often mine was of food, or birds, or the beauty of water. But sometimes I dreamt of men. I seen one man alone on a strange shore, a place where it rained a lot. I saw another man hitting a woman, and a child cowering under a kitchen table, watching. These visions did not trouble me, however. They was bear dreams, and forgotten as soon as my mind moved on to something else.

I was by myself on the island, but I didn't lack for company. More often than not, the raven would find me. One time I was munching on a red salmon I'd caught, with several seagulls lurking nearby. I bit off the head and chewed it and swallowed. Then one of the gulls got too close, so I jumped at him. He skittered off with his wings lifted high in the air, but when I turned around there was three more of them pecking away at my meal. I charged them and they flew off, but then two others come in and stole even more food. This went on for some time, but then there come a *"Ggwaakk ggwaakk ggwaakk,"* and all the seagulls tore off like scalded cats. I wheeled to find him staring at me.

He said, "I scared off all them seagulls for you. You mind if I eat the rest of this fish?"

"That's my fish," I said. "You keep off it."

"I come down here to tell you something."

"I reckon you come down to bum a meal."

"That too," he said. Quick as a wink he pulled off a strip of fish skin and jiggled it down his gullet.

I sniffed at him. He had a strange scent. The closest human equivalent I can think of is old stale tobacco smoke that lingers in your clothes. But there was other things, too. Rotten meat, punky birch wood, elderberries. And a vague smell of wild roses, like he'd used it to try and mask the other odors instead of taking a bath.

"What'd you come here to tell me, then?" I said as he picked off a piece of orange flesh and swallowed it, then another.

"There's seals hauled out on the beach on the south lobe of the island. If you killed one we could eat."

"You look like you're doing pretty well right here."

If I had been a man and a raven started talking to me, I might have recalled the old stories I heard from Lucky Jim and George Washington, the ones where Raven, the Black Bird, could talk to people and other animals. But I was a bear and not bothered with such notions. He was just a bird come to talk to me. An annoying bird who helped himself to my food.

"This fish aint going to last forever," he said. "You'll need to get another one. Or get us a seal."

"What's this *us* shit?"

He just laughed and stuck his beak into the innards of the fish and pulled out the heart. He didn't waste no time when there was food in front of him, that's for sure.

"There must be other ravens on this island," I said.

"They're all assholes."

I watched as he gobbled up almost all of my fish, and then I lost all patience and stamped my paws at him. He flew into the air like he was shot from a cannon, shouting, "*Ggwaakk ggwaakk!*"

When I looked down, there was just the backbone and guts with a few bits of flesh.

Sometimes I went for days without seeing him. Other times he would hang around, jabbering about the goings-on of the island as if under the impression that I was fascinated by his opinions. One time when I went out onto the sand-flats to dig razor clams with my claws, he hung around poking and sniffing at the empty shells I left behind. There was no way he could get in close to steal anything, and I sucked every single shell clean as a whistle. He got disgusted at this and cussed me out, saying I wasn't no kind of friend.

"Go dig your own clams," I said, and he flew off, still cussing. I didn't see him again until the fall.

As I've said, there weren't no bears on the island except me, but I did not have the place to myself. Kalgin is a well-used spot. Folks use it as a stepping stone for the Inlet crossing. Me and Yasha stopped there any number of times ourselves over the years. From time to time there would come men putting their boats in along the beach to hunt seals or dig clams or just to rest up and wait for the tide to turn. I stayed clear of them as much as I could, but eventually word must have got out that there was a brown bear living on the island, for men started coming into the woods with rifles looking for my tracks. I never did let them get so much as a good look at me, but I will confess that the island did seem like a very small place at times, especially with that raven leading them to me. His motivation was the same as when he would tell me where

KRIS FARMEN

I could find some food—he wanted to eat his share at the gut-pile. But I didn't hold it against him. We all have to eat.

Most of the time, though, I lived well. When my belly was full I would lie in the grass watching the songbirds. Sometimes they would land to talk, but mostly they seemed to enjoy fluttering around me, and I loved studying their pretty colors as they chattered at one another in their own language. Sometimes when I got bored with the birds I would watch the streams flowing or the wildflowers waving in the breeze. When it rained I got wet. When the sun shone I was hot and panting. The bugs deviled me in the early summer until the dragonflies hatched to eat them.

One fall as I was getting my den ready for the winter's dreaming, the raven startled me from the boughs of a nearby spruce tree. I hadn't known he was there; I was just working away when suddenly there come his loud *Ggwaakk!* I turned and charged at him, but he was just out of my reach and knew he was safe.

"What do you want?"

"Didn't you used to live up on the Sixmile?"

"I can't recall," I said, truthfully.

"Lots of men crawling around there these days. You got anything to eat?"

I went back to cropping dead grass with my mouth and carrying it to the den where I dropped it in a pile. I would push it down into the hole later.

"Who told you that?" I said.

"A halibut," he replied, twisting around to scratch between his feathers with his beak.

"A halibut."

"She said you should know."

"My indifference would fill the den," I said.

"You're real fancy talker, you know that?" He shifted his feet on the bough where he'd perched, and a cascade of snow slid down. "You sure you don't got nothing to eat?"

I crawled into my den and started spreading out the grass.

Once again I slept all winter with my dreams. The man on the rain-slashed beach was taken north. The other man who kept hitting his wife and the child moved them to a new home. Two abandoned cabins and a field where men buried their dead.

I had these visions, but I was detached from them. My woes over Hack and Polly, Sixmile and my family was left far behind me in the distant hazy past. But it was just as Lucky Jim had warned me so long ago. My desire to ever be a man again faded with time.

In fact, by the third summer I had completely forgotten that I ever had been a man. It had no more meaning in my life. I had nothing and no-one. I was lost to the island as my sorrows was lost to the wind and tide.

My raven chum kept coming around, though. Whenever I killed a seal, he would appear out of the air and flutter down to the ground and stroll right in for a beakful. When I fished in the creeks, he would watch me from the top of a spruce tree. Sometimes he was around every day, all day long. Other times I didn't see him for a whole season. Most of the time he jabbered about the weather, or commented on my hunting and fishing skills, or complained about some other animal whom he felt had slighted him. He was particularly fond of spreading unseemly gossip about other the ravens he knew.

Every now and again there would be some mention of his halibut girlfriend. How she wanted me to know things that meant nothing to me.

"Like what?" I would say.

"I can't remember," he'd reply.

I lost count of seasons. I ceased to care. Each summer rolled into fall, and another winter's slumber into another spring's awakening. But sometimes, when I was alone without my uninvited companion, I could not understand why I felt so heartbroken when I looked out at the evening mountains, or heard the call of a thrush deep in the woods, or saw the sunlight flashing upon the feathers of a hummingbird.

Eventually, though, I ceased to wonder about even that.

"*Ggwaakk!* Wake up!"

I ignored him.

"*Ggwaakk ggwaakk!* You got to get up now, buddy."

I had been enjoying my midday nap. Now I was awake and pissed off. I didn't open my eyes. "Are you back again?"

"There's men coming," he hissed.

"I've heard that one before."

"I aint kidding this time."

I sighed. "If there was men here, you'd be doing somersaults in the air and trying to lead them to me."

He was getting anxious, I could hear it in his voice. "Not this time!"

I sighed again and considered rolling over, but my belly was full of blueberries, and it seemed to be so much effort.

There was a whistling of wings. "*Ggwaakk ggwaakk ggwaakk ggwaaakk!*"

I opened my eyes to the rock where his voice had come from. He was gone. Then I heard crunching in the beach gravel. Men's feet.

My pulse raced, and my heart thumped against my ribcage as I stole a look over the tips of the grass. There was two of them. They were coming toward me but hadn't seen me. I sank back down in the grass, figuring to let them walk right past. Then I'd cut for the tag-alders and give them the slip.

I let my eyes follow the sound of their footsteps as they come closer, then stopped. This was an unwelcome development. I watched with my head down low and was dismayed to see one of them climb onto a drift log. I could just see his head as he scanned the beach. Then his gaze settled straight on me. He shouted something to the other one as I wheeled and bolted for the trees. There was a great deal of shouting behind me, more than normal when I came across men, but this was no doubt a tactic to scare me. I punched into the brush at the edge of the beach and bowled my way through the spruce and devils club and then across a boggy muskeg flat where I took refuge on a hummock of scraggly black spruce. This was a hideout that had served me well on previous occasions. I pressed myself down into the willows and tea-bushes and watched my backtrail.

After a while I seen the men come up to the edge of the bog. They hunkered in the alders, whispering at one another. One of these men was female, which struck me as odd, but all I really cared about was getting to the thicker timber. Slowly, I crept back through the spruce to the far side of the hummock. The trees thinned out, giving little cover between my position and the edge of the surround-ing bog, but I reckoned I could slip out undetected.

As I started moving, one of the men walked out into the bog and stood with his arms spread out and yelling across the distance. I paid it no mind but kept on my course, ducking and slipping low and quiet through the brush. I still had the crest of the hummock to hide me. It was not much, but it was enough to cover my escape. I was fairly sure I had not been spotted, and I dearly wanted to be somewhere else.

They must have seen me, though, for there came more yelling. This time it was both of them shouting and waving their arms. This was odd behavior for men. I was maybe a stone's throw from cover, but it was over the most exposed part of the bog. I bunched my legs, then sprang, running hard and splashing and sucking in the soggy moss and cottongrass. Plowing toward the shelter of the trees that came closer and closer with each jump—twenty foot, then ten—and that's when I heard the crack of the rifle, and the world went black.

———

At first I heard the surf on the beach, and I thought, *This wind is whipping up into a storm. I should get into the timber. And what a peculiar dream I just had.*

I was on my back, which struck me as an odd position to fall asleep in, all four feet sticking up into the air.

Must have been one hell of a dream. This thought in and of itself seemed strange to hear inside my head.

I pushed my eyes open and rolled onto my side. My head hurt like hell, and I had a sour stomach to boot. There was something draped over top of me that hindered my movement. Whatever it was, it smelled like men.

There come a cry, then some murmurings as I rolled onto my four legs. Then the men was there beside me, trying to touch me. Talking to me in low tones. Panic filled me as I realized it wasn't no dream I'd been remembering—these men had captured me somehow, and I had to get away. I let out a roar and took a hard swipe at them, but to my horror it had no more effect than a stiff tickling. My claws had changed—they was pale and flexible. I roared even louder, but pain shot through my head and everything clipped to black again.

Somewhere in that blackness I heard my own voice for the first time in many years, and I realized I was dreaming. But not bear dreams. Men's dreams.

I was talking to someone. I sat up and found myself in a hemlock glade where the trees had grown crooked and twisted from the wind. I could barely see them, for it was night. The only light came from a small campfire whose light flickered upon the trunks and the rain-smelling boughs overhead.

It was Lucky Jim. He sat by the fire with his knees drawn up before him and his arms resting upon them. His neck was draped with necklaces of dentalium shells, and his long hair was piled up behind his head in a large bun, dressed with seal oil, red earth and goose down.

"Granddad!" I said. I was overjoyed to see him.

"Aleksie," he said, "have you been listening to me? What I'm telling you?"

"What's that?"

"The time has come for you to be a man once again."

"I don't want to, Granddad. I'm happy the way I am."

My attention was caught by a movement, and there come a hawk owl, sailing up to perch on a limb above Lucky Jim. Then I seen a cow-moose looking into the globe of firelight. A couple river otters wrestling each other, and a wood frog sitting on the root of one of the hemlocks. Indeed there was every animal in the forest—marten, mink, beaver, wolf, caribou, even sheep come down from the mountains. And all manner of fish, birds, and insects, too many to name here. They was there with us, gathered round the fire and listening to Lucky Jim as a counsel of elders.

My jaw hung open as I watched them change into human beings. Every single one of them. They stood watching me with the pale firelight upon their faces and glittering in their eyes. I knew suddenly that these was all my Indian kin, all those in Lucky Jim's mother's side of the family who had our talent, our power, our affliction, whatever you choose to call it. Every single one of us stretching back to the dawn of time when the Black Bird created the world.

"We both know you aint happy the way you are," said Lucky Jim. "Feeling nothing is hardly the same thing as happiness."

I looked up at the stars. Orion the hunter. The Big Dipper. They was brighter than I'd ever seen them. When I looked back at him there was Opal the halibut-girl standing behind him with her arms around his shoulders.

"Opal," I said.

She nodded. "AC."

"Where you been?"

"The bottom of the sea."

"Muscle Sam was right."

"All alone in a prison with no walls," she said. "I sent you some company, though."

"You mean him? That Black Bird?"

"Yes. There's things that need to be done. You've been putting them off."

"But I don't want to leave," I said. I didn't believe it, but I clung to that thought out of habit.

"Yes you do. You're miserable living here as a big animal. It's not the life you was meant to live, and there are people who need you. I sent word to you. Didn't he tell you what was going on?"

"Sometimes," I said. "But he's got a habit of talking in riddles."

Opal rolled her eyes. "I told him to quit doing that. Sometimes I don't know why I even bother with him."

"They're all liable to be gone," I said, looking at my bare feet.

"You mean your people."

"Yes. They're likely dead or run off by now. I been gone a long time."

"Not so long," she said. "They're looking for you."

I turned this over for a moment. "Granddad, I want to stay here with you."

"You'll see this country soon enough, Aleksie. But now it's time to stop being selfish."

I looked at Opal and seen the belt of Orion reflected in the dark pools of her eyes. I stared at this for longer than seemed polite, but then the earth turned upside down, and I was falling into the night, between the stars in her eyes, with no notion of what I might find when I landed.

*

$\mathcal{AC}$ ceases to speak. Becky watches him for a long time, wondering where this man acquired such a vivid imagination.

"I didn't imagine none of that," he says. "It happened."

"AC, how—" She searches for words. "Do you read minds as well? Don't tell me a bird flew up and told you."

"No bird this time. You're just an easy read."

She stares down at her notebook, where she has not written any notes past his description of changing into a bear after he fled Kenay town.

"You can ask around on the Peninsula," says AC. "Ask folks about the bear that used to live on Kalgin Island. They'll know exactly what you're talking about. They'll tell you that his tracks showed up right after I disappeared. And that he just up and vanished from the island a couple months ago."

"And that was you."

"It was."

Becky finds herself rather suddenly annoyed by his outlandish claim. "That doesn't prove anything."

"I don't got to prove a goddamn thing to you. You wanted to know all about my affliction and what it's like to be a bear. So I told you. Don't get all huffy with me cause it aint what you wanted to hear."

She can feel her very human desire to believe bumping heads with her hard-won scientific skepticism.

"I'm sorry, I wasn't trying to be rude. It's just—"

"Just what?"

"Can you understand that everything that you've told me is rather hard for me to accept? Can you appreciate that?"

"I suppose. But I aint really asking you to accept it. My time is near, and—"

"And?"

"I want to leave a record," says AC. "Of my days on this earth."

Becky sighs. "That's not really what I'm here to do."

"You could write it down. So people can read it."

"You've got the notebook I gave you," she says. "You could write down your own story."

"You're better at that kind of thing. And besides, I've already told most of it to you. Time's getting short."

"Well, if you think of anything I haven't put down."

"Yeah."

She watches him. "So."

"Yes?"

"You obviously became human once again."

"I did," he says. "There was people that needed me."

KRIS FARMEN

CHAPTER IX

I woke in the gray light of midnight. Rain was falling. There was a fire; I could see it between the spruce trees. A man and a woman sat beside it underneath a tarp. I was tucked into blankets, with another tarp strung over top of me. Rainwater dripped from the lower edge. My head still hurt, but I felt less queasy. I pushed my arm out of the blankets to feel my skull, and I winced when I touched the furrow in the top of my scalp. It had been salved and stitched up.

"He's awake," said the woman to her companion. The man rose and followed her as she ducked under the canvas and knelt beside me. I blinked at them as the rain drummed on the tarp above us. It was Polly. And Yasha.

"How you feeling, AC?" she said.

"Like shit. Scuse my French."

She smiled, and my heart fluttered at the sight.

"Yasha," I said. "Jesus."

He laughed. "Sorry about that head wound."

"Pardon?"

"Yasha had to shoot you," said Polly.

"What now?"

"We couldn't get you to stop running. So he took aim and creased your head to knock you out."

"It was all I could think of to do," Yasha said.

I tried to grin, but it hurt. "I missed you, partner."

"I almost missed you, too."

He looked different than I remembered. His hair had been shaved off sometime recently and had regrown to a half-inch of stubble. It made the veins on his temples stand out. His eyes looked more serious than I remembered, and his face was creased with worry and hardship.

But his grin was the same. There was no doubt it was my old partner Yasha Izaakov.

"Where the hell you been?" I said.

"All over the world."

They had clothes for me. Yasha give me a hand with suiting up, and they both helped me over to the fire. The movement made me dizzy, but this settled down when they propped me against a spruce tree. Polly got the kettle going for tea, and Yasha passed me a Ball jar of smoked eulachon. When I was fed up and full of tea, he loaded me a pipe, and we sat there smoking and watching the fire. After a while, the stories came.

———

Yasha had indeed been all over the world. He had been keen to put his harpoon arm to the test when he signed on to that New Bedford whale-ship, but he got little opportunity for this—the crew used a newfangled cannon to fire the harpoon rather than throwing by hand. Yasha didn't think too much of his shipmates or of this industrial method of killing.

After a three-month Arctic cruise they pointed south to the Sandwich Islands, the kingdom of Owhyee that I had read about in *Roughing It*. But when they called into the port at Honolulu the customs agents seized the vessel. It seems the owners was long since in arrears to the local government for customs fees. Stranded, and with no money, Yasha found these islands to be murderously hot and muggy, no place for an Indian from Cook Inlet. So he signed onto a British-flagged whaler called the *Resonator* from faraway New Zealand, headed for the Southern Ocean by way of Japan. They was still harpooning the old-fashioned way, and Yasha's skills was quickly discovered. The harpooners was all New Zealand tribesmen, and they was most keen each of them to get the first strike at a whale. They give no quarter in this contest

KRIS FARMEN

and ridiculed any throw that missed its mark. Yasha won their confidence by being among the boldest of harpoon-men and wound up with his right arm covered in their strange south-seas tattoo marks.

There under the spruce trees, he pulled off his jacket and rolled up his shirtsleeve to show me.

"God almighty," I said. I'd never seen nothing like it. His skin was filled with intricate curly-cue patterns from wrist to shoulder.

"Them New Zealand Natives told me it would keep my arm strong," Yasha said.

Polly watched us, saying nothing. The rain had slacked off, and we could hear the drops plopping against the leaves and the tarp above us. A gust of wind shook the water through the trees. Polly reached up with a stick and pushed on the center of the tarp so that the water collected there slid off the edge.

"So what happened then?" I said.

Yasha opened another jar of eulachon and made a sandwich by breaking a pilot cracker in two and laying an oily fish between the halves. He took a bite, chewing around his words as he spoke.

"I got shipwrecked."

Five months into his southern cruise, the ship ran into a storm off the Straits of Magellan, and the ship foundered. The crew put into the whale-boats but was dashed against some rocks in the moonless dark. Yasha made it to shore, but he found no trace of the others. He wandered in this wet rainy wasteland for many days until he was saved from starvation by a band of local Indians. Their forest, he told me, was made up of bizarre trees that seemed to have come out of a dream, and the animals was tiny dwarf-sized things. His rescuers was strange folk as well—they wore no clothes, only fur robes and cloaks of home-spun wool from an animal something like a deer that they killed up in the high mountains. Over many months, Yasha learned their language and got on with their ways.

I said, "You mean to tell me they ran around bare-assed naked? In that cold?"

He nodded, as if he still had a hard time believing it himself. "Those was some tough Indians."

He stayed with these people for more than a year, hunting and fishing, and wondering how he might possibly get home. Then one morning they woke to gunfire. It was the Chilean army coming down on them. The soldiers marched Yasha and his friends to a town where the local magistrate, who was actually a Britisher, told them they was all criminals, guilty of HOSTILE INDIAN-ISM. He called them enemies of the state. They was to be executed, even the women and children.

"He was a Britisher?" I said.

"He was. But he spoke Spanish."

"But it aint part of Victoria's empire."

"Not officially. Chile's its own country, but lots of Britishers live there. Anyway, the Army goes after the Indians."

"So what happened?"

Yasha had only known these Indians to be peaceful folk. They had never attacked white people, and in fact went to great pains to avoid them. When this charge of HOSTILE INDIANISM and its sentence was translated to Yasha and his terrified friends, he spoke up in American, unmindful of the consequences.

"Now just wait a minute, damn you!" he said to the judge.

The courtroom fell silent. The soldiers looked at one another and then at the magistrate. At his signal the soldiers brought Yasha front and center and pushed him down to his knees. His clothes was all rags. He had an iron collar round his neck and chains on his hands and feet.

The magistrate looked down from his bench and asked Yasha where he come from, as it obviously wasn't Patagonia.

"Alaska," said Yasha.

The magistrate was educated enough to know that Alaska was a United States possession. He called the army captain over and conferred with him in Spanish. The captain turned and barked some orders at his men, and two of them come up and unshackled Yasha. They frog-marched him into a jail cell where they kept him for ten days. Then they brought him out and give him some used clothes and boots that was too big for his feet. They put him on a ferry up the coast, then a train with the same two soldiers as armed guards.

Yasha spoke no Spanish, and his guards spoke no American, so he couldn't ask where he was going or what happened to his friends. The train was bound for the capital city, so Yasha figured he was being transferred to prison there. His spirits was near rock bottom at that point, and he suddenly wanted very badly to see Cook Inlet once again.

It was a grand surprise when in the capital the soldiers marched him up to a tall building with the stars and stripes flying out front. It was the United States consulate. The Chilean soldiers saluted the marines guarding the front door, then they unlocked Yasha's wrist shackles and turned and left.

"I tell you what," Yasha said. "I was never in my life so happy to see the Yankee flag."

"Did they get you back to Alaska?" I asked.

He shook his head. "I'm an Indian. Not a U.S. citizen. So there wasn't much they could do for me. But they treated me good. They give me a meal and a bath and passed the hat to scare me up some travelling money."

"So how'd you get home?"

He shrugged. "I started walking."

Yasha told me how he stuffed newspaper into the toes of his oversized boots and made his way out of the capital, heading for the coast. There he found a British-flagged Canadian ship with a cargo of nitrate bound for Vancouver by way of San Francisco. He signed on as an able seaman, and when they reached Frisco town he invested his sea-wages into a modest outfit and a steam-ship ticket to Seldovoya.

"How long you been back?" I asked.

"Since March month. I built a new summer cabin up at the mouth of Rabbit Creek. Don't know what I'll do for the winter. Maybe go trapping up on the Little Su."

The rain had started again. I leaned my head back against the bark of the spruce tree and listened to the drumming on the canvas above. I closed my eyes, then opened them again. I had trouble focusing my gaze and my head was foggy. My sense of smell seemed to have deserted me, and this was difficult to get my mind around. To a bear, the world is an avalanche of sounds and smells, but now the forest seemed flat by comparison.

Polly watched the fire. I noticed the crows' feet that had begun to form at the corners of her eyes, just like Yasha's, and it made me wonder what I looked like. I had no idea how long it had been since I had seen my own face.

"What year is this?" I said to her.

"Eighteen ninety-four."

"Ninety-four you say?"

She nodded.

"I been here for five years?" It was hard to fathom such time. Fatigue had started to overtake me. It seemed I had never been so sleepy.

I looked into my empty tea mug, then back at her. "Polly, what are you doing here?"

She finally met my eyes. "We come here to find you."

I felt my lids sagging. It was a struggle to stay awake.

"There's been stories of a bear here on the island," she said. "Everyone's heard them. But it wasn't until Yasha told me about your—"

Her gaze fell away back to the fire, and I could plainly see she was having difficulty accepting what she must have witnessed earlier in the day.

"Let's call it your peculiar ability," she said. "It wasn't until Yasha told me about it that we put two and two together."

Looking at her, I seen for the first time that there was something horribly wrong behind her brave face. She was a married woman, and plucky though she was, she certainly didn't have no business hunkering under a tarp in the rainy woods on Kalgin Island with two reprobates, one of which had just spent five years in the skin of a brown bear.

"Polly, what's going on?" I said, working harder than ever to keep my eyes open. "How come you're out here to fetch me?"

I recall hearing her voice, but the weariness overtook me, and I slipped back into night.

———

They must have carried me back under the first tarp, for I woke in the early hours of the morning next to Yasha. It was a raven calling across the treetops that pulled me out of sleep. I lay there, listening to the air whistling under his wings as he flew overhead on his way to somewhere. Polly had bedded down beneath the second tarp, next to the fire, which was only proper.

It was still raining, and I rolled onto my back, watching the leaves of the tag-alder and devils club dance up and down as the rain drops pelted them. Nature was calling me, so I slipped out from the tarp and walked into the woods, staying under the big spruce trees so as to keep dry. When I finished and turned to come back, Polly was moving through the trees toward me.

My guess was that she was answering her own call, so I merely nodded at her and made to pass politely by. Instead, she put a gentle hand against me.

"Hello Polly," I said.

"Good morning. How is your head?"

"Better. My scalp still hurts, but I feel more clear-headed."

She motioned for me to bend over. "Let me see."

I done so, and she stood on a deadfall for better vantage. Her fingers gently brushed my hair out of the way. I rolled my eyes up to watch her, thinking of how the last words she'd said to me before I'd left Kenay was to go to hell.

She finished her ministrations, and I straightened up, fighting a brief wave of dizziness.

"So how do you feel?" she said.

"What, in general?"

"Yes. I mean, considering what you've been up to."

"I feel odd. You ever read that story about Rip Van Winkle?"

"Yes. After five years I'll bet you do feel a lot like him."

"I thought I'd never see your smile again," I said.

"A lot's changed on the Peninsula since you've been gone."

Of that I had no doubt, but it was not what was on my mind just then. "Polly, I'm awful sorry about what I done to Hack there at Kenay town."

"What's done is done, AC. I forgave you long ago." She patted her hand against my chest. "You should take it easy for a couple days. Yasha really rang your bell."

"I'm just glad it wasn't Scotty doing the shooting."

A pained look crossed her face, and then to my surprise she buried her face in her hands and started to cry. She sank down against the deadfall. I was dumbfounded by this. All I could think of to do was to kneel down and put my arm around her.

"What's the matter, Polly?"

Her voice was wavering with tears. "I tried to tell you last night, but you fell asleep."

I had a vague recollection of hearing Scotty's name as I drifted off, but nothing beyond that. "I'm very sorry. I was having a tough time staying awake."

"It's alright. It's not that."

"What then?"

She sniffed and pressed the heels of her palms against her eyes. "Scotty's dead. Greg killed him."

"Beg your pardon?"

"And he's taken Max, and Scotty's daughter Lindsay."

"What the hell?" This was a lot of information to work through, and my head was not yet fully accustomed to human thought. There was still some of the bear living in my skin. I could feel him sniffing around at the world and the dark corners of his domain.

"Polly, what is going on? Where has he taken Max and Lindsay? And why would he kill Scotty?"

"I don't know where he took them. That's why we come here looking for you. We need your help."

I sat for a moment trying to make sense of this. It was distressing indeed to be informed that one of my best friends had been murdered. There was a brief wish that I could just go back to being a bear, but I pushed it away. I started to ask Polly how this came to pass, but she spoke first.

"AC, there's something else I have to tell you."

"What's that?"

It took her a long moment to find her voice. All I could do was watch the side of her face in the gloom of the rainy woods.

She took a deep breath. "Maxim is your son."

I opened my mouth, but could find no words so I shut it again.

"That night on the beach at Deep Creek," she said.

"Max is my son?"

She nodded, and a trace of her old dimpled smile flashed across her face. "He looks so much like you now."

"But Hack."

She took another long breath. "I confess that I was something less than virtuous when I was younger."

"You was exercising a couple different options," I said.

"I suppose you could say that."

I peered through the wet brush toward the open expanse of the beach where a lighter shade of gray announced the coming of a new day.

"But why didn't you tell me?"

She wiped fresh tears from her eyes and covered her face again. "Forgive me, Aleksandr. I'm so sorry and ashamed of what I did. What I kept doing. I should have told you that he was your son. I should have let you claim him and give him your name. I knew he was yours from the moment I found out I was expecting. But I was young and scared. I had nothing and no-one, and I thought Hack was the better prospect."

This might have stung me at some point in the past, but it seemed unimportant just then.

"Please forgive me, Aleksandr," she said. "I've deceived you all these years, and my soul must surely be damned to hell for it. God won't forgive me, but I hope you can."

"You know it's blasphemy to presume what God will or won't do," I said.

"I'm a little past that stage."

"Is my aunt Klara still alive?"

She nodded, still pushing tears out of the way with her fingers.

"Well," I said, "she once told me that women often have to make some very tough choices. I was just young and wet behind the ears when all that happened between you and me. I can certainly see why Hack would have looked like a more suitable husband. Or why you might not have wanted to move way up to Sixmile to live in a sod-roofed trapping cabin."

"That sort of thing never mattered to me, AC. I've dreamed many times over the years that I was your wife."

"I guess that makes two of us," I said, smiling a little. I still had my arm around her. I drew her in close and touched her cheek with my fingertips. She closed her eyes.

"I told Hack I wanted a divorce," she said to the forest. "That's why he took Max. When I told him that I wanted my son he started smacking me. Punching me. He said he'd kill me if I tried to take Max away from him. He said—"

"What? What did he say?"

"He said he would never let me see my son again."

My head was working more clearly by this point, and it come to me that I had only heard bits and pieces of a much larger story.

Polly looked past me toward our camp. "Yasha is up."

He was building up the fire and getting the morning tea ready. I said, "I think the three of us need to have a chat."

"First things first," said Polly, and before I could react she tilted her mouth up to me and gave me a kiss. It felt like breathing color into a photograph. She loosed the barest of giggles, and that was more than I could handle. I took her up in my arms once again after so long, and it was right, so right. As if I had returned home at last after so many years of being lost in the woods.

The story my friends had to tell was that Greg Hackham and several other captains of the placer mining business had, over the years, staked claims up and down Tutsilitnu and Sixmile Creeks. Men was working these claims in a fever for sluice gold, and there was talk of a new town being platted at each creek mouth.

"What of our old place?" I asked Yasha.

He shook his head. "Some miners moved in not long after you left. I heard your cabin caught fire and burned to the ground."

"You heard?"

"I aint had the heart to go up and see it for myself."

Hack and Polly had a new log house at the Tutsilitnu camp, which was apparently being called Hope. When Hack made his threats, Polly fled the camp, taking Max with her. Yasha had gone into business market hunting sheep across the Arm and selling the meat to the miners, and he happened to be at the diggings that day. He took Polly and Max in his dory down the Arm to Scotty's new home at the mouth of the Tutsahtnu, which is apparently now being called Chickaloon River.

Scotty had returned to Cook Inlet back in 1892. He had a fish trap in the river, catching and drying salmon to sell for dog feed. Polly and Max sheltered with him and his wife and young Lindsay in their two-story log house.

"Wait a minute," I said. "His wife?"

Yasha managed a smile. "It's true. Her name's Ekaterina. She's a Creole gal. Mednovsti and Kolosh Indian on her mother's side. Scotty met her when he was market hunting for a timber camp there on Baranov Island."

"Scotty," I said. I wanted to give him a ration of shit over this and was saddened to realize I would never get to do so.

Of course, Greg Hackham was not the type to stand still for this sort of behavior from his wife. He went to Scotty's place with two armed men and banged on the door as the family and their refugees was getting ready for bed.

Scotty opened the door, and Hack said he had come for his son. By then Polly had spilled the beans about Max's pedigree, so Scotty informed Hack that he was welcome to kiss his ass and get the hell out of his yard. Hack drew a pistol and pushed his way into the house with his goons behind him. Both of them was armed. Hack went upstairs and retrieved the two children.

"Damn you, Polly," he said when he returned. "You go ahead and run off if I'm not good enough for you. But you won't take my son. Any judge in a divorce court will back me on that."

"Oh for Christ's sake, Hack," Scotty said. "Any man with eyes in his head can see he aint your son."

But Hack was a proud man and was not willing to bear the shame of having been duped into raising another man's child. He had other plans in mind.

Over the barrel of his pistol he said, "This is my boy. He carries my name, and he's going to carry on with my work building up this godforsaken territory."

At this Polly jumped up and tried to pull her son away from him, but Hack belted her across the face and she fell to the floor. He pushed Max at one of his hired men, then grabbed Lindsay by the hair. "Scotty," he said, "your little halfbreed brat is coming with me as insurance. In case you get any bright ideas about following me."

Scotty lunged at him, shouting, "You take your fucking hands off my daughter!"

Hack shot him straight through the chest. Then the five of them backed out the door and headed down the inlet, no doubt with the screams of Scotty's family in their ears as my old friend's final breath faded into the air.

"Jesus," I said. It was hard to accept that my good friend was murdered for nothing more than Greg Hackham's pride. The world seemed to be spinning a lot faster than it had when I left Kenay town.

Yasha looked over at Polly. "You told him?"

"I did."

"Hack's got your son and Scotty's daughter held hostage," Yasha said. "We come here to find you so we could get them back."

"Where's his wife at?"

"Ekaterina's with Mike and Klara," said Polly. "Sava and Belukha Pete got the word out for folks to be on the lookout for Hack. And not to let him anywhere near her."

"Big Nick went to sniff around and see if he could find where Hack took the kids," Yasha said. The world was indeed spinning faster. This seemed to be a mixed blessing at best.

"How long ago was all this?" I said.

"Six days," said Polly. "But there's something else you need to know."

"This is getting awfully complicated."

She and Yasha looked at one another, then back at me.

"It is complicated," said Polly. "I'm sorry to have to unload all this on you at once, but you've been gone a long time."

"So what else do I need to know?"

Yasha folded his arms over his chest. "Sava told us that Hack sent men to fetch the federal marshal. He's claiming that I'm the one shot Scotty."

"What?"

"That's what Sava said."

"We got time," I said. "The marshal's in Sitka. It'll be weeks before he can get here."

"They got a second one now. He's based out of Kodiak."

"Hack's accusations won't stand up," I said. "There's four witnesses."

"I don't care to find out one way or another," said Yasha. "I aim to just steer clear of the Yankee law."

I nodded at him and looked down into the coals. The teakettle had long since boiled, and Polly moved it off the fire and dropped the tea ball into it.

"So Yasha," I said.

His eyes looked huge with his hair cropped short.

"I heard you got drunk after you left Nikishka."

He watched me for several long seconds. "I did."

"They tell me you talked about things. About my affliction. About our row at Sixmile."

Yasha looked down at the teakettle. It took him a moment to collect himself. "I might have mentioned something about it. But I haven't had a drink since."

"Does anybody believe it?"

"I do."

"Folks just thought it was a crazy story," said Polly. "I certainly didn't believe it when I heard it. Everyone just figured Yasha had gone mad with grief."

"So it's not the talk of the town?" I said.

Polly shook her head. "I haven't heard anyone mention it for years. I had completely forgotten it until Yasha mentioned it to me just the other day."

"What did folks say when you left to come find me?" I said.

"We just said we had an idea where you was," said Yasha. "They asked where, and I didn't say."

I let out a mirthless laugh. "Hell. Who would believe it anyway, right?"

There was a crowd gathered when we put in at the Kenay beach landing. They no doubt had been watching for Yasha's sail. All faces was grave and downcast, and I was unsure what to make of them as I leapt over the bow with the mooring line. I did notice, however, that there was very few American faces there to greet me.

I mentioned this to Yasha and Polly. Polly rucked up her skirts, and I helped her down over the side. "It's been tense here in town since the incident," she said.

Yasha's voice came from the stern of the boat. "Most of the Boston Men have sided with Hack."

"And they're all out looking for Yasha," said Polly.

I turned to the crowd. Sava Golinov made his way to the front. He put out his hand and we shook.

"It's good to see you, Aleksie," he said.

"You too, Sava." His hair had gone white, and he walked with a cane. It made me realize just how long I had been away.

"Are you well?" I said.

He shrugged. "I'm getting old. Your aunt and uncle are waiting for you up at the house."

I paid my respects to everyone in the crowd as Yasha tied up the dory. Then we headed up the bluff path, which now seemed to be more of a proper road. It was disorienting to be among so many people again, and indeed, to see a town. I had not laid eyes on a house, a store, or coal-shed for five years.

The skyline of Kenay had changed. There was more buildings, and most of them was frame constructions with false fronts. There was horses and wagons in the streets, a rare sight when I'd left. We did not linger in town, but took the trail across the little gully and up to the hill where the old familiar sight of Mike and Klara's house greeted me. My heart give a leap when I seen it. It was clean and smart-looking as ever.

The crowd had trailed away to where it was just me, Yasha, and Polly, with Sava hobbling along behind us.

Mike and Klara met us at the door. Mike's hair was thin atop his head, and Klara had more than a little gray in her own locks, but there was no doubt I was home. I hugged my aunt and shook hands with my uncle.

"I thought we'd lost you," Klara said, wiping tears from her eyes.

"Never," I replied.

We went inside, and I blinked my eyes at the old familiar wallpaper and wainscoting. Klara led us into the parlor, where a woman sat on the sofa, dressed in black.

"This is Ekaterina Keogh," Polly said.

I offered my hand to the widow, but she stood and embraced me. "Daniel told me so many things about you, Mr. Campbell."

"Daniel?"

"It was his Christian name."

I almost smiled. "I don't think I ever heard it before, ma'am. Everyone just called him Scotty."

"I know," she said.

"I'm very sorry we have to meet like this. Scotty was a good man, and one of my best friends."

She nodded. There was lines and dark spots beneath her eyes from grief and worry.

"We'll find Lindsay," I said. "You have my word on it."

Klara had the samovar ready. She poured tea and set out cookies as Mike brought in extra chairs. Polly sat down next to Ekaterina and put an arm around her. Mike offered Sava his own easy chair, and Klara insisted I take a place on the sofa next to Polly. She flashed me a knowing look as I sat down.

Klara took a sip of tea, then spoke. "I take it Yasha and Polly have filled you in regarding the situation?"

"They have," I said. "I reckon they've told me what I need to know."

"Any news from Big Nick?" said Yasha.

Mike shifted in his seat. "He come by yesterday afternoon. Said he seen Lindsay with Hack up at Hope."

"What about Max?" Polly asked.

"No solid word on the boy," said Mike. "Nick reckons there's three or four places he could be."

I took a cookie from the plate on the coffee table. I was the only one who done so, but God help me I was famished.

"Where might those places be?" I said.

"Maybe Kodiak town. He might have sent him down with the men who went for the marshal. Or maybe the beach plant at Anchor Point."

"Greg has a cabin up at New Knik," said Polly. "He might be there."

Mike scratched the back of his head. "Nick said that was another possibility. Or he could be up at Hope with Lindsay, and Nick just didn't get wind of him."

"This could take some time," I said to Yasha.

"There's a lot of places to check."

It was hard not to dwell on all the men they said was out combing the Inlet for us. We would have to be careful.

Sava cleared his throat. "Well, we know Lindsay is at Tutsilitnu. And we know that Maxim might be there as well. So it seems to me that Hope is the first place to look."

"Yasha," said Klara, "you won't be able to stay on the Peninsula. Or even the west side. Not with the government looking for you."

Mike nodded. "She's right. I'm sorry to have to say it, but once you've found the children Yasha will need to skedaddle."

"I been planning on it anyway," said Yasha. "I figured I'd head over the mountains to the Iliamna country."

"That sounds familiar," I said.

Everyone looked at me.

"I'll be going with you, Yasha."

"You don't have to. You got a family to think about now."

"I know it. And you're part of that family. You always have been."

His face softened into a momentary smile.

"I'd like to go with you, too," said Polly.

I turned to her. She was still holding Ekaterina's hand. "Where you go," she said very quietly, "I go. I should have done that a long time ago."

It seemed that here before me was the prospect of the family I should have had all along. Like maybe a second chance had been offered after so many years. It was the only bright spot in a very dark situation.

"Alright," I said. "When we get back with the children we'll head over the mountains together. To start over."

"You shouldn't come back here," said Sava. "The law will be watching for you."

"What do we do with Lindsay then?"

"We'll arrange for Big Nick to meet you at Iliamna Bay on the west side. Where the portage to the lake begins. You can hand the girl off to him, and he'll bring her here."

"I guess I just got here," I said to Klara.

"I know," she said putting a hand over her face. Mike reached out and took her hand, and she buried herself against him. The rest of us waited patiently for her to get hold of herself. On the wall above the window directly across from me hung the icon painting of Jesus, also weeping.

I scanned each face in the room, finishing up with Polly. "So it's Tutsilitnu then?"

"Tutsilitnu," said Yasha.

"Hope," said Polly.

*

"*Wait* a minute," says Becky. "You were convicted of killing Scotty Keogh."

"That's true," says AC.

"But it seems pretty clear from what you've told me that Hackham did it, not you."

"My lawyer said that was hearsay."

"Then how were you convicted of the crime?"

"They was told that a Kenaytze Indian killed Scotty. I was the closest thing they could find."

Becky rises, walks three paces, then returns to her chair. "That is hardly a fair trial."

"The judge said that because Hack wasn't among the living he couldn't testify that I was innocent of Scotty's murder. Not that he would have, the lying son of a bitch."

"He murdered Scotty in front of his family and kidnapped his daughter as well?"

"Yes."

"That's horrid!"

"He was a horrid man. Though everyone around here seems to think highly of him. That don't exactly fill me up with confidence in the American judicial system."

"Did you tell them what you just told me?"

"What do you think? They said there was no evidence, and no-one could testify to having witnessed the act."

"What about Scotty's wife? And the children?"

"She's three-quarters Native. The judge wouldn't allow her on the stand to testify against a white man. As for the kids—"

The cellblock door slams against the log wall. Lieutenant Henderson stalks up to the cell. Maddox is right behind him, carrying a carbine.

"Lieutenant Henderson," says Becky. "What is going on?"

"Miss Ashford, I'm afraid I'm going to have to terminate your visits with this prisoner."

She rises from her seat. "Whatever for?"

"I think you know."

"Do tell, please."

Henderson points at AC. "He assaulted the Reverend Robinson. In your presence. Which, I might add, would make you an accessory should he choose to press charges."

"That's preposterous! I never touched the man."

"But you failed to inform the guard. You chose to cover up for this filth."

Becky glances at AC, who stares steadfastly at the floor between his moccasins.

"I have work to finish, Lieutenant."

"Your work is finished right now. You are no longer permitted to visit him."

"Lieutenant, please."

"I'm sorry, no. You have become a threat to the security of this facility. And your infatuation with this siwash is hardly appropriate."

Becky steps up to him and plants her hands on her hips. "Excuse me?"

"Escort Miss Ashford out of here," Henderson says to Maddox. The private doesn't meet her eyes, or AC's, as he steps around behind her.

"Let's go, Miss," he mumbles.

Becky looks at him, then back at Henderson. Silently fuming, she gathers her things, stuffs them in her briefcase, and stalks toward the door. AC lifts his eyes and watches her go. She pauses at the door and turns back to him.

"Out!" Henderson bellows, stabbing a finger at her.

She turns and leaves with Maddox at her heels.

Henderson turns to face Campbell. "Bashing a preacher," he says. "God almighty. The sooner you hang the better, you sorry bastard."

Aleksandr Campbell rises to his feet in one smooth motion. He stands at the cell door and speaks in a flat, even voice.

"You're one tough son of a bitch when there's these iron bars between us."

Henderson draws his revolver from its holster, cocks it, and points it directly at Campbell's forehead. The muzzle is not six inches from his skin.

Campbell does not flinch. He does not even blink. "How bout you open this door and we'll find out who's the real hardass."

"I've had enough out of you, Campbell."

"Then do it."

A bead of sweat breaks out on Henderson's temple. His finger takes up the slack on the trigger. Campbell does not move, nor do his eyes.

There is a fluttering at the window, a rustling of air. Henderson's eyes flick over to see the raven perched on the tiny windowsill, peering into the cell as if it were some other dimension. Studying him with eyes like wet oil. Campbell turns to the raven just as it opens its beak and utters a gurgling question. Campbell answers it, talking raven-talk from deep back in his throat. The giant black bird nods once, then hops backward with the grace of an acrobat and takes to wing, out over the fields of crimson fireweed, tag-alder and puschki weed, flying north and calling, Ggwaakk ggwaakk ggwaakk!

Henderson lowers his revolver. Shaking his head, he holsters it, then exits the cellblock.

When he has gone, Campbell goes over to his mattress and withdraws the hidden notebook and pencil. He opens it to the blank page and stares at it, thinking about what the Raven said.

Becky will be coming back.

KRIS FARMEN

CHAPTER X

*B*ecky I am real sorry that you was ordered out by Henderson. He's a first-rate piece of work who takes delight in bossing others around, especially someone like me. He reminds me in no small measure of my old schoolmaster Watkins. You may take comfort in the notion that there will never be a shortage of assholes in this world.

A bird told me you would be coming back. I do not know how you will manage this, but for the time being these writings are the only way I have to leave a record of what happened and how I come to be sitting in this jail cell, waiting my appointment with the noose. I will do the best I can with it, both for you and for myself.

———

We made the most of our brief time in Kenay town. Klara cooked us a huge meal, and while she was working at the stove Mike took me down to the AC store so I could get outfitted. I got only the basics—extra clothes, a packboard, axe, knife, and a used Winchester repeater in .40-60 caliber. I had figured to make these purchases on credit and started to tell Mike that I would send payment as soon as I could, but he waved a hand at me.

"Don't worry about it, AC," he said. "You just find those kids."

Standing there I thought of all the years between us, the good times and the bad. There was a swell of emotion inside me, and all I could think of to say was, "Thank you, Mike."

We left the next morning on the tide as the first rays of the sunrise broke over the bluff edge.

"Godspeed, Aleksandr," Mike said as he shook my hand.

I nodded at him, and then I give Klara a hug. "Be careful," she said in Russian. "I love you, Aleksie."

"I love you too, Aunt Klara," I said. "I'll come back to see you someday. You got my word on it."

"If it is God's will," she said, but we both knew it was most likely His will that I would never return.

Polly had elected to come with us to Hope over the objections of Mike, Klara and Sava. Mine as well.

"The children won't know you," she said to me. "And they barely know Yasha. I should be there for them."

Yasha helped her into the boat as I lingered with Mike and Klara, watching the new frame buildings along the bluff. So much had changed, and it was hard not to think that all of this unpleasantness might have been avoided if I hadn't been so selfish with my life and stayed on the island lost in myself all those years. But there was no help for it now.

"Good bye," I said with a final wave. Then I pushed the boat off and leapt in. Mike put his arm around Klara. Yasha got the oars into play and rowed us out from shore.

We caught a lucky southeast wind near the forelands that brought us up to the mouth of the Swanson River by noon. We lined the boat up the river channel through the mudflats and waited out the ebb tide on the sandspit below the trees. The wind held, and on the next incoming tide we rowed back down through the flats and cruised northward past Point Possession. I wanted to stop, but Yasha and Polly convinced me it was better not to. They reminded me of the men looking for us—we had passed two sails far out across the Inlet, which we only avoided by skillful boatmanship and good luck. So we kept moving.

We had aimed for Yasha's new cabin at Rabbit Creek. Looking over the water, it was a cute little place set up on a bench of white spruce trees above the creek. But as we got closer I spied two boats pulled up in the landing.

Yasha let out a string of Kenaytze oaths.

"You know any of those boats?" Polly asked.

"No," he said pulling the tiller around. Polly ducked as I swung the mast and boom over to the starboard rail, and Yasha steered us for Fire Island. It was tough going, for we was running abeam to the wind, and there was a lot of chop. Yasha had to lean hard against the tiller to keep us pointed on course. The wind in the sail threatened to push the leeward rail down under the water, but we was nearly out of tide and required speed above all else, so we dared not shorten sail. I had Polly move to the port side while I lashed a line to the mast, threw on Yasha's slicker against the sea-splash, and hung myself out over the rail to try and balance us.

"They really are after you," I called over the wind.

"We had to detour over to Old Kuskatan on the way to the island to get you," shouted Yasha. "Too many sails after us. It's getting harder and harder to move around without getting caught."

Of course Yasha and me had the advantage of knowing Cook Inlet's treacherous tides, winds and currents from our earliest days. I was pretty confident we could outfox them.

We pulled in the sail and dropped the mast as we rounded the western point of the island, then we rowed into shore through the pocket of slack water behind it. I worked the oars while Yasha rode in the bow, sounding the bottom with a long pole to make sure we didn't run aground in the shallow mudflats. We pulled up into the mouth of a creek that was just barely deep enough to float us, turned the boat around, and made fast to a drift log. Our boat would look like any other vessel pulled up to shore for the night.

We pitched a quick camp, something we could disassemble in a hurry if we had to. After supper I give Polly a kiss and left her to her dishwashing and walked down through the beachgrass to the end of the point where it ran out into the Inlet. Knik Arm was back to my right, Turnagain Arm to my left. I sat on a drift log, looking up toward Sixmile. Scotty had been at the edge of my thoughts all day, though I hadn't had much time to dwell on him. Now that I had a moment of peace and quiet, it was hard to accept that he was gone, never to be seen again in this life.

The clouds had broke up to the south, and the rays of the sunset beneath them had turned the sky pink and yellow. After a while, Yasha come up behind me and sat down to load his pipe.

"What you doing out here?" he said in the Kenaytze tongue.

"Saying good-bye to Scotty, I guess."

"I miss him. He was as good a friend as you could ask for."

"At least you got to see him again," I said. "When you come back."

"He was doing well with his life," said Yasha. "Ekaterina and Lindsay was a steadying influence on him. Fatherhood suited him."

"Where'd he get buried?"

"Kussilof. Big Nick arranged for it."

We watched the sky as the pink and yellow blended into a peach color that washed across the undersides of the clouds. The snow on the high peaks picked up the color and seemed to glow from it. Our lucky wind had died, and the Inlet was flat calm.

"What's Sixmile and Tutsilitnu look like these days?" I said.

Yasha blew some air through his lips. "It's turning into a big place. Lots of miners. Lots of tents and a few cabins. Hack owns half the placer claims in the valley, one way or another."

He struck a match and lit his pipe.

"What about Belukha Pete? And everyone at Possession town? How have they made out with all this?"

"Not much left of it. They had the chicken-pox there a couple years ago. Lots of people died, and most of the survivors moved up to the Matanushka River. Pete's up there too."

I looked across the water where the dark line of Point Possession seemed to slide out halfway across the Inlet. There was a lump in my throat, and it was hard to speak.

"This is all my doing," I said.

"How do you figure?"

"I'm the one that had the bright idea to buy our outfit with gold back in eighty-five. If I'd kept my word nobody would know about the gold at Tutsilitnu, and none of these miners would be here."

"You shouldn't be so hard on yourself," said Yasha. "There's more Boston Men in this country than ever, and they would have found that gold anyway."

There was something in his eyes that hadn't been there when we lived at Sixmile. It was not sadness, nor was it happiness. It was as if he'd found some measure of peace in the world, and I could only envy him that. For my part, I could hardly wait to be gone from the Inlet, and this was a depressing thought in and of itself.

"But I didn't have to help them," I said. "I give my word to Lucky Jim, and I didn't keep it. Now I have to go to sleep every night thinking about that."

"I don't blame you, AC. Pete neither. Nobody does, so you need to just let go of all that. Otherwise you're just liable to start drinking again."

"I don't want that," I said.

And believe me, I didn't. There in the colors of that sunset I could suddenly see how I had wasted my younger days, slowly poisoning myself with booze. I suppose I might have blamed Big Nick and Scotty for that, but it was not them who lifted the bottle to my lips.

We was quiet for a while, smoking.

"We had some good times here," I said after a while.

Yasha's mouth hooked up slightly. His eyes stayed fixed on the vision of glory before us. "Didn't we, though?"

I recharged my pipe. "It's a bum deal that you got to give up your brand new cabin."

He seemed unperturbed. "I imagine there's plenty of cabin logs over the mountains."

"George Washington used to say that Iliamna Lake is so big it's like a freshwater sea."

"I know. I'm looking forward to seeing that."

I struck a match and lit up.

"AC."

"Yeah?"

"I'm sorry I took off on you. It was the wrong thing to do. And I'm sorry for running my mouth about your power."

"Don't trouble over it," I said.

"Fedosya and Semyon was already gone when I got to Nikishka."

I said nothing.

"You're my partner, and I should have stuck by you when you really needed me. You was only trying to help me when you tried to keep me from going."

"Yasha," I said, "you're the closest thing I got to a brother. I can't hold nothing against you."

A shower floated down way across Turnagain Arm, near the mouth of the Tutsahtnu where Scotty had been killed in his own house. From afar it looked like a curtain stretched across the country. It caught the fading sunlight in streaks of rainbow color, staying for five minutes, maybe a little more. Then it pulled back up into the sky like it had never been. Off to our right the mountains on the west side was a jagged blue line with the sunset behind them. The wet mudflats glowed gold and orange.

"It's beautiful, aint it?" I said.

"Hush," said Yasha. "Our mouths aint big enough to speak of all that."

———

Polly and I slept that night curled up under one of the tarps. It will come as no surprise that she was worried sick about our son and Lindsay, and I gave her whatever comfort was in my power to give. Somewhere in the night the rain come back and drizzled upon us, though we stayed dry beneath our coverings. I woke in the dim hours of the morning with Polly next to me. The rhythm of her breath told me she was asleep, which was good, for she needed the rest. I kept my head under the tarp and focused my attention on the light that spread under the folds. There was something I needed to say to her before I left, and the thought of it filled me with both dread and joy.

The rain slacked off, but the grass was still wet as me and Yasha left Polly. She drew me into her arms as Yasha stood amidships setting out the oars making ready to row to Tusilitnu at half tide.

"Bring our son back," she said into my neck.

"If he's there I'll find him."

"And be careful. I just got you back, and I don't want to lose you again."

I took in her scent. "I love you, Polly. I never stopped loving you."

She pulled my forehead down to hers. "I love you, too, AC. Always and forever."

My pulse filled my ears. The world I had returned to seemed to be pulling me along like the tide. And you cannot fight the tides of Cook Inlet. You can only get out of the way when they're not moving the direction you wish to go. When the tide turns your way you must hold on tight and never hesitate. You have to charge hard and trust to luck and use every bit of skill at your command.

"Polly," I said.

"Yes?"

"Would you be my bride when we make it to the lake?"

She nodded, then wiped at a tear. "Yes," she whispered. "Yes I will, AC."

———

What happened next has been the subject of a great deal of testimony and deposition. Almost all of it was lies told to box me up in this jail cell. Here is the truth of the matter.

Yasha rowed halfway up the Arm, and then I took over. The rain come down again as we left Polly on the beach and pulled away from Fire Island, but it slacked off and quit as we approached Tutsilitnu. The clouds above showed no sign of clearing. I had steeled myself for my first look at this new camp they called Hope, but even so it was a cold slap across the face when I seen the white spots of the wall tents and the stump-field that ringed them in the cloudy distance.

I worked the oars and turned us stern first so I could get a better look. Yasha sat sideways on the bow thwart, leaning against the mast where we'd lashed it down for rowing.

"Lot of people here now," he said.

"No kidding."

"It's starting to feel like America."

"What's America like?"

He propped his moccasin feet on the rail. "It's like this. Only more Americans."

"Jesus Christ." I studied the tent city, working the oars to keep us pointed into the channel.

"I know," said Yasha.

"So where is Hack's place in all this mess?"

He pointed up the west hill. "You can't see it just yet, but it's up there. Put us into that little cove. We can just slip in without being spotted."

The cove he pointed to was an indentation in the coast with a scrap of gravel beach above the mud. I had sailed past it countless times in *bidarkas* and dories, never thinking much about it. Now it was to be our hideout. Times had certainly changed.

I turned the bow around and rowed backward with a foot against the aft thwart for power against the tide-flow. We had timed our arrival so we could make our getaway on the falling tide, which meant the clock was ticking. I put us into the cove, and we anchored the dory and made ready for the quarter-mile walk to Hack's place. I slicked my skinning knife over a sharpening steel, then checked my rifle to see that it was loaded. Yasha watched as I done this, and when I looked up I seen he was unarmed.

"What?" I said.

"We aint murderers, AC."

"Things could go to hell."

"Then they go to hell. We aint going up there to kill Hack. We're going to fetch them kids."

"Yasha, they could try to nab you for the marshal. Hell, for all we know he could be there already."

"Then we'll deal with that some other way than killing. Besides, the marshal's boat wasn't pulled up at the waterfront."

Out in the Arm, the tide was rolling. We had no time for idle argument. Yasha was right and I knew it.

"All right," I said, laying my rifle in the boat.

We took to the woods bearing no arms but our pocket-knives. You will note, Becky, that this is contrary to the lies presented to the court at my trial. The prosecutor claimed we was murderous savages, armed to the teeth and out for Hack's scalp, but it was the complete opposite. May this record show that Yasha Izaakov was a peace-loving man who convinced me to lay down my gun.

We moved fast and quiet, following moose trails through the rain-soaked mossy woods until we came to the edge of the stump-field. It saddened me to recognize the dead stumps of many of my favorite trees. We halted just inside the timber to get the lay of the land.

It was even more disheartening to see the invasion of our country up close. There was close to thirty boats at anchor in the creek mouth. The camp's early risers was stirring.

"It's even worse up at Sunrise," said Yasha.

"You mean Sixmile?"

He nodded.

This amounted to a very sour homecoming.

Yasha pointed to a cabin up near the top of the field. "There's Hack's place."

It was a one-story place with a loft, a tin roof, and three glass windows. It looked to be the nicest place in town. It had a commanding view of the camp and diggings below.

"Leave it to Hack to have the biggest house in a tent camp," I said.

Polly had drawn us the layout of the cabin on a slip of paper so we would know the interior as soon as we opened the door. It had a kitchen in the front with a small separate parlor in the rear.

"Someone's home," Yasha said. "There's smoke in the chimney."

KRIS FARMEN

Hack was asleep in his suit in a chair in the parlor when we eased the door open and crept inside. I hadn't seen him since the fight in Kenay town—his nose was flatter, and he'd grown his beard to hide his crooked jaw. But it was him, no doubt about it. Yasha stayed in the kitchen just inside the open door, keeping an eye on the tents downhill from us.

Both kitchen and parlor was well furnished. That would have been Polly's doing. My eye lingered a moment on the shelf of books against the north wall. I had no notion of why Hack had chosen to take his night's rest sitting in a chair, but I did see the revolver that lay on the side-table next to him. Evidently he was expecting company. Such is the life of a wealthy and jealous man.

I moved to the table and took up the pistol and stuffed it into the back of my waistband beneath my moleskin jacket. Quietly, I pulled up a second chair so that I sat facing him with our knees almost touching.

He mumbled something and stirred. I was watching him when his eyes fluttered open. He started, jumping back into his chair and bumping it against the wall.

"Time to wake up, Hack"

"You!"

His eyes darted to the side-table, but of course his pistol was no longer there. He looked back at me, and I knew he had received word that I was back in the world and coming for him.

"You know what I'm here for."

He just watched me, saying nothing.

"Where are the children? I aint going to ask you twice."

"Fuck you, Campbell."

I backhanded him across the face. "By God, I busted your pretty face once, and I'll happily do it again."

There come a stirring on the loft boards above. Yasha shot a worried glance at us. Hack never took his eyes off me. They was full of fear and hate and loathing. Such a creature I might have pitied had he not kidnapped my son and murdered my friend.

"Upstairs," he said with a smirk.

I heard Yasha's moccasins on the ladder. There was a rustling, then a sharp cry, then a shotgun blast tore through the morning.

"Yasha!" I shouted. Hack took the opportunity to topple my chair and pin me to the floor. All at once there come the screaming of a girl upstairs and the thump of someone falling down the loft-ladder. Yasha cussed and dove away as another shotgun blast ripped into the kitchen door, punching it wide open. The child screamed again, crying and whimpering. Hack was on top of me with his hands at my neck, working to cut off my air. I had the pistol but it was beneath me where I couldn't get at it. I tried to twist around and get my coattails out of the way, but he got a knee onto my chest and slammed me down against the floor, bearing down on my throat. I drove my own knee up into his sweetmeats, and he screamed and let go. I threw him off me and shucked the pistol and held it on him as he balled up in agony on the rug.

Boots clumped down the ladder. Yasha bolted out the door with the shotgun man on his heels. I heard two pistol shots, then a sickening crunch. Then there was silence.

"Yasha!" I called.

A dark shape moved through the door, and I threw up the pistol. It was Yasha. "Whoah," he said, holding up his palms.

"You alright?"

"Yeah."

Hack was still doubled up and writhing, so I lowered the shooter. "What happened?"

"Maybe you better come see."

I grabbed Hack by the hair and lifted. "On your feet!" With the pistol I pushed him staggering out the ruined door.

"Hell's bells!" I said when I seen the shotgun man. He lay face up with a kindling hatchet buried straight into his face between the eyebrows. One of his legs flopped around violently, but he was dead as a doornail.

Yasha's hands shook as he pointed at the nearby chopping block. "He come at me with his pistol. I grabbed that hatchet from out of the block and let him have it."

"Well, it was self-defense," I said. "Any fool can see that."

"Let's hope we don't have to put that to the test."

This killing was pinned on me as well in the early stages of my trial. I never caught the man's name at the time, but apparently it was George Stafford. Curiously, the prosecutor and the judge concluded there was not enough evidence to link me to his killing. They made this decision speaking legal Latin, and while my attorney translated it for me I still don't entirely understand it. Not that it matters. They can only hang me once.

From around the corner of the cabin we heard a tiny voice: "Yasha?"

We looked over, and there was a girl, maybe seven years old, standing in front of the doorway in a torn pinafore dress.

"Lindsay!" said Yasha. He rushed over and knelt down, saying, "It's alright, honey. We've come to take you home to your mother."

She threw her arms around him, and he held her close, making sure to shield her from the awful sight of Stafford's twitching corpse.

I shoved Hack behind the corner of the house where Lindsay couldn't see. He slumped against the log wall still clutching his baubles.

"Where is my son?" I said.

He glared at me and said nothing. A spark shot out from beneath my ears. I cocked the pistol and pushed it under his chin. "WHERE IS MY SON, DAMN YOU!" I had just tightened up on the trigger when Yasha come up behind me and stayed my hand.

I swallowed the sparks.

"There's men coming up the hill," he said. "They got guns. And we got to make the tide."

He had Lindsay in his arms with her face pressed into his jacket so she would not see what was happening.

"Partner, we got to git."

"What if Max is here?" I said. "I aint leaving without my son."

Lindsay mouthed some words against Yasha's chest, but we couldn't make out what she said. He hefted her on his arm and stroked her hair. "What is it, honey?"

She was crying, but Yasha gently wiped her tears away. "Say it again. What is it?"

Lindsay sniffled. "Max is at Anchor Point."

Yasha looked smart over at me and I at him. We had not a moment to spare, but here before me, delivered into my hands, was the man who had brought so much grief into my life, and the lives of so many others. The man who could prove Yasha's innocence.

From down the hillside we could hear men shouting to one another.

"We got to go, AC," Yasha said. "*Now.*"

I had to make a decision, right or wrong. So I made it. We lashed Hack's hands before him with a length of rope, then I reached into my jacket pocket and withdrew a coil of moosehide line. This I fashioned into a leash, the kind the Indians used for prisoners back in the old days. I slipped the loop over Hack's head and snugged it up tight so that it would cut off his air if he struggled.

"Come on," I said, giving him a not-so-gentle tug. "You're going to answer for the shit you've pulled."

And with Yasha carrying Lindsay we ghosted into the trees, following the moose trails back to the dory.

We slipped out of Turnagain Arm with no-one behind us. Those fellows charging up to Hack's place did get their boats into play, eventually. But by the time they figured out what had happened, we was long gone.

Polly was waiting for us on the beach when we made it back to Fire Island. Lindsay seen her straight off, and she was over the bow and running across the silt and gravel to her before the keel even hit. Polly scooped her up into her arms, covering her with kisses. The child put her arms around her like she meant to squeeze the daylights out of her. Hack sat in the boat, sullen and hateful as Yasha and I tied up and put out the anchor.

Polly's motherly look turned to alarm when she seen Hack and realized that we did not have Max with us.

"Where's Max?" she said as I grabbed Hack by his coat and dragged him over the gunwale and dumped him on the silt. His hands was still bound.

"Things didn't quite go as planned," I said.

"What do you mean?"

"Everything's fine," I said. "Max is at Anchor Point. Hack had Lindsay up in the loft, and there was a bit of a scuffle."

She looked from me to Yasha, then back again. "A scuffle?"

Yasha leaned against a drift log. He was still shaken by what had happened, and to be frank, so was I.

I went up and touched her cheek. "We're both fine, don't worry."

"What's he doing here?" she said.

"I'm going to haul him in to the marshal."

Hack stirred. "You keep your hands off my wife, Campbell."

Yasha got up and nudged him with his toe. "Aint noone talking to you."

"We're still married," Hack said. "You fool around with her, and it's adultery. I'll kill you for it."

I turned to face him. "How 'bout you just keep your mouth shut. I can always send Lindsay and Polly into the trees while I go to work on you."

"That aint the plan," said Yasha in a low voice.

"We can turn him over to Big Nick if nothing else," I said. "The time's come for him to pay for his crimes. All of them."

Polly give me a rather queer look over the top of Lindsay's hair.

"It would make us look more like law-abiding citizens if we brought him in," I said.

Yasha frowned.

"It's the right thing to do, partner. And besides, he can testify to your innocence."

Hack struggled onto his back and sat up. "So just where the hell did you show up from, Campbell?"

"Kalgin Island."

"What pray tell were you doing there?"

"He was a bear," said Yasha.

"Oh yes, that's right. You and your magical powers. Lord help us all."

I ignored this remark. Yasha looked sheepish and stared off at the water.

"I reckon our best bet for now is to head to Anchor Point," I said to Polly and Yasha. "Finding Max is most important."

Hack twisted his wrists in the bindings. He was trying to stand up. I went over and shoved him down again with my foot.

"They're not going to arrest me for what Yasha done," he said looking up at me.

"You're mad," said Yasha. "I watched you shoot Scotty. So did Polly and Ekaterina. Lindsay, too."

His mouth twisted into an unpleasant smile. "I've got men who were with me who will testify in court that you were the one that drilled Scotty."

"Like that fellow with the shotgun?" I said. "I don't think he'll have much to say."

"I got plenty of others."

I folded my arms. "Hack, you might as well come clean. There's four witnesses to what you done. You're sunk."

"We'll just see about that, Campbell."

The solid tone of his voice give me pause, I must confess. I had no way of knowing that he had several attorneys in his employ. Indeed, the word *attorney* was almost unknown to me. I had read about them in books, but book learning only takes you so far in this life. There was forces I could barely comprehend that was about to be unleashed upon me like the hounds of hell itself.

We hoped for a strong north wind to take us all the way to Anchor Point, but we got only the barest of breezes. We stuck to the west side where we was less likely to bump into the Kodiak marshal or any of Hack's friends. We kept Hack in the bow where we could watch him. His hands had begun turning purple so I cut his lashings, but I made it clear that we would tie and gag him in a trice if he opened his mouth again.

We passed the west forelands around midnight and fetched up at the cemetery near Old Kuskatan. The village had moved sometime before I was born to the north side of the forelands, but someone was keeping up the old Russian crosses and grave-houses with fresh paint and flowers. Spending the night at a graveyard is hardly my idea of fun, but the tide was turning, and it was the most convenient place to land where we wouldn't be spotted.

As we was getting set for the night, I heard Lindsay ask Polly about the graves. "Are these doll-houses?"

"No, honey," said Polly, "they are the monuments the Indians build for their departed loved ones."

"Oh."

Hack passed the night lashed to a tree, and I heard Lindsay say to Yasha, "He's a very bad man." I did not disagree with her assessment. Scotty's daughter was a pretty sharp little girl, and it brought a smile to my face thinking of him. She'd gotten old enough that I could see his face in some of her features, and I made up my mind then and there to always make sure his child was looked after.

Tired as we was, neither Polly nor I could sleep, so I asked her to tell me about Max. "Not what he looks like," I said. "I mean what he's like."

She smiled a little as we lay beneath the sheltering boughs of a spruce tree. "He's very clever," she said. "He likes to take things apart to see how they work. He ruined one of Hack's pocket-watches like that, but quite often when he puts things back together they work just right."

"Did Hack treat him alright?"

She looked away and said nothing. I stroked her golden curls, fascinated by the color of them.

"He might have a hard time trusting you," she said.

"We'll deal with that when the time comes. Is he a healthy lad?"

"For the most part. But he does have a problem with his ears."

"A problem with his ears?"

"He says he gets a crackling feeling underneath them sometimes. I took him Outside last winter to see a doctor, but he couldn't find anything wrong with him."

My voice seemed to have deserted me.

"AC, what's wrong?"

"He gets that from me," I whispered.

———

There was blue sky above as we pulled out with the southbound tide, but we had to tack against another southeasterly wind, and this ate up a lot of time. Halfway across the water Polly sighted a steam plume up near the East Foreland.

"Marshal Tomlinson has a small steam-ship," she said.

I was once again leaning out over the rail, holding onto a line and trying not to fall in the drink as we beat across the wind. "You reckon that's him?"

She stood up and shielded her eyes from the sun-glare. "No way to tell from this distance. It could be him. Or it could be Captain Lathrop with his freight barge. Or any of a half-dozen other ships."

This was true to the letter, but deep inside I reckon we all knew it was Tomlinson, come to hunt down Yasha. Yasha himself stood at the tiller saying not a word and watching the smoke most intently.

Later, the wind came about north by northeast with a couple hours left on the tide. This was good for sailing, and it meant I could ride inside instead of hanging over the rail, but it brought with it a thick overcast sky and the possibility of more rain. It also blew up a field of whitecaps, which made it a rough ride, but we was in the middle of the Inlet and had to go somewhere. We put out all our canvas and drove hard for Cape Starichkof. Hack rode quietly in the bow, not looking at anyone.

I took the tiller from Yasha so he could have a break. As we cruised along I got to daydreaming about walking down the beach of Iliamna Lake with my son and telling him about bears and cranes. If he had the sparks in his ears then he most likely had the ability to change just as I did and Lucky Jim before me. I wondered what manner of beast lived in his skin. There was an urgency to get to him now, for this was not something I wanted him to face alone. There was also the hope that I could help him to not make the same mistakes with his life that I made with mine, namely turning to drink to control the sparking.

These was the thoughts in my head when Lindsay sang out that there was something floating in the water up ahead. All eyes all looked where she pointed. Off the starboard bow was a dark shape, barely visible for the waves breaking over it.

"What is it?" Lindsay said to me.

I shook my head. "I don't know."

"Might be an upturned boat," said Polly.

I leaned into the tiller, steering us toward the object. It looked flat and slick-backed like a dark-stained pan of river ice, though this was unlikely in August month. Yasha gripped the mast and climbed up with his toe on the boom.

"I'll be damned," he said. "It's a great big flat fish."

By this he meant a halibut. Indians of course, consider it bad luck to use an animal's name when looking right at it.

"You boshing me?" I said, for everyone knows that halibut live on the bottom of the ocean and never come up to the surface unless pulled up on a hook and line.

"I'm looking right at it," said Yasha.

"Good lord, it's huge!" said Polly.

I got up on the stern thwart and braced the tiller against my knee. My hands were cold in the wind and I cupped them over my mouth and blew on them. With the extra height I could see that it was indeed a halibut, a giant old hen. Five hundred pounds if she was an ounce. We could have climbed over the side and strolled around atop her.

Lindsay turned to Yasha. "Is it dead? "

"No," he said. "I can see its eyes blinking."

"You ever see such a thing before?" Polly asked us.

Me and Yasha could only shake our heads.

Hack had not moved. He watched this astounding phenomenon with studied indifference.

"We're low on grub," I said to Yasha.

"I know it." He started reefing in the sail so we wouldn't scoot right past. This was way more fish than we could use, but it was food, and we didn't have no time to debate the evils of wanton waste. The fish was far too big to gaff and haul aboard—hell, it was bigger than the boat—so Yasha took Hack's pistol from behind my waistband and bellied up to the rail to shoot it through the head. We would have to butcher it leaning over the side, which was tricky, though certainly preferable to going hungry.

I steered us in close, watching the fish and thinking of how odd this was. Just as Yasha cocked the pistol and aimed, I recognized the eyes.

"Opal," I said to the wind, for it was none other than her. "Wait!" I sang out.

Yasha looked over at me. "What?"

"I know that fish. We can't kill her."

Down in the water, Opal watched me with her twin eyes, saying nothing.

"We need grub, AC," said Yasha.

My limbs started to shake for some reason that I could not name. "Yasha, we can't kill this big fish. I know her, and she's been real good to me."

Opal blinked, still watching me from the top of her watery home. She didn't look at the others, only at me.

There come a thump from the bow and we all turned just as Hack made a lunge for Yasha and the pistol. Before I could react he'd knocked him down into the bilge and got a hand round the gun's action and was pushing his shoulder into Yasha's face, trying to get a forearm across his throat. The boat rocked dangerously from the waves and their struggle as Yasha tried frantically to thumb back the hammer and get a shot into him.

I turned loose of the tiller and threw myself onto Hack. He was shouting and kicking, and Yasha got off a shot, but it flew wild and clipped the top of the transom. Lindsay screamed. Hack wrenched the pistol from Yasha's grip. He cocked and aimed and loosed a shot at me. I felt the wind of it as I dove down. Polly grabbed Hack's thighs, and I knocked the pistol aside and punched him hard in the gut. He stumbled back, tripping over a box of fishing tackle. He flailed his arms and stumbled in the pitching boat, trying to right himself. I grabbed for his collar but missed as he tumbled backward over the rail. My fingertips touched his waistcoat but nothing more and he splashed into the water.

"Hack!" I shouted, throwing out a hand to him.

"I can't swim! I can't swim!" he cried. He thrashed all about, gasping in shock from the ice-cold water. I grabbed the fish-gaff and thrust it out at him, but the waves and wind and current had already pushed him too far away.

"She's gone!" said Lindsay. "The halibut is gone!"

Hack's panicked eyes locked onto mine as he flailed in the water. The cold was rapidly sapping his strength. Frantically I looked around for something I could throw out to him. Then Polly cried out.

"Look!"

The overcast sky to the northeast was yellow and orange down to the horizon. It colored the water and hid the mountains. Hack was splashing and shouting and starting to go down. There was a flash of sliding water around him, the boiling of something huge and monstrous coming to the surface. Then there was Opal, back atop of the ocean, right in front of him. The water broke over her as she studied him for a moment.

Then she struck. Her jaws must have had a good twenty-four inch spread—one of her cheeks would have filled a good-sized skillet and hung out over the sides. She clamped down onto Hack's head; there was no sound but the thrashing as she bucked and twisted him every which way. It was not unlike a smaller fish grabbing a half a herring on a hook. One of Hack's hands reached for us, then Opal dove, and the two of them was gone. There was nothing left but the whitecaps, the wind, and the skim of Hack's blood upon the water.

I turned around from the rail. Polly hugged Lindsay close to her while she and Yasha stared first at one another, then at the water, then over at me. I once heard of a salmon shark that grabbed a Russian officer's dog that had jumped overboard for a swim, but I never in my life expected to see such as we had just witnessed. Many men have called me a liar over this, but I don't give a damn what they think. I watched it happen with my own eyes, and they can all go to hell.

My heart sank to my feet as we stood there, struck dumb and watching Cook Inlet's choppy skin with the wind whipping through our rigging. Hack was the only white man who could testify to Yasha's innocence, and now he was gone for fish fodder.

"*Ggwaakk ggwaakk ggwaakk!*"

I looked up to see a raven shooting past with the wind over top of our vessel. The fiery sky behind us looked like the end of days.

———

The wind refused to make up its mind that afternoon. We was almost within sight of Cape Starichkof when it swung all the way around to the southwest and with no warning built into a gale of ten foot seas. Then the tide turned, and we was left with no choice but to backtrack until we fetched up on the south end of Kalgin Island. Here we made camp as the rain began to pelt down, just as it had the previous week when Yasha and Polly had first come for me.

This was a bitter disappointment, for all around us was the very obvious feeling that we was right back where we started from.

I recall standing at the edge of the timber and staring into the forest where I had spent so many years imprisoned by my own selfishness and melancholy. In that moment I heard the Devil whispering in my ear once again, telling me that all the difficulties of this hunt for the children and the venomous legacy of Greg Hackham would cease to trouble me if only I would just let myself change into a bear once more. Abandon my friends and keep company once again with the Black Bird. I felt the barest of crackles in my jaw, and for a moment I craved a drink. I will allow that I was tempted, but in the end I clamped down my teeth and swallowed the sparks and turned my back on those years. I had family counting on me.

We strung tarps between the spruce trees and retired early. We was exhausted and hungry and troubled by the day's events. Me and Polly lay under our tarp listening to the raindrops slap more and more insistently upon the canvas.

"We're in a heap of trouble, aren't we?" she said.

"We are."

She curled her fingers against me. "We can't go to the marshal now. If we do they'll hang Yasha."

Hack had plenty of friends, and it didn't take a genius to see that either me or Yasha would get charged with his murder, which is of course what happened. But at that moment I was still a free man, and neither of us knew what was about to unfold.

"We still have to get Max," I said.

"I know," Polly said putting her face against my shoulder. "I know."

✳

ootsteps once again enter the cell block, and Campbell hastily slides the notebook and pencil under his mattress. He thinks it is Heinz's turn on watch this morning, and he composes himself to have his noon meal flung at him. Tomorrow, he is to hang.

There is a woman's voice. "Good day, AC."

For just a half second he thinks it is Polly, and his heart skips a beat, but he is almost as pleased to see who has come.

"Becky?"

"How are you?"

She stands before the bars with her briefcase hanging from both hands in front of her skirts. Campbell smiles. The chains of the shackles around his wrists rattle as he rises to his feet. "I figured you'd be back."

"Did a bird tell you that?"

"Yes."

"They have you in irons, I see."

AC holds up his bracelets. "They said I was a threat to the guards."

"Ah."

"How'd you manage to get back in to see me? You poison the Lieutenant or something?"

Her eyes flick down to the floor. "Never you mind."

AC shrugs and smiles, and she pushes her own smile back at him. She glances toward the door. "I think Corporal Heinz has your dinner."

Heinz appears with his cap pulled low over his eyes. He nods at Becky Ashford, then bends and slides Campbell's tray beneath the bars. It is beans and cornbread, with a tin mug of coffee.

"Is there a chair I might borrow?" she asks as he straightens up.

"Yeah, I guess." He disappears out the door and returns with her usual seat. He sets it on the floor, leaving her to place it to her liking. She slides it into her customary position. AC retrieves his notebook and sits with his back against the wall and his left shoulder just inside the bars.

"I been writing for you," he says.

"Really? May I have a look?"

KRIS FARMEN

AC tips it through the bars to her, then takes up his plate and begins eating. His irons clink softly against the tin. Becky is silent, flipping through the pages, but he reckons he can hear her mind at work. The image of cogs and gears and steam chambers inside her head brings a smile to his lips as he chews and swallows.

She has finished reading by the time he is on his coffee.

"You actually have very good penmanship," she says.

"That would be Mailman Mike's work. I was surprised how fast it come back to me."

Becky examines the pages again for a moment. AC watches her.

"I do appreciate your efforts," she says after a moment. "There are some interesting data in here."

"I wrote it down so you would know what happened and why I'm in here. I thought maybe you could put it into a book or your government monograph."

She looks at him over top of the notebook.

"So there would be a record of what happened to me," says AC. "And of how things were here in this country when I was younger. So that—"

Becky watches.

"So that my son can know where he comes from. Who his people are."

Becky molds her face into a very prim posture. She opens her mouth and considers her words. "I have to tell you that most of what you've written will be of no real interest to the Bureau. I came here to record information on your belief that you can change yourself into a bear, not your frolicking with a married woman."

Something in her demeanor has changed, though AC cannot put his finger on it. It is as if the light has gone out inside her. Or is being hidden beneath a mask.

"I never got to tell Max about his power," he says.

"His power?"

"It's in there," he says, gesturing at the notebook. "Polly told me that he gets the crackling sparks under his ears. He needs to know what's happening to him, and he won't have nobody to explain it."

Becky purses her lips and studies the tips of her shoes.

"I loved Polly," says AC. "And I want Max to know that. Is it not a beautiful thing that we was reunited after all those years?"

"I suppose it is. Like something in a novel. But I'm not after romance, I'm here for scientific data."

She reaches up and brushes a strand of hair away from her eyes. "And besides," she says, "I doubt the reading public would see things the way you do. They will see a married woman dishonoring herself and her family."

"That aint the position I'd expect a modern woman like you to take on the matter."

Becky looks down at her shoes again. She hates herself for making the bargain she had to make to see him once again. The deal with Marshal Tomlinson. There was no science in it. Lieutenant Henderson was right about her, and she knows it, and just as Campbell told her the other day, being wrong about oneself has a particular sting.

"It is the position I take, regardless."

AC sighs and rests the back of his head against the wall. "Then do what you will with it. You asked me to write things down, so that's what I done."

They sit. Aleksandr Campbell wonders just what she had to do to get her access to him reinstated. Becky Ashford wonders how to turn the conversation around to the direction she has promised to take it. It makes her want to cry, a feeling she detests. She loves the rhythms of his language and how different they are from everything she knows. How different this far-flung land is from everywhere else she has been. She wonders if, in another place and time, this man before her might have been another Quanah Parker or Louis Riel.

"You're looking very hard at that notebook, Miss," says AC.

"I'm just looking over your writing again."

"You're liable to burn a hole in the paper."

Miss Ashford makes a conscious decision not to bite her lip. She has begun to wish desperately that she had met this man somewhere other than his condemned cell. Her eyes come to rest on the veins on his forearms, his hands, his fingernails. There is the wish that she could unlock the cell door and remove his irons and have him take her far away from all of this.

She can feel Campbell watching her. She clears her throat and decides to go for broke.

"Mr. Campbell, could you tell me where you hid Greg Hackham's body?"

"I beg your pardon?"

"I said, can you—"

KRIS FARMEN

Campbell feels a spark shoot out from beneath his right ear, then another. Slowly, he realizes what has happened.

"Can you tell me –"

"Not you," he says.

"I just—"

He shakes his head. "Not you, Becky. Don't tell me you believe that horseshit."

"Just tell me. Please, AC. He has family that need to know where he lies."

He rises and stalks across the cell. "Did Tomlinson put you up to this? Or Henderson?"

"No."

"Don't you lie to me!"

She feels the vapors spreading behind her nose. A tear spills from her eye, and she hates herself for it.

"Please, AC. Just tell me."

"I did not kill Scotty and Hackham!" he shouts at her. "How many fucking times do I have to say it?"

Becky wipes at her tears, a fast involuntary motion. Heinz's bootfalls approach from the office.

She looks up and Aleksandr Campbell is gone. In his place is a bear, enormous in the small space and advancing with its eyes locked upon hers. The pale tips of its fur tremble in fury, and the shackle-chains drag across the puncheon floor as it moves, catlike, to the center of the cell. The notebook drops from Becky Ashford's hand. She sits frozen in place, her eyes wide and refusing to process what they see.

The bear's mouth does not move, but a voice fills the entire building: GET OUT!

Becky Ashford lets loose a tiny cry and is somehow aware of Heinz in the cellblock doorway. The bear bellows again at her, and she spills over backward as it charges the bars and stamps its front paws at her. It pops its teeth and slams once more against the iron, shaking it in its moorings. The bear is so close she can smell its breath and feel the wind from its charge. She crab-crawls backward with her fashionable shoeheels catching and tearing her petticoats. She finds her feet and scrambles to the door where Heinz stands, slack-jawed. Their eyes meet for a moment, and there is a perfect understanding, not of what has happened, but in the knowledge that neither of them can really comprehend what has happened.

She squirts past him and out the door. Heinz looks after her, then back into the cell. The bear is gone. There is only the convicted murderer Aleksandr Campbell, slumped against the cell bars, working his jaw up and down.

Heinz does not see the notebook that he has pulled into the cell and hidden.

KRIS FARMEN

CHAPTER XI

*B*ecky I apologize for frightening you earlier today, it was uncalled for. I did not kill Scotty or Hackham, no matter what they have told you, and as I consider you a friend it upset me greatly that you would ask such a thing. My guess is that you was put up to this by Tomlinson, because frankly Henderson aint smart enough to think of it. I have heard the Marshal is still in town, and this is not the first time they have pressed me to reveal the whereabouts of Hack's body, which of course is at the bottom of the Gulf of Kenay in the form of halibut shit.

I got no idea if you will ever read this, but it's obvious to me that you want to know what happened at Anchor Point, and this is the only way I have to inform you. These events are unpleasant to revisit, but I have chose to write it down for the reasons we discussed during your last visit. They tried me in front of a petit jury, which is six Americans instead of the usual twelve. I had a defense, but the attorney they brought over from Sitka for me was a drunk who had his law license revoked in three states before he washed up in Alaska.

When I told him what I have told you, and what I am about to tell you, he just looked at me and said, "Son you need to understand something here. The law aint got nothing to do with truth or justice."

In other words, my trial was all about what was erroneously referred to as THE FACTS. These so-called facts, as presented by the prosecutor—a man named Fenton—was that I had murdered Scotty in cold blood in his house at the mouth of the Tutsahtnu River and then abducted Hack and murdered him and dumped his body in a secret location. Fenton also took great pains to point out that I showed no remorse for these crimes, but then how could I show remorse for murders that I had not committed?

They was far more concerned with Hack than with Scotty, and my attorney told me my case rested on the principle of *habeas corpus*, which means they had to produce a dead body in order to accuse me of murder. Fenton countered this by arguing that *habeas corpus* only applies in what he referred to as THE CONTIGUOUS UNITED STATES EXCLUSIVE OF ITS OVERSEAS POSSESSIONS, and the judge agreed.

I recall most particularly Fenton in his dark suit turning to me while making his closing arguments. He said, "This Russian siwash is representative of the depravity of his race. It is an established scientific fact that individuals of mixed race lack the intellectual capacity to control their base urges. I ask the jury to hand down a verdict of guilty to send a message to these half-breeds that such murderous behavior will not be tolerated by the government of the United States of America."

The petit jury took less than ten minutes to hand down its verdict, which of course was GUILTY. The next day I was brought forward in my irons to stand before the judge and receive the sentence which is to be carried out at ten o'clock tomorrow morning.

So here for the record is my account of how we recovered my son, Maxim Campbell, and of the aftermath that brought me to this cell.

The southwest storm with its contrary wind and heavy seas kept us weather-bound on the island for almost two days. Yasha harpooned a harbor seal just outside the surf, so we at least had meat. On the afternoon of the second day the storm slacked off, and we caught the ebb tide and a westerly wind for the drive straight down to Anchor

Point, but halfway across our wind sputtered out. The tide pushed us southward almost to the mouth of Kachemak Bay before it turned and we was able to get onto the oars and pull for the Anchor River.

Anchor Point is not so much a point, but a bend in the coast where the Inlet curves around from Kachemak Bay back to the northeast. Hack's gold workings along the beach lie just to the south of the river mouth. I watched the men at work as Yasha took a breather at the oars, letting the tide carry us along shore toward the river.

I'd never seen such a large sluicing plant. The grass was all tore up, and they'd leveled most of the trees for timber to build the oversized steam-driven rockers that shook the beach sand. They'd excavated a giant crescent-shaped hole into the beach between the point and the river mouth, and it looked like the river might burst its way straight through to the sea any day. Men moved this way and that, with teams of horses pulling drays piled high with sand up to the hoppers where men with shovels pushed it into the steam-rockers. Behind all of it was a clutch of rough cabins and wall tents.

I looked for Max, but there was several young lads among the work gang, and I couldn't pick him out at such a distance. Not that I would have recognized him—he was only two or three the last time I seen him. Then, to my surprise, Lindsay, who was sitting next to Polly, sang out.

"There's Max!" she said. "Mrs. Hackham, I see Max!"

I looked where she pointed but could not pick him out. Polly hushed the girl and looked over at me.

"That's quite an operation," Yasha said.

"This plant moves a lot of sand to find gold," Polly said. "Most of those men are immigrants and their sons from San Francisco who will work for pennies."

Just up from its mouth, the Anchor River bends to the south and runs parallel to the shoreline for a good mile. With the tide coming in we was able to row upstream to the boat landing in back of the mine.

"We clear on the plan?" I said.

Everyone nodded.

The plan was for Polly and me to go find Max. Polly would say there was a family emergency, and that I had been sent to escort her and Max back home. Lindsay was to stay in the boat with Yasha to keep her quiet. I disliked having the girl anywhere near all of this—we originally thought to leave her with Yasha on Kalgin Island, then come back and pick them up on our way to meet Big Nick, but she would have none of it. She said there was ghosts on the island. This might have been something Scotty filled her head with, but after five years' residence there I could scarcely disagree with her.

Me and Polly climbed out onto shore. "We won't tarry," I said. "So stand by to shove off."

Yasha nodded.

"And keep your face hid," Polly said. "They're most likely on the lookout for you."

"I think maybe I'll take a nap."

Lindsay watched me with her large eyes. To her I said, "We need you to be a good girl and stay quiet. Can you do that?"

She said nothing, but nodded at me most solemnly.

Yasha shed his jacket, for the day was warm in the lee of the beach ridge. "Good luck, AC."

There was a great welling inside my breast as we walked up the trail from the landing to the mining plant. My desire to see my son and claim him as my own was so great I could barely keep myself inside my skin. But there was nothing to do but take it easy. No good would come of going off half-cocked at this stage of the game.

The miners had all seen us row past and turn up the river. The foreman and another fellow in a dark suit come walking down the trail to meet us halfway and see what news we brought. They both wore pistols, a new sight for me. I've read that in America everyone carries a hand-gun, but this has never been the custom in Alaska. This led me to the uncomfortable conclusion that they was indeed on the scout for Yasha. I didn't know too many miners, but my bet was that, as a general rule, the man-agement didn't make a habit of wearing revolvers at their desks. These fellows was strangers to me, but they both obviously knew Polly. The foreman touched his hatbrim. "How do, Mrs. Hackham."

Neither of us looked too dapper after several nights of sleeping out under the spruce trees. But she made a good show of things all the same.

"Good day, Mr. Lewis."

Lewis inclined his head toward his companion. "I believe you know Marshal Tomlinson."

It took a great deal of effort not to show the fear that clutched me. I studied the water to compose myself. Up at the mine workings, one of the immigrant workmen was yelling at a team in a language I didn't understand. My eyes strayed to the steam rocker and the awful racket it made, the plume of steam and smoke that rose from the giant boiler.

"Yes," said Polly. "It's been a while."

"It has," said Tomlinson. "But you shouldn't be travel-ling. There's a dangerous man on the loose."

"Oh?"

"Some low-down Nate murdered that Irishman Keogh up at Chickaloon Bay," said Lewis. "Hank and his two Kodiak deputies have been up and down the Inlet conducting the manhunt." He glanced down at the pistol he wore. "He swore me in, and some of the men. Just in case."

I took it that Hank, or Henry, was Tomlinson's Christian name. It did not bode well that he was on a first-name basis with the camp foreman. I glanced over at the landing, but did not see a steam launch. Tomlinson must have sent it out looking for Yasha.

"There's no telling where this suspect will show up next," said Tomlinson.

Polly nodded. "Well, I have this man and another with me as an escort."

Tomlinson looked me up and down. This was my first encounter with an active peace officer—Polly's father had been long retired from the business—and I have to say I did not care for this man's presence. His eyes was flat and hard and bore the look of a man who would reach right through you to get what he was after.

"I don't know you," he said.

"This is Alex Kashevarov," said Polly. "He's an old friend."

Tomlinson's eyes lingered on me for a half-second, then he looked back at Polly. "So may I ask what brings you here?"

"I've come for Max. Has there been any word from Greg?"

"Not since he sent Max here," said Lewis.

"There's been a family emergency," said Polly. "I need to take him down to the States."

"A family emergency," said Tomlinson.

"I'd prefer not to go into it." Polly was working hard not to cry, and it seemed to me that it was not entirely a show. Hardly surprising, considering everything she'd been through.

"I just want to get my son and go," she said. I kept my own mouth shut.

Judging from their reaction, word of Hack's disappearance had not yet reached Tomlinson and Lewis. Assuming it was Tomlinson's boat we'd seen that morning, the storm that kept us weathered on the island would also have kept them from coming back here with the news. This at least stood in our favor. We still had a chance to get Max and make tracks.

The look on Lewis' face was genuinely sympathetic. "Fair enough. Come along and we'll go fetch him."

I moved to go with them, but Tomlinson stopped me. "Why don't you introduce me to your friend down there in the boat."

"He's napping."

"I'm sure he won't mind."

"Alright," I said. If nothing else it would put me closer to my axe and loaded rifle. Polly and Lewis were already moving up the trail through the tall grass.

Yasha seen us coming. He lay sprawled in the bow as if he had not a care in the world, but I could see him watching us from under the brim of his slouchy clerk's cap.

"This is Marshal Tomlinson," I said. "He's keen to meet you."

"How do," said Yasha. Lindsay stood at the transom. She had been plaiting several strands of grass together but stopped to stare at our visitor. Tomlinson glanced at her, then went back to studying Yasha who had not moved except to shift his hat brim a little so he could get a better view.

"I'm looking for an Indian named Yasha Izaakov," said Tomlinson. "You know him?"

"I do," said Yasha.

"Any idea where he might be?"

"No."

I stole a glance back toward the camp and mine workings where the men and boys was moving around the diggings like so many ants. The teamster had finally got his animals moving, and another had replaced him at the hopper. I wondered what would become of all this now that Hack was dead. I hoped to see some sign of Polly coming our way with Max, but so far there was nothing.

"What's your name, boy?" said Tomlinson.

"Lukas," said Yasha.

"That's only half a name."

"Lukas Fedorov."

"You always this horizontal?"

"I don't follow."

"It means you need to stand your red ass up when I'm talking to you."

"Easy now," I said, pointing a thumb at Lindsay. "Little pitchers has big ears."

Tomlinson glanced over at me, then back to Yasha. Just then Lewis appeared coming back down the trail with Polly behind him, leading a boy in ragged work dungarees that was too big for him. Despite our desperate circumstances my heart leapt at the sight of my son. Naturally he was quite a bit taller than I remembered, and his face had lost the chubby features of a toddler. I could look at nothing else as they come up to the boat.

I got in and Polly made to pick up Max by the armpits and hand him over to me, but he pulled away, saying, "I can do it, Mama."

This made me smile. My son boosted himself onto the rail and slid into the boat.

"We'll be off then," Polly said. "While we still have the tide. Thank you for your help, Mr. Lewis."

Lewis touched his hat-brim. "No trouble, ma'am. We'll keep an eye peeled for Hack."

"Thank you."

Tomlinson watched silently as Lewis give Polly a hand climbing in and set his shoulder to push us off. I felt fleet of foot and light of spirit as I moved to the oars, and I dared for just a moment to think that we might have actually pulled it off. That we could make the rendezvous with Big Nick across the Inlet that evening and be over the divide and into the Iliamna country within a few days, where me and Polly could be married and watch our son grow up.

Max and Lindsay was obviously chums. From the way they carried on, you would never have guessed the terrible thing they had witnessed just the previous week. We was no more than six feet out from shore when together they clambered over the seats to the bow and Max dug into his pocket and pulled out an agate, speaking the five words that sent all my hopes tumbling to hell:

"Yasha, look what I found."

I did my best to play it easy, but I seen the look Yasha shot me. The jig was up.

"Stop that boat!" shouted Tomlinson. He charged into the water with Lewis right behind him. I was just digging the oars to turn us downstream when he lunged forward and caught the bow-line. The water was up to his knees, and he dug his feet into the gravel as Lewis splashed up and got his own hands on the rail, pulling us into the bank. Yasha swung a punch at him but the rocking of the boat took the power out of it.

"Get it into shore!" Tomlinson ordered, turning to drag us back to the landing. I tried to work the oars to pull us away but Lewis stood in the way of the starboard stick and we spun in a circle, half-dragging Tomlinson around with the bow. Yasha grabbed his rifle and levered a round into the chamber and Lewis drew his pistol with one hand still on the gunwale.

"Get down!" I shouted at Polly and the kids. I dropped the port oar and pulled the starboard one out of its oar-lock and jammed it hard into the side of Lewis' head. It glanced off his skull but it was enough to knock him down. He fired as he fell and the children screamed as he splashed into the river. I felt the bullet fly past my armpit.

Tomlinson was grunting and cursing, trying to manage the boat on his own. The water was up to his thighs now, but we was barely an oar-length from the bank. Lewis got his feet under him. He jumped up and leveled his shooter at me. His free hand clutched the side of his head. Blood streamed out from his hair.

"Don't fucking shoot!" shouted the marshal. "You'll hit those kids!"

He was just yelling for Lewis to grab the rail when Yasha fired at Lewis. He seen it coming and ducked and the bullet slammed into the mud. Working the action, Yasha spun and fired at Tomlinson, but he too ducked down. The marshal had his hands full with the bow-line, but Lewis snarled like an animal and lunged over the rail and grabbed the back of Yasha's waistcoat and yanked him assward so that he dropped the rifle in his struggle to get free. Lewis wrapped an arm around Yasha's neck, then handily flipped his pistol around so he was holding it by the barrel and started clubbing Yasha with it.

I went to grab hold of Lewis and pull him off, but just as I laid hold of him I heard voices on the bank above. There was a dozen workmen jumping down and plunging into the river toward us. Most of them was armed.

Lewis swung a savage blow at Yasha's shoulder, probably trying to bust his collar-bone, but Yasha twisted away from it. I grabbed the fish-gaff and swung it with both hands like a sword at Lewis' face. It cracked hard against his cheek-bone and he slid off the rail. Two miners grabbed onto the bow-line behind Tomlinson. We had no chance if we stayed with the boat.

"Over the side!" I said. Yasha needed no encouragement, he snatched up his rifle and rolled overboard. Polly was right behind him. I pushed Lindsay into her arms, then clambered after them with Max and my own rifle tucked under my arm like a load of sticks.

"Get in the grass!" I said. Sparks shot out from my ears, and I clamped my jaw down against them as Lewis staggered to his feet, glaring after me. Polly high-stepped through the water, holding up her skirts with her free hand. Me and Max was right behind her.

Yasha hauled Polly up onto the bank, then me. "We should have sliced the bow-line."

"Too late now," I said, pushing him into a run.

We made for the river mouth—there was nowhere else to go. We was on the ocean side of the stream, which of course made it a natural trap where we would be pinned against the water, but we didn't exactly have the time to plan our moves with precision. We stayed in the low spots as much as we could, using the tall grass and puschki weed to keep us hid. All the same, they was not far behind, and we was damn near beat when we come to the end of the grass and broke out onto the bare gravel of the sand spit at the river-mouth. The soft sand sapped even more strength from our legs, and I could feel myself starting to stagger as two rifle-shots sailed past me and Max.

Behind me, I heard Tomlinson yelling again at the men to quit shooting at us, lest they hit Polly or the kids.

There was big drift logs everywhere, strewn by the tide. We ran for one of them near the water's edge. Yasha pushed out ahead of us and dove behind it. We was but three steps away from him, then two, then I heard another rifle shot and Polly cried out and stumbled, spilling Lindsay onto the gravel.

"Polly!" I shouted. Another bullet whapped past my head. Lindsay scampered behind the log. I threw Max after her, then got down on the sand and pulled Polly to cover. I rolled her over and propped her head against the log. I sucked in my breath when I seen the dark red stain spreading out from beneath her bosom and the beach sand that clung to it.

Tomlinson was close. "Don't these god damn Bohunks speak English?" he screamed, probably at Lewis. "TELL THEM TO QUIT FUCKING SHOOTING AT THOSE KIDS! We got the boat coming down to flank them, so just sit tight!"

"Polly," I said.

Her eyelids fluttered. She reached up and touched my cheek.

Max crawled over to her. "Mama! Mama, are you alright?"

Lindsay was right behind him. "Is she alright, Mr. Campbell?"

"Yes, honey," I said, though I didn't believe it. I looked over at Yasha. "How many rounds you got left?"

"Thirteen. A few more in my pockets."

"We got to get across that river."

He blew on the action to clear it of sand. "Gonna be cold."

I laid my rifle over the log and peered over the sights. Tomlinson and the men was spread out maybe a hundred yards to the south, all of them behind drift logs like ours. The river mouth was at our backs, and the tide had just turned, heading out, which was likely to make things tricky. It had to be ten or twenty foot deep, so this was a swimming proposition. And that was only the first hurdle, for we still had to get across the bare gravel on the other side, and then behind the cover of the bluff edge.

"What about you?" Yasha said.

"I got a full magazine. Fifteen shots." The sparks in my head was making it hard to think. I worked my jaw up and down against them as they spread around my neck.

"After that?" said Yasha.

I shook my head. I had two boxes of shells in my pack, but that was sitting in the dory and may as well have been in San Francisco.

Yasha let out a quiet curse. Out across the beach I heard Tomlinson yelling, "Wait for the boat! They aint got nowhere to go!"

Polly was looking skyward, her eyes trying to find me and our son. Of all things, when I caught sight of her eyes the crackling tapered off, then evaporated like mist. This might have been a fascinating development in other circumstances, but I hadn't any time to mull it over just then.

She reached for Max and patted his arm with a weak hand.

"You got to take the children," I said to Yasha.

"What?"

"Get them across," I said. "Then I'll bring Polly. We'll get up into the woods and cut for Starichkof."

Yasha cast a glance at Polly. He knew just as I did that it was a slim chance. But sitting there on the beach we had no chance whatsoever. Once the boat got around behind us, that would be the end of everything.

He took a deep breath. "Max and Lindsay, come on."

Lindsay was game, but Max shook his head. "I'm staying with my mother."

"There aint no time to argue."

"I aint going."

Polly's eyes held mine. Her lips moved, but she couldn't find her voice. But I knew in an instant what she was saying.

"Max," I said.

He pretended he hadn't heard me.

"Max, look at me."

He done so and I put my hand on his cheek. "Maxim, I'm your father. Your dad."

His brow furrowed. "No you aint."

Polly might have corrected his grammar, but there was no time for that. All we had was my colonial Creole voice.

"Max, I am your father, not Greg Hackham. You was deceived all these years, just as I was, but I don't want you to hold it against your mother. She was only doing what she thought was best."

He tried to turn away, but I held him fast. "I don't hold it against her, do you understand me? And you can't neither."

Someone called out that they could see the boat coming.

"Max?"

Polly stroked his arm. When she found her voice it was barely a whisper. "I love you Max, I love you so much. It's true what he says. Your name is Campbell."

Yasha took hold of Max. "We can't wait no more!"

"Go on, partner," I said. "If something happens to me, you take him to the Iliamna country and give him a good home."

I seen in Yasha's face that we was both thinking of Semyon and Fedosya, and of me and Suzanne's lost child. Then they was gone, sliding down the sharp cut in the gravel and into the water.

"They're swimming for it!" someone yelled.

Yasha and the children was under cover in the lee of the bank, but it wasn't long before they was out in the open with nowhere to hide. Upstream, I could just see the boat nosing around the corner with two armed men in the bow and a third bending hard on the oars.

I levered a shell into the chamber of my rifle and started firing at them, slow and deliberate. Not trying to kill nobody, just to make things harder for them, keep them pinned down. The effect was immediate—the oarsman spun the boat and pulled them back behind the bank.

I looked back and to my horror seen that Yasha and the kids had lost their footing and was caught in the current and being swept out to sea.

"Yasha!"

The children was floundering in the cold and going down. Yasha tried desperately to keep their heads above water, even letting them climb onto his shoulders while he struggled to tread water and hold onto his weapon and keep them all afloat. By then they was so far out they was no more than dark shapes against the water.

I swore and thought I might actually weep with frustration, but then as I watched there come a swirling of the waters beneath them. It could barely be seen, but then it grew wider and wider—something was pushing the water up from beneath, as if an entire sandbar was rising up from the depths—and as I watched, all three of them was lifted clear of the water.

I blinked my eyes, hardly daring to believe it. But there she was, plain as day. It was Opal, the halibut-girl.

The water spilled off her back with Yasha clutching at Max and Lindsay, all of them lying atop her, coughing and sputtering as she worked her flukes and carried them beyond the far bank and got them out of sight. That was the last time I seen my partner. Or my son, Maxim Campbell.

There was chaos among Tomlinson and his deputies. They was just as stupefied by what they'd seen as I was. Polly started coughing, and I could do nothing as frothy red blood collected on her lips and chin. I ran a hand through her hair, trying frantically to think of how to get her across. There was little doubt that the shock of the cold water would be the end of her. But I could not leave her side.

Tomlinson had somehow managed to crawl closer. "Kashevarov!" he called.

It took me a moment to remember who he was talking to. "What, damn you!"

"I can see to it Mrs. Hackham gets to a doctor!"

"In exchange for what?" I said, though I knew perfectly well what he wanted.

"In exchange for you coming out quietly. Otherwise we will flank you, and it won't be pretty when we get a good sight on you."

I closed my eyes and rested my forehead against the salt-pocked log. I could hear the small surf on the beach. The wind blowing through the grass just as it had that day at Deep Creek when Polly and I first seen each other. It seemed like a thousand years ago.

Tomlinson's voice: "What's it going to be?"

For the second time in my life I decided to change into a bear. I closed my eyes and searched for the sparks, even one, that I might multiply into a million.

And I couldn't find them, just like that night at Skilant when Sava came to fetch me. They were gone, with no explanation until I opened my eyes and seen Polly was looking up at me. It made me sick to think I had discovered this so late, that I had spent so many years as a drunk when all I needed was her eyes. Now everything was snatched away from us. She was going fast, and our time left together could only be measured in moments.

She said nothing, she just reached out and touched my arm. I studied her blue eyes, the patterns of her soul inside them. Taking my hand from my rifle, I reached out to touch her golden curls one last time. I bent down to kiss her, and she breathed her last breath into me.

There were no sparks. I stood my rifle in the air by the barrel and threw it onto the sand. Polly was still in my arms when they come up and pulled me away.

KRIS FARMEN

ecky Ashford sits at the roll-top desk in the parlor of Mrs. Rudikov's boarding house with the unexpected sight of morning sunshine spilling through the windows, through the lace curtains, and onto the pages spread before her. Papers and notebooks are stacked in various piles, her notes from her ethnographic work in different locales across the territory. The notes from the Campbell interviews are on top, open at various places. In front of her are the water-crinkled pages that Private Maddox delivered to her last night with a late evening knock on the front door.

"Campbell asked me to bring you these," he said, standing under the portico in his slicker and hip boots. Water dripped off his army slouch hat and onto his shoulders.

Standing in the open doorway, Becky Ashford took the notebook he held out to her. It was the same notebook she gave to Campbell earlier in the week. She recognized the pattern embossed into the cover.

She opened it. The pages had gotten wet from the rain on the way over, despite being beneath Maddox's raincoat, and she had to be careful in turning them. Thankfully, his writings were in pencil and not affected by the moisture. Once again, she noticed Campbell's good penmanship.

Swallowing hard, she closed the notebook and clutched it against her chest. "Thank you."

He touched his hatbrim and turned to leave, but stopped just inside the drip-line of the portico. "I've heard some of the Nates here saying that he's some kind of medicine man. That he can turn himself into a grizzly bear."

Becky listened to the rain drumming on the roof shakes. Behind her she could sense Mrs. Rudikov walking past, stopping to watch. Wondering, no doubt, who she was talking to and why she was letting all the heat out into the October night.

"So I've heard," she said.

"You sail tomorrow, then?"

She nodded. "At two o'clock. The captain delayed the sailing."

"For the hanging?"

"Yes. Henderson needed him to be an official witness."

Maddox frowned, then settled his gaze on the porch, studying the watery tread marks left by his boots on the weathered spruce planks.

"They put me on the hangman's detail tomorrow," he said. "I'm not too happy about that."

"I guess there's precious little in life to be happy about sometimes."

"I guess so."

Becky held up the damp notebook. "Thank you again."

"Good night, Miss." Maddox turned into the rain and clumped down the steps and onto the gravel street. She stood there for another half-minute, listening to his footsteps splashing in the puddles and watching the skewed rectangle of lamplight from the parlor window that glistened on the wet lawn.

———

Now she sits with her trunks and her grip stacked on the porch, waiting for the porter who will arrive any moment. Everything has been packed; only her briefcase and its contents are still laid out before her. She was up late, reading his story again and again, well past midnight.

Her elbows rest upon the desktop as she sets her forehead on her hands. She yawns from fatigue, staring down at her shorthand and at Campbell's longhand, the representations of his time on this earth. A time all too brief, though it passes too quickly for everyone.

Becky sits thinking about his son, Maxim Campbell, and his statement that the crackling beneath his ears faded when Polly looked at him.

Aleksandr Campbell wanted her to write a book for him. That was why he kept letting her interview him. Or one of his reasons, at least. She closes her eyes and pictures her tiny basement office. There is no doubt that such a book with its rough language and scandalous behavior would not endear her to her superiors, and she already has a difficult time getting them to take her work seriously as it is. Not for the first time, thoughts of love and marriage fill her mind. Thoughts of the men who have come into her life, then left when they perceive that it is not in her nature to play the obedient wife. Of the idea that she will most likely wind up her days as an old maid, a label that she despises on both moral and personal grounds,

KRIS FARMEN

but which seems to suit the moment. At times like these, her life seems like a dark path through a forest of regrets.

She hopes she will someday outlive the question of where his power came from. The sight of the bear that appeared in his jail cell and told her to get out. Her eyes stare past the words on the final page and focus on the lacy pattern of the sunlight sprawled across it.

———

Out of long habit, Aleksandr Campbell wakes early. He lies in his bed listening for the wind, but it is silent.

"Don't tell me it's calm," he whispers to his empty cell. He rolls his head back to look out his tiny window and is surprised to see blue sky above the sharp line of the hillside. His shackles hang heavy on his wrists as he climbs to his feet and makes use of his bucket one last time. What little he can see of the sky is perfectly blue over the ragged silhouette of the dead grass, ferns, and fireweed that forms his limited horizon, not unlike the untrimmed edge of a page in a book.

He looks down at Becky Ashford's copy of Roughing It *where it lies next to his mattress. He should have sent it back with Maddox, along with the notebook, but he didn't. A small regret to add to the list. He considers opening it to read again about the Sandwich Islands, but decides against it. There is too much to see this morning.*

It has rained during the night, but now there is frost on the grass and on the forbs that stand and will keep standing until the first decent snowfall. The golden cottonwood leaves have piled like feathers among the stems, and the rainwater cupped inside them has frozen into delicate lenses with tiny liquid pools trapped beneath.

Nothing moves in the morning. A sheet of sunlight creeps westward across the tiny patch of yard and the walls of the houses beyond, liquefying the frost that has gathered in the night. Campbell smiles as the light moves toward him. He stands on his tiptoes and his chains bump against the log wall as he reaches his hand out to touch the dawn.

True beauty needs no words to describe it. This is what his grandfather told him many years ago. He stands enraptured by the sunlight, a rare commodity on this island. From across the yard an outhouse door clatters shut. A householder tosses a basin of washwater out the back door. There is the punctuation of stove wood being chopped, a whiff of coal smoke in the chilly air.

Aleksandr Campbell smiles, watching his hand and his steaming breath in the morning sunlight. Then the smile fades as he remembers. Today at ten o'clock he is to hang.

He moves away from the window and lies down on his mattress. He shuts his eyes and thinks back to lying beneath the poplar trees in the woods near Skilant town. How brilliant and gold their leaves looked against the blue September sky as they shimmered in the breeze. He wishes for perhaps the ten thousandth time that he had been in the room when Hack pointed his pistol at Scotty. Or that he hadn't shaken his head at Yasha that spring day next to the Kenay River just before the wedding. That he thought to cut the bow line at Anchor Point, or that his skin was white so he would have been believed.

He is sitting upright upon the mattress when the cellblock door scrapes open. There is the familiar sound of boots, and the scent of men fills the narrow hallway. Lieutenant Henderson is flanked by Maddox and Heinz. Both of them carry carbines.

"On your feet, Campbell," says Henderson.

Aleksandr Campbell does not look at them as he stands up and crosses the cell to where Henderson fiddles with the ring of keys. The prisoner stands patiently with his head down as the officer tries first one key, then another, cursing when he gets to the last one and finally the lock turns. He pulls on the iron gridwork and motions for Campbell to step forward so his shackles can be removed.

"Heinz," says the Lieutenant, "Did you bring the short irons?" These are shackles with only a half-dozen chain links between them, used for executions. The hands of the condemned will be cuffed behind him so he cannot reach up and grab the rope.

"No, sir. I guess forgot them."

Henderson turns to him. "You seem to forget an awful lot, Corporal."

Heinz gropes for an excuse, but fails. "They're in the cabinet. I can go get them."

"Stand fast. We'll get them on the way out."

Campbell's lips move and Henderson's ears pick up a mumbled word.

"What's that?" he says.

Campbell says nothing as Henderson fits the key into one of the bracelets. He opens it, then the other, and drapes them over the bars of the cell to be retrieved later.

"Maximum what?"

KRIS FARMEN

Campbell's eyes stay fixed on the floor.

Henderson shrugs, then takes the lead with Maddox following, then Campbell, then Heinz. He has just reached the cellblock door when he hears the sound of something large behind him. There is suddenly less air in the room. Heinz lets out a small cry that is cut off by an animal roar that quivers his bowels. Henderson wheels as a rifle fires, deafening in the confined space. The ringing swells in his ears, and through the gunsmoke he can just barely see the improbably giant shape that launches itself at Heinz. The bearded corporal screams and drops his empty weapon, then he is on the floor with the bear snarling and chomping at him, slamming him this way and that with its paws as the long pelt-hairs ripple over its body.

Bright blood smears the floor and walls. Lieutenant Henderson's mouth falls open.

Heinz lets out another scream as the bear clamps its jaws onto his head and smashes him like a rag doll against the cell bars. His neck breaks with an audible snap. The shackles slide and clatter to the floor.

The bear spits Heinz out in a heap. Campbell is nowhere to be seen.

Henderson gapes from Heinz's corpse to the bear, then over to Maddox. The big animal's bulk fills the hallway as it approaches. The youth clutches his rifle to his chest, wide-eyed as the bear stands up on its hind legs, bumping its head against the roof. It plants its forepaws on the wall on either side of Maddox's head. He can feel the heat emanating from its fur, see the blood of Heinz's miserable life glistening upon its chops.

Henderson's voice comes as a whisper. "Shoot it." But Maddox cannot move as the bear sniffs at him with a great snuffling of breath. Then it drops to all fours again and turns to Henderson, popping its teeth.

"Shoot it, Private!" he orders, backing up as the big animal advances upon him with its head down and ears back. First one deliberate shambling step, then another. The bear's eyes do not waver from Henderson's as he paws frantically at the flap of his holster, now shouting, "Shoot it, damn you, shoot it!"

He freezes when he recognizes the eyes. Then there is movement, and all he can see is teeth and hot wet breath and the fur that wraps around him.

"Shoot him!" he screams, gargling, strangling, pleading. "Shoot him!"

FIN

ABOUT THE AUTHOR

Kris Farmen is a novelist, historian, and freelance journalist. His first novel, *The Devil's Share*, drew high critical praise. His writing has also appeared in *Alaska* magazine, *The Anchorage Press*, *The Surfer's Path*, and *Mushing* magazine, among others. He lives in Alaska, on the lower Kenai Peninsula.

Publisher's Note

The names and spellings of places, towns and some geographic references have been preserved as they were in the late 19th and early 20th century. In cases where the original name was so obscure or where the name change into the modern name or spelling occurred close to the time period in the book, the modern spellings are used.

The transliteration of Russian words and place names has been done in a manner consistent with the colonial Alaskan dialect of Russian, which lacks the V consonant and replaces it with the W. Place names in the Dena'ina (formerly Kenai'tze) Athabascan language have been rendered with simplified English spellings reflective of late 19th century linguistic conventions.